About the A

Julie Stock is an author of contemporary romance novels, novellas and short stories. She's a proud member of the Romantic Novelists' Association's New Writers' Scheme and she's also a Member of The Alliance of Independent Authors.

She blogs every week about her path to publication on her website, 'My Writing Life' at www.juliestock.wordpress.com. She would love to hear from you.

You can also connect with her on Twitter, Goodreads and Facebook.

If you would like to be the first to hear about her new releases and other news, you can sign up via her website to receive her occasional newsletters.

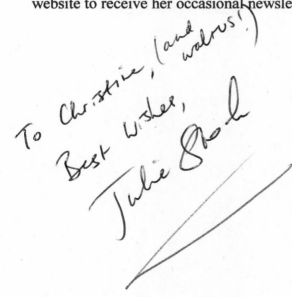

FROM HERE TO NASHVILLE

By Julie Stock

Clued Up Publishing

Published by Clued Up Publishing

A CIP catalogue record for this book is available from the British Library.
ISBN 978-0-9932135-0-2

Cover Design: Design for Writers
Editing: H&H Editorial Services
Proofreading: Wendy Janes
Printed and bound in Great Britain by Clays Ltd, St Ives plc

To Simon, Hannah and Laura.
Thank you for believing in me and for constantly reassuring me through all the ups and downs of this new writing life.

CHAPTER ONE

Poole, Dorset, England
Rachel

'It's time for our last session of the evening now, folks. We're proud to present to you the next big thing in UK country music. Please give it up for local band Three's Company!'

The crowd applauded in response and I took a deep breath to try and stop my heart from racing as I walked over to the microphone. It didn't matter how many gigs we did, I still felt nervous every time. With a quick glance round I checked that Sam, the guitarist, and Matt, the drummer, were ready. I tossed my hair over my shoulder and moved my guitar into position, running my fingers gently over the strings to reassure myself before the growing audience.

The boys played the opening bars of Lady Antebellum's 'Need You Now' and I relaxed, letting my voice take over and lead the way. As the song ended, the crowd gave another good round of applause so we went straight on to our second number. About halfway through, I spotted a man watching me intently. He was tall, with broad shoulders and he had a healthy-looking tan. His dark brown hair curled invitingly around his face and his jaw was covered by a fine layer of stubble. He smiled encouragingly so he didn't put me off my stride and reluctantly I looked away. But I was intrigued.

By the end of the song, the crowd was singing along. More and more people had started to come in, drawn by the sound of our music, which boosted our confidence still further so I felt the time was right for some introductions.

'Hi, we're Three's Company and it's great to be here

1

tonight.' I had to pause and wait for the cheers to subside. Smiling, I carried on, 'I'd like to take a minute to introduce the band. Sam's on guitar and that's his brother, Matt, on drums.' They both grinned and gave a little wave. 'I'm Rachel and next up, is a song of mine called "My Turn".'

I settled myself on the stool at the front of the stage, making sure I was comfortable before playing the introduction so that I could focus and get my first public performance of this song perfect. I'd written it with my mum in mind and I only wished she could see me sing it now.

'All my life, I've been waiting, waiting for my turn,
Wondering how much longer it's gonna be…
And when it comes, I'm gonna make sure I take it,
Make the most of it, live my turn to the limit.'

I didn't look up until I reached the end of the song and when I finished singing, there was complete silence in the pub, feeding my fears for a brief moment. This was swiftly followed by thunderous applause though and I could not believe the crowd's reaction.

When we broke for the interval, I rushed to hug Sam and Matt, flushed with our success. Standing at the crowded bar a few minutes later with my heart still pounding and a huge smile on my face, I suddenly felt the hairs stand up on the back of my neck.

I turned slowly to find myself staring up into the most beautiful pair of brown eyes I'd ever seen. The gorgeous man who'd been watching me earlier now stood before me and my breath caught as I studied him close up. He towered over my petite frame, his soft, wavy, dark brown hair falling over his forehead, hands slung low in his pockets and cowboy boots peeking out from beneath his jeans.

'Er, hi,' I managed to stutter out, reminding myself to take a breath.

'Hey there,' he drawled in the most luscious American accent. 'I heard you singing and I wanted to find out more about who that fabulous voice belonged to.' He smiled and as he did, I noticed the way his lips turned up invitingly at the corners.

'Thank you. I'm glad you liked it,' I replied, trying to appear calm and to bring my focus back to his eyes.

And then he chuckled. God, he knew how to make a chuckle sound sexy. He oozed confidence too, with his broad shoulders pulled back and his head held high.

'You British, you're so damn polite,' he said, raising his eyebrows. 'You sounded great up there.'

'Yeah, the crowd had a great vibe tonight. I can't quite believe it.'

'Well, you have no reason not to; the proof's all here. I loved your own song by the way. You have a real talent there.'

I blushed then, an honest-to-goodness shade of pink that made him chuckle once more, locking eyes with me as he did, so I knew the compliment was sincere.

'I'd love to hear more of your singing. Have y'all any more gigs coming up?'

'We've got another one next Tuesday at a local pub down on the quayside. Do you know where that is?'

I gave him a cheeky smile, feeling like I'd somehow been transported to an alternate universe where I flirted with handsome Americans all the time, and he rewarded me with a playful grin by return. Wow! His grin was almost sinful. I didn't know how much longer my legs would support me, after the excitement of being on stage and now this unfamiliar feeling of attraction. I took a step back and reached out to hold on to the bar behind me.

'Well, I'm staying with my cousin, Tom. He's the bartender here so I'm sure he'll help me get to the *quayside*, whatever that is.' He tilted his head to one side endearingly and frowned a little as he considered the possibilities.

3

'It's down at the waterfront.' I smiled again, picking up on his confusion. 'Tom lives a couple of doors away from me actually so he knows how to get to most places.'

'Great, I'll look forward to it. I'm Jackson by the way, Jackson Phillips.' He held out his hand towards me.

'Rachel Hardy,' I responded, placing my hand in his. The warmth of his skin against mine set my pulse racing once more, as he held my hand and my gaze for what seemed like an eternity.

By this time, Tom had made it over to us. 'What can I get you two to drink?' he asked, bringing us both back to reality. 'Fantastic set, Rachel, by the way. The crowd loved it.'

I asked for a lime and soda, as did Jackson. When Tom brought the drinks back a moment later, Jackson insisted on paying for them and I took a long sip while I collected my thoughts.

'Where are you from then, Jackson?' I turned to face him and found him already looking at me, with that intensity that had caught my attention when I was singing.

'I'm from Nashville. Do you know it?'

I coughed and spluttered as I tried to swallow the sip of drink I had taken at just the wrong time. He reached out to pat me on the back, looking concerned by my reaction.

'You okay?'

'Sorry,' I managed, 'it's just that was the last thing I expected you to say. I've always dreamed of going to Nashville.' I could only hope that my face didn't have a silly teenage look on it.

'Well, it's good to have a dream to work towards and I can heartily recommend it to you. I'm over here for Tom's wedding to Meg at the end of the month, I'm going to be his best man.'

As I cast my eyes over his perfectly toned body, a sudden wicked vision of Jackson in a morning suit appeared before me. I must have given myself away because he was now looking at me quite differently. My face warmed under his scrutiny. Thankfully, my best friend, Jenna, chose that moment to come over and introduce herself.

'Rachel, found you at last!' She pulled me in for a quick hug, forcing me to tear my attention away from Jackson for a moment. 'You guys sounded brilliant out there. All those practice gigs over the last few years have paid off, you know. I felt really proud of you all, even those two brothers of mine.'

'We did a pretty good job tonight, didn't we?' I admitted before turning back to Jackson. 'Jenna, this is Jackson Phillips, he's Tom's cousin and he's over here from *Nashville*.' I raised my eyebrows slightly, knowing she would get the connection. They said hello and then I had to down my drink quickly because it was time for me to get back to the stage.

I cast a final look in Jackson's direction and he tilted his head gently towards me, giving me another charming smile. His gaze followed me all the way to the stage and the attention made my stomach flutter.

We started the second half with our version of 'Killing Me Softly With His Song', keeping quite faithfully to Roberta Flack's original, before going on to some other covers, including 'This Kiss' by Faith Hill.

All too soon, I sat down at the piano to introduce our final number. I'd chosen another one of my own songs to finish with, called 'Don't Let Me Go'.

'How can things have turned out like this?
I thought you'd be here forever
But now you've gone and I'm on my own.
I couldn't make you stay but promise me one thing
Don't let me go...'

The crowd cheered their approval for this final song. People came up for some time afterwards to congratulate us on our success before going on their way. Finally, only Jackson remained, smiling at me and waiting for me to finish receiving all the compliments. Sam and Matt had already started taking the gear out to the van so it took a few minutes before I could introduce them to him.

'Sam, Matt, meet Jackson, Tom's cousin. He's over here from America for Tom's wedding.'

'Whereabouts in America are you from?' asked Sam, as he put his guitar carefully back into its case.

'Nashville,' Jackson explained.

'As in, Nashville, Tennessee, Music City,' I reinforced.

'Yep, the very same,' Jackson laughed. 'That's how I know you guys sound so good. I've heard a few bands in my time,' he said.

'Nice to meet you and thanks,' Sam replied, shaking Jackson's hand.

'Hello, Jackson, glad you enjoyed the gig,' Matt said, a bit breathless after packing his drums away. 'Rachel, sorry to interrupt but do you want a lift home?' he continued. 'Jenna's waiting in the van.'

'No, I'll walk back as it's such a lovely evening, but thanks anyway.'

'If you only live a couple of doors away from Tom, I can walk you back to make sure you get home safely, if that's okay with you, Rachel,' Jackson offered, looking first at me and then at Sam and Matt as if he knew they acted as my protectors.

'Is that okay with you, Rachel?' asked Sam. The sullen look on his face caught me off-guard. I was used to him being protective of me in the absence of a brother of my own, but this wasn't the same and I couldn't quite put my finger on it.

'Yes, of course,' I said, pushing my worries away. 'Thank you, Jackson and thanks guys, for an awesome performance tonight. I'll call you tomorrow for a post-gig analysis!' I gave them both a hug and a kiss and they turned to leave.

I looked at Jackson and blew out a long, slow breath.

'A penny for your thoughts?' he asked.

That made me laugh, to hear this typically English phrase coming out of his mouth. I studied his face for a moment.

'I'm not quite sure what to make of you. I've never met anyone from Nashville before and you're taking me a bit by surprise.'

'And that's a good thing, right?' His eyes twinkled. 'Shall we go?'

Jackson took my guitar for me and we walked back slowly along the quay, delighting in all the sparkling lights and the buzz from the tourists out enjoying meals on the warm summer evening. Once or twice, his hand brushed mine as we walked and I wondered if he felt the same tingling sensation I did every time our skin touched.

'Have you always enjoyed singing?' he asked.

'Oh yes, since I was young, my mum and dad encouraged it. We always had music in the house.'

'And were your parents there tonight?' he asked.

For a moment, I couldn't answer. 'My parents have both passed away,' I whispered and found myself stopping in the street.

He took my hand.

'I'm really sorry. Sorry that happened to you and for being nosy.' He groaned.

'Don't worry. It was a natural question to ask and I don't mind talking about them.'

We started walking again and he let go of my hand. I missed the warm, reassuring feel of it.

'Did they ever hear you and the band sing?'

'No, they didn't get the chance.'

'Well, they sure would have been proud of you tonight.'

To my relief, he didn't ask me how they'd died. My family's past was my burden and not something I chose to talk about very often.

Before I knew it, we'd reached my gate and it was time to

say goodbye but there was still so much I wanted to say.

'Your next gig is on Tuesday, you said. What's the name of the pub?'

'It's called The Cork and Bottle and we'll be on at eight again. I'll have to make sure we play some different songs then if you might be coming,' I joked.

'I'll definitely be there.'

My heart flipped over at his confident reply.

'Great, it will be good to see you again.' I paused, uncertain of what to say next. 'Well, I enjoyed meeting you tonight, Jackson,' I said, looking up at him one last time, 'and thank you for walking me home.' I reached out to touch him lightly on the arm, letting my hand linger for a moment before pulling away.

'The pleasure was all mine. Goodnight,' he replied softly, his deep voice caressing me right till the very last minute. Then, he handed me back my guitar, turned and continued on his walk home.

Watching him go, I had the feeling that my life had just taken a turn for the better.

CHAPTER TWO

After some breakfast the next morning, I called Sam to talk over last night's concert, still buzzing with excitement from all that had happened.

'Hello, Rach, how are you feeling today?' his gravelly voice resonated down the line.

'I still can't get over how brilliantly it went for us last night, can you?'

'No, better than we could have expected really, given that we're still quite unknown.' He fell silent at the other end of the phone, making me wonder what he was really feeling. He didn't seem his usual laid-back self.

'Hey, Sam, is everything all right? You seemed a bit upset with me at the end of the gig last night and I didn't know why.'

There was an awkward pause while I waited for his reply.

'I'm feeling a bit tired, that's all and I've got a sanding job to finish today as well. I'll be fine later on, I'm sure. Do you want to meet up for a drink tonight as usual?'

'Yes, I'd like that, shall we say six o'clock?' I was sure he was bluffing but I didn't want to push him over the phone.

'See you then, bye.' He rang off quickly as though he couldn't wait to get away.

I remembered the strange look I'd seen on Sam's face last night when Jackson had offered to walk me home and a seed of doubt began to niggle away in the back of my mind.

As I closed my wooden gate and stepped out on to Green Road for the short walk into town to see Jenna before meeting up with Sam, I could see what a wonderful August afternoon it was. The sun was shining, warming my skin and my soul, and the sky was such a vivid blue, it made me smile. I walked along the quay, watching the boats bobbing in the harbour and the tourists eating fish and chips, studied eagerly by all the seagulls flying around overhead.

I turned right, up the cobbled High Street towards the museum and Jenna's thriving florist's shop. Outside I saw buckets and jugs full of brightly coloured roses, tulips, chrysanthemums and lilies, and pots of all shapes and sizes as well, containing everything from lavender bushes to sage and thyme. The heavenly smell outside the shop always lifted my spirits. As I opened the door, the bell tinkled and she automatically looked up to greet her next customer. Her friendly face lit up when she saw it was me and she came round the counter to give me a hug.

'Hey, you're looking very happy this afternoon! Could this have anything to do with your great gig last night and maybe a certain gorgeous hunk you met?' Jenna knew me so well, I couldn't hide anything from her.

'I can't think who you mean,' I said, trying to look nonchalant but grinning at the same time.

'And how come I don't know anything about this guy?'

'Hang on, I only met him yesterday at the gig but I knew you'd want to hear the full story,' I said and then filled her in on how we'd met.

'And he's from Nashville too, that's pretty cool.'

'I know, I could hardly believe it. He's here to be best man at Tom's wedding. They're cousins.'

We had to pause our conversation for a moment while she served a customer who had picked up one of the bouquets from outside the shop. Jenna wrapped the flowers and told the customer briefly how to look after them so they would last longer.

'What happened at the end of the evening then? I heard he

10

walked you home.'

'You don't miss a thing, do you?' I laughed. 'He walked me home, that's all, no big deal.'

'If it's no big deal, why have you come to see me straight away, why are your eyes shining like that and why are you smiling all over your sun-kissed face?' She reached out to pat me playfully on the cheek.

'I know I'm probably getting ahead of myself a bit but I really liked him, I felt attracted to him even and that hasn't happened in such a long time, you know.' I paused to let my mind wander to the gorgeous image of Jackson I had already tucked away in my brain. 'Still, I shouldn't get my hopes up, it's not like he'll be around for long and you know what my track record with men is like.'

My face fell and my shoulders sagged as the reality set in. Jackson would be gone in a couple of weeks and that would be the end of that.

'Don't you dare feel sorry for yourself. Just because things didn't work out with Nick, it doesn't mean every relationship you have will be the same. Give yourself a chance. What difference does it make if it's only for a couple of weeks?' Jenna scolded. 'Have you made any plans to see him again?'

'He wants to come to our gig on Tuesday.'

'He sounds keen. Make sure you look your fabulous best and he'll be blown away. Changing the subject, are you seeing Sam tonight?'

'We're meeting at the pub. Do you want to join us?'

'God, no. Too knackered. I'll see you tomorrow for Sunday dinner.'

I gave her a goodbye hug and set off to meet Sam.

Sam was already there when I arrived, sitting at a bench outside the pub with a pint of beer in front of him and a chilled glass of rosé waiting for me on the side. He stood up to greet me, giving me one of his enormous hugs and a kiss on the cheek. He smiled at me so I guessed things couldn't be as bad as all that.

'You definitely know the way to a girl's heart.'

Sam laughed. 'In your case, it's easy because you're a creature of habit. You *always* have a glass or two of rosé on Saturday nights in the summer, changing over to red wine in the winter, simple! If only I could predict all women so easily.'

'So you're saying I'm predictable? Charmed, I'm sure.' To my relief, our friendship seemed to be on its usual footing again.

'Only on the wine front, of course, not in any other, more significant way, I hasten to add.'

'Okay, you can stop digging, I'll let you off. What about the gig last night? We were great, weren't we? And I still haven't recovered from the audience's reaction to us.' I was babbling on, I knew, but I wanted to talk it all over with him and if I could postpone any other sort of conversation indefinitely, that would be a bonus.

'Yeah, the crowd really seemed to approve. Anyway, I thought it went better than the last show so maybe we need to think about that when booking venues in the future. No point going back to places where we didn't get a great reception.' He paused to take a sip of his beer. 'I think your voice sounded amazing last night though and that clearly made a difference.'

'I don't know that I sang any differently. I did get a real buzz from the crowd's reaction in the first half, which spurred me on later so perhaps that helped. I think we ought to play a different setlist if we can for next Tuesday so if anyone comes again, they don't hear the same stuff.'

'I agree about different songs for Tuesday. Perhaps we could chat to Matt about it to see what we can come up with. Have you written any other new songs you'd like to play? They really seemed to go for the new material.'

'I have plenty but I'd need to practise on my own and then again with you guys. Is there enough time for all that? I know it's easier for me because I'm not working at the moment.'

He pulled a face before saying, 'Don't remind me about your lovely long holidays!' I smacked him on the arm, knowing he was trying to wind me up with the 'teachers and their long holidays' rant. 'As long as you don't spring anything too difficult on us, I think we'll be okay,' he continued, giving me his usual twinkling smile in reassurance.

We fell silent for a moment, taking in the view. I noticed that the breeze had picked up a little because I had to keep brushing my hair out of my eyes and the sky was a bit overcast now. I shivered, wishing that I'd brought a jumper along.

'What about Tom having an American cousin and from Nashville too? That was a bit of a surprise.' There, I'd said it and I turned to look at him to see if I could gauge his reaction.

'Yeah, I guess,' he replied looking miserable all of a sudden.

'I take it you didn't like him then?'

'I didn't have time to decide whether I liked him or not. It seemed a bit ridiculous, that's all, someone from Nashville coming along to one of our shows, you know, and then offering to walk you home too, Mr Charming himself.'

'Hey, he *was* genuinely charming and I don't think it's that ridiculous. I don't understand why you're so irritated about it. What harm is there in having someone who has obviously seen a lot of bands in his time coming along to our gigs and being positive about them?'

'That's not the point, Rachel.' He'd gone all quiet.

'What *is* the point you're making then?'

'Look, it doesn't matter, let's drop it. Do you want another drink?' His face was gloomy with frustration.

I handed him my glass because I didn't know what to say. While he was gone, I thought about it though. He was obviously irritated by Jackson but he wouldn't say why. I had an idea that he was being even more protective of me than usual. I watched the man I'd known for years and grown up with, as he weaved his way back through the crowd towards me a few minutes later. He didn't notice any of the admiring glances his tanned, fit body received from the women he passed. He could be out with any one of those women now, I thought to myself, but he's here with me. None of those women knew that we were just friends though and that's all we ever would be in my view. Sam was like a brother to me and although I could see how attractive he was, I wasn't going to let myself be attracted to him.

'Thanks,' I murmured as he handed me my drink.

He sat down, pushing his curly blonde hair out of his eyes. Not for the first time, I marvelled at the gorgeous, self-assured man he had become. Despite all my efforts, my thoughts strayed back to *that* night. I closed my eyes in an effort to block them out. We'd never talked about it and I didn't want to start now.

'Did you get your sanding job finished today?' I asked, breaking the awkward silence that had fallen between us. He nodded but didn't say anything. I looked away, wondering how long he was going to keep this sulk up and heard him take a deep breath.

'Are you coming over for lunch with us tomorrow?' he asked, avoiding the issue.

'Yes, I'll be there.' I paused, summoning up the courage to speak again. 'Sam...I...' I didn't know how to bring the subject up without causing an argument and the look he gave me confirmed that he wanted to steer clear of it too. 'I have to go,' I said instead and stood up.

I waited for him to stand up as well, fiddling with my bag handle while he manoeuvred his bulky frame out of the small wooden chair. I looked up at him, hoping he would say something to sort things out but he just bent down, kissed me briefly on the cheek, mumbled goodbye and sat down again. I turned abruptly on my heel and walked away.

CHAPTER THREE

I wrapped my coat tightly around me as I walked to church early the next morning and, as always, my thoughts turned to my mum and dad on the way. Sunday mornings were my favourite when my dad still lived at home because we'd always indulge in a fried breakfast all together, listening to the latest songs on the radio and singing along at the top of our voices. Despite the difficulties caused by my dad's drinking, we still shared some happy times before he left and the memory made me smile. The smile faded quickly as my thoughts turned to my mum. She'd been so selfless, keeping the pain of her cancer hidden from me after my dad's early death and it still hurt to think that I had lost both my parents in such a short space of time.

As the worship began, I relaxed into it, enjoying the familiarity of the words of both the service and the hymns. Walking back to my seat after the Communion, I glanced around the pews to check for any other people I knew but had missed, smiling and nodding at one or two. For a moment, I thought I saw Jackson at the back of the church but then I shook my head slightly, thinking I must have been mistaken and it was simply that he'd been on my mind a lot since Friday.

I said my goodbyes quickly afterwards and made my way out to the churchyard, picking up the flowers I'd brought with me from my garden on the way. I always went to see my mum's and dad's graves on these Sundays, to tidy them up, to lay new flowers and to offer up some prayers. I closed the door of the church and turned towards the path, only to find Jackson

15

standing there.

'It *was* you at the back of the church! What are you doing here?' I demanded. None of my close friends knew I came here, it was private to me and I looked away, hoping he would get the message. He raised his eyebrows in surprise.

'Specifically, I'm waiting for you but I was out walking this morning, heard the music and decided to come in to see a Church of England service for myself. It's a bit different to what I'm used to at home.' He smiled.

'Jackson, it's lovely to see you but I…'

'What is it, Rachel? Do you want me to go?'

'Yes, no, oh, this is difficult. Okay, deep breath.' He looked a bit confused as I stumbled over my words. 'My mum and dad are buried here and I've come to see them,' I explained.

'I'm sorry, I didn't mean to intrude.' Realisation dawned on his handsome face and he made to leave.

'Jackson!' I called after him. 'Would you wait for me on the bench by the gate?' He turned back and nodded. I walked off in the other direction and spent a precious ten minutes with my parents, before discreetly wiping my tears and making my way over to him. He saw my face but, tactfully, didn't mention it. By the time we left the little lane leading up to the church, I'd managed to pull myself together.

'Thank you.'

'What for?' he asked me gently.

'For being there and for understanding how important that visit is to me. It's nice to have someone here with me afterwards. I'm sorry if I was sharp with you at first.'

'I'm sorry, I realise it must be a private thing for you.'

We made our way back to the quayside and Jackson suggested stopping for a coffee as it had warmed up a little.

'What's new since Friday?' he asked as we sat down, smiling his megawatt, shiny, all-white teeth American smile at me.

'I've been thinking about our next gig, talking over with Sam what our setlist should be on Tuesday. I'd like to try out some more new songs but I'll need to find time to practise before then.'

'That's great that you have more of your own songs. I can't wait to hear them. You might well be pushed for time though, especially if you have to work tomorrow.'

'No, I'm a singing teacher and I'm on school holidays at the moment so I have time to practise during the day but Sam and Matt do have to work of course. Anyway, it'll be okay because we've been playing together for a good few years and we can be ready quickly when we need to.' I paused to take a sip of my coffee and to take a moment to study his features. In the daylight, I could see that he was a bit older than me, probably closer to thirty, I decided. 'How about you, what do you do for a living that allows you to come to Dorset for the best part of a month?' I smiled, hoping he would tell me more about himself.

'I run a small business in Nashville which I've left in the hands of my very capable team so it's okay for me to be gone a while. I have some business interests in London so I've been up and down there a few times during my visit to earn my keep.' I noticed he didn't tell me what his business was in but I didn't want to seem rude by asking too many questions. 'Tom was telling me about a singing competition that's going on here over the summer,' he continued. 'Have you heard about it? It's called "Open Mic", I think he said.'

'No, I haven't heard about it but it sounds interesting. Do you know any more about it?'

'He said it's a nationwide competition and there's an audition process. You guys would have no trouble getting through, I'm sure.'

He glanced out to sea as he finished talking so I couldn't see his face to get any clue about how strongly he felt about this. I had the sense that he was trying to be neutral about it but

I wasn't sure why.

'I'll have to look it up. Thanks for telling me about it.' I smiled.

We continued chatting for a bit longer and then walked back to the cottage. We stood face to face across the gate to say our goodbyes.

'I'll see you on Tuesday then, if not before,' he said, without making any move to go. My hair was blown by an unexpected gust of wind across my face and he gently reached across to tuck it behind my ear, touching my face with his thumb as he did.

The sensation was as electric as it had been before and I experienced a reawakening of desire within my body that I'd not felt since my days with Nick. I didn't remember ever feeling it so strongly with him though.

When I looked up at him, I was pretty sure that my eyes were giving me away.

'Goodbye,' I replied breathlessly.

It would seem like forever between now and Tuesday.

Jenna's family had lived in the same terraced Victorian house for as long as I could remember. Jenna was waiting on the porch when I arrived with Matt and his family and she welcomed me with open arms. We walked through the sunny, terracotta-tiled kitchen and soon everyone was gathered together in the back garden. Sam smiled at me but he still didn't seem to be quite his usual outgoing self. There was no laughing or joking about today and I worried that whatever had upset him yesterday, had not gone away completely. I decided I would try and have a quiet word with him again later. Jenna's parents both shooed me away when I offered help with the cooking so I sat down on a bench to admire the garden. Sam came over to join me soon after and I swallowed nervously in anticipation of our conversation.

We kissed cheeks and greeted each other before falling

into silence. Neither of us wanted to be the first to broach the subject of last night's conversation. Then we both started talking at once.

'You go first,' he said.

'I know I upset you last night but I still don't understand why.'

'You didn't upset me. It's just that I care for you and I don't want you to get taken in or maybe, even hurt, by some big, flashy American who won't be here for long anyway.'

He pushed his hands through his hair, looking embarrassed.

I grabbed his hands. 'Hey, I don't want to get taken in or hurt either but I can't live in a cocoon for the rest of my life. I need to move on from the way Nick treated me, I can't let it dominate me any more.'

'But is this guy, Jackson, the right person for you to move on with?' he asked, gently pulling his hands free and turning to look at me.

'I don't know, I've barely even talked to him. Who knows if anything more is going to happen?'

I couldn't tell him how much I was attracted to Jackson, it didn't feel right to talk about that kind of stuff with him.

'Be careful, that's all.'

'Listen, your friendship means everything to me but you don't have to worry about me, I can look after myself.'

I blew out a sigh of relief to think he'd only been looking out for me, nothing more, and I relaxed back into my chair. I noticed that he sat in the same hunched-up position though on the edge of his seat. I had the feeling that there was more he wanted to say but we didn't talk about it any more that day.

We rejoined the rest of the group shortly afterwards and the afternoon passed lazily in a wondrous blur of good food and wine. The band and I discussed the upcoming gig on Tuesday and agreed to have a quick rehearsal at mine the next evening after the boys finished work. Jenna and her parents all said they would come on Tuesday and we told them about the success we'd had so far. I brought up the subject of the "Open Mic" competition to sound the guys out about it.

'Do you think that's something you might be interested in doing?' I asked them.

'I'd like to know a bit more about it first, but it sounds interesting,' Matt replied and Sam nodded his agreement.

'Jackson said it's a nationwide competition and that we'd have to audition but he didn't think we'd have any trouble getting through.'

Sam stood up and walked off then, as though I'd said something to upset him again. No-one else but me seemed to notice, leaving me to struggle with my own confused thoughts about his behaviour.

Was he jealous of Jackson? If he was, he certainly had no right to be.

I spent most of the next day refining the songs I'd chosen to sing at the gig on Tuesday night and trying to decide on the cover songs I would sing this time. As the first band on, we planned to perform six songs again, four covers, a mix of country, rock and pop and two of my own songs, confident that this formula would work after the success we'd had on the previous Friday.

These gigs meant such a lot to me, probably more than they did to either of the guys. In my mind, it was clearer now. I had mourned my parents for four years and although that ache would never go away, it was becoming more manageable with every passing day. I liked my job but not enough to work it for the rest of my days. Since my feckless ex-fiancé, Nick, had abandoned me after my mum died, preferring to travel the world, I had no-one that held a special place in my heart. I knew the time was right for me to pursue my dream of a music career at last and I needed it now more than ever.

Later on, I fired up my computer to see if I could find out

more about the "Open Mic" competition Jackson had mentioned. It seemed that it was a nationwide singing competition for unsigned singers and bands, and auditions were being held all over the country this month! I looked up where our nearest audition location was and found out there was one coming up in Bournemouth.

The downside was that it was this Friday and I didn't know if there were still places left, let alone if we could be ready in time.

On impulse, I sent off an email asking if we still had time to apply. Shortly afterwards, I received a reply:

'Dear Miss Hardy,

There are still a few places left for the audition in Bournemouth on Friday if you would like to apply. Can you tell us some more about your act please? We'd love to hear from you.

Regards,

Natasha, for "Open Mic" Competition.'

I sucked in my breath as I read her reply and although I wanted to answer at once, I knew I'd have to wait and talk to the guys before committing myself any further. When they finally turned up at six o'clock, I could hardly contain myself, bouncing lightly on my toes as I let them in. I filled them in on all the details.

'I feel excited about this opportunity. I believe that the time is right for us now, especially as the gigs are going so well. How about you?'

'I don't suppose there's any harm in auditioning,' said Sam. 'Are you up for that, Matt?'

'We have nothing to lose,' Matt agreed, smiling.

I'd have liked a more enthusiastic response from them but decided that it was a man thing and they were keeping their inner thoughts to themselves. The rehearsal went well and after the guys had gone, I sat out in the garden, thinking about all that had happened over the last couple of days. The combination of a successful gig and meeting Jackson, who had enough confidence in us as a band to encourage us to enter this competition, was an intoxicating one. Why shouldn't we go for it now?

CHAPTER FOUR

The insistent ringing of the phone woke me early the next morning and it took me more than a moment to get my bearings. Groggily, I reached out for the handset on my bedside table and picked it up.

'Hello?' I mumbled, rubbing my eyes with my free hand.

'Rachel, it's Jenna, I'm sorry to call this early.'

'What time is it?'

'It's seven o'clock, you know I wouldn't call unless it was urgent. The thing is, Mary's called in sick and I wondered if you might be able to help me in the shop today? I'm desperate.'

'Okay, what else can I say but yes, but you owe me for calling me at this ungodly hour when I'm on holiday. I'll be there as soon as I can.' I grumbled but I would do anything for Jenna and she knew she only had to ask so I stumbled out of bed and into the shower, ate a quick slice of toast and set off for the town. I knew that there was a lot of preparation to be done before the shop opened as well and Jenna wouldn't be able to do it without my help.

As I set off towards the seafront once again, I enjoyed the feel of the early morning sun on my face and the gentle breeze through my hair. I would never grow tired of living by the sea, with the particular salty smell of the air and the sound of the water lapping against the harbour walls. As I walked, my mood lifted immediately, banishing the pain of the early wake-up call. I paused for a moment to take in the red, yellow and blue-coloured boats bobbing in the harbour and their shimmering reflections in the water.

The shop kept Jenna and I steadily busy throughout the morning and it was nearly eleven before we had time for a cup of tea. I left Jenna serving while I went into the back room where she kept a very small kitchen area. As I was stirring the sugar in, I heard the bell go, then, Jenna in conversation with a very familiar-sounding American.

'Jackson!' I exclaimed.

I smoothed down my hair and apron, grabbed the cups and headed back. Jackson's face lit up when he saw me which put me at ease.

'Hey, what are you doing here?' he asked in his lazy drawl, reminding me of one of the reasons I liked him so much.

'She's helping me out for the day because my assistant called in sick. She's been an absolute star,' Jenna jumped in before I could reply.

I beamed at Jackson, revealing my pleasure at seeing him again so soon.

'That's real kind of you,' he replied, keeping his gaze fixed on me. 'I hope you won't be too tired for tonight, though, I'm kinda looking forward to it, you know,' he said, making it clear that he couldn't wait to see me again either.

I couldn't bring myself to look away from him, knowing it would break the spell he had me under.

Jenna sucked in her breath. 'Oh, Rachel, I completely forgot about your gig. You'll have to go early to get yourself ready. Thanks for reminding me, Jackson. Is there anything else we can help you with?'

Jenna was ever the business woman and I had to admire her. It gave me a moment to study Jackson too, without him being aware. I noticed his muscled arms, on show today because of the sunny weather and wondered what exercise he did to keep himself looking so good. His white polo shirt fit him perfectly and I spent a pleasant few minutes imagining the toned chest underneath it.

'I came in to get some flowers for Tom's fiancée,' he

admitted. 'Meg's been having a few problems with the wedding arrangements. She's getting all stressed out so I thought some flowers might cheer her up.'

I could have swooned at his feet right there. I hardly ever received flowers and it seemed like he was so thoughtful.

'You're very quiet today,' he said, drawing me out of my daydream. I hadn't even noticed that Jenna had disappeared to put a bouquet together for him.

'I had an early start and I'm out of the habit. And Jenna was doing a fine job of speaking for me anyway.' I rolled my eyes a little and he chuckled by return. 'By the way,' I went on, 'I told Sam and Matt about the competition when we rehearsed yesterday and we've decided to apply for the audition this coming Friday.'

'That's great news, I think you've made the right decision, if you don't mind me saying. Tonight's gig will be a good practice as well.'

Jenna returned then with a delightful bouquet. I could see that Jackson was impressed.

'Will you be there as well tonight, Jenna?' he asked, as she handed him back his change.

'Yes, I'll be there. In fact, I'm bringing the whole family, so we'll see you later.'

He gave me one final glance as he left and if he'd been wearing a hat, I'm pretty sure he would have tipped it at us.

I didn't leave the shop till four, hoping that would be enough time for me to get myself over to the pub without being late. After a quick shower, I did my make-up, applying only mascara and a hint of lip-gloss, before getting dressed. For this gig, I'd settled on a dark brown, tiered gypsy skirt made out of a light corduroy and a pale brown scoop necked blouse that tied up at the front. Lastly, my old cowboy boots completed the outfit.

I gave my long chestnut brown hair a quick blast with the

hairdryer and let it fall loosely down my back and then popped in some gold hoop earrings and clipped my lucky bracelet around my wrist. Giving myself a final look in the mirror, I went downstairs to run through a quick warm-up with my guitar. It was a little after half past five as I closed the door behind me, guitar case in hand, and set off for the quay for the second time that day.

When I arrived at The Cork and Bottle, to my relief everything was all set up. I went downstairs to the stage area. Following a quick soundcheck with the boys, we were on stage by seven. We'd decided to open with a classic Carpenters' song, 'Superstar', that everyone would know and could sing along to. I tried not to let it bother me that I could only see a handful of people in the audience as I stepped up to the microphone. As the song went on, more and more people came downstairs to listen and by the end, the room was about half full.

I had a quick glance around for Jackson but there was no sign of him. I did spot Jenna with her mum and dad and they all gave me huge smiles, which was reassuring. I sat down at the piano, taking a moment to focus and was soon lost in my next song, Roberta Flack's 'The First Time Ever I Saw Your Face'. One of my favourite songs, it required all my concentration. So I was a bit taken aback when I finished and stood up to find the room full of people, with some even standing on the stairs. I smiled broadly as the applause filled the air. That was when I spotted Jackson, standing in a corner and clapping as enthusiastically as everyone else.

Next, I'd planned to sing one of my own songs. As I glanced at Sam, he winked at me and smiled. I introduced 'Love Me' as a song I'd written and waited for the crowd to settle before playing the introduction on my guitar.

'This is who I am, what you see is what you get,
I wear my heart on my sleeve and hope you'll do the same,

Accept me with all my faults and don't try to make me change,
Just love me, love me, take me as I am, love me...'

When the audience joined in with the chorus, I knew that the song was a success and the deafening applause at the end of the first half confirmed it. I couldn't believe it. I stood and watched with surprise as everyone dashed upstairs to get a drink in the interval, looking like they wanted to be sure not to miss the second half. Sam and Matt came over for a group hug and I found I had tears in my eyes. They offered to brave the scrum upstairs to get us drinks and I turned to the piano to sort out my music for the second half.

'Excuse me...' I looked up into the face of a smiling stranger. 'I loved the first half. You have a great voice.'

'Thank you, that's kind of you to say.' I blushed at my first compliment from a fan.

At that point, I remembered Jackson and looked around to see if I could find him but the room was virtually empty. Perhaps he'd gone upstairs to get a drink too. Sam and Matt reappeared a few moments later with drinks for us and Matt filled me in on the news.

'That guy Jackson's here again, did you see?'

'Yes, I saw him when I was singing.' I feigned nonchalance but I'm not sure if I got away with it.

'He's upstairs now and he said to tell you that you were fantastic. I think he thought he'd see you upstairs. Jenna's up there too with Mum and Dad and they all sent you hugs. They said they'd catch us all at the end.'

Matt was bubbling over with infectious excitement. Sam, on the other hand, was strangely quiet.

At least Jackson hadn't just left then. I saw him come back downstairs shortly afterwards and gave him a quick wave and a smile.

He pulled a funny face then from afar, grimacing and gesturing at the crowd at the same time as if to explain that it

27

was chaos so he would talk to me afterwards.

Jenna and her parents came down a minute later and they all gave us a big thumbs up. I turned to check that the guys were in place, getting a scowl in return from Sam but a quick nod from Matt. I didn't have time to wonder what had upset Sam now but I supposed it would have something to do with Jackson being there. I shrugged and let it go for the time being.

The second half went as well, with us singing 'The Right Kind Of Wrong' by Leann Rimes, followed by 'Breathe' by Faith Hill to a great response from the crowd but it seemed like it was our own material they were waiting for and we didn't disappoint them. Our last song, 'Too Late' was a really new one and I wanted to try it out to see how it sounded.

'I thought my time had come and gone, baby,
And then you just came along,
You made me feel special
Like no-one else had ever done before,
And just when it seemed like it was...

Too late, too late, too late for me
I found love with you
And now there ain't no turning back
'Cos I ain't never gonna let you go.'

Once again, the crowd joined in with the chorus and there was a real buzz in the room. The applause at the end of the song went on for several minutes and then someone shouted 'encore' and we did. People came up and talked to us for so long afterwards, I thought we might never get away! It had been such a great night once again and the adrenaline continued pumping through my veins long after the crowd had dispersed to get drinks before the next band came on.

Jenna threw her arms around me and squeezed me tight by way of congratulations.

'You're an absolute star,' she cried. 'I can honestly say that I have never heard you sing so well.' I stepped back to talk to everyone.

'Wow, thank you and thanks to all of you for coming. It was so wonderful to see you all out there in the audience.'

Jenna's parents echoed her congratulations too before they all left for home. Jenna promised to call me tomorrow, nodding in Jackson's direction before she went. Finally, only Jackson remained and I went over to find out what he'd thought of our set.

'You were incredible tonight! I've never seen a crowd in a bar respond so well to a new band and I'm sorry but I couldn't get anywhere near you, there were so many people! It was wild.' He laughed a deep, rich laugh full of his pleasure at our success.

'Wow, that's really good to hear. I mean, we felt the excitement too but being in the crowd must have been even better. Thank you for coming.'

'Would you mind if I walked you home again?' he asked all of a sudden.

'I'd love that, thank you,' I replied, my gaze lingering on his deep, brown eyes.

CHAPTER FIVE

I was still on such a high as we left the pub and didn't want to go straight home. Jackson must have read my mind because a moment later he suggested going to get a drink somewhere to celebrate the success of the gig.

A few minutes later, we were sat side by side at a table in a new wine bar I'd seen further down the High Street. I could feel the warmth from his thigh resting lightly against mine, making it hard for me to concentrate properly.

'How are you feeling now you've had time to process your brilliant success tonight?' Jackson asked me, putting his glass of fizzy water down on the table.

'It still hasn't sunk in, to be honest. We're just doing our thing and we've been doing it for a while. I can't think what's changed.'

'Have you always performed your own songs?' he asked perceptively, turning to face me. 'I think the crowd really enjoyed them tonight.'

'Yes, we have but not at every gig and maybe, only one song at most. Perhaps that's it, the audience is getting more of a feel for us from our own songs and it seems that they like them.' I smiled warmly at him, raising my eyebrows in amazement at our good fortune. I took a sip from my glass of wine.

'Do you write the songs together as a band or is it only you who does the songwriting?'

'It's mainly me but the guys help with the music sometimes. You seem to like all this stuff, are you musical?'

'Me, no!' He laughed out loud at the mere idea. 'No, I

don't play anything and you wouldn't want to hear me sing but I do love music, it's true.'

'I happen to think that everyone can sing, even if it's only a little bit. I've heard enough people try in my teaching career to know.'

'That's right. I remember you saying you were a singing teacher.'

'Yep, singing teacher by day, would-be singer/songwriter by night.' I laughed at how crazy it sounded. I moved to brush my hair out of my face, drawing Jackson's attention to my bracelet.

'That's pretty,' he said, reaching out to take my wrist in his hand. He bent his head forward to study the charms, touching one or two of the musical ones with his long, slim fingers. I wanted to tell him about it but I couldn't seem to find my breath. He released me and turned to look deep into my eyes, inviting me to reveal more about myself.

'My mum gave it to me for my 18th birthday and I wear it for luck whenever we play.' I could feel tears beginning to form and I dipped my head, willing them to go away. As if sensing my sadness, Jackson put his arm around me and drew me close to his body. I put my hand to his chest to steady myself and let his clean, masculine smell wash over me. Neither of us spoke for a moment, just enjoying the feeling of holding each other. After a few minutes, I pulled away from him and reached for some wine to calm my beating heart. I heard him clear his throat and glanced over to see him take a long drink too. He had managed to comfort me and set my heart racing all at the same time.

'I guess you'll be preparing for the audition for the "Open Mic" competition on Friday now?' Jackson resumed the conversation.

'I'll have to confirm that tomorrow, if it's not too late. I've been really busy today.'

'I'm sure it'll be okay. Have you any more gigs lined up

for me to come to?'

'Matt organises all the bookings. He probably has some plans in mind. Anyway, haven't you had enough of us already?' I teased.

'It's been a pleasure for me to come and hear you sing,' he said, leaning towards me and pressing his thigh more firmly against mine. 'As soon as you have another date scheduled, I hope you'll let me know because I've been enjoying myself going to gigs again. I don't seem to get the time any more.' He moved back again but my heart was pounding at his touch.

'I'm glad you've enjoyed them and I promise to let you know about any new dates.'

We left the bar shortly afterwards and walked down to the quayside once more, drawn by the sound of the waves and the glowing lights. There were lots of people milling around, chatting and laughing as they enjoyed the warm summer evening. As we reached the water, Jackson took my hand in his, wrapping his fingers around mine and stroking them gently with his thumb. I was aware of how our hands fit perfectly together, as we swung them gently back and forth. We wandered slowly back to the cottage but, once again, we'd reached my garden gate before we knew it.

As we came to a stop, Jackson blurted out, 'Would you be free for dinner tomorrow night? We could celebrate your success with the gig tonight when you're feeling a bit more rested.'

'I'd like that.' I didn't even need to consider it.

He smiled broadly and took out his phone to exchange numbers.

'Shall I pick you up at seven?'

'That sounds like a good plan,' I agreed.

He took a step towards me and gently leaned in to kiss me on the cheek. His lips barely touched my skin but it was enough to make me want more of the same. Instinctively, I put my hand where his lips had been, as if wanting to keep the kiss there, and the crooked smile he gave me was irresistible.

'Goodnight, see you tomorrow. Sweet dreams,' he called, looking back one last time before I opened the door and went inside. God, I thought, I'd only known him for a short time, but I could no longer deny it: I was in danger of falling for him and it had been a long time since I'd let myself experience feelings like that.

There was a knock at the door the next morning. As I opened it, all I could see were flowers in an arrangement so enormous, even the person delivering them was virtually hidden from view. The sweet smell of sunflowers, orange gerberas, creamy chrysanthemums, luscious pink roses and so many more filled the air that I couldn't take them all in.

'Oh my goodness, Mary, are these for me?' I recognised Jenna's assistant from the shop when she poked her head out.

'Yes, and there's a card attached,' she said, grinning. I thanked Mary, told her I was glad she was better and brought the beautiful flowers into the kitchen. I didn't think I had enough vases for all of them. I noticed the card tucked into the middle of the bouquet, pulled it out of the envelope and read the message.

'Hey, gorgeous. Just to remind you that you rocked last night and I can't wait to see you again later. Until then, Jackson x'

I almost fainted with delight. I'd never been sent such a romantic message, nor such a fabulous bouquet. I decided to text Jackson there and then to thank him. But how should I phrase it? I didn't want to be too forward but then again, maybe I did!

'Thank you for the lovely flowers, what a wonderful surprise! Your message has left me speechless, not something that happens to me often. Looking forward to seeing you too, Rachel x'

Next, I called Jenna.

'I just received the flowers, they're absolutely wonderful.'

'I'm really pleased you like them. When Jackson came in and ordered the bouquet for you this morning, I wanted to make them special because you deserve it.'

'Oh, Jenna, thank you for being such a good friend. I don't know what I would do without you.'

'And what about the message on the card?' she teased me. 'He must really like you. Where are you going for dinner?'

'I don't know, we didn't discuss it.'

'Sounds like Jackson's sweeping you off your feet.'

I laughed. 'I know and it feels great! Would you like me to bring you some lunch in later so you can help me plan a course of action for tonight?'

'That's a brilliant idea. Shall we say twelve thirty?'

'That's another date for today!' We both giggled as we hung up.

As soon as I'd put down the phone, I fired off a quick email to Natasha at the competition telling her a bit about our band and confirming that we would like to attend the auditions on Friday. Her reply came back straight away.

That's great, Rachel. We look forward to seeing you in Bournemouth on Friday. Soundcheck is at half past five and the auditions start at seven. The auditions are not open to the public so I'm afraid you won't be able to bring any guests.'

I bit my lip as I read through her message. It all sounded very real now and it was too late to even think about changing my mind. Anyway, I wanted the band to take full advantage of this opportunity and, in my heart, I couldn't wait for Friday to come. I decided to ring Sam on his mobile to let him know that it was all booked for Friday and to see if we could fit in a rehearsal before then. It took him quite a while to answer and I wondered where he was.

'Hey, what's up?'

Sam sounded like he was busy working. I felt a bit guilty

34

for disturbing him but I ploughed on.

'I've confirmed that we'd like to attend the auditions on Friday. Could we fit in a rehearsal before then?'

'I'll need to talk to Matt about it as well. Can I call you back?' He didn't sound very pleased about it. My grip tightened on the phone. All at once, I'd had enough of his pettiness over the past few days.

'I won't be here later, I'm going out tonight with Jackson. You don't sound like you're that pleased anyway, so there's no point in you calling me back.'

He sighed. 'Sorry, I can't talk right now but look, you shouldn't get your hopes up about this audition. To be honest, Matt and I are only doing this for you so let's take it easy and see how it goes.' He paused. 'And why are you going out with that Jackson guy?'

'That's none of your business. And if you have nothing positive to say, I'll let you get back to your work.'

I ended the call and threw my phone to the other end of the sofa. Why did he have to say that he and Matt were only doing this for me? Sam's poor attitude made me more appreciative than ever of Jackson's support. At least he was showing an interest.

Around midday, I set out for town to see Jenna, eager to get some fresh air to clear away my bad mood after the call with Sam. I walked into the shop twenty minutes later, carrying two huge sandwiches from the deli. We went out to the back room to eat and catch up, leaving Mary in charge of the shop.

'First of all, congratulations again on the gig last night. You guys were fabulous and the crowd loved you,' she began. I nodded, a bit embarrassed by all the praise. Then she went on, 'Secondly, have you decided what to wear tonight?'

'You mean from my vast wardrobe of top fashion designs?' She nodded back at me. 'Well, no, I haven't. It is a bit tricky when I don't know where we're going.'

Just then, my phone buzzed as it received a text. When I looked at it, my eyes widened in surprise.

'It's from Jackson.' I read it out to her.

'Do you like seafood? If you do, I'm standing outside a great looking place on the High Street. Let me know what you think.'

'He must be outside Simply Seafood. Quick, let him know,' she said.

'I love seafood. Are you at Simply Seafood? I'm with Jenna at the moment, if you want to pop in. Otherwise, see you later and thanks.'

'No kiss then?' Jenna teased, looking over my shoulder.

'Well, he didn't do one either and I don't want to be too flirty.'

'Why the hell not?'

A few minutes later, the doorbell tinkled and I held my breath, wondering if it was him. Jenna poked her head round the corner from the back room to check and then disappeared. When she reappeared, she had Jackson in tow. His huge frame filled the room, leaving little space for anyone else. It meant he had to stand incredibly close to me though, definitely a bonus.

'Thank you again for the lovely bouquet,' I began, looking up into his handsome face. 'That was kind of you. I can't remember the last time someone gave me flowers.'

'I'm especially glad I did then, if it's been so long.' He was close enough to touch but I didn't think it would be right in front of Jenna so I had to satisfy myself with ogling him instead. He paused for a moment before saying to Jenna, 'You know, Meg said she was having a few problems with the flowers for the wedding. Would you mind if I recommended you to her?'

'That would be fantastic, Jackson, thank you. I haven't been going long so all positive feedback is appreciated.' Jenna smiled. 'Here's one of my business cards if you'd like to pass it on and I'll wait to hear from her.'

'I'd best leave you ladies to your lunch and make my way back. I booked the restaurant for half past seven, Rachel, so I'll pick you up at seven. Is that okay?'

'Yes, great, thank you.'

Jackson flashed me another smile before ducking his head to go back to the main shop.

Once he'd gone, I stared at Jenna, hardly able to believe my good luck in meeting him. She stared back for a moment, equally unable to believe that she might soon be planning her first wedding. Then we both squealed in delight before going back to thinking about what I should wear.

'I think you should wear a dress, if you have one. And something that will show off a bit of cleavage too,' she suggested.

I almost choked on my drink.

'I think I have a dress or two but none that I'd like to wear in public!' I sighed. I never had the money for clothes shopping after paying all my bills each month, but I did have a little put aside so maybe I should indulge myself.

'I might go for a wander round the shops on my way back home and see if there's anything that catches my eye.' I fell silent then, wanting to ask her about Sam but not knowing how to go about it.

'What's the matter? Why the miserable face all of a sudden? You must have something to wear.'

'No, it's not about clothes.' I hesitated before taking the plunge. 'Look, tell me if this is awkward but I wanted to ask you about Sam. He's been a bit off with me lately.'

'Go on,' she said, the smile fading from her face.

'I tried asking him about it on Saturday and again on Sunday, but all he said was that he didn't want me to get taken in or hurt by Jackson. I wondered if he might be a bit jealous of Jackson, actually. Then I spoke to him about doing the audition before coming down here to see you and he was blunt about it, saying he'd only gone along with doing it to please me. Do you know what it's all about? I'm obviously missing something.'

'I probably should have told you this before but I didn't know how.' She paused and studied me for a moment. My mouth went dry. 'You're the only person who doesn't realise that Sam has a thing for you. He has had for quite a few years so I'm sure he is jealous of Jackson who's succeeding where he's failed.'

My face paled and I sat down on the nearest stool.

'As for the competition,' she went on, 'you know Sam better than anyone. He's a home-loving kind of guy, he's happy being a carpenter, going where the jobs take him. He's not after fame and fortune.' She looked at me with sadness.

'I wish someone had told me,' I said, 'because I honestly had no idea. I love Sam like a brother and wouldn't want to hurt him for anything but why hasn't he told me this? It's not like he hasn't had plenty of opportunity in the past, before Jackson came along.'

My hands were clammy now with the realisation that I might have made a big mistake with Sam in the past. I wanted to tell Jenna what had happened between us that night but I didn't know how she would take it so I kept quiet.

'I don't know.' She came over to give me a hug. 'Talk to him about his feelings and about the competition. Tell him how much it means to you. That's all you can do.'

CHAPTER SIX

Jackson looked me over as I closed the door behind me, his smile broadening as he took in my outfit.

'Wow, you look stunning.'

I'd been saved in the end by a maxi dress that I'd bought in the sale late last summer. It had a lovely ethnic print, all blues, pinks and greens and an interesting neckline that showed off some cleavage without overdoing it, I hoped.

'You look pretty handsome yourself.'

My eyes wandered greedily over his soft, brown leather jacket, worn over a pale yellow button-down shirt and chinos. He was wearing his cowboy boots again but there was still no sign of a Stetson.

He took my hand and we set off together for town. We walked in silence for a while along the quiet residential street. I was enjoying the reassuring feel of our hands together. When we arrived at the quayside, we stopped to stare at the dazzling array of expensive-looking yachts moored in the harbour. The sun shone down on the still, blue water and there was hardly a cloud in the sky.

'I'm ashamed to say that I know very little about Nashville,' I said, 'apart from the music connection. Are you close to the sea there?'

'We're about eight hours from the sea in most directions,' he explained, 'so not what you'd call close, no. But I like going to the beach and I try to get there quite often. I have a beach house at Charleston, which isn't a very long flight away.'

'You have two homes then, one in Nashville and another in

Charleston?'

Jackson seemed to hesitate. 'Actually, I have some other homes as well. I prefer not to stay in hotels when I travel.'

'Okay, you have to tell me now,' I said, laughing. 'Exactly how many homes do you have?'

'That's not important,' he fudged. He looked distinctly uncomfortable so I decided not to push it and turned to look out at the sea again.

'That's Brownsea Island over there,' I said, pointing. 'It's a lovely place, full of wildlife and the views are stunning. I spent hours there as a kid but I haven't been for a few years. I ought to go back with my camera some time soon.'

'Maybe you could take me there, show me the sights?'

His arm was leaning against mine and the warmth of his body, through his jacket, caused a tingling sensation deep within me.

'I'd love to do that.'

When we arrived at the restaurant, a waiter led us to our table straight away. Jackson handed his jacket over before sitting down, giving me the chance to admire his arms in his short-sleeved shirt. I looked up to find that he was watching me watching him and smirking at my attention. My cheeks heated a little from being caught in the act so I smiled quickly before looking down at the menu. I chose clams followed by sea bass and Jackson went for the local oysters and plaice. While waiting for the starters, I decided to try and find out a bit more about him.

'Do you mind me asking how old you are?' I began.

'Not at all,' he said easily. 'I'll be thirty this October. How about you?'

'I turned twenty-six this March. And what do you do for a living?' I went on.

He debated for a moment before admitting, 'I'm in the music business actually, like you.'

'Ah, now I see why you know so much, but I'm hardly in

the music business. I'm a singer/songwriter destined to play pub gigs for the next few years until I give up and sink into oblivion.'

I looked up at Jackson to find him frowning at me.

'What's the matter?'

His jaw clenched. 'How can you even joke that you're going to give up when you're so talented? If you do this audition, you stand a good chance of getting through to the regional final too and maybe even winning,' he argued.

'Thank you for your confidence in me but you don't know any more than I do whether I can make a go of it, do you, to be fair?'

He paused, took a deep breath and said, 'When I said I'm in the music business, I actually own an independent record label in Nashville and I've managed to sign some of the most up-and-coming artists to the label over these past few years.' He stopped to let this information sink in. I wasn't sure if he'd intended to give that much away because he was looking down at his lap now.

'And your record label has made you rich, right? So rich that you have several homes?'

'Yep,' he answered looking down at his lap again.

'And so, is your interest in me purely business-related? Is that why you're wining and dining me and encouraging us to enter the competition?' I suddenly felt very naive and worried that I'd misunderstood what was developing between us.

His head snapped back up at that criticism.

'I would like to get to know you better. But it so happens that you're a great singer/songwriter and I own a record label. Those two things could be mutually beneficial, yes.'

He stopped talking when our starters were brought to the table.

'Let's toast then to mutually beneficial relationships.' I raised my glass by way of apology. We talked about our love of food as we ate our starters, sharing tastes of each other's meals and steered clear of the serious topics we'd strayed into.

Once our main courses had arrived, Jackson tried again with a more meaningful conversation.

'I'm serious about you being talented, you know. Your own songs were really moving. They sound like they're based on personal experience, which is what country music's all about of course. So, are they, you know, based on your own experience?'

'Well, my childhood wasn't great in many ways. My dad used to drink a lot and finally, after years of putting up with it, my mum had had enough and they split up when I was fourteen. But my dad carried on drinking and eventually his body couldn't take it any more. He was only fifty when he died. I still can't understand how he could do that to himself.' I paused to consider the futility of it all. 'My mum died a year later from cancer. She knew she had it but had kept it secret from me because of what had happened to my dad. That was about four years ago but I still miss them both such a lot.'

Tears were in my eyes as I finished telling him about my family. He reached out and took my hand. I looked up at him and saw him swallow, as if my story had touched him deeply.

'And of course, I've been incredibly unlucky in love. I'm doing what I want now, no men involved,' I went on jokingly to try and change the atmosphere.

'Maybe you haven't met the right person yet,' he offered, gazing into my eyes.

'Maybe you're right. I'm a glass half-full kind of girl so I'm ever hopeful that I'll find someone I can trust.' I paused for a moment to collect myself. 'How about you? Have you been over to the UK before?'

'Yes, my mom and Tom's are sisters. We used to see each other all the time when we were little. My sister, Shelby and I spent the first few years of our lives in Bournemouth. Then when I was seven and she was three, we upped and moved to Tennessee, which was where my mom met my step-dad and we've been there ever since. But I've kept in touch with Tom over the years.'

'Wow, what made your mum move to Tennessee from Bournemouth? That's quite a leap.'

'After my dad left, things were quite bad for us. It was a constant struggle for my mom, trying to bring up two young kids on her own. When one of her cousins in the States suggested she come out to give life over there a try, I think she jumped at the chance of a fresh start.'

'What about your real dad? Have you kept in touch with him?' I asked.

'He disappeared one day, the year I turned five and never came back and I haven't seen him since. My memories of him are vague now. I've always seen Bob, my step-dad, as my real dad.'

'Have you any brothers or sisters from your mum's marriage to Bob?'

'Hell, yeah,' he laughed. 'Two brothers and two sisters. They're all quite a handful and I'm the eldest so I'm expected to be the role model, which doesn't always work out, you know.'

He winked at me then, giving me a warm feeling right at the pit of my stomach.

The waiter asked whether we would like dessert. I wasn't bothered so Jackson asked for the bill while I went off to the toilet.

I stared at myself in the mirror, wondering what on earth he could see in me now I knew his background. Our lives were very different and he would be going soon anyway. I told myself to try and enjoy it while it lasted and not to think too much about the future.

When I returned to the table, Jackson had paid the bill and I decided not to argue and thanked him as graciously as I could.

On our leisurely walk back to my cottage, I asked, 'When

is Tom's wedding?'

'It's a little over two weeks away. Have you been invited?'

'Goodness, no. I don't know either of them that well.'

'Would you like to come as my date?'

I was stunned. 'I'd love that. Thank you.'

He stopped and turned towards me then but didn't say anything. Turning to face him, I looked up at him expectantly, hoping that he would kiss me because I was too shy to be the one to make the first move.

As I looked into his dark eyes, he leaned towards me, tilting his head to one side. My heart beat a little quicker in anticipation of a kiss and suddenly his warm lips were on mine, brushing them gently at first. His kiss was so inviting that I responded naturally, moving closer, taking in his wonderful manly scent. I was very aware of his hands, one resting on my hip, the other clasping the base of my neck. I slipped my arms around his waist and the kiss deepened. He traced my lips with his tongue and when I opened my mouth a little, he took the hint and started to explore further.

I closed my eyes and a moan of pleasure escaped me. He groaned too, pulling me closer. The stubble on his cheek tickled my face and I wondered what it would feel like if he was kissing other parts of my body. My face burned at the thought of it.

Perhaps sensing my increased passion, Jackson chose that moment to pull back. 'Rachel?' he said huskily.

As he stepped away, I opened my eyes, shivering from the loss of his warmth. I knew that I had never been kissed like that before. Nick, my ex-fiancé, had never managed to awaken such strong feelings in me and that realisation was both frightening and exciting.

I could see the desire in Jackson's eyes and knew that it was reflected in mine.

There was no hesitation in my heart when I asked him, 'Would you like a coffee before you go?'

He nodded, his gaze intense on my face.

When I brought out the drinks, we sat together on my cushioned bench in the back garden. I decided then to be bold and ask him about his love life.

'Do you have a girlfriend back home that I should know about?'

'I wouldn't be here with you if I did,' he said immediately. 'I was in a relationship with someone until a year ago; in fact, we were also engaged but she cheated on me.'

'I'm so sorry.'

'It has been hard for me to get over, I have to admit. You're the first person I've kissed in all that time.'

I was surprised by this confession and didn't know what to say.

'How about you, Rachel? Are you seeing anyone?'

'No, I haven't dated for a long time. I have to say, I'm a bit out of practice.'

He was silent for a moment, as though considering that information. Then he put his arm around me and pulled me against him.

'Thank you for a wonderful evening, I've really enjoyed it,' he murmured and kissed me again briefly on the lips. I had the feeling he was deliberately trying to restrain himself.

A few moments later, he stood up, drawing me up with him. We said goodnight but as I watched Jackson raise a hand in farewell and walk away down the street, I found myself wishing he had chosen to stay.

CHAPTER SEVEN

I'd booked a taxi late Friday afternoon for the short ride to Bournemouth International Centre where the "Open Mic" audition was taking place. The driver dropped me off at the designated entrance for performers, much less fancy than it sounded, and I went inside to look for Sam and Matt who had come in the van with all the gear.

I checked in with a woman at the registration desk and she directed me towards one of the smaller conference rooms, where I found the guys waiting for me. I was starting to feel a bit daunted by the sight of so many other acts rushing around trying to get ready for their performance tonight, so seeing Sam and Matt calmed me down and I greeted them both with a big smile.

They led the way into a soulless conference room, which was not what I was expecting, and my initial excitement faded a little. It was a medium-sized square room with a stage rigged up at one end and some tables and chairs for the judges at the other. The sides of the room were taken up with cheap-looking tables and chairs, next to bright orange curtains and separated by an overly patterned carpet. I would have to exercise amazing willpower to stop myself being distracted by all the overwhelming colour in the room.

We'd carried out our soundcheck by six o'clock, giving us time to grab something to eat. We went out to have a look around the venue and found a little café but I could only manage a coffee because of my nerves.

'How are you both feeling about the audition?' I asked once we'd found a table. They both seemed much more

46

relaxed than I was.

'We had a great rehearsal yesterday and the setlist we've planned is just right for the audition,' Sam replied, with a small shrug.

'I've got some good news for us too,' Matt broke in. 'I had a text today from that new wine bar we signed up with. They heard about our success at The Cork and Bottle the other night and they want us to play there tomorrow night. I know it's short notice but it means that word is spreading about us.'

'Wow! That's amazing. I'm definitely up for it if you two are?' They both nodded.

'I am up for it,' said Matt, 'but Natalie's not that impressed by all these extra rehearsals and shows we're doing at the moment.' He sighed.

I frowned, thinking about Natalie but I didn't say anything, knowing that only he could deal with that problem. Everyone fell silent and I found myself wishing that Jackson was there to boost my confidence. He'd sent me a text earlier in the day to wish me luck but I would have loved him to be there with me. Thankfully, we had to be back by half past six so it wasn't long before we were in the hall outside the conference room again, getting ready to audition.

When we arrived, we found a woman from the competition organising performers with military precision. We checked with her when we were due to perform. We were act number six and as each act had to limit their performance to two minutes, we didn't have long to wait. My stomach churned at the prospect of performing in front of these industry judges and I wished that I could hear some of the acts to give me an idea of what we were up against. Instead, all I could hear was the sound of my own heartbeat thumping furiously as I became more and more apprehensive.

Our turn came round soon enough and once I was in the room walking towards the stage where my trusted guitar waited patiently for me, my spirits lifted. It took only a few minutes for each of us to get into place and when I raised my eyes in the judges' direction, I found them ready for us. I coughed nervously before introducing the band.

'Can you tell us a little bit about your experience please?' one of the male judges asked me.

'I'm Rachel and I write the songs for the most part and I sing, play guitar and play the piano as well. Sam's on guitar and Matt plays the drums. We've been playing pubs in the local area for about the last four years.'

'Great, Rachel, thanks. What are you going to play for us today?' asked the only female judge. I didn't know any of the three judges.

'We're going to play a new song I wrote recently, called "Too Late",' I replied.

'When you're ready, then, guys. Give it your best shot,' said the remaining judge.

This was it then. No turning back if Three's Company wanted to get through to the regional final and definitely everything to gain by giving it our all. I took a deep breath and began to play my guitar. For the next two minutes, we gave our performance everything we had and the judges looked like they were really getting into it from the positive-looking glances they exchanged. All too soon, we'd finished and were making our way out again. We found a table outside and collapsed into the chairs, relieved that it was all over.

'How do you think it went?' I asked, looking at Sam and then Matt for confirmation.

'I don't think we could have done a better performance than that,' Matt replied. 'If we don't get through, it's not because we're not talented. It will only be because other acts are better than us and to be honest, tonight, we were at our peak.'

'It's great to hear you say all that, thank you.' I looked at Sam to find him nodding in agreement and my heart soared. I reached out to take their hands and give them both a squeeze.

During the interval, we removed our gear from the stage to make way for the performers in the second half, and the guys began loading it into the van. I checked with one of the organisers that we were free to leave and was told we'd be informed by email of how we'd done. Now all we had to do was get through to Monday.

In the van on the way home, Sam took hold of my hand. I didn't pull away, even though I knew I should because my hand seemed to belong in his. He hadn't said anything to me about having feelings for me but that small act spoke volumes. We needed to talk about it, to clear the air but how to do that without ruining our friendship?

'Will you come in for a quick coffee?' I asked, as Matt drew the van up outside the cottage. Matt glanced nervously at his watch but followed me and Sam inside anyway.

While the kettle was boiling, I came straight to the point.

'I need to talk to you both about the "Open Mic" competition now that we've done the audition. You both know, I think, how much it means to me to pursue this and I know that neither of you wants it like I do. I don't want to push you to do something you don't want to do so I need you both to be honest with me please about what we'll do if we get through the audition.'

I stared at them both, squashed side by side on my tiny sofa. They looked awkward and didn't say anything. I made the coffees and when I returned, Matt spoke up.

'Look, Rachel, we do know how much it means to you but take me, for example, I have different priorities. I'm married with a young baby, I can't be gallivanting off to do shows all over the place. I'm worried that if we get through the audition, it's going to get serious and I didn't sign up for any of that. I just wanted to have a bit of fun, playing my drums and doing the occasional gig. I'm sorry.'

'And how about you, Sam? You said that you only agreed

to do this to please me so do you feel the same as Matt?' I asked.

'I suppose I do, yes,' he said quietly. 'I know I'm not married but I want a quiet life, you know. I like gigging for fun but not for anything more serious, I'm sorry if I didn't make that clear before.'

They both looked sorry for themselves. I went out into the garden to think about what they'd said.

'Rachel, I'm sorry, I have to get back. I'll see you tomorrow at the gig.'

I didn't turn to look at Matt, I just nodded and said goodbye. I sensed Sam come up behind me and put his arm around my shoulder. I turned my face towards him, unable to stop tears from springing to my eyes. He lifted his hand and gently wiped my tears away with his thumb, only making me cry more. He wrapped his arms around me and I fell into his embrace gratefully. We stood silently together for a few moments, neither of us daring to speak. Finally, I stepped back and wiped my eyes again.

'You know this is my dream and this is probably my last chance to try and make it happen.' He nodded at me. 'That's why I want us to make the most of this competition. Perhaps we should wait and see what happens about the audition because if we don't get through, none of this matters anyway.'

'Let's do that and see where we are afterwards,' he agreed. He smiled tentatively but both of us knew that we were putting off another difficult conversation later on. I waited for him to say something to me about his feelings but to my disappointment, he said nothing, leaving shortly afterwards. What was he so afraid of?

CHAPTER EIGHT

After a restless night, I settled on the sofa with my guitar and started playing a few favourite songs. I moved on to a more poignant one of my own, closed my eyes and let myself become drawn into the music. All of a sudden, the sound of someone knocking at my front door startled me out of my reverie. I opened the door to see Jackson standing there, looking absolutely gorgeous in black jeans and a grey t-shirt, his wavy hair still damp from the shower.

'Jackson, hi!'

'Did I wake you up? If I did, I'm sorry.' He grinned at me but I couldn't understand what he meant at first.

Then it hit me, I was still wearing my pyjamas. Never had my camisole top and pyjama shorts seemed so revealing. My face grew suddenly hot.

'Oh my goodness, no!' I exclaimed. 'Look, come in. I'll go and get changed.' I ran upstairs as gracefully as I could, leaving him to fend for himself for a moment, and changed into some yoga pants and a more appropriate t-shirt. I pulled my hair into a ponytail and took a few calming deep breaths before going back downstairs again.

'Sorry about that,' I said when I walked back into the lounge. 'I was busy singing and time slipped away from me.' I risked a little glance at him and found him smiling reassuringly at me. 'Would you like a drink?' I asked.

When he said no, I sat down in the armchair opposite him and tucked my bare feet up underneath me.

'How did the audition go yesterday?' he asked me, giving me one of his breathtaking smiles and a glimpse of his perfect white teeth.

'It went really well. We all agreed that it was one of our best performances.'

'Do you know when you'll find out whether you got through?'

'They said they'll email us on Monday so I need to keep myself busy till then. The gig at the wine bar tonight will help with that.'

'Is that a gig you haven't told me about?' He raised his eyebrows in query and I realised I hadn't had the chance to tell him the good news about the wine bar coming to us and asking us to play, rather than the other way round.

'I hate to say I told you so,' he said, 'but it was only a matter of time before this started happening. You guys are so good that word was bound to spread quickly round town. What time is the gig tonight?'

'We're on first at eight but I'll be getting there early, as always for the soundcheck. Will you be able to come?'

'Of course, I wouldn't want to miss another chance to hear you sing.'

He stood up then and so did I, finding myself standing very close to him. The heat radiated from his body and I looked up at him, staring into his dark brown eyes, not quite knowing what was going to happen next. My body seemed to have already made up its mind, as I leaned involuntarily towards him. He reached out to steady me, placing his hands on my waist, and bent his head to whisper in my ear.

'Just so you know, I definitely preferred your pyjamas.' I could feel his smile as his lips kissed their way slowly down my neck and my knees almost gave way at his sensual exploration of my skin. He held on tight to me and as I buried my fingers deep in his hair, pulling him even closer to me, I heard him sigh with pleasure. When the kiss came at last, the softness of his lips was intoxicating and as our tongues met, the desire I was feeling intensified further. I laid my hands against his chest, enjoying the feel of his firm muscles under his shirt and his heady, male scent. Just as I was imagining what his skin would feel like if his shirt wasn't there, he broke away and we both inhaled deeply. His pupils were dilated and I guessed mine looked the same. I stared into his seductive brown eyes and waited to hear what he would say next. Instead, he took my hand and led me upstairs where my bedroom beckoned.

At the top of the stairs, Jackson moved to one side to let me lead the way. Once inside the room, I turned to face him, desperate for reassurance that we were doing the right thing.

'Jackson, I...'

He put his finger on my lips. 'Shh. Do you want this?' I nodded and suddenly his lips crushed mine in another deep kiss. His passionate embrace was all I needed to confirm that he wanted me as much as I wanted him. His fingers slipped underneath my t-shirt and his warm hands against my skin made me tremble with anticipation. I began to pull his t-shirt out from his jeans but he saved me the job by pulling it out himself and then over his head in one swift movement.

I stared at him, my breath trapped by the sight of his now bare chest covered with a sprinkling of dark, curly hair. I moved closer to him again, raising my hand to trace the muscles I'd felt there earlier and then placed a soft kiss right in the middle of his chest. A low rumble in his chest told me how much he liked it. In that moment, I knew I wanted to feel his body against mine and I couldn't wait any longer. As that thought went through my mind, he reached out to remove my top and then we rushed through our remaining clothes, both of us eager for the same sensation of skin on skin.

'You are so beautiful,' he whispered, gazing at me with what looked like admiration. He held out his hand towards me and as we lay down together on the bed, our bodies entwined and our lips joined once again. In that moment, I knew I had never wanted to make love with anyone before as much as I wanted to with him right now. His fingers and lips ignited my body with their every touch and my back arched towards him so it wasn't long before our two bodies became one. We set up a slow, sensuous rhythm between us then, caressing each other inside and out, until we both reached the brink of our release and when that moment finally came, the sweetness of it brought tears to my eyes.

We lay side by side afterwards, both of us quiet. When I looked up, Jackson was watching me as though he could read my thoughts.

'How are you feeling? No regrets, I hope?' he asked.

'Being with you was everything I'd hoped it would be and more,' I replied, taking his hand and bringing it to my lips.

'That's how I felt too.'

I smiled to myself as I remembered our lovemaking, knowing I had never felt such deep emotion with anyone else.

As much as I would have loved to spend the rest of the day in bed with Jackson, I had a gig to play. I had no memory from my earlier trip to the wine bar with him, of any area that could be used as a stage for bands to play on so I didn't quite know what to expect when I turned up later that afternoon. The guy behind the bar pointed me towards the back where Sam and Matt were already setting up. I could see that there was a raised area for us to play on and a small, intimate space with some tables and chairs around it. This looked good and the customers in a wine bar would be a slightly different group than we'd experienced this far.

'This is nice, isn't it?' I said in welcome, waving my hand around.

'Yeah, it's a bit different to what we're used to. The crowd will be as well, I expect.' Sam grinned at me.

I returned it a bit awkwardly, worrying that he would be able to see that I was still buzzing after making love with Jackson only a short time ago. I felt sure I must be giving off some sign about what I'd been up to but, if I was, neither Sam nor Matt seemed to notice. I carried on as normal, giving them a hand with bringing the rest of the gear in from the van and we performed a quick soundcheck before going off to get something to eat.

When we returned, the wine bar was filling up nicely and people were beginning to settle in around the stage area. By eight o'clock, every table was taken and the audience was buzzing. I couldn't see Jackson anywhere but I knew he would slip in unnoticed by the crowd. It had only been a couple of hours since I'd left him but I longed to see him again.

I'd chosen a Dolly Parton song to start with, 'Here You Come Again', knowing it would be a good choice for our usual crowd. What I wasn't sure of was how well the song would go down in this new setting and a flicker of doubt crossed my mind. As I sat down at the piano, I concentrated on putting all my energy into it, emphasising some of the funnier lines from the song and hoping that they'd respond. I reached the end and pushed back from the microphone, scanning the room to gauge the audience reaction. I was disappointed to see that a lot of people weren't even looking our way and we received only a polite ripple of applause. It could have been because we were only the support band but, instinctively, I knew that wasn't the reason.

I looked quickly at Sam and Matt to see what they were thinking. They both gave me tight smiles in response, which I took to mean that they felt as worried as I did about the seeming lack of interest. Nevertheless, I ploughed on, ever the professional, sitting down at the front of the stage with my guitar this time and strumming the opening chords of Eva Cassidy's version of 'Fields of Gold'. As I began to sing, I spotted Jackson standing up at the back with a grim look on his face. He must have been there for the last song as well and heard the mediocre reaction. His presence was reassuring though and when he caught my glance he gave me a crooked smile and my heart skipped a beat.

This song was probably more familiar to the audience and I noticed that people were starting to pay attention to us now. At the end, the applause was stronger, which gave me renewed enthusiasm for singing one of my own songs. As this gig had come up at such short notice, we'd decided to play it safe and stick to songs we knew well so the first of my own songs was 'My Turn'. It meant such a lot to me and regardless of their response to it, I was determined to sing my heart out, putting all the emotion I had into every word and note. I knew I'd done it justice but would they feel the same? Luckily, our own material did the trick again and the crowd seemed more interested in us afterwards. The applause was better, with a few people standing up to encourage us further. We broke for the interval feeling a lot more confident than we had at the beginning.

Jackson came over to talk to us, giving me a soft kiss as he arrived, and I sensed Sam stiffen beside me. God, I'd had enough of that but now was not the time to mention it.

'How do you feel after the first half guys?' He looked concerned.

'I'll go and get some drinks,' Sam interrupted, 'and see if I can find Jenna.'

'She couldn't make it,' I told him. 'I'd love a drink though. Why don't you go with him, Matt?' I suggested so that I could talk to Jackson on my own. He turned to watch them go.

'Is it me or is there some tension here?' he asked, taking my hand.

'Let's not go there right now.' I sighed. 'What did you think about the first half?'

'What you did was great, as good as in your last two shows. It's just that this audience is a bit more sophisticated, I think, and they want to hear your material, they don't want covers. What are you planning for the second half?'

'Two more covers and one of my own songs.'

'Would you be up to doing one cover and two of your own songs?'

'I'd need to agree it with the guys but I'm pretty sure that would be all right.'

After a quick check with Sam and Matt, it was decided to give Jackson's suggestion a try, although Sam didn't look all that pleased about it. There wasn't time to debate it so I started the second half with one of my favourite recent songs, 'All your Life', by The Band Perry which I hoped was a bit more up to date for this audience. It was a good choice because they looked more animated and some people were even singing along. That was a real confidence booster for me and I'm sure for the boys too. I glanced over at Jackson and he was smiling encouragingly back at me.

I went on to introduce 'Too Late' and all at once, there was a new air of anticipation in the room as they waited to hear what this next song of ours would be like. It had gone down so well on its first outing that I was hopeful of it being as popular here. Jackson nodded at me as if approving my choice. I had the feeling he liked this one himself, professionally and personally. I was pretty proud of it too and I belted it out with as much passion as I could muster. The crowd joined in and at the end, the applause made it clear how much they'd enjoyed it. Lots of people stood up and the clapping went on for several minutes. There were lots of cries for 'more' and we were happy to oblige.

We finished the set with 'Love Me', a completely different song but judging by the crowd's reception, another great success. By the end, we had turned things around and there was no doubt that Jackson had given us some good advice. As soon as we'd taken our applause and I'd spoken to a few members of the audience, I made my way over to him.

'You did a fabulous job in the second half there. You really had them on side.'

'Thanks but it was your advice that made the difference,

you know.'

'Your own material is so good that you should be singing more of that now than the covers you've been doing, I think, if you don't mind me giving you my opinion.'

'Of course I don't mind, you know your stuff and I appreciate your help.'

'Can I walk you home again, if that's not getting old?' he asked.

I leaned towards him for a kiss and he responded, dipping his head to meet my lips. It was only a second though before he was wrenched away from me. I looked up in surprise, unsure of what had happened, only to find Sam standing there with a very moody look on his face. He was holding on to Jackson's arm until Jackson pulled out of his grasp and came to stand by my side.

'What the hell is going on?' I demanded.

'I might ask you the same thing,' Sam spat back at me. 'What are you doing kissing this guy you barely know?'

He took a step towards Jackson again and I instinctively stepped between them, uncertain of what Sam was about to do. Matt came forward then too, perhaps sensing the danger in the air, and he pulled Sam back but Sam's eyes never left mine. The hard look in his eyes was unsettling and I wanted him to go because his attitude had already started to get on my nerves tonight and now he had made things even worse.

'Sam, please, don't be like this,' I pleaded with him.

Abruptly, he turned on his heel and walked off with Matt trailing behind him. We'd managed to postpone talking about our relationship up to this point but I knew we couldn't leave it much longer if we were to salvage anything from our friendship, and I had the feeling that I needed to put him straight about a few things sooner rather than later.

Once we were outside, with Jackson holding my guitar again, I broached the subject of Sam with him as we started the walk back home.

'I'm really sorry about Sam's behaviour towards you tonight. He was rude and aggressive. I've never seen him like that and it's unforgivable.'

'Don't you worry about it, it's not your fault.'

'He's worried about me, that's all, we've known each other a long time and he doesn't want me to get hurt again.'

He stopped then, touching my arm so that he could look me in the eye. As I turned to face him, I was a bit wary about what he was going to say next but I'd brought the subject up so now I'd have to deal with it.

'Does he have feelings for you? Have you two ever dated?'

'No…no,' I stuttered, wondering whether to tell him the rest. I pressed on. 'We've never dated but Jenna told me recently that Sam has had feelings for me for a while. Apparently, I'm the only person he hasn't told about that fact,' I said, closing my eyes briefly to hide my irritation.

'And how do you feel about him?' Jackson wasn't giving up easily.

I started walking again while I considered what to say. I didn't have the courage to tell him that we'd slept together after a drunken night when things had escalated beyond our control and, besides, I hadn't even talked about that night with Sam yet.

'He's been like a brother to me all my life, I know that sounds clichéd but it's true, so I care for him very much.'

I was being economical with the truth, I knew but I couldn't tell him everything that had happened between me and Sam in the past. I risked a peek at Jackson to see how he was taking all this. He looked pensive. We were almost back home by this point.

'I'm not stepping on any toes then by getting to know you better?' He looked pointedly at me, giving me the chance to explain but I shook my head, saying nothing. 'Okay, this is how I feel,' he continued. 'I know you and I come from completely different lives but we shouldn't let that get in the way of us getting to know each other better. We don't know where this might go between us but I think we could enjoy finding out, don't you?'

'I do think that but what will happen when you have to go home?'

'I hear what you're saying and obviously I don't want either of us to get hurt but we won't know if we don't try. And there's always a risk in opening up your heart to someone new. Why don't we try and take it one step at a time and enjoy ourselves along the way?'

I nodded but that worry still lingered in my mind, even though I said nothing more about it. I'd also kept the full extent of my relationship with Sam a secret from Jackson and I knew I'd have to face up to that before too long.

'Are you going to church again tomorrow?' he asked me, as we arrived at my front door.

'No, not tomorrow, I don't go every week. I'm having Sunday lunch with Jenna's family in the afternoon again, so I won't get back till later in the evening.' On an impulse, I made a new suggestion. 'Would you like to spend the day sightseeing on Monday? We could take a picnic and go over to Brownsea Island, if you'd like.'

'That sounds like a great way to spend the day. But right now, I'm thinking about how we're going to spend the rest of tonight.' His voice was husky behind me and I turned round with a gasp. The playful grin was back on his face and I couldn't get the door open quickly enough.

CHAPTER NINE

After a tense lunch at Jenna's house the day before, I was looking forward to spending today with Jackson and getting away from things for a while. Going out would also help take my mind off the audition results which should be coming through some time today. The start of the new week was a bit misty but it was meant to be another sunny day later on.

Jackson picked me up right on nine o'clock as we'd agreed in a quick chat the night before, and hoisted the bag I'd packed for our picnic easily up on to his shoulder for the walk down to the quay. I'd made sure to take my camera with me this time, in the hope of spotting a red squirrel at some point during the day. We stopped for some breakfast on the quay, by which time the weather was already brightening up.

'How was lunch at Jenna's house yesterday?' Jackson asked once we'd got settled at a table.

'Not very good actually.' I frowned as I remembered the strained atmosphere from the day before.

He raised his eyebrows, inviting me to tell him more.

'Well, Sam had apparently been called out on an emergency job so he wasn't even there and Matt's wife, Natalie, decided to have a go at me about the amount of time Matt was away from home at the moment because of all the extra rehearsals.' I sighed heavily, wondering what I had done to deserve all this trouble lately. Jackson winced in response and reached across the table to take my hand.

'It's a good thing we're going out for the day today then, isn't it?' He smiled and gave my hand a little squeeze. 'Aren't you supposed to hear about the results of the audition today?'

I nodded as I swallowed a sip of coffee.

'I don't want it to take over the day. Let's forget it and focus on having a good time.'

We bought our return tickets at the kiosk on the quayside and waited for the ferry to be ready. Soon we were on our way across the harbour towards the island, the wind blowing gently in our hair. I looked across at Jackson to find him taking in the view. His handsome face was even more striking in profile and I noticed a fine stubble growing over his jaw which was especially inviting. He turned then, saw me studying him and leaned towards me for a kiss, pulling me gently towards him at the same time. With his arm round my waist and the warmth of his body next to mine, I decided that this had the makings of a perfect day.

It was only a short journey across to the island and once we'd paid our entrance fee we headed into the woods to walk across. It was only a twenty-minute walk from one side to the other but we stopped so many times along the way to look at the church, the wildlife, the lily pond, the trees, taking photos all the while, that it was almost midday when we reached the beach on the far side. We sat down to admire the view from the island back towards the town and to look at the photos I'd taken.

'This is a beautiful island,' Jackson said. 'The views are fantastic and it was wonderful to see the wildlife in the woods.'

'I'm still hopeful about seeing a red squirrel on the way back too.'

We were so hungry after our walk that we started our lunch early, tucking into the hearty picnic I'd prepared. Afterwards, I lay down on the grass to stare at the crystal blue sky and Jackson followed suit. As I lay there, I summoned up the courage to ask him the one question I didn't want to know the answer to but would have to ask anyway.

'Jackson?' I started tentatively without looking at him.

'Mm-hmmm?' he replied. I could sense that he had turned his face to look at mine.

'When are you flying back to Nashville?' I bit my lip waiting for his reply.

'On the 26th August, just after the wedding,' he said, turning on to his side and propping himself up on his elbow to see my reaction. My face fell, even though I knew it was inevitable that he would be going back. 'Let's enjoy today and not worry too far ahead as we agreed.'

He kissed me softly, stroking my hair away from my face, then lay back down without saying anything more. I knew I was starting to like him and I thought he felt the same, even after a few days, but neither of us knew what we could do about the future. His life was in Nashville and mine was here and not only that but our lives were poles apart. Jackson took my hand and squeezed it and I tried hard not to let this new information spoil the day.

When we set off again, we followed the coastal path around the south of the island, made famous by Lord Baden-Powell, and stopped to look at the monument and read the inscription. I glanced up in the stillness after I'd finished reading and found myself looking straight at a red squirrel in a nearby tree. I got my camera ready as quickly as I could and snapped off a few shots before it disappeared. Jackson looked up as I finished, completely oblivious to the squirrel's presence. I showed him the photos as proof and he pulled a funny face.

'Oh boy, I wish I'd seen that,' he said. I laughed at his face but he shrugged it off.

We were wandering back towards the ferry when Jackson asked me about my plans for my singing.

'What do you want to do with your singing? You know, let's say you guys get through the audition, win the regionals and go on to the national final. What would you like to happen next?' It was very reassuring to see that he took me seriously.

I waited a moment or two before answering and then sighed as I said, 'In my dreams, I'd like to make a go of it as a singer and songwriter because I've wasted too much time thinking I couldn't do it, that I wasn't good enough. If we get through to the final, I am going to give it everything I have.' I paused, knowing that I ought to tell him the rest. 'The thing is, Sam and Matt don't feel the same way as I do about the competition, they made that clear to me the other day.' I looked up to see Jackson's feelings about it but his face was passive, taking it all in.

'What have you decided to do?' he asked at last.

'We agreed to wait and see whether we get through to the regional final first. If we don't, none of it matters anyway but if we do, we'll have another difficult conversation to deal with.'

'Have you checked your phone to see if you've had a message yet?' he went on.

'No, I'm out with you so I haven't checked my phone.' I rolled my eyes at him but he persisted.

'You know you want to and I don't mind at all. Go on, have a look.'

I tutted at him before removing my phone from my bag and switching it on. It took a minute for it to catch up with the texts and emails received but my eyes were drawn at once to the email symbol and the number next to it. I gave it a tap to see what was there. What I read next took my breath away. 'We got through!' I cried, looking up at Jackson to see his response.

'That's fabulous, well done, I knew you'd do it,' he replied, lifting me off my feet and swinging me round in the air. As he set me down, he gave me one of his best smiles. 'When is the regional final?' he asked as I quickly sent off texts to Sam and Matt, promising to call them later.

'It's on Friday at the same place.' I could hardly keep still, I was so excited at the news.

Jackson paused for a moment before saying, 'Listen, I have to go to London on business for a few days tomorrow but I'll be back on Friday so I won't miss the regional final, that is if you'd like me to come?'

'Of course I would.' Even so, my smile faded at the thought of him going away, which I tried to hide but didn't quite succeed. I knew I would miss him but I had to admit to myself that it might allow me to get my head around all that had been happening and to try and regain a sense of normality.

We made our way back to the ferry shortly afterwards. I was still reeling from the good news as we set off for home. I couldn't stop smiling and even though we didn't speak much, I knew Jackson was pleased for me too.

'Would you like to come in for a drink?' I asked once we returned to the cottage, flashing him what I hoped was a persuasive smile.

'Sure, a cold drink would be nice.'

We went on through to the kitchen where I made two drinks and took them outside to the garden.

'What will you be doing in London?' I asked, handing him his drink and sitting next to him on the garden bench.

'I'll have a couple of face to face meetings with some of my music partners over here. It will make a change from always having to deal with them over the phone. I have a couple of potential new artists in the pipeline as well so I need to meet with their managers too. And then there'll be dinners so I'll be kept quite busy.' He took a sip of his drink and stared at me expectantly, sensing that I had more questions.

'Do you have somewhere to stay in London? I mean, one of your homes?' I tried to ask as if it was the most natural thing in the world to me to have lots of homes.

'No, I don't have a home in the UK. I'll have to slum it and stay at a luxury hotel instead.' He grinned disarmingly and my stomach performed a little somersault.

He moved up closer to me then and put his arm around me,

pushing my hair gently over my shoulder.

'How about you? What will you get up to without me to keep you occupied?' he asked softly, eyes glittering.

I swallowed before whispering, 'I think I'm really going to miss you actually, it will be hard not spending time together.' He was still gazing at me with his dark brown eyes and listening carefully to what I was saying. 'Have I said too much?' I asked when he didn't reply.

He kissed me lightly on my bare shoulder, sending a ripple of desire right through my body. I put my arms round his neck and drew him in closer so our lips and tongues could meet in a fiery embrace. When we paused, his eyes were smouldering and I felt flustered by the depth of my feelings.

'Rachel, I'm feeling the same connection between us that I think you are and I've enjoyed this time with you, more than you can realise. I'll miss you too but I'll be back before you know it, you know. I have an early start in the morning so I can't stay tonight, I'm sorry.'

He stood up then to go, pulling me up for one last kiss. He smelt so divine, like he'd just stepped out of the shower, it was all I could do to keep my hands off him, but I let him go in the end and saw him to the door.

'Take care, see you on Friday.'

'Bye, see you soon, sweetheart,' he said in his honeyed voice before disappearing along the street.

I closed the door and leaned back against it, blowing out a long breath. I had no idea what to do next. I liked Jackson but the reality was that I hardly knew him. It had been a whirlwind romance so far and I'd enjoyed every bit of it, but in two short weeks he would be gone and I might never see him again. So should I continue seeing him and get my heart broken when we had to say goodbye or should I break it now by deciding not to see him any more? Neither option was appealing for obvious reasons.

I decided that it was high time I found out exactly where

Nashville was and maybe, the devil in me thought, I could Google Jackson as well (hush my mind!). I knew this was probably dangerous but at least I would have a better idea of what I was dealing with.

I made myself another drink and opened up my laptop. I started with Google maps to find Nashville, Tennessee. When it came up, I was surprised to see that it was closer to the eastern coast than I'd expected and in the Deep South. I could make out Charleston in South Carolina where Jackson had said he had a beach house. I then Googled beach houses in Charleston and could not believe my eyes when I saw the cost! We were talking millions of dollars for some of them but they did look fabulous. It seemed a bit out of my comfort zone to be looking at these luxury houses but I didn't let that stop me for a minute.

Next I typed his name into the search engine and hovered over the enter button. I wasn't sure if I ought to do this but on the other hand, better to know any bad news sooner rather than later, right?

I pressed enter and went straight for images.

Before I knew it, the screen had filled up with pictures of his lovely face. About half of them were of him on his own but most of the remainder seemed to show him with one particular woman, Stephanie Shaw. When I investigated further, I confirmed her as the fiancée who had cheated on him just before their scheduled wedding day a year ago. I flicked back to read some of the articles but they were mostly from gossip magazines and not worth bothering with.

I clicked a link to find out more about his record label though, which led me to another one telling me his net worth.

My mouth fell open. Jackson was worth twenty million dollars!

CHAPTER TEN

As I came downstairs the next morning, I was already feeling miserable at the prospect of three days without Jackson. I went to pick up the post and as I turned the largest envelope over, I saw that it had "Open Mic" Competition stamped across the front. I tore it open, desperate to read the contents. Inside, I found the arrangements for the regionals taking place in Bournemouth on Friday. I was finishing reading through all the details when the phone rang, making me jump. I was quite taken aback when I heard Sam's voice at the other end.

'Hey, Rachel, how are you?' He sounded nervous, as if he knew I might be cross with him.

'I'm okay, thanks.' I sounded frosty, I knew but I couldn't help it. I *was* cross with him since the gig the other night when he'd been so rude in front of Jackson.

'I was ringing to see how you are because I missed you on Sunday.'

I softened at once because it seemed like he genuinely wanted to talk to me and also, I'd never been one to bear grudges. 'I'm good, especially now we know we've got through to the regional final. I was going to ring you actually to ask if you and Matt could fit in a rehearsal before Friday?'

'Yep, no problem. How about tomorrow?'

'That sounds good.' I paused. 'Did you manage to sort out your emergency on Sunday?' I asked suddenly remembering about it.

'Yes, I did, thanks.' He fell silent for a moment and I waited for him to continue. 'Listen, we need to talk, you and I but I can't do that with Matt there.'

'I agree, we do need to.' At last, he was facing up to the fact that we needed to talk this all over. 'Have you got any time this week during the day?' I asked.

'No, I'm busy on a job over in Bournemouth all week and Matt gives me a lift home when we come to you. Could we make a date for lunch on Saturday maybe?'

'Okay, let's do that if we can't meet any sooner.'

'I'll see you tomorrow for the rehearsal then. Take care, bye.'

Later that evening, Jenna came round for dinner and a catch-up.

'So,' she began after I'd shown her into the kitchen/diner, 'how did the picnic on Brownsea Island go on Monday?'

'We had a wonderful day and I took some fabulous photos,' I replied, as I poured us out a glass of wine each. 'We even saw a red squirrel, well, I did, Jackson missed it.' I laughed. My arrabbiata sauce was simmering nicely and looked almost done so I gave it a final stir and moved it to a lower heat.

'It sounds like you two are getting on famously. What about you and Sam? Have you managed to have a chat about things?'

'No, we couldn't meet on Saturday night because of the gig but we'll be meeting this weekend because he says he wants to talk. Even though I'm not looking forward to it, I am glad that we'll be getting things out in the open because what with that and the competition, which is also proving to be a bit of a sticking point between us, things aren't too good right now.'

'Yes, I'm picking up odd vibes from him at home at the moment. He seemed quite off when I spoke to him last night.'

'Did he tell you the good news?' I asked.

'What news is that?'

'We got through to the regional finals!'

'Wow!' she squealed. 'That is wonderful news. Well done!'

'Well, I'm really pleased about it but Sam and Matt, not so much, which is why things are difficult. That's probably why he didn't tell you about it too.'

I paused to consider that for a minute before going on. 'And now, Jackson's away for a few days on business and I feel I need a bit of time to try and get my head round some things.'

'It sounds like you might need a bit of help with that, so go on, what's up?'

My oven beeper went off, so I drained the pasta and served up dinner before telling her all my insecurities about where the relationship might or might not be going.

'Mmm, this is delicious,' she mumbled, finishing a mouthful of pasta. When she'd finished eating, she went on, 'Okay then, you like Jackson and he seems to like you, yes?'

'Yes,' I agreed.

'But you have some worries about where it will all lead and that's natural, but it shouldn't stop you from trying.'

'I know but Sam was right about one thing at least: Jackson will be gone soon and I'm already starting to feel something for him and all I can see is me getting hurt down the line if I give in to my feelings. Then there's the competition. Sam and Matt have told me that they don't really want to come with me to the nationals if we win on Friday at the regional final in Bournemouth. If we do win, what will I do? I don't know if I'm up to carrying on alone or if it's even allowed within the rules.' I groaned. 'Everything seems such a mess.'

We cleared the plates away and sank down on to the sofa. Jenna topped up our wine glasses and we were both silent for a moment as we pondered the situation.

'I understand how you feel about Jackson,' she said after a minute. 'It is a risk of course but you can't avoid that where your heart's involved. If I said to you that you could never see him again, how would you react to that?'

I grimaced, which gave her the answer.

'Exactly. My advice is to see where it goes with Jackson and deal with whatever else happens along the way, as it happens. All you're doing is worrying about what might happen. And it's the same thing with the competition. Concentrate on the regional final first. If you do win, then you'll have to think about what to do next but wait till that happens before getting in a state about it. Try taking things one step at a time.' She smiled a rueful smile. 'Did anyone ever tell you, you worry too much?' She winked at me, knowing full well that it was something she had said to me many times over the years.

'Thanks for talking it over with me, Jenna. I will try to follow your advice, I promise but I don't think the next few days are going to be easy. Anyway, changing the subject slightly, have you heard from Meg at all about the wedding flowers?'

'Yes, I have and she's coming in to talk to me tomorrow. I'm really excited about the prospect of doing her flowers. If it works out, it could lead to so much more work for us.'

'Well, you really deserve it. I know it will all go well tomorrow but you will let me know won't you?'

'Of course. I'll want to shout it from the rooftops if she gives me the job!'

We carried on talking and catching up for a while longer over coffee before, all too soon, it was time for her to go because of her early start in the morning. I saw her to the door and hugged her again before she climbed into her car and drove away. I got into bed shortly afterwards and as I drifted off, my dreams were of a tall, handsome American from Nashville.

The day of the regional final arrived and I could hardly concentrate on anything else all morning. Jackson had texted to say he would be back by lunchtime and would pop in to see me as soon as he arrived. When he finally knocked on my door at midday, I was a nervous wreck.

'Hey, Rachel, how are you?' He beamed at me but then his face fell, as he looked at me more closely. 'Are you okay?'

'Not really,' I confessed, holding open the door to let him in. We went through to the lounge and I sat down on the edge of the sofa. Jackson took a chair opposite me and waited for me to explain. 'It's just that I'm really nervous and I can't seem to control it, I don't know why. I'm not sure I can deal with this all the way through to this evening.'

'You do know that this is perfectly normal, don't you?' he asked, smiling at me. 'I know it's not pleasant but you will get through it and soon you'll be on the stage and it will all melt away.'

'Do you promise?' It felt better already, having him there to reassure me.

'I sure do.' He stood up and pulled me up to him for a hug and a long kiss. His eyes locked with mine and his strong arms enveloped me. As our lips touched, I breathed in his familiar smell and I swear that kiss brought me back to life after several days of absence. 'What time do you have to leave?'

'Sam and Matt are setting off in the van at four and our soundcheck is at half past five so I planned to get a taxi from here at five. I have to try to keep going till then.'

'Would you like me to come with you in the taxi?'

'That would be great, yes, please. You should be able to get a seat as our guest too. We're allowed to bring two people and I know the guys aren't bringing anyone. I'd have loved Jenna to come but she'll be working.'

'How about I dump my bags then and we go get some lunch down on the quayside? That should while away some hours.'

We were back in plenty of time for me to get ready for the

evening performance. I went for a simple sundress that I'd dug out from the depths of my wardrobe, teamed with my favourite pair of wedges. I was finishing drying my hair when the doorbell rang announcing Jackson's return. He gave a low whistle on the doorstep, smiling in appreciation of my appearance. I quickly popped in my hoop earrings, grabbed my bag and my guitar, following him outside to take the taxi for the short drive to Bournemouth.

By the time the driver pulled up in front of the Bournemouth International Centre fifteen minutes later, it had started to rain. We dashed inside and went in search of the guys for our soundcheck. This time, we were in the main auditorium on a much bigger stage. It was filled with all the accompanying amps and microphones and other musical instruments needed for a gig like this, so the pressure had definitely stepped up a gear.

I breathed a sigh of relief after everything went according to plan with the soundcheck. Once Jackson was in his allocated seat, I went to wait with the other performers backstage.

We were scheduled to play right before the interval, after two other similar bands. There would be three more acts in the second half and finally, the result. Everyone was very friendly but as nervous as me by the look of their faces, with the exception of Sam and Matt, who didn't seem at all worried. Perhaps that was because they didn't have so much riding on their performance. I couldn't resent them, I was just glad that they'd accompanied me this far.

We watched the other performers on a big-screen TV in the communal dressing room. The first two bands were as accomplished as us, although they mostly sang covers. We'd decided to go purely with my own songs tonight, which I hoped would make the difference.

Before I knew it, I was standing in front of the microphone once again, taking lots of deep breaths to help myself adjust to the setting before me. I could almost taste my own fear at this point. Although I was growing more comfortable with bigger audiences, this one was the biggest so far and the noise level was incredible. It was so heartening though and I took strength from the support the fans were showing, cheering and whooping our arrival.

I adjusted my guitar to make it comfortable, then checked that Sam and Matt were ready. We launched into our first song, 'Love Me', which was catchy enough to get the crowd singing along. The applause was fantastic and we had to wait quite a few minutes for it to die down after the song ended. I was grinning from ear to ear at their response.

Once things had quietened down, I put my guitar on the stand and sat down at the piano to sing 'Don't Let Me Go'. A hush fell over the audience as I began to play and, in my mind, I was in the arena on my own, singing to myself. When I sang the final note and stopped playing, I turned to the audience, eager to hear their reaction. I ought to have been used to the moment of silence that often followed the end of a great performance but as it was, a sliver of panic started in my stomach as the doubts started to form.

The almighty roar that broke out then, quelled that fear at once and I readied myself to sing the final number. I slipped my guitar strap back over my head and moved my long hair out of the way, trying to stay calm. Even if we didn't proceed to the national final, this had been such a great experience and I would never forget it. I had pursued my dream and I'd given it my best shot so there could be no regrets.

We gave 'Too Late' our all and the crowd loved it, joining in with the chorus and rising to their feet to dance as well. The applause lasted for several minutes once again and I was reluctant to leave the stage. We thanked them before going and went back to join the other performers in the dressing room where they'd been watching us on the TV.

'Well done, you guys, you were fab!' one of the other

female singers congratulated us, pulling me to her for a hug and a peck on the cheek. Her band mate shook hands with Sam and Matt, clapping them on the back too.

'Your songs were fantastic, you deserve to win, guys,' one of the other solo artists praised us before heading towards the stage herself.

We watched the remaining three acts in the second half, who were all solo performers and then settled down to wait for the results. I'd expected it to take some time and for it to be a tense wait to find out what the judges had thought. In fact, they made their decision in record time and ten minutes later we were listening to the compère start his announcement.

'In third place, Deena Barker. In second place, Quiver. And in first place, following a brilliant performance tonight...' He eked it out as long as he could. 'Three's Company!' The crowd went wild and I stood there in shock, quite unable to believe that we had really won.

The moments following the announcement went by in a blur.

We went out on stage to receive the crowd's applause once again and to hear that the national final would take place the following Wednesday in London. The crowd cheered and applauded non-stop for at least five minutes. I tried to find Jackson's face in the crowd but the lights were too dazzling. We were soon back in the dressing room once again.

'Hey, Rachel, well done. I'm really glad you won.' I looked round to see Deena, one of the runners-up grinning broadly at me.

'You were brilliant too. I'm sorry you didn't get through to the final,' I replied, giving her a hug.

'No worries. It is what it is.' She shrugged. 'Good luck for Wednesday,' she called out as she left, swinging her guitar case on to her shoulder.

The band who had come second, Quiver, would also be joining us in the final. Sam and Matt both gave me a hug and went off to pack up our gear, without discussing the inevitable problems I would now face going on to the national final on my own. I didn't blame them, now was the time for celebrations, not arguments. Once they'd gone, I went in search of Jackson in the auditorium but his seat was empty. I did a quick scan of the ground floor of the arena and spotted him by the judges' table, talking to one of them there. I approached slowly, hoping they would have finished talking by the time I got there but also wondering how it was that Jackson knew the man. He must know him through the music business, I concluded. As I drew nearer, Jackson looked up, hurriedly finished his conversation and ran over to me, sweeping me up in his arms for a hug.

'Well done, I knew you could do it!' he cried and his enthusiasm was infectious. I found myself laughing and crying all at once. 'You were fabulous tonight, there was no doubt in my mind that you would win.'

'I enjoyed it so much and the crowd were amazing which really helped. I can't wait for the final now.'

We turned to go and I noticed the judge he had been talking to was still looking at us, a small frown on his face. I smiled at him to try and break his mood but he turned away, shuffling his papers.

I shrugged, putting the incident out of my mind.

'Let's go and look for a taxi, shall we?' I suggested and I looped my arm through Jackson's.

CHAPTER ELEVEN

The next day, I arrived at our usual pub on the seafront a few minutes late to find Sam sitting outside, drinks at the ready.

'You look a bit out of breath.' He stood up to greet me and moved to kiss me on the cheek.

'I'm fine, I was taking some photos up by the park. Thanks for the drink.' I was puffing a little as I tried to catch my breath.

'Shall we order now because it's starting to get busy? I brought a menu out for us.' I chose something quickly and Sam went off to place our order.

While he was gone, I gave some thought as to how to approach things with him when he returned but I didn't come up with anything better than going with my instinct.

'What did you want to talk about?' I asked as soon as he'd sat down again. I wasn't going to make things easy for him by doing all the talking. He needed to explain himself.

'It was about the competition.'

My mouth fell open in surprise. I thought he was going to talk about his feelings for me but he was still avoiding that topic, clearly. I closed my mouth quickly and waited.

'I am proud of our success so far,' he went on, 'but honestly, I don't think we have any real chance of winning the national competition.'

'What?! How can you say that?' I couldn't stop my voice from rising in anger at his attitude. 'It doesn't matter what you think though any more, does it? You obviously aren't going to change your mind and come with me so I'm going on my own. Contrary to what you might think, I believe I have a very good chance of winning, otherwise I wouldn't bother.' I folded my arms and glared at him.

'I'm sorry. I think it's best to be honest, that's all.'

'Thank you for that vote of confidence. It's a shame you can't be honest about everything you think.'

'What's that supposed to mean?' It was his turn to glare at me.

'I think it's time we talked about you and me and *we* were honest with each other.' I looked at him pointedly and he had the grace to look a bit guilty. I took a deep breath and plunged in. 'You've been grumpy since Jackson came on the scene and last week when I asked you about it, you said that you don't want me to get hurt but that was all you said, apart from a slightly sarcastic reference to "me not getting it", which I didn't understand.'

He looked like he was going to interrupt me but I held up my hand because I didn't want to lose my courage. 'Then, during the week,' I went on, 'I met with Jenna and asked her if she knew why you were so annoyed with me and she told me that you've had a thing for me for years and that I must be the only person who doesn't know it!'

My voice had risen unwittingly towards the end of my little speech but petered out on a pathetic sob at the end. I swallowed and tried to pull myself together. 'You haven't ever given me any hint that you felt like that about me, Sam, not even after that night we spent together.' And there it was, out in the open. When he didn't react, I continued, 'Until now, when someone else is showing an interest in me and to be honest, I'm pissed off with you when you've had all the time in the world to let me know.'

I stopped and took in a deep breath. I'd been wringing my hands together and my knuckles were white so I made a conscious effort to stop doing it, staring at my hands in my lap to try and help me calm down.

The waiter arrived at the table with our food at that point, giving us both something else to focus on for a minute. Once the waiter had gone, I knew that this was Sam's moment to tell me how he felt.

'I'm sorry that I've never said anything to you before,' he said, staring down at his plate. 'I suppose I was hoping that you'd realise by the amount of time I choose to spend with you and by the obvious way I care for you. I didn't realise I needed to spell it out.'

He glanced at me just as I rolled my eyes at that last comment but he carried on anyway. 'So, yes, I've been grumpy because Jackson has turned up and done in a couple of days what I've been trying to do for the last four years! I care about you, more than you seem to realise and I would love to take things further but I have no idea whether you'd even want that from me.'

'Couldn't you have tried telling me and then listening to what I said?' I tried but failed to keep the sarcasm out of my voice.

'If you remember, you ran out on me the morning after that night, which I took to mean that maybe you regretted it so that's why I've never been brave enough to bring the subject up again.' He fell silent then, having said as much as he felt he could right now, I supposed.

I sighed, knowing that this next part would be hard.

'I've always thought, since we were kids in fact, that you cared for me like a brother. Apart from that night, which I thought *you* regretted because you never mentioned it again, I've never had any signal from you that you had more involved feelings for me. The fact that neither of us made the effort to discuss what happened that night, maybe shows that we didn't want to start a relationship of any other kind.'

'That's not what I felt,' he whispered. My head snapped up at that.

'What did you feel?' I wasn't sure I'd want to know but curiosity got the better of me.

'It was one of the best nights of my life but I truly believed you regretted it because you'd gone when I woke up.' I closed my eyes then at the pointlessness of it all. 'What about you?'

'I remember it being a good night.' I paused, embarrassed to discuss something so intimate with him. 'But more than that, I remember feeling worried that we would lose our friendship and that meant more to me than a one-night stand.'

'You don't feel for me what you already feel for Jackson, is that it?'

'I don't know how I feel about Jackson or about you.' I didn't want to hurt him by saying any more and I didn't have the courage anyway.

'Have you thought what it's going to be like when Jackson goes home? I think there's a real danger of you getting hurt.'

'Of course I have and I know it's a risk getting involved with him but as I said before, I need to take that risk with someone if I'm ever to have any chance of happiness in my future.'

He looked so crushed by that statement that tears sprang to my eyes.

'Please don't hate me,' I whispered.

He hugged me to him then. 'I could never do that,' he said fiercely in return. 'But I do wish you could feel more for me.'

He didn't say anything more and I didn't know what else I could say. We ate our food for a few minutes and I pondered what was happening between us.

'The trouble is that the competition is threatening to come between us and I don't want that, Sam. I want to share this success with you guys. I know I can do it on my own but I'd rather do it with you so that you're a part of it with me through till the end.'

He tutted slightly then before saying, 'We've been over this, I don't want to do it and Matt can't do it for obvious reasons.'

I nodded miserably, knowing there was no point in

discussing it any further.

We finished our lunch very quietly, both of us subdued after our conversation, and shortly afterwards we stood up to say our goodbyes. We hugged again and I watched as he walked off in the opposite direction.

As I walked home, I went over everything that had happened. I told myself that I'd tried to be honest and not lead him along with the promise of something I couldn't deliver but I'd seen in his face how much he felt for me and, suddenly, I was confused.

As for the competition, I didn't know whether to carry on without them or to simply give up.

By the time I reached the cottage, I'd decided to call Jackson and ask for his advice. Before I could ring him, my phone buzzed with a text from Jenna.

'When were you going to tell me the good news?! Congratulations, I'm really pleased for you all.'

'Sorry! Thank you, me too. Just a shame that Sam and Matt don't want to go on to the final with me.'

I knew it was unfair to dump them in it with their sister but I couldn't lie about it either.

'What?! Let me get back to you x'

Bless her, that's what friends are for. I wasn't that optimistic about her chances of success though.

'What do you think I should do?' I asked Jackson on the phone, after explaining that Sam had confirmed they wouldn't be coming with me to the national final.

'I think you'll have to contact the organisers but you may not be able to get hold of anyone on a Saturday. I can ring around some of my contacts to see if I can organise a guitarist and drummer from session players, I'm sure that won't be a problem. The difficulty is whether the organisers will accept them joining you as a partly new band. I think you should emphasise that you wrote all the songs and the music so Sam and Matt aren't integral to the sound.'

I winced to hear him say that but I knew he was right.

'Can I leave you to make some calls then please? But don't confirm anything until you've come back to me again. And I'll send an email to the "Open Mic" people explaining the situation to see what they say. I'm not going to wait to see whether Jenna manages to sort things out. Even if she does, at least I'll know what all my options are.'

'That's a good plan. Listen, while we're talking, do you fancy going out for dinner tonight?'

'Where did you have in mind?'

'How about eating out in Bournemouth for a change?' he suggested. 'We could set off a bit earlier so that we can have a wander first, if you like.'

'That sounds like a lovely idea. What time shall we meet?'

'How about six o'clock? I'll arrange a taxi to take us there. I can fill you in later on any news about session musicians too.'

On the way to Bournemouth, Jackson told me he had managed to find some session musicians for me who were on standby while I made up my mind about what to do. The driver dropped us off opposite the re-modernised pier. We walked towards the seafront and we were soon strolling along the promenade, looking down at the golden sandy beach I loved so much as a child. It was still full of people taking advantage of the early evening sun.

'Do you remember all this or is it too long ago?' I asked Jackson as we strolled hand in hand.

'Are you trying to tell me I'm getting too old to remember stuff?' He teased me.

'I didn't like to say but you are approaching the big 3-0 and that seems ancient to me!'

He grabbed me round the waist then as if about to pay me back for that insult but kissed me full and deep instead, almost taking my breath away. As I pulled back, I had to grab his arm to stop myself from losing my balance.

'I'm glad to see that your advancing years have not affected your kissing ability,' I said rather huskily and my cheeks reddened a little at the lustful sound of my own voice.

He grinned at me and made sure I was steady again before letting me go.

'To answer your question, I don't remember a great deal, no, but it doesn't seem to have changed an awful lot. It seems as lovely a seaside town as it ever was.'

We wandered for a while longer before deciding that we were both hungry enough to look for somewhere to eat. We turned around and started walking back towards the pier and we managed to find another seafood place near the pier itself which had a free table.

'Are you sure you don't mind having seafood again?' Jackson asked me.

'The seaside is the best place to have it, I always think, and I love it anyway, as long as you don't mind.'

Having settled that worry, we sat down at a table outside and enjoyed the view as we waited for our drinks. The clear blue sea and the rise and fall of the waves had me mesmerised until the sound of Jackson's voice broke the spell.

'You looked like you were someplace far away then. What were you thinking about?'

'About the situation with Sam and Matt.' I sighed, remembering my conversation with Sam earlier that day. I didn't want to tell Jackson about that though. 'Thanks for sorting out the session musicians for me, I appreciate that,' I said instead. 'I still haven't heard anything back from Jenna. I would prefer to go with Sam and Matt of course but I can't force them to come with me. I'm not sure I'm up to going to Jenna's for lunch tomorrow with all this hanging over us.'

'Yeah, that could be kind of awkward. Hopefully, you'll know before you have to go tomorrow.'

We watched the sun setting as we ate, the assorted shades of orange reflecting off the water and we both tried to keep things light, to think only about the here and now.

Jackson put his arm around my shoulder as we walked back along the seafront and I leaned into him, enjoying the feeling of having his arm close against my body. After a while, we ended up by the taxi rank and set off back home. Once we were settled in, I became aware of the beginnings of a headache and I rested my head wearily against Jackson's shoulder. I must have dozed off because the next thing I knew, Jackson was gently shaking me.

'Honey, we're back at the cottage. Are you all right?'

'I've got a slight headache, that's all.' He came round to help me out of the car after paying the driver and I was grateful for his firm hold to support me.

He followed me into the cottage, guiding me towards the kitchen and then pouring me a glass of water. I swallowed down some headache tablets, hoping to stop it getting any worse.

'I'm sorry to spoil the end of a lovely evening,' I said. 'I probably just need a good night's sleep to get over this.' I pressed my fingers to my temples, trying to ease the pain. I looked up at him with regret, knowing that the evening was being cut short and that I probably wouldn't see him the next day either.

'Are you sure you'll be all right on your own?'

I swayed on my feet, feeling suddenly faint. Jackson's arms wrapped around me at once and he lifted me effortlessly towards him. The last thing I remembered was him carrying me up the stairs towards my bedroom.

CHAPTER TWELVE

I woke in the middle of the night with an overwhelming need to be sick. I dashed off to the bathroom and only just made it before my stomach started heaving. I washed my face in cold water afterwards and rinsed my mouth out, trying to take the awful taste away. I stumbled back to bed and took refuge under the covers, shivering with cold. I glanced at the clock on my bedside table and groaned when I saw that it was three o'clock. As I turned back round towards the bed, I thought I saw Jackson sleeping in the wicker chair in my bedroom but I dismissed it as my mind playing tricks on me. I tossed and turned for some time before falling asleep again as the sun was coming up.

I was startled awake by the phone ringing what seemed like only minutes later. I groaned as I rolled over, my stomach churning as I did.

'Hello,' I mumbled.

'Rachel, you sound awful! Are you okay?'

'Thanks for that, Jenna. No, I've been up in the night being sick and I still don't feel good. I'd better not come over for lunch today, I don't think.' I slumped back against the pillows, worn out just through speaking.

'No, sure, don't worry about that. Do you want me to come over and look after you?'

'No, no, I'll be fine. Is there any news about Sam and Matt though?'

'That's what I was ringing about. They've agreed to come with you but Natalie's not very happy about it and that might have been awkward so I wanted to warn you to watch what

85

you said.'

'Perhaps it's best then that I won't be coming. Thank you for talking to them anyway. I'd better go, I'm feeling rough again.'

'Take care and let me know if you need anything.'

I experienced another nasty visit to the bathroom before crawling back into bed again. I wanted nothing more than to curl up in bed all day. Shortly afterwards, there was a knock at the front door. I groaned, resenting the fact that I now had to go downstairs. I grabbed my dressing gown and plodded unsteadily down the stairs.

'How are you feeling now?' Jackson's attractive face was etched with concern on my behalf.

'Not great to be honest, I just want to be in bed.' I clutched at my stomach as it made another ominous gurgling sound.

'How about you let me come back in and look after you?'

'Honestly, I don't want you to see me like this, thanks all the same.'

'I have seen you and it doesn't bother me.' He stared patiently back at me.

'What do you mean, you *have* seen me?' I frowned, struggling to concentrate on his words.

'I was here with you all last night. I've been home for a shower, that's all. Now I'm back to look after you because the thought of you being on your own when you're not well worries me.'

He raised his eyebrows at me so I held the door open and, sighing heavily, made my way back upstairs. Even in my feeble state, the fact that he had stayed with me during the worst of my sickness made me realise how much he cared for me. I climbed back into bed, listening to the sounds coming from the kitchen. I had no idea what Jackson was up to down there.

A few minutes later, he appeared at my bedroom door with a jug of water and a glass, waiting for me to invite him in. I waved him in with my hand, not having the strength to speak. I gratefully took the glass of water he held out to me and drank it all down.

'Mmm, that was good, thank you,' I said, wiping my face with the back of my hand in a way that I was sure didn't look very attractive. I lay back against the pillows, listening to my stomach growling unpleasantly. I watched as he squashed his manly body into the dainty chair at my bedside and I had to smile at the sight.

'I wonder if it was the seafood that made you sick?' he asked me. Up until then, I hadn't even considered that.

'Probably, but who knows?' I mumbled. 'You didn't eat any did you?' He shook his head and I closed my eyes. The next time I woke up, two hours had passed and I knew I needed to go to the bathroom again. I didn't have time for embarrassment, I just ran. As I leaned over, preparing for the worst, Jackson appeared next to me in time to lift my hair out of my face, giving me the greatest sense of relief that I wouldn't have to try and do that for myself this time. He was kindness itself, helping me up afterwards and offering me everything I needed to clean myself up. He took my arm and gently led me back to bed. Then he made me drink some more water.

'I'm sorry that you've seen me at my worst,' I said to him once I was settled back in bed again.

'You were pretty fierce with me last night, refusing to let me help you. Is that what you mean?'

My mouth fell open and I was lost for words for once.

By teatime, the worst seemed to be over and I was beginning to feel a bit better. I'd dozed throughout the afternoon but whenever I woke up, Jackson was there. This time, he had a book in his hands and I was glad to see that he had found something to do while I kept on dozing. I was only sick one more time and things seemed to calm down after that.

'Have you had something to eat? You must be starving.'

'Don't worry about me, I'm fine.'

'Thank you for looking after me today. It's been good having you here. And thank you for staying last night. I'm sorry if I was horrible to you.'

'I'm glad I could help you out today and that you would let me.' He smiled at me in that playful way of his, lips twitching up so enticingly and I couldn't help but smile back.

'I think I might be up for something simple to eat now and maybe we could rustle up something more substantial for you too.'

I pulled my dressing gown on once again and slipped out of bed. By the time I reached the kitchen though, I needed to sit down again and thankfully, Jackson took over, making some toast for me and some pasta and sauce for himself. I watched him as he worked and marvelled at the ease with which he moved around my humble kitchen. If I didn't already know he was a multi-millionaire, I would find it hard to believe. He turned suddenly and caught me staring at him.

'Penny for them?' he asked me.

'It's funny to see you cooking in my little kitchen.'

He sat down opposite me and pulled a face.

'I can look after myself, you know. I don't do much cooking, I have to be honest, but I quite like it when I do. Anyway, eat your toast, it'll make you stronger.' He was bossing me about but I knew he was right and I kind of liked it anyway.

'Jenna rang this morning to tell me that Sam and Matt have agreed to come with me to the national final on Wednesday after all. I think she probably gave them what for about letting me down.' I took a mouthful of toast and then chewed it very slowly.

'I'm real glad to hear that. I know you could have managed without them but I'm pleased that you don't have to.'

'I know I should be grateful that they've changed their minds but it feels awkward. I don't believe their hearts are really in it.'

'What about the organisers? Anything from them yet?' I shook my head and pondered what on earth I was going to do.

In no time at all, it was Wednesday morning and I was packing a bag for London. As Jackson had some business to attend to yesterday, he'd already gone up, saying he would meet me there. He'd told me that he would sort out the hotel arrangements, recommending that I stay over after the final, returning to Dorset tomorrow.

Having had the go-ahead the previous day from the organisers to continue on to the final without Sam and Matt, I felt as if a great load had been lifted from my shoulders. I still wished they were coming with me but I was happier knowing that I wasn't forcing them or causing problems in their lives. I'd talked it over with Jenna as well to get some perspective and she'd given me the benefit of her wisdom, as always.

'Even though I persuaded them to say yes,' she'd told me, 'Sam and Matt don't want to go and it would make life a lot easier for Matt especially, if they don't have to. So if Jackson has sorted out the problem of the missing band members and the organisers have agreed to it, there's nothing else stopping you now, in my view. Do this for yourself and stop thinking about Sam. Go to London and see what happens.'

I caught the train from the station a little after nine o'clock, due to arrive at Waterloo just before half past eleven. Once the train was on its way, I took the opportunity to go over my songs before the rehearsal that Jackson had organised with the session musicians later this morning. I'd decided to sing the same three songs I'd performed at the regional final, 'Love Me', 'Don't Let Me Go' and 'Too Late'. 'Too Late' was still quite a new song so I went over the chords on my manuscript paper a few times until I was sure of what I wanted to play, making revisions as I went. As a result, the time flew by and when I next looked at my watch, I was surprised to see it was nearly eleven. I quickly visited the Ladies' to check how I looked before meeting Jackson again.

The train pulled in at Waterloo bang on time and suddenly I felt nervous about seeing him in a different setting. I took a deep breath, grabbed my suitcase and walked to the nearest door.

After descending the steps, I turned towards the barrier and even at that distance, I could see Jackson's tall, handsome figure looking out for me. I caught his eye and grinned and he returned the favour with his most dashing smile. It was all I could do not to run along the platform and fall straight into his arms.

As soon as I reached him, he took my suitcase in one hand and led me gently to one side with the other and, putting the suitcase down, he pulled me towards him. I could see the longing for me in his eyes. He cupped my face gently with his hands and bent his head towards me, his eyes never leaving mine. My body melted into his and as our lips touched, the desire I felt for him sent shivers down my spine. He tasted every bit as good as I remembered and I couldn't get enough of him. My heart was beating so loudly I was sure that he could hear it too.

'It's good to see you,' he said huskily, pulling back at last and looking at me as though he'd not seen me for years.

'It feels like it's been ages, not a couple of days. I've missed you, you know.' I smiled with delight at him.

'I thought we'd go back to the hotel briefly to drop your bag off and then go straight to the studios for the rehearsal, if that's okay with you, sweetheart?'

He had no idea that I would do anything he asked of me as long as he continued to call me his sweetheart. I nodded and he took my hand as we left the station in search of a taxi.

After a short journey, we pulled up outside the hotel. It looked truly luxurious, with uniformed doormen outside waiting to tend to our every need. I seemed to remember reading something about it in a glossy magazine a while back. I hoped that I wasn't under-dressed in my simple cream blouse and tailored grey trousers. After paying the driver, Jackson came round to open my door and took my hand as I stepped out of the taxi. He carried my suitcase as we walked inside, ever the gentleman. Placing his hand on my back, he guided me straight over to a separate lift in the corner of the lobby.

'Which suite are you staying in?' I plucked up the courage to ask.

'We're in one of the penthouse suites.'

'That sounds like more luxury than I'm used to,' I replied.

'I'd like you to get used to it because you're more than worthy of it.'

We came out of the private lift straight into an internal lobby and as we entered the suite, my breath caught as I glimpsed the sweeping staircase leading to a second floor. The lounge even had a chandelier! It was sumptuous and I was overawed by the grandeur of it all. I turned to find Jackson watching my reactions and I blushed as I realised how provincial I must look.

'Sorry, I'm not used to this kind of hotel at all. It's magnificent.'

He kissed me then ever so gently and I knew that I was falling in love with this man despite all the barriers that there might be to our future together.

I went upstairs to unpack the few things I'd brought with me. The bedroom was stunning too, with an enormous bed covered by an attractive, blue silk throw. Under other circumstances, I would have loved to spend the rest of the afternoon in bed with Jackson, but I had the final to think about and it was the only thing I could concentrate on for now. Still, I hoped that we could explore it later.

I went back downstairs to join Jackson on the roof terrace. He was admiring the view of London spread out below. I put my arm around his waist and he pulled me in close to him.

'What a fabulous view! I've never seen London like this before.' I marvelled at the sight before us, pointing out the London Eye across the river and, glancing the other way, we could see St. Paul's Cathedral in the distance.

I gazed up into his eyes and saw only happiness reflected there. Time seemed to stop for a moment, the way it only does when you're falling in love, I think. I heard Jackson sigh before saying,

'Shall we get off to the studios then? I can't wait to hear you sing again.'

'That would be great. I'll feel better with the rehearsal out of the way.'

We made our way back to the lobby where the doorman called us another taxi to take us to the studios in Shoreditch. Once inside the studios, the sound engineer came out to greet us and to introduce himself.

'Hi, guys, I'm Jim and I'm at your disposal today.'

He took me through to meet the session guys then. Ed, the guitarist and Max, the drummer were clearly very experienced and picked up on what I was trying to achieve very quickly. It wasn't long before we'd gone through all three songs and with a few tweaks, we were pretty close to what Three's Company would normally play. I didn't keep them any longer than I had to because we had to be at the West London venue by half past five again for the soundcheck.

Once we were on our way back to the hotel, I decided to ask Jackson what he thought my chances were.

'When I met with Sam the other day, he told me he didn't think I had any hope of winning tonight. Is that what you think?'

'Hell, no! What a stupid thing for him to say, if you don't mind me saying. I wouldn't be supporting you like this if I didn't think you had as good a chance as the next performer of winning this competition tonight and everything I heard at that rehearsal only confirms for me that I'm right. Put that comment out of your head if you can.'

I sighed and leaned back against the seat of the cab. 'At least you'll be there for me and that's a comfort to know.'

He cleared his throat but didn't say anything.

I glanced round and found him looking a bit uncomfortable. 'What is it?'

'The thing is,' Jackson admitted, 'I can't come with you tonight. I have a prior commitment that I can't get out of. I'm really sorry.'

I stared at him, shocked. Suddenly, I was alone and vulnerable.

CHAPTER THIRTEEN

As soon as we arrived back at the hotel, I shut myself away in the bathroom to get ready for the final. In truth, I was close to tears because no-one I loved or cared for would be with me tonight. It took all my strength not to give in to them. Jackson's absence was the last straw and I didn't want to talk to him any more either. Just as I was learning to trust him, he'd let me down.

About an hour later, Jackson knocked softly on the door. 'Rachel?'

'Yes?' I called out in reply, not bothering to actually go to the door.

'I have to go now. I wanted to wish you good luck for tonight.'

'Thanks, bye.' I knew I was being petty, not going to the door but I didn't trust myself not to say something I'd regret later.

'I'll see you later. Take care now.'

I went through to the bedroom and sank down on to the bed as I heard the door to the suite close behind him. I had no idea how I was going to get myself together for tonight's performance.

I was still sitting there some time later when there was another knock, this time on the door to the suite. I hauled myself up and went to answer it. On opening the door, I found myself looking at a glorious bouquet of flowers. The bellboy peeked out from behind them to give me the card and I asked him to come in and put them on the table while I found him a tip. Once he'd gone, I took a look at the card.

'Wishing you all the very best of luck for tonight, Rachel. You'll be fabulous! Love Jenna, Sarah, Dave, Sam, Matt and family xx'

The tears fell then.

I knew that Jenna would have organised these flowers but it meant such a lot to see the names of my closest friends all written there like that. I pulled myself up and wiping my eyes, I went to finish getting ready.

An hour later, I stood on the stage at the venue for my final soundcheck with Ed and Max but they were nowhere to be seen. I waited anxiously for a few minutes, looking all around the arena. As I was about to go in search of them, I spotted two men walking down from the left-hand entrance door to the stalls. It was only when they got closer that I realised that it was Sam and Matt walking towards me with big grins on their faces. My mouth dropped open in surprise but I was so pleased to see them. I gave each of them a quick hug before we all moved into our positions for the soundcheck.

Within twenty minutes, we'd finished and we were back in the waiting area with the other performers.

'What are you doing here?' I asked them as soon as we were on our own.

'We couldn't bring ourselves to leave you on your own for the final. We wanted to see it through to the end,' explained Matt.

'We knew we wouldn't forgive ourselves if we missed the final, so here we are.' Sam shrugged endearingly at me.

'I'm really glad you changed your mind,' I replied smiling at them both. 'Did you tell Ed and Max? Were they all right about it?'

'Yeah, they were cool.'

And that was that. Still, I was grateful for their change of heart and their company.

The guys went off to get a drink and I found myself alone

again, trying desperately not to give in to my nerves. I noticed that the room was fairly quiet and presumed that everyone else was feeling like me. Looking around at their faces, I could see this was true. We were all nervous and wanted to do our best. The marketing people buzzed around, making sure everyone was ready and had what they needed for their performance.

The only comfort I had while waiting was my guitar, which I hadn't wanted to leave on the stage with this many people around. I found a corner, sat down and lifted it out of its case and on to my knee. I didn't want to play, I only wanted to feel it, to let it comfort me. I placed my fingers on the strings, marking out the familiar chords without actually playing and let my mind do the rest. I held my pick in my mouth, tasting the worn plastic and enjoying the sensation. I closed my eyes and let everything wash over me, calming myself before the storm.

'Excuse me, are you Rachel Hardy from Three's Company?' A brisk voice interrupted my thoughts.

My eyes snapped open and I found myself looking at one of the PR clones.

I removed the pick and confirmed my name. We went through some basic details and she told me that the final would be starting soon.

I glanced over at the big-screen TV and could see that the crowd in the auditorium was warming up nicely. Sam and Matt were working their way through the crowd towards me now and I knew it wouldn't be long before it was our turn.

'We're on last in the first half,' Sam told me.

I nodded and followed them towards the screen as we heard the first act being announced by the presenter. The band walked on and we could see them arriving on the stage in front of the audience who went wild. The camera panned around to take in the judges as well as the audience and it was then that I nearly fainted with shock.

Jackson was sitting at the judges' table. He was a judge!

That's what he meant by a prior engagement. Suddenly, everything clicked into place. He must have been scouting for talent when I first met him at the pub and he'd probably been one step ahead of us all the way. I'd taken such a sharp intake of breath that both Sam and Matt were looking at me with concern. They obviously hadn't noticed Jackson up there.

'Are you okay?' Matt asked me, taking my arm to support me. 'You've gone pale.'

I led them over to one side, trying not to draw any further attention to myself.

'I just noticed that Jackson is one of the judges and I had no idea of that until I saw him then,' I whispered.

'The lying…' Sam blew out a long breath, turning round to look at the TV again.

We all understood at once the significance of what I had seen.

'And what are you thinking of doing about that?' asked Matt hesitantly.

'What do you think I'm thinking?' I retorted. 'We all know Jackson and I know him especially well. He even told us about the competition and now we're in the final and he's judging it. It's probably as close to cheating as you can get. There is an absolute conflict of interest here. I don't think we can perform, it wouldn't be fair.'

'Let's not be hasty,' said Sam. My mouth fell open in surprise. 'Everything you're saying is true,' he continued, 'but we might as well go out and perform anyway now we're here and in the interval we can tell the organisers that we're withdrawing if you still feel that strongly.'

I looked at him, considering his advice and then walked away to think about it. As I stood gazing out the window, I struggled to contain my fury. It was just as well that Jackson wasn't there in front of me because I thought I might have punched him. I released my fists from their clenched position.

Sam was right, I concluded. We owed it to ourselves to go

out there and deliver the performance of our lives. After this was over, I would have plenty of time to tell Jackson exactly what I thought of his deception. I just had to hope that my dream wouldn't be at risk because of his lie.

I stood on the stage facing the arena and the biggest crowd I'd ever performed to. My body was trembling and I took a moment to try and compose myself before giving the band the nod to show that I was ready. At least I couldn't see Jackson because of all the lights. After all that had happened, I was an emotional wreck but I didn't expect to get another chance like this and I wanted to give it everything I had, for myself and for my absent family, not for anyone or anything else.

I launched into 'Love Me', feeling the guitar strings against my fingers and loving the sound that they made as I picked out the chords. Once again, the audience joined in with the chorus and I knew from that feedback that we were doing well. The applause lasted for several minutes, as I made my way over to the Kawai piano at the back of the stage. The arena became quieter as I sat down and prepared to play. This crowd was more excitable than the one at the regional final and soon there were whoops and calls of support, all of which boosted my confidence as I sang and played another one of my songs. It crossed my mind that the show was probably being recorded at that point but I didn't let it bother me.

All too soon, it was time for my final song, 'Too Late'. I had come to love this song in the short time since writing it and I hoped that this audience would love it as much as all the others had so far. As soon as we started playing, the crowd jumped to their feet, swaying to the music and then, joining in with the chorus. My heart was pounding at that moment and I knew I'd done the right thing by taking Sam's advice to go on and perform, in spite of everything Jackson had done to deceive me. The song was as popular with this crowd, who were still applauding and hooting even as we left the stage.

I thanked the guys as we came off and went to get my guitar case so I could pack up my things and go. I didn't want to stay for the results. All I wanted to do was to savour the joy of our performance, without it being sullied by accusations of cheating.

Tears came to my eyes but I swiped them away, lifting my head high. As I came out into the corridor, many more people were milling around because it was the interval and I found it hard to get through. Then, all of a sudden I was free and walking towards the down escalator, a few minutes away from the exit and my escape from this nightmare.

That's when I heard Jackson calling my name.

I stopped but didn't turn round.

'Rachel, where are you going?' he asked when he caught up with me.

I frowned at him as if he were stupid.

'Where do you think I'm going?' I hissed. 'I'm leaving. I'm not going to stick around to be accused of cheating when they all find out that I know one of the judges. I won't let you do that to me. You've betrayed me enough already.'

I moved around him to continue on towards the escalator but he reached out his hand and took hold of my arm. I looked down at his hand, unable to hide my disgust.

'Please remove your hand and let me go.' I glared at him but he didn't give up.

'Please listen to me and then if you still want to go, I'll not stand in your way.'

I stood absolutely still, my eyes locked with his until he removed his hand. 'Nothing you have to say is of interest to me any more.' I looked away but I couldn't bring my feet to move.

'I know I should have told you I was one of the judges but I knew you wouldn't have taken part in the competition if I had. And you were so talented, I couldn't bear for you not to audition. I knew you could get through to the final.'

'So you led me along anyway with no concern at all for my feelings?'

'Things spun out of my control! We started seeing each other and having…feelings for each other and there was never a good time to come clean. I don't want to spoil this for you when you've made it this far, that wouldn't make any sense at all so tell me what you think I should do and I'll do it. Please, Rachel. You have a great chance here and I don't want you to miss it because of me.'

'You mean I had a great chance and you've ruined it.' A single tear escaped and rolled down my cheek. 'We're involved and you're one of the judges, for goodness' sake! How can I possibly get out of that with my dignity intact? If you tell them we're involved, they'll probably disqualify me. If you don't tell them, then we're cheating and I can't live with that. Either way, you will have caused me great shame and embarrassment because you put me in this position. I've asked Sam and Matt to tell them we're withdrawing to save myself from that.'

'Um, well, I spoke to them before I found you and I asked them to hold off for the moment when I realised that you'd left and why.' I opened my mouth to speak but he held up his hand. 'Listen, this is my mess, I know and I want to put it right. I think there is another option: I could withdraw from the final judging, saying I have a conflict of interest because I know one of the performers. I haven't been involved with any of the regional finals so it is possible that I wouldn't have known about that conflict until today. I don't want to jeopardise your chances so if I simply pull out of the judging, I won't and you'll be able to have a fair crack at winning. You're so honest and I respect that. Please let me do this for you.'

I bowed my head and my shoulders sagged. I was really tired by everything but I could see that this was a way out and I needed to make a decision soon. Reluctantly, I turned around and started walking back to the dressing room, feeling Jackson right behind me.

As the second half of the show began, I noticed that Jackson was still on the judges' podium. I had no choice now but to trust him to keep his word and bow out when it came to the judging process. I remembered the judge he'd been talking to at the regional final and the frown the man had given me when Jackson had hugged me after our win. It all made sense now and I kicked myself for my stupidity. I watched with Sam and Matt as the other acts took their turn on the stage, enjoying the variety of talent and marvelling at the high standards in this final. I knew we couldn't have done any more but was very aware of how we compared to the other performers out there. I was sure that the judging was going to be very difficult. Whatever happened, at least I could be confident that the outcome would be a truthful one and that meant a lot to me.

Soon it was all over and I saw all the judges, except Jackson, stand up and leave the arena. He must have told them about his conflict of interest then, I decided, and I was relieved to see that. Everyone in the dressing room started wandering around wishing each other luck before the final announcement came. A bell rang somewhere to signal the judges' return to the arena. The presenter went out on to the stage again and the crowd fell quiet in anticipation.

'Before I announce the winner of the "Open Mic" competition and the runners-up, I have been asked to read out a short statement from the judges.

One of our judges discovered tonight that he had a conflict of interest because he knows one of the acts that performed in this evening's final. He therefore withdrew from the judging process so that all the acts could be judged equally and fairly. The three judges who have come to the final decision have not been informed which act this concerns so that they too can be confident that they were treated fairly.

There were a few wolf-whistles but nothing major and the presenter carried straight on with his announcement.

'In third place, Daniel Eaton, in second place, Three's Company. And the winner of the "Open Mic" competition is...The Cavaliers!'

The audience went crazy on hearing the winner and I had to admit that they had been really good. I was happy to have come second to such a good act and to have done so well overall. Everyone cheered as The Cavaliers went out to take their bow and to sing once again and there was lots of hugging backstage as we recovered from the tension we'd been sharing all evening.

'We did well, guys. Thank you both so much for coming to support me. It really did mean a lot, especially with everything else that has happened.'

'We're going to get straight off home again in the van. Are you sure you don't want to come with us?' Sam looked at me with concern.

'No, I still have some things I need to sort with Jackson and my stuff's at the hotel anyway. You take care and I'll see you both soon.'

As I was approaching the exit, one of the marketing people called me over again. I tried not to roll my eyes at him, wanting nothing more than to get back to normal. I'd taken a chance on success and had my moment of fame but all I wanted now was to go home.

'Hi there, Rachel, well done on your second place! I wanted to talk to you about your prize and how to claim it.' He beamed at me in a way that wasn't entirely natural.

'I didn't realise there was a prize for second place.'

'Ooh, yes and you wouldn't want to miss out on this. Here are the details. Well done again.'

He handed me a piece of paper and zoomed away to tick off the next item on his to-do list.

I looked down at the piece of paper and had to smile as I

read it. My prize was to record a demo CD at the expense of The Rough Cut Record Company, owned by one Jackson Phillips.

CHAPTER FOURTEEN

We hardly talked in the cab on the way back to the hotel. I was so let down by the way Jackson had lied to me, even though he'd tried to put it right by not taking part in the judging of the competition.

I went straight upstairs to the bedroom when we returned to the suite, intending to close the door firmly behind me so that there could be no possibility of any further discussion between us. Jackson had other ideas though and followed me right up the stairs, catching the door before it had the chance to swing shut completely.

'We need to talk,' he said quietly behind me.

'I don't want to talk any more.' I couldn't bring myself to turn around and look at him, knowing that once I did, I wouldn't be able to stay angry with him for long.

'I'm deeply sorry for what I did. I only had your best interests at heart, I hope you know that.' His voice sounded closer but still I didn't turn.

'You lied and that was unforgivable.' My voice caught on a sob and I felt his hands on my arms, caressing my skin, trying to make everything better.

'Haven't you ever made a mistake like that, Rachel?' His accent was even more pronounced than usual and it was lulling me into forgiving him, even though I didn't want to.

At last I turned to face him and as I expected, his dark eyes were full of sorrow. I took a step back trying to distance myself.

'Of course I have. But I trusted you and you let me down. And that hurts so much.' I sat down on the edge of the bed and let the tears fall. He had no idea how deep-rooted my trust issues were after being abandoned before by Nick.

He knelt down in front of me, passing me a tissue to wipe my tears with.

'If I hurt you, I'm truly sorry. I certainly never meant to do that. Please can you forgive me?'

Even kneeling down, his eyes were level with mine and the power of his gaze had me trapped with nowhere to go.

'Maybe.' His lips curled into a sexy smile and as he rested his hands on my thighs, I knew that I would give in.

He leaned towards me and kissed me lightly on the lips, before sitting back on his heels, waiting for a further signal from me.

'I do understand that you had the best intentions. I'm just unhappy about the way you went about it.' He nodded, looking serious now.

I reached towards him, grabbing his jacket and pulled him back for another, deeper kiss, a kiss of forgiveness. Our tongues met and the taste of him touched all my senses. The next thing, we were lying side by side on the bed, and I remembered that earlier I'd thought I was falling in love with Jackson. I touched his lips with my fingers and he kissed them lightly before moving in closer to me.

'Can I show you how sorry I am?' He grinned wickedly and I felt the heat of my passion for him burn deep within me. As he started to undo the buttons on my blouse, I knew I could no longer resist him.

We took an early train home the following day, taking seats opposite each other. Every time I looked up, I found him looking straight back at me, waiting for me to say something about yesterday so that we could finally move on. I folded my arms and stared resolutely out the window at the passing countryside. Although we had indulged in fantastic make-up sex last night, I still felt resentful about all that had happened.

'Did they tell you what the prize was for the runner-up last night?' he asked me eventually, when we'd been travelling for a while.

'Yes, they did.'

'And?' He raised his eyebrows at me, inviting a reply but I shrugged. 'Don't you want to make a demo CD with my label?'

I didn't answer and he seemed to give up then and leave me alone.

I retreated into my own thoughts and wondered why it was that I felt guilty when I'd done nothing wrong. Today was Thursday. Tom's wedding was on Saturday and I was supposed to be going as Jackson's date. Not only that but Jackson would be leaving next Monday. I needed some time to decide what I was going to do.

When we were nearly home, I overcame my anger with him to ask the question that had been on my mind since being offered the prize.

'If we did want to go ahead and record a demo CD at your expense, and I'm not saying we do, but hypothetically, if we did want to, where would that happen? Would you book that studio we went to in London the other day, for example for us to go and do it at our convenience?' My resolve was already weakening and I'm sure he knew it.

'Actually, I've had an idea about that. It does involve you forgiving me completely though.' He smiled at me and waited.

'Don't push your luck. Get on with it.'

'Well, as you know, I'll be going home to Nashville next Monday, which doesn't leave any time for recording the demo before I go, what with Tom and Meg's wedding and all. And I'd like to be there when you do it, so I'd like to propose that you come over to Nashville to record a demo of say, three of your own songs, in our studio over there. No strings or promises attached, we could try it and see, but it would also give us the chance to carry on getting to know each other better. What do you say?'

My mouth had dropped open so I didn't have anything to say at that precise moment. He was laughing at the expression on my face so I quickly closed my mouth.

'I...I don't know what to say to that. That's a big step to take. I mean, what about my job and how would I even pay for myself to get to Nashville and to stay there indefinitely in a hotel or something?' I garbled in a rush, forgetting for the moment that I was still cross with him.

'Well, as far as your job goes, only you can make that decision. But obviously, I will pay for your flights and you'll stay with me, not in some hotel or something, as you put it.'

'I'm going to need some time to think about all of that,' I replied, although inside I was bubbling with the excitement of that prospect.

'I know. And you do understand that the offer would only be for you to come, not for Sam and Matt, don't you?'

'I suppose so, yes,' I replied, although I hadn't quite processed that until he spelt it out for me.

'Perhaps you could let me know on Saturday when we go to the wedding, that's if you'd still like to come with me?' He looked humble and full of regret, striking right at my emotions.

'Yes, okay, I'll come with you but only because I don't want to let Tom and Meg down.' I held my head up high but I noticed the way his lips twitched up, confident that he was breaking down my defences.

The next couple of days passed in a blur of final arrangements for the wedding. As Jenna had been asked to do Meg's flowers, I hardly saw her because she was so busy with preparations but I did text her to let her know the outcome of the competition.

I'd finally found my dream outfit in a little boutique in Bournemouth, an amazing red sweetheart off-the-shoulder dress, so I busied myself with going to collect it on the Friday morning.

Meg and Tom had asked the band to play at the wedding so we had a rehearsal early on the Friday evening. It was the first time I'd seen them since the national final and I had the feeling they assumed that now I'd tried my shot at fame and failed, everything would just go back to the way it was before. More than that, I knew they'd be expecting me to have broken up with Jackson after all that had happened so I had some explaining to do about the prize and Jackson's offer to me. Once our rehearsal was done and I'd made them a cup of coffee, I decided to broach the subject.

'I haven't had the chance to tell you both yet that there's a prize for being the runners-up in the competition as well.' They both waited patiently for me to continue. I took a deep breath. 'The prize is to record a demo CD of my songs at a professional studio, paid for by Jackson's company. The thing is, he's offered to pay for me to go out to Nashville to record it at their studio over there.' I waited for their reaction. When a minute had gone by, I couldn't wait any longer. 'What do you think then, guys? Do you think I should give it a shot?'

'I definitely think you should make a demo CD,' said Sam carefully. 'You have the talent and he obviously has the connections. As for going to Nashville, I'm not sure that's a good idea.'

'Why not?' I asked, knowing what he was going to say.

'Because you hardly know him and that's a long way to go with a stranger, especially after the stunt he pulled the other night. I can't believe you're still with him to be honest.' He paused, looking at me for an explanation.

'We made up after he apologised for deceiving me. I still feel a bit annoyed about it but I know he had our best interests at heart.'

'I presume the offer is only for you to go to Nashville, not for us?' he asked then. I nodded. 'Can't you do it over here? In London, for example? Then we could record it with you. You surely don't need to go all the way to Nashville to record a demo CD?' He was getting irritated now.

'No, I don't have to go all the way to Nashville but that would be a dream come true for me and it might be the lucky break I need. And Jackson's not a stranger, that's not fair.'

'I think you should go, Rachel,' Matt interrupted. 'You have a real chance here and you've proved yourself through doing so well in the competition. If you stay here, I don't honestly think I could remain in the band because of the impact it's having on us as a family right now and I would always feel guilty if I dropped out and left you in the lurch. I'm pleased for you.'

He stood up then, getting ready to go, so I went to give him a hug, noticing the way Sam was glaring at him as I did.

'Thanks for those kind words, Matt. I appreciate it.'

'I'm going to go and give Natalie a call to say we're on our way. Good luck with it all, Rachel.'

'Rachel, this is madness, please don't go,' Sam began once Matt had left the room. 'You can record a CD here and I bet there'll be plenty of record labels interested in you if you send it out to them.'

'But Sam, you don't understand. I've always dreamed of going to Nashville and now I have the chance. It would be crazy to turn that down.'

'I know you have that dream but this is about more than that for me.' He paused, collecting his thoughts. 'Look, I haven't been completely honest with you, I guess. You know that I care for you but the thought of you leaving makes me realise how special you are to me and I've wasted so much time already.'

He fell silent for a moment and swallowed, and my sense of foreboding grew even stronger.

'What are you trying to say?'

'I love you, Rachel, I always have, I've just never had the confidence to tell you. I know I should have told you before

109

now and I wish I had but despite the timing, I have to let you know how I feel. It's probably too late but if I never told you, I'd regret it for the rest of my life.'

I swallowed then, taken aback by his confession and reached out to take his hands in mine.

'Sam, I love you too but I don't know if I could love you in the same way you love me.'

He pulled me close to him and I knew that we were in a dangerous place. He leaned towards me, his curly blonde hair falling over his eyes as always and I sensed that he was going to kiss me. I knew I should pull away because I didn't want to give him false hope but I didn't want to be that brutal either. As our lips met, I closed my eyes, trying to remember how it had felt to kiss Sam before. It was a sweet kiss, gentle at first but then more probing and I couldn't help but respond. All at once, I came to my senses and pulled away.

'I…I'm sorry, I didn't mean to pressure you. Tell me honestly that you didn't feel anything and I'll walk away.'

I stared at him for a long moment, then I shook my head. I watched as his face fell.

'We should have taken our chance long before now but we didn't and I think it's too late now, I'm sorry.' I smiled at him but although he returned it, his eyes were sad. 'I think we want different things from life, you know. I want to travel, to see the world and try my luck at having a music career before I settle down, whereas you're happy being a carpenter and living at home.'

'I'm ready to settle down with you though, if you'd have me, I'd even be prepared to get a proper job.'

He laughed then and so did I, neither of us believing that for a minute.

'I don't want to tie you down, any more than I'd want you to make me give up my dream before giving it a try. I wouldn't have been able to do any of this if it weren't for you and Matt. I mean that, Sam, you've both been so great and it pains me to hurt you like this.'

Tears had sprung into my eyes and now Sam reached out to take my hand. I never imagined it would go like this when I told him about Jackson's offer.

'Look, I can't pretend that I'm not hurt but I do understand that you want to give this a try. I wish you didn't feel the need to go all the way to Nashville to do it though. All I can do is wish you good luck, I guess, and remind you that I'll always be here for you, if you need me.'

I looked up into his soulful eyes and knew that he meant it.

'The thing is, Sam, I'm going to be scared witless without you two to hold my hand!' We both laughed then and that broke the tension.

I kissed him on the cheek and watched him as he walked towards the van where Matt was patiently waiting. They came back in to collect all the gear, driving off into the night shortly afterwards.

CHAPTER FIFTEEN

Finally, Saturday, 24th August dawned bright and clear. The wedding was at eleven o'clock at Meg's parish church over in Longfleet. Tom, Jackson and I were going to travel together by taxi to the church. At ten, Jackson knocked on my door to collect me. He looked absolutely divine in his black morning suit, grey waistcoat and pink paisley tie, as I'd known he would all those weeks ago. As I turned to face him, he extended his hand towards me. It only took me a second to decide whether to take it and confirm my forgiveness by doing so.

'You look stunning, Rachel,' he whispered in my ear, his warm breath sending a wave of desire rushing through my body. I took a moment to compose myself before getting into the waiting taxi where Tom was already seated looking very nervous. I kissed his cheek and reassured him that everything would be fine. Thankfully, Jackson sat in the front, allowing me to avoid my raging feelings for at least a short while.

We were at the church in no time and the two ushers Tom had chosen to help guests find their places were already there. I noticed their buttonholes and said a silent congratulations to Jenna for having pulled it all off. One of the ushers helped me find my place to sit inside the church, along the same row as Tom and leaving a spot for Jackson next to me. Soon, other guests were arriving, including Jenna who looked lovely in a floral chiffon dress.

'Jenna, the flowers look fantastic, you should be proud of yourself,' I said in greeting as she sat down next to me.

'Thank you, I am pleased with the results I've seen so far.

I'm absolutely shattered though. I don't know if I could cope with a number of weddings on the go at the same time!' She pulled a face at that idea but then glanced around, happily appraising her work.

Soon, everyone was seated and we were waiting for the bride to come. She was only a few minutes late and when she entered the church, the music played and we all stood as one to welcome her. Tom and Jackson had arrived to take their places a few minutes earlier and now we all turned to see Meg walk up the aisle with her dad at her side and her bridesmaids behind her. She looked radiant in an ivory strapless satin chiffon dress, with a beaded bodice and train. Her bouquet had a sunny yellow theme, including roses, freesias and gerberas, all bound together with a golden ribbon. It looked absolutely stunning.

Tom and Jackson moved forward for the service, with Jackson rejoining me once he'd handed over the rings. He looked relieved that he'd fulfilled that job without incident and I smiled at him in approval. The rest of the service passed smoothly, finishing with the signing of the register.

Afterwards, we followed the newly married couple and their families outside for photos. At last, Jackson and I were called for a photo together of friends of the groom. He took my hand and guided me to a good spot towards the back where we could be seen without being too obvious.

'I love a good wedding, don't you? The celebration of love and a new life together,' he said, giving my hand a little squeeze.

'Yes, it was lovely to see them so happy together.'

We didn't have the chance to say anything else because the photographer took charge then but I had the feeling that Jackson definitely had more on his mind today.

We watched Meg and Tom depart for the reception in the elegant burgundy and black Riley hired especially for the occasion. They looked confident and happy as they drove away. Jackson and I hitched a ride with Jenna to the reception, all of us bundling into her ancient Fiat Punto. As we were a small wedding party, Meg and Tom had decided to hire out a restaurant in the Old Town for the reception. It was soon time for the speeches and Jackson chinked his glass with his knife to encourage everyone to listen. I was very eager to hear what he had to say.

'As y'all probably know, Tom and I have known each other since we were kids together and our friendship has lasted throughout those years and even across oceans and continents. He's like a brother to me and I'm really pleased that he's found the woman he wants to spend the rest of his life with in Meg. I may have only known Meg for a short while but I know in my heart that she is "the one" for him and now he's found her, I hope he hangs on to her and never lets her go. Please raise your glasses to toast the bride and groom, Meg and Tom!' The rest of his speech passed in the usual jokey manner of best men's speeches but without any awfully embarrassing revelations. Tom wasn't that kind of guy, he was simply a lovely man and Meg was very lucky.

As Jackson came to sit back down, I needed to go and get ready with the band so, once again, we didn't have a chance to talk any further.

While everyone finished eating, we did a quick soundcheck and prepared to play. I'd decided to change into a more relaxed outfit of skinny jeans tucked into my cowboy boots and a simple checked blouse over the top, and then we were ready to go.

As soon as the opening notes of our first song began, everyone seemed to turn their attention towards us. I could see their expectant faces as I started with my newest song, 'Too Late'. People began tapping their feet, others clapping their hands along to the catchy country-pop beat straight away and some even joined in with the chorus. I had a great feeling about this song. When I looked over at Jackson, raising my eyebrows at the crowd's response, he nodded in confirmation and smiled like it was a secret only we knew. We played for about half an hour in total, a mixture of my songs and some covers but it was the new material that the crowd enjoyed the most. I was amazed at how quickly they picked up the words of the songs, joining in with me time and again. They cheered and whooped at the end of every song, showing their appreciation for our sound. When we'd finished, I gave Sam and Matt a hug before they started to pack away.

'We were really good together tonight, guys. The crowd loved us,' I cried over the rising noise at the reception.

'There was a great atmosphere at this one, you're right. It must be the love all around,' Matt replied with a wink, before going off to load stuff into the van.

'Thanks for coming to play with me again, Sam. I hope we'll get the chance to do it again soon.'

'Have you made up your mind about going to Nashville then?'

'Not totally but…' He stared at me as I faltered, then gave his head a gentle shake before following after his brother.

I wasn't quite sure what to make of that reaction but I didn't intend to let it bother me. I dashed off to get changed again and then went to rejoin the party.

Jackson found me almost at once, wrapping his arms around my waist from behind and swinging me round to face him. He looked at me for a moment then leaned towards me for a long, slow kiss. I lifted my arms and looped them round his neck, bringing our bodies close.

'You guys were fantastic, you had the crowd eating out of your hand. If I were your manager, I'd suggest that "Too Late" should be the first song you release from your first album. It would be such a hit, I'm willing to bet on it.'

'Well, you should know, I guess.'

'Would you like to dance to celebrate?'

'Do you dance?'

'Only with you, sweetheart.' He led me on to the dance floor.

Meg and Tom had had their first dance and now, they were playing 'Close to You' by The Carpenters, as he took my hand and started to guide me around the room. I gazed up into his eyes and his hand squeezed mine in reassurance. I never had been much of a dancer but it was surprisingly easy when you were dancing with someone who knew how to work the floor.

'I thought your speech went well. It was interesting,' I began as a way of making conversation.

'How do you mean, interesting?' He smiled his cheeky smile at me.

'Well, I liked the bit about hanging on to that one woman if you find her and not letting her go.'

'Yep, I truly believe that. The only difficulty is in finding that one person who's meant for you, someone you can put your trust in.' I nodded in agreement.

'Too true,' I replied.

The next thing I knew, his lips were whispering in my ear again, making every one of my nerve endings stand to attention.

'Do you trust me, Rachel?' He pulled away a little to hear my answer.

I was speechless for a moment, thinking back to how I'd felt the other night but I'd moved on now so I nodded and he held me tighter still. I rested my head on his shoulder and enjoyed the feel of our bodies moving as one. As much as I hoped the song would never end, we came to a stop as the music faded.

Soon, it was time to see Meg and Tom off on their honeymoon and we followed everyone else outside to wave them goodbye. Before getting into the car, Meg turned away from the crowd, bouquet in hand, and as tradition demanded, she threw it over her head to the next bride-to-be. It was with some surprise that when I next looked down, I found that I was holding that same bouquet of flowers. Before I could say anything, Jackson had swept me up in his arms for a breathtaking kiss. I could hear people cheering in the background and my cheeks burned with embarrassment.

'Jackson, put me down. Please!'

He was laughing as he set me down but I wasn't. I didn't want to be the centre of that kind of attention.

'What's the matter?' he asked me, noticing the scowl on my face.

'I hate these silly traditions. People are staring and laughing at me.' I bowed my head.

He put his fingers beneath my chin and gently lifted my face up so I had to look at him.

'They're staring because you're beautiful,' he told me, gently stroking my face. 'And they're laughing with you because they know it's only a matter of time before you get a marriage proposal.'

I opened my mouth slightly to protest but he placed his finger to my lips, staring deep into my eyes. 'I love you, Rachel.' My eyebrows shot up and I gasped though it was only confirmation of my own feelings.

'I love you as well,' I replied without the slightest hesitation and his lips claimed mine.

The next day, Jackson and I walked hand in hand into town for the last time. We were both quiet on the journey along the residential streets, each lost in our own thoughts. Now that we had told each other our true feelings, everything felt so much more complicated. I knew I would have to give him an answer today about joining him in Nashville because soon he would be gone and maybe I wouldn't have this chance again.

As we approached the sea, the question weighed even more heavily on me. The waves looked choppy today which seemed appropriate for our mood.

We stopped in for a lazy lunch at one of the bustling restaurants on the quay.

'Have you made any decisions about coming over to Nashville to record your demo with me?' he finally asked me, as we were finishing our meal.

'I thought I had but now I'm nervous about making the decision because it means leaving behind everything I have in my life.'

He narrowed his eyes at me then.

'Well, that sounds like you've already made up your mind not to come,' he said, looking forlorn at that prospect.

'No, I haven't. It's a lot to think about, that's all.'

'Let's break it down then. What's the thing you're most worried about?'

'The biggest hurdle to overcome would be my job at the music service of course. The earliest I could come to Nashville would be the end of October when we have the next school holiday, if I don't want to let schools down. I could mention it now so that they're forewarned and if it all comes to nothing, it won't matter.'

'I seriously doubt that it will come to nothing, trust me.' He smiled reassuringly. 'Personally, I'd prefer you to come as soon as you can. Why don't you ask how soon they would be prepared to let you go when you go back to school?'

'What do you mean, hand in my notice before we've even recorded the demo?'

'Maybe, or if that's too big a step, how about asking for some time so that you can come over to Nashville and see how things go?' he suggested.

'I could ask, I suppose. They can only say no.' I paused to let that sink into my mind.

'What's next on your list?'

'The cottage, which is mine but there would still be bills to pay which would be difficult if I wasn't working.'

He smiled at me then, a knowing look that said he had already solved this problem.

'No, absolutely not, you are not going to pay my household

bills, as well as everything else you're doing for me! That's too generous.'

He folded his arms and pouted at me and I had to laugh at his doggedness.

We paid for lunch and set off along the shoreline towards the bay. I noticed that the sea had become a bit calmer but there were a few grey clouds in the sky and I thought it might rain now. We admired the wonderful array of boats and yachts in the marina as we progressed around the bay. It had started to rain when we decided to stop for a drink at the marina's café before starting our walk back. As we sat down to drink our coffees and indulge in a slice of cake, I brought us back to our earlier conversation.

'How about this as an idea? When I go back to work, I ask for a term off, before they allocate me to students, a kind of sabbatical if you like. At the same time, I suggest to Jenna that she could live in my cottage, rent free, as long as she pays the bills during my absence. If all of that comes together...' I paused as I blew out a long breath, 'I would be free to come to Nashville and give the singer/songwriter plan a go.' Jackson leapt up and pulled me out of my seat to hug me to him.

'That sounds like a damn fine plan to me, sweetheart!' He kissed me. It started softly but soon became more demanding. We both knew it might be some time before we would see each other again.

We sat down again and I gulped in some air. This was a big step for me but I had this chance and I knew I might never get one like it again. I would be putting my future in Jackson's hands and now, it was time for me to take a leap of faith and put my trust in him. We talked the idea over some more before starting the walk back to the cottage in the drizzling rain.

By the time we returned, it was nearly six o'clock and we were tired but happy after a long day's walking and talking. Neither of us was hungry so the question came up of how to spend our last evening together. I'd been thinking about something for a while and now was my last chance to suggest it.

'I know there are other things we might want to do now,' I said with a cheeky grin. 'But I wondered if you'd like to hear any more songs that I've written,' I suggested quietly, not knowing if he could really hear me. I guess he did though because he sat up very suddenly from the position he'd been lounging in on the sofa.

'You have more songs? How could you have kept this quiet for so long?'

I grinned sheepishly and stood up to get my guitar.

'How many songs are we talking about? This is great news.'

'Well, I think I have about a dozen more I could play you right now.'

He didn't say anything for a moment so I looked up to check his reaction. It was safe to say that he looked like he might explode with the excitement of this new knowledge. Finally, he found his power of speech.

'I can feel an album coming on. Play them for me please,' he begged.

And I did and it was the best concert I'd ever given, even though it was to the smallest audience.

He had nothing but positive comments to make about each and every song. Even his suggestions for improvements were constructive. He loved my music and I knew that a new phase of my life was about to begin.

That night, we made love as though we might never see each other again. For the first time in my life, I shed tears when our lovemaking was over.

'Sweetheart, why are you crying?' he whispered softly into the half-light of my bedroom.

'I'm not upset, it's okay,' I replied, trying to make sense of my emotions. 'It's like, like you've reached deep inside me, to a place I didn't even know was there.'

He pulled me close to him and nuzzled my hair and I wished the night would never end.

CHAPTER SIXTEEN

Nashville, TN, USA
Jackson

My driver, Greg, was there to greet me when I got back to Nashville International.

'Welcome back, Mr Phillips. You look well, sir.'

'I'm very well, thanks, Greg.'

The first thing that hit me as we exited the airport building was the humidity. A few weeks away had made me forget that typical aspect of a Nashville summer night. That was another thing I was going to have to get used to again, along with being on my own once more. Greg led me to where he'd parked the Lexus and took my bags from me before I climbed into the backseat of the car for the drive home.

As he drove, my mind went back to that morning when I'd kissed Rachel one last time before the cab turned up outside her cottage.

'I'll see you real soon, sweetheart,' I'd told her, praying that I would be right. I'd held her to me as she started to cry, wanting to soothe her tears away but at the same time, loving the feel of her soft body and all its curves pressed against me.

'Bye, Jackson,' she'd whispered. 'Thanks for giving me the time of my life these past few weeks.'

It had been such a wrench to leave her after the time we'd spent together, especially after we'd become so close in the last couple of days. I had enough great memories to last me a while but I wanted more and I hoped that she did too.

I leaned back in my leather seat with a sigh, wishing that Rachel was with me so I could share my life with her.

My loft was located in one of the historic neighbourhoods of downtown Nashville, not far from the Cumberland river and a short walk to our offices, and most other places I wanted to go.

The open-plan design of the living space had appealed to me at once, and with just two bedrooms and one bathroom, it was more than enough for a single man like me. I'd kept to simple furnishings because I loved the character of the place and I didn't want to cover up the hardwood floors with rugs and the like. My biggest indulgence had been the pieces of original artwork I'd purchased to decorate the walls with scenes of Nashville's musical life.

Most of all, I loved the district. It was a bit seedy for some, especially at night but when I pushed open one of the large windows in the lounge, I could feel the heat of the day on my skin and hear the noise from the street below as the city came alive. I left the window open and let the familiar smell of fried chicken waft in, making my mouth water as I thought about it.

I headed off for a shower, not feeling like I could sleep yet, despite it being after midnight Nashville time. It took only a minute for the water in the walk-in shower room to heat up, and as the powerful jets from the extra-wide shower head pounded my skin with water, I felt my tired muscles start to relax. I crawled into bed just before one o'clock and tried to picture Rachel back in Dorset. I would call her in the morning to catch up and to hear the sound of her voice. I already knew that I didn't want to be separated from her for much longer.

Just before ten o'clock the next day, I went out to speak to my assistant, Annie.

'Is everyone okay for this meeting?'

'Yes, they're all waiting for you in the meeting room, Jackson.'

'Would you like to order in some lunch for us today so that we can catch up, if today's good for you?'

'Of course, I'll get right on it. I hope the meeting goes well for you.'

'Thanks, Annie, and thanks for setting it up.'

I almost saw Annie as equal to my mom in the office and she'd been a good friend to me over the years, especially when everything had fallen apart after Stephanie.

When I entered the meeting room, my creative Vice-Presidents were ready and waiting for me. I gave them a big smile and thanked them for coming. They all turned to me expectantly.

'It's great to see you after a month away but I've called you together now to tell you about a bit of a development. When I was away, I met an amazing new singer/songwriter via the "Open Mic" competition I was involved in. Her name's Rachel Hardy, she's twenty-six and she has a whole heap of fantastic songs already written and she plays guitar and keyboard. She won our prize to record a demo CD of her songs and I've offered her the chance to come over here to record it. Hopefully, she'll be here within the next few days but in the meantime, I'd like you to listen to the rough recording of her performance from the competition final last week and give me your thoughts.'

Taking a deep breath, I walked back along the corridor to my office, rubbing my now slightly clammy hands together. It meant such a lot to me for them to want the label to sign Rachel like I did. Of course, it was my company and I didn't need to consult anyone but that wasn't my style. Some of my employees had been with me since the label had started eight years ago and I took a lot of pride in knowing that they respected me.

I'd been working at my desk, going through all the paperwork that had mounted up in my absence and checking my emails, when my cell buzzed as it received a text from Rachel.

'I can't believe I missed your call. Are you free now? Would be good to talk to you xx'

I called her straight back and she answered on the first ring.

'Hey, sweetheart. How are you?'

'Better already just hearing your voice. Is it good to be back home?'

'In some ways, except that I miss you. I hope you can make it over here soon.'

'Well, I went to meet the head of the music service this morning, that's where I was when you called earlier. Unfortunately, he wasn't at all receptive to the idea of me taking some time off. In the end, he said that if I wanted to go, I'd have to resign and he would release me from my contract.'

'Man, talk about an ultimatum.' I rubbed my hand against the back of my neck and blew out a long breath. 'What do you think you're going to do?'

'Either I stay and accept his terms or I hand in my notice. I don't want to let them down, of course but I would obviously like to come out to Nashville. I did wonder whether there might be someone I know who could cover my lessons so that I could hand in my notice but that would be a big step for me.'

'I'm sorry that you're faced with this choice now. You know that I'll support you if you decide you do want to take me up on my offer.'

'I know and I appreciate your offer of support but I don't want to be totally dependent on you.'

'How about Jenna, did you put your idea to her about staying in the cottage if you came to Nashville?' I said, trying to change the subject slightly.

'Yes. She'd love to be nearer the shop so that would be one problem solved.' She paused and I jumped in to give her some good news.

'I've left my team listening to the recording of your performance at the final. They should be getting back to me with their thoughts soon.'

'That sounds great,' she replied. 'I wish I could be there

with you now but hopefully, it won't be too much longer.'

'I sure hope so, sweetheart. Take care and bye for now.'

I felt for her as I put the phone down, knowing that she wanted to do the right thing for herself, as well as for her employer.

Not long after saying goodbye to Rachel, I sat back down at the conference table, eager to get my team's feedback.

'What did y'all think?' I said brightly, trying not to betray my feelings.

'I thought she had a distinctive voice and she's an accomplished musician with her own individual sound, which could be interesting for our market,' said Todd, my A&R guy. 'She's clearly a talented songwriter too if these are all her own songs. I'd definitely like to see her in person.'

The others all chipped in then with similar positive comments.

'We'd really need her to come here for a while so we could get a better idea of how to market her sound if she's British. I'm not quite sure how that would work, you know? It would obviously help if we could get to know her better,' said Will, my head of Marketing.

'When will she be here?' asked Todd.

'That's a problem at the moment because she's a singing teacher and has obligations so I'll keep you informed of the situation. Thank you everyone for your feedback and confirmation that I still have the magic touch for spotting a good artist when I hear one!'

By the time the meeting was over, it was time for lunch but I wanted to let Rachel know how things had gone. I sat down and dialled her home number once again, eager to give her the news.

'I have some great news,' I began.

'That sounds exciting,' she replied in her lovely English accent. It still turned me on to hear the sound of her voice.

126

'Well, my Vice-Presidents all loved the recording I played them of your performance from the final. They said you have a rich, individual sound and you're obviously a talented singer and songwriter and they can't wait to meet you! How about that? It's not just me who thinks you're great you see, sweetheart.'

'Wow, that sounds brilliant, although they probably went along with you, seeing as you're the boss,' she argued.

'No, I purposely let my VPs make up their own minds. Most of them have been with me since I started the label so I really trust their opinion.'

'I know nothing of this kind of business. I guess I'm going to have to get used to being a little overwhelmed by all these changes.'

'Hey, that's what I'm here for. I'll look out for you and guide you every step of the way, I promise.'

'Well, let's hope I hear soon about my job. Will I speak to you tomorrow?' She sounded so sweet and tentative.

'You bet. Shall I try and call around lunchtime again?'

'Yep, that sounds good.'

'I'm having dinner at my parents' house tonight and I'm going to tell them all about you as well,' I told her.

'Now you're making me really nervous.' She laughed and we said our goodbyes.

CHAPTER SEVENTEEN

My family home was out in Bellevue, on the outskirts of the city and I still experienced a familiar, happy pull every time I approached the house along the gravel driveway. With Greg driving me, I could take the time to really appreciate the view of the antebellum-style house as I approached, with its red brick façade and pillars either side of the entrance. I walked up the steps to the green front door and let myself in. I called out to tell everyone I was home and in no time, my mom, Michelle, my step-dad, Bob and my younger sister, Maggie were all around me, hugging me and welcoming me back.

'Jackson, you look really well, there's something to be said for that sea air. What did you think of Dorset, going back after all this time?' asked my mom. 'I wish we could have gone with you. Still, summer school was great fun this year.'

We wandered into the kitchen as we talked and my stomach rumbled from the wonderful smells of my mom's cooking. Over dinner, I told them all about Dorset and about the wedding, answering all their questions as patiently as I could. When there was finally a lull in the conversation, I took a deep breath before plunging in with the most important news.

'I met someone while I was there. Her name is Rachel.'

They all looked up, my mom and sister gasping in surprise, while my dad just looked happy for me.

'Oh my goodness!' Maggie squealed before bombarding me with a hundred questions. 'How did you meet? How old is she? What does she look like? What does she do? When's she coming over?'

Dad held up a hand to quiet her.

'Let Jackson tell us in his own good time, Maggie. Don't crowd him. It's probably been hard enough telling us that bit.' My dad smiled kindly at me.

Over dinner, I told them everything about how we'd met and how talented a singer and songwriter she was. I told them about the demo and how we were trying to get her over to Nashville to record it as soon as possible. After we'd all helped clear away, Maggie went off to her room saying she needed to study, but perhaps sensing that I needed some time alone with Mom and Dad.

'Jackson, is it serious with you and Rachel?' my mom asked.

'I think it could be. We tried to keep it simple and to have fun without getting involved but since I came back, I've hated being without her.' I scrunched my face up for a moment.

'Try not to get too frustrated about it,' my mom reassured me. 'From what you say, she's doing everything she can to get here, which means she cares for you too because that's a hell of a commitment to come all the way to Nashville. What do her family think?'

'Her parents have both passed and she has no other family. She has some really solid friends and they've looked out for her but in a way, I think she feels she has nothing to lose by giving things in Nashville a try.'

'Well, let's keep our fingers crossed that she gets here soon. I can't wait to meet her. Sorry to ask but does she know about what happened with Stephanie?'

'Yes, I told her that but I haven't told her about what happened to me afterwards. I haven't had the courage because her dad was a drinker and died from it. I didn't know where to start with that explanation.' I looked at my mom for reassurance.

'You need to tell her at some point, Jackson, it's better not to have any secrets.'

My dad nodded in agreement.

'Yeah, I've not been doing too well on the secrets front.' I told them about the competition then and how angry Rachel had been with me for keeping my involvement with it a secret.

'Well, you did the right thing then. Don't beat yourself up about Stephanie, son. You had a tough time and you got through it the only way you knew how. Now it's over and you never have to see Stephanie again. You've moved on with your life and that took a lot of courage.'

'Thanks, Dad. I know you're both right but I still don't relish that conversation.'

We chatted for a while longer about their news. My parents were both lecturers at the university and so they had just come to the end of the long holiday and were now getting back into the swing of the new semester. Maggie attended Vanderbilt as well now. She'd only just started and was bound to have lots to tell me so I excused myself and went off to find her. I tried her room, knocking gently as I arrived.

'Hey, Maggie, how's college?' She pulled me in for a chat.

'It's great, Jackson. I haven't had many classes yet but I'm really enjoying concentrating on the one thing I love, writing.' She beamed a big smile at me. 'I'm really pleased about your news too, it's lovely to see you looking so happy and so well again. We were all really worried about you before you went away. You were working too hard and didn't seem to have any life outside that at all. I can already see the good effect that knowing Rachel has had on you.'

'Hey, when did my little sister get so wise all of a sudden?' I teased her. 'I do feel happier, Maggie.' I gave her a quick kiss and a hug and promised to see her again soon.

As I put the phone down after speaking to Rachel the next morning, I had to stifle a yawn. I went over to stretch out on the sofa in my office, planning to read through some of my paperwork, and closed the door on my way. Next thing I knew, my sister, Alex was gently shaking me awake, saying it was twelve thirty and time for the lunch we'd planned. I sat up quickly, annoyed at myself for sleeping so long.

'Jet-lag still getting to you, huh?' she asked.

'Yeah, I woke up at five this morning. Hang on while I go to the bathroom to freshen up a little.'

I did feel better for a bit more sleep and was looking forward to my lunch with her. We strolled down to our favourite midtown café and ordered a couple of club sandwiches and some drinks before settling in to catch up. As we began to chat, my shoulders relaxed and the tension began to ease away from me. I was very close to Alex. I think it helped that we both worked in the music business and we were very like each other in many ways. I told her all about meeting Rachel and how much I'd enjoyed getting away from everything for a while.

'You really needed it, you were working yourself to death before you went so it probably came at the right time for you. Rachel sounds lovely, I can't wait to meet her. When's she coming?'

'Soon I hope, it's all a bit up in the air at the moment because of her job. Anyhow, I played Rachel's performance from the final to my VPs yesterday and they loved it. Ideally, I want Rough Cut to sign her but, and this is where you come in, I want her to know that she has a choice, that she doesn't have to sign with us if she doesn't think that's the best deal for her and for that, she'll need a manager.'

'And you're thinking that I could be her manager?' Alex asked with a slight frown.

'Yes, I think that would make a lot of sense.'

'I think I should hear her sing first of all and then we'll need to meet as soon as she comes over. These things can't just be decided, we might not even get on for any number of reasons.'

'I think that's unlikely but I take your point. All I'm asking is that you'll keep an open mind for me. Do you want to stop in for a copy of her performance on the way back then?'

'Yep, that sounds like a good idea and I'll call you with my thoughts later today. Listen, I'm really glad that things are going so well for you both but don't rush it, you know. Give yourself some time to get used to being in a relationship again without any strings,' she advised.

'But I really like her, Alex, and I don't want to lose her because of my past. She already means a lot to me.' I frowned again, miserable at not being with Rachel.

Alex patted me on the arm. 'Take it easy, that's all I'm saying.' She of all people, knew how badly I'd been hurt before.

When I arrived at work the next day, I felt relaxed and happy for the first time in ages. I'd started working a more sensible day, much to Annie's surprise, leaving at six o'clock last night and not arriving till nine this morning. I'd even gone for a run yesterday evening, which was something I used to do all the time before Stephanie had set out to ruin my life. Meeting Rachel had made me realise that I'd let too many things go since then, and now I wanted to get back on track and put what had happened with Stephanie behind me once and for all. I was confident that Rachel would be able to come to Nashville and we might even know for sure today.

At ten, Todd appeared at the door of my office for the meeting that Annie had set up between us. He'd obviously been busy in my absence, listening to lots of demo CDs and attending a number of singer/songwriter and "Open Mic" nights at different venues to see who was new on the music scene. He'd picked out three new acts that he was interested in and we spent some time discussing their relative pros and cons and how they would fit together with our other artists.

We also talked about the individual financial implications of taking on each of these artists, what the costs of development, marketing and sales might be and when we could expect to recoup our costs.

I asked Todd to bring the three CDs along to the meeting this afternoon so the whole team could listen to them together and discuss where we thought we could go with them. I moved on then to talk about Rachel.

'I suppose realistically, we're looking at the same level of analysis for Rachel, aren't we, if we're to keep this strictly business?' I asked Todd.

'Jackson, I hope I'm not speaking out of turn,' he replied. 'But are you and Rachel an item? You seem to speak very fondly of her.'

For a moment, I wondered how much to reveal but I decided it was best to be honest all round. 'Yep, I think you could say that we are.' I smiled broadly and he did too.

'Well then, yes, we are really, except that you have a bit more personally invested in Rachel's success.' He smiled ruefully. 'You know that we'll give her the same level of attention as any other new act so she wouldn't lose out,' he reassured me.

'I just want her to get here and then you guys can all meet her and make your own minds up and we can get her out on the circuit.'

By the time we'd finished, it was midday. I invited Todd to walk with me to the deli on the corner to pick up a sandwich and we wandered out into the sunshine. When we got back, we went out to the roof garden to eat lunch and catch up. I'd just sat down when I saw Annie weaving her way towards me looking intent on something.

As she drew closer, I could see she was holding my cell.

'Jackson, I've brought you your cell because it buzzed with a text while you were out. When I glanced at it, I could see it was from Rachel. I hope you don't mind. I thought it might be important.'

'Thanks, Annie, I appreciate that.' I took the phone from

her. When I opened the message, it said,

'I have news. Please call me as soon as you can.'

I stood up, gathered my lunch and apologised to Todd for abandoning him, then strode back to my office. Rachel answered straight away and I could sense her excitement.

'Hi, sweetheart, what's the news?' I hardly dared to breathe, waiting for her answer.

'They've agreed to let a friend of mine replace me. She was looking for a job anyway so I've handed in my notice and now I'm free to go!'

'Oh, that's fantastic news. I'm proud of you for deciding to take that leap. I won't let you down, I promise.'

'Thank you, I know. I'm really excited now, I can't wait to see you more than anything else. So tell me, what do I need to do?'

'Okay, well, first of all, I'm going to ask Annie, my assistant, to wire you the money you'll need for the plane ticket and other expenses. You'll need that before you can do anything. Is your passport all up to date?'

'Yes, my passport's valid for a few years yet, I'm sure but I'll check it. What about a visa, do I need one?'

'No, there's a Visa Waiver Program now. Anyway, I'll get Annie to contact you with all the relevant details if you give me your email. Then it's just a question of you getting packed up and coming over. This is awesome. We'll be seeing each other in a few days now. I'll ring you in the morning again and we can see where things are at that point, okay, sweetheart? Hey and thank you for calling and letting me know.'

'I can't wait. Speak to you tomorrow.'

The next couple of days were long, hot and drawn out, with me whiling away the hours until Rachel's arrival, which was going to be on Sunday. I spent Saturday with my folks, finally returning home around midnight, conscious of the fact that over in Dorset, Rachel would soon be setting off for Nashville. As I listened to the distant sound of the live music from the honky-tonk bars on Lower Broadway through my open window, my excitement grew. I would be able to show her the real Nashville very soon and I knew she would love it.

CHAPTER EIGHTEEN

The next day was another long, drawn out affair, during which I became more and more impatient to see Rachel and yet the hours seemed to be twice as long as normal. I tried all my usual distraction techniques, going for a run, having a tidy up around the condo (already as tidy as it could possibly be), making a few calls, having a long lunch but it was still only three o'clock by the time I'd finished. I finally decided to slump on the sofa and watch a bit of TV and promptly fell asleep in front of a movie. When I woke up, it was nearly six so at least that had killed a few hours. It wasn't long now till Rachel would be landing in Fort Worth and so I sent her a text asking her to call me when she arrived.

'Hi Jackson, it's me,' her tired but still lovely voice said a short while later.

'Sweetheart, hi, how are you, apart from dog-tired?'

'Yeah, that's a good description. I am really tired but I don't think I could sleep, do you know what I mean?'

'It's crazy isn't it? I felt the same. Have you had something to eat?'

'I'll try and get something while I'm here perhaps. How are you doing? It must have been a long day for you and you still have ages to wait until I get there.'

'You are well worth the wait. I'm trying to pace myself so that I don't go mad before you get here.' I laughed and so did she and it sounded wonderful.

'I must tell you that I could seriously get used to travelling first class. What an eye opener! I do feel a bit like an impostor though.' She chuckled.

'As I've told you a million times, you deserve it as much as the next person and I'm glad you like it.' I smiled. She was like a kid in a sweet shop.

'You'll be coming to meet me at the airport then?' she asked.

'Of course, I wouldn't miss it. I'll be the one with the red carnation,' I joked.

'Ooh, cheesy, it'll be just like in the movies and will you be holding up a card with my name on it, for good measure?'

'Hmmm, I hadn't thought of that, I'll see what I can do. I will sweep you away in a luxury vehicle as well, ma'am.' I exaggerated my accent just to make her laugh.

'You really know how to spoil a girl.' She sighed and my heart skipped a beat.

'That's one of the things I'm looking forward to doing over the coming weeks,' I said and this time, my voice sounded a bit husky.

'Well, that sounds just what I'm after, thank you. I probably ought to go and look for something to eat now, my stomach did just rumble,' she said a bit reluctantly, 'and I'll see you very soon.' It was her turn to sound excited by that prospect.

'Okay, sweetheart, take care and remember that it won't be long now,' I said.

'Yes, see you soon. Bye for now.' She blew me a very sexy kiss down the phone. Phew! That had me heated up in all the right places. I decided to go and have a shower and get changed so I looked my best when she arrived.

A couple of hours later, the concierge called to let me know that Greg was waiting for me in the lobby so I grabbed my things and set off to meet him for the short ride to the airport.

By the time we arrived, Rachel's plane would be landing and I would be ready and waiting for her as soon as she came through. There were a lot of people waiting for loved ones in the arrivals hall and soon passengers started to appear.

I rubbed my hands over my face, worrying that things might be a bit awkward between us at first. I knew this was silly because everything had been exactly the same when we'd spoken on the phone, I was just jittery with anticipation.

Then, all of a sudden, there she was, her long chestnut hair framing her pretty face, which was looking desperately for me. When our eyes met, hers lit up with pleasure and I imagined that mine did the same.

She walked as quickly as she could towards me, flinging her cases at my feet and throwing her arms around my neck. Our lips met and the kiss we shared was like coming home. It was a long time before we stopped to draw breath and I only pulled back a little, not wanting to let her go for one second. She smelled so inviting and the feel of her skin against mine filled me with desire.

'Hey, Rachel,' I whispered, 'I sure am glad to see you.' I smiled at her lovely face.

'Back at you, Jackson. I've missed you, I don't think I was aware how much until I saw you then.' We shared another kiss, our bodies drawn irresistibly to each other. I buried my fingers in her long, wavy hair and felt her sigh. I knew at that moment that all I wanted to do was to get her in my bed and show her all the love I had for her.

'C'mon, let's get you home,' I said, breaking the connection for the time being. 'I see you can travel lightly!'

I teased her and she gave me a look that said she could probably meet any challenge I might throw at her. I picked up her bags in one hand and took hers in the other and we set off for the car.

'I can't get over how humid it is here, even this late at night,' she said as we walked.

'I know, baby, it takes some getting used to. It even surprised me when I came back but I think I've adjusted now.'

I stowed her luggage in the trunk after opening the rear

passenger door for her. When I jumped in, I pulled her close to me as we set off for the condo.

'Who's that?' she whispered, nodding at Greg.

'Rachel, meet Greg, my regular driver.'

'Pleased to meet you, ma'am. I hope you'll enjoy your stay in Nashville.' Greg smiled at Rachel in the rear-view mirror.

'Pleased to meet you too, Greg,' she replied a little shyly before nestling back against me. I sighed as we relaxed back into the seat for the journey home.

As we got out of the car, Rachel stood transfixed, staring at the affectionately named 'Batman' building, an icon of the Nashville skyline.

'What is that building? It looks like…like…'

'Like Batman?' I offered, amused at the look of confusion on her face.

'Exactly,' she said, still unable to look away from the view of the city at night.

I chuckled.

'That's what everyone calls it, sweetheart.' I took her hand and watched as she tried to absorb it all.

'And something smells delicious. What is it?'

'That, sugar, is good ol' southern fried chicken. We will definitely make sure you get to try some while you're here.'

'Wow, what a fantastic sight!' she said, going straight to the terrace for the night-time view of downtown Nashville's skyscrapers, from above this time. 'I love that Batman building. The spires look so cool lit up like that!'

I set her bags down and followed her out there, slipping my arm around her waist.

'Yeah, the view was one of the things I liked most about this place. I love being in the heart of the city, with the mix of old architecture and modern skyscrapers side by side.' I pointed out the Cumberland river to her and the famous Shelby Street bridge.

She turned then to look at me and, as I looked down into her eyes, the strength of her love for me made me catch my breath.

'Jackson, I...' she began but then faltered.

'What is it?' I asked, drawing her to me and tracing her lower lip with my fingertips. I could hear concern in her voice.

'Are you sure you still feel the same way for me as you said you did in Dorset?'

I leaned down and kissed her softly on her full lips, breathing in her now familiar floral scent. 'I love you, as much as I did before, if that's what you're asking me,' I said, gazing down into her eyes. 'You're gorgeous and it's all I can do to restrain myself right now. But we can take our time and let you get settled in first.' I smiled, trying to lighten the mood a little.

She nodded, a faint blush creeping up her cheeks.

I grabbed her hand then and took her on a whistle-stop tour of my loft, finally bringing her to my bedroom. I put her bag down on the floor and turned to face her.

'Would you like something to eat or drink or do you think you'll be able to sleep?' I asked her.

'I'm not really hungry right now but I don't want to sleep either.' She pulled at her lower lip with her teeth and raised her eyebrows at me.

I took a step towards her. 'What do you have in mind then, Miss Hardy?' I hoped that I had picked up her signals correctly.

'I think it's time we both showed a bit less restraint,' she said, with a grin.

I swept her up in my arms then, tasting her lips again before laying her gently on the bed. She looked adorable with her hair fanned out on the pillows around her, staring up at me and I wanted only to make her mine once more, to share with her the passion I'd been holding in while we'd been apart.

'How about having something to eat now?' I asked again,

some time later, propping myself up so I could see her more clearly.

'I wouldn't mind something because I didn't eat at the stopover in the end. But you must be tired. You'll have to get up tomorrow won't you?'

'I had a snooze in front of the TV earlier, so I'm not too sleepy and I can go in whenever I want. I am the boss, you know.' I put on what I imagined to be a typical boss face, knowing I was nothing of the sort.

She laughed then and smacked my arm playfully. I swung out of bed, pulling on my boxers and went into the kitchen, with Rachel following a minute later, dressed in one of my t-shirts. I fixed some salad for her and poured out some sparkling water. I nibbled at some chips while she tucked in.

'Can I ask you something?' she said after a quiet moment.

'Sure, although this sounds a bit ominous,' I replied.

'Are you teetotal?' she asked. 'I'm only asking because I've never seen you drink alcohol.'

'Yes, I am and I have been for the best part of a year now,' I replied after the slightest pause.

'Does that have anything to do with your break-up with Stephanie?' she asked intuitively.

'Unfortunately, yes it does.' I sighed, running my hands through my hair.

'You don't have to tell me about it now, if it makes you feel awkward. It's just something I've wondered about.'

'You never make me feel awkward and you have a right to know about my past.' I paused again for a moment, gathering myself before I went on. 'I loved Stephanie and I'd expected us to settle down and make a life together, you know. She was so glamorous and self-confident, she completely took me in. I'd moved into her apartment after a few months but I'd left something at home that day so I went back to get it in the afternoon, only to find the two of them having sex in our bed.' Rachel winced as I described that awful moment.

'I'm still ashamed of how I acted then. I was so angry I completely lost it and started hitting this guy until she managed to pull me off him. I know I said some terrible things to her and then I ran and kept on going to get as far away from them as possible. I remember sitting on a park bench in the evening finally and breaking down. Everything we'd planned had been shattered in an instant and I couldn't imagine how I would rebuild my life.' I grasped Rachel's hand and she squeezed mine in reassurance.

'I ended up in a bar then and drank myself into oblivion. Fortunately, someone there recognised me and helped me call my sister Alex. She came and took me home with her. But that was only the beginning. I kept on drinking solidly for the next three months, trying to forget what she'd done to me. My family worked so hard to care for me through that dark time and there must have been many times when they thought I would never come through.

Then one day, I woke up with yet another terrible headache and furry mouth and I decided that she wasn't worth all this. If anything, I'd had a lucky escape and now it was up to me to get on with the rest of my life. So I broke all ties with her, I went out and bought this place and I cleaned up, deciding to try never to drink again. That's when I took Greg on as my driver too and I've stuck to that promise to this day. I haven't seen Stephanie again since and I hope I never do see her again because I'm not sure I could trust myself to be a gentleman in her presence.'

Rachel's eyes hadn't once wavered as I was telling her my story. If anything, she seemed stronger with each word, as though her respect for me was growing as she listened. As I finished, she stood up and came round the breakfast bar towards me.

'You are one hell of a good man, you know, and I'm lucky to have met you when I did. I'm sorry that she hurt you but you should be proud of yourself for getting through that nightmare. Thank you for being honest with me.' She kissed me, looping her arms around my neck.

'I don't know what I did to deserve you, but whatever it was, I'm sure glad I did it.' I beamed at her. 'I have to be honest and tell you that I don't know what I'd do if I did see her again. I worry that it would send me straight back to drinking.'

'Is it likely that you'll see her again?'

'I think she left town after what happened. She hated the bad press she was getting because they found out she cheated on me. I don't have any idea where she went though.'

'All we can do is deal with that if it comes up but it doesn't sound like it will. As long as you're honest about your feelings, it'll be okay.'

As I came downstairs into the lounge the next morning, I saw Rachel sitting on the terrace. She looked stunning, with her chestnut hair cascading down her back and all her luscious curves outlined by her silk gown.

I stood for several minutes, drinking in her loveliness and remembering how good her skin felt to the touch. My body was already responding to that memory when she turned to look at me, obviously sensing I was there. I looked down sheepishly, caught in the act of staring but when I dared to look up again, she was smiling brightly back at me.

I walked towards her.

'Hey, good morning, sleepyhead,' she said, taking my hand and bringing it to her lips.

'What time did you wake up?'

'Five o'clock or some other ungodly hour. I've been sitting here quietly, watching the sun come up and waiting for you to surface. Shouldn't you, you know, be at work now?'

'No, I've sent a text to Annie to say I'm working at home, at least for this morning. They're slowly getting used to me not being such a workaholic since I met you.'

'Since you met me?' Her eyes widened. 'What do you mean?'

'Well, after Stephanie, I threw myself into my work, living and breathing it to try and help myself forget all the pain. And I kind of expected the same of everyone else, which I'm not proud of. But since I came back last week, I've started to rediscover my true self a little. I think that's down to meeting you.' I smiled. 'I'm hoping that you're going to help me continue that trend over these coming weeks, sweetheart.'

'It would be my pleasure.'

She came over to me and kissed me. From that point on, I was lost in her and I knew it was only a matter of time before we would end up back in the bedroom so that I could show her what I was feeling.

I suggested that we go out for lunch once we were finally dressed so that Rachel could start to get a bit more of a feel for Nashville. I decided to keep it simple for her first day and so we wandered round to my favourite sandwich shop on Union Street. It was midday by the time we got there and already feeling pretty humid but the line outside wasn't too bad and once we sat down inside, it was fun advising Rachel about what to have.

'What do you recommend? It all looks and smells great but there's so much choice!' Her eyes widened as the table next to us received their order, including the most enormous sandwiches. She laughed along with them at their surprise.

'Yeah, you're right but I've tried most things over the years. I'd definitely recommend one of the hot sandwiches but honestly, it's all good. You must try and leave some room for a brownie, they really are to die for.'

Our server came shortly after and, with her friendly encouragement, Rachel finally went for the Angus Po'Boy and I had my regular, Wicked Chicken for the spicy chipotle and green chilli sauce. We ordered a couple of lemonades too and sat back to people watch for a minute while we waited for our orders to come.

As always, the restaurant was bustling with both tourists and regulars but no-one seemed to mind being packed in because the food was so delicious. I watched Rachel's face as she took in all the cowboy hats in the room, smiling as her eyes lit up at the sight. Music was never far from her mind though.

'What have you planned for me, musically, I mean, over the next few weeks?' Rachel asked, breaking us out of our reverie. She had a glint in her eye as she posed the question. I smiled before replying, knowing exactly what her double meaning was but then focussed on the real question.

'I thought that it would be good for you to come in with me to the office tomorrow and sing a few of your songs for us live so that they can see what you're like in real life, if you'd be up for that?'

'That sounds like a good idea,' she agreed but she was twisting her hands together.

I reached over and took one of hers in mine.

'Hey, you don't need to worry about anything. I'll be there to look out for you and they're all nice people, honestly. I'd also like to invite my sister, Alex, if that's okay? She's a music manager and I've already given her the CD of your performance at the final, which she told me she thought was fantastic, by the way.'

'Hang on, why do I need a manager when I have you?' she queried.

I took a deep breath before answering.

'You don't have to answer to me about anything. This has to be your journey and if you have your own manager, you'll be taking independent advice, and don't think that because Alex is my sister, she'll do what I say. Nothing could be further from the truth, which is why I spoke to her because I know she'll look out for your best interests. She's had several years of experience already, despite only being twenty-four.'

'Okay,' she said reluctantly. 'Well, I'd like to meet Alex of course but I'm not sure that I need independent advice like you're suggesting. I haven't even recorded the demo CD yet.'

'Listen, sweetheart, I want you to do what's right for you. You won't offend me by signing with someone else if that's what you finally decide down the line, you know.'

'Jackson! How can you even think that I'd do that? I'm shocked by that idea, I really am. I know I'd be upset if you did that to me. Anyway, you're getting way ahead of things.'

'What can I say? This is business, you don't owe me anything but it is a good idea to think ahead so we're prepared.'

She pursed her lips and folded her arms, letting her body tell me that she didn't like that idea one little bit. The look she gave me made it very clear that she had her own opinion about how she wanted things to go. Her determination made me smile, even if it meant we wouldn't always agree on everything.

'Why are you smiling at me?' she demanded.

'It's just that you're so sexy when you're cross with me.' I grinned at her, knowing I'd caught her off-guard.

Then our food came, taking our attention away from the discussion for a moment at least. It was delicious as always and for a while we simply indulged our taste buds. When we both paused to let our food go down, she went straight back to the point.

'I know you want to look out for me but I think this impartiality is misguided. *You* found me and *you* made this all happen for me and I want you to be by my side as I go through this whole thing.'

'I will be by your side, I'm not suggesting otherwise.' I paused. 'Look, let's not get bogged down by this, please. How about we take it slow and see what happens and deal with things as they come up?'

She nodded but I could see that I'd unsettled her and that

From Here to Nashville

was the last thing I'd meant to do.

CHAPTER NINETEEN

It was mid-afternoon by the time we returned and Rachel went straight off to unpack her stuff while I checked in with the office to arrange things for tomorrow and to deal with some emails. I found it hard to concentrate after our disagreement. I wanted only to do what was right for Rachel but she hadn't taken it that way. I would have to tread carefully not to throw her off balance again.

After an hour of being apart, I went to look for her, hoping that she'd had enough time on her own to process our earlier conversation by now. I went into the bedroom only to find her fast asleep in semi-darkness, with the blinds closed. I knew I should wake her because it would be better for her to sleep at night but I couldn't resist watching her sleep for a few minutes longer. I held my breath as I watched the gentle rise and fall of her chest and I noticed the contrast of her flushed cheeks against the cream pillowcase. I sat down on the bed next to her and reached out to caress her cheek, making her sigh.

'Sweetheart, time to wake up,' I whispered, and I kissed her lips softly before sitting back again.

She stirred and squinted at me, then sat up suddenly, her face close to mine.

'How long have I been asleep?' she asked, moving away a little.

'Only an hour, I think. Shhh, it's okay,' I reassured her. 'I didn't think it would be good for you to sleep too long.'

'I think I'll have a quick shower to wake myself up.'

She headed off to the bathroom before I could say anything further and I went back out to the lounge, wishing I'd climbed into bed with her instead of waking her up. I found myself thinking of all the contours of her body while she was in the shower, which only made my frustration grow but I didn't think she was in the right mood for me to join her in there yet.

A short while later, she reappeared, with her hair damp from the shower and her skin smelling even sweeter, if that was possible. She'd changed into fresh clothes as well and looked more relaxed. She wasn't smiling at me though.

'Are you still mad at me?' I asked.

'A little,' she said honestly, 'but I do understand your reasons, I don't agree with you, that's all.' She smiled a crooked smile. 'The important thing is that we keep talking about it all, okay?' she asked.

'Of course we will,' I agreed and I went towards her and took her in my arms. 'I wondered if you might like to go over to my parents' house tonight so I can introduce y'all? My mom is dying to meet you! What do you think?'

'Yes, that would be nice, I think.' She was biting her lip though as if she wasn't sure.

'It won't be formal or anything, my folks aren't like that, honestly.' I kissed her again, craving a taste of her. 'Shall we head over there about six?'

We made our way downstairs soon afterwards to meet Greg again for the short ride to my parents' house. I pointed out some landmarks to Rachel on the way, wanting to share all the things I loved about my home town. As we approached Centennial Park, I waited to see her reaction to our very own Greek temple in Tennessee.

'Goodness, what is that amazing building in the park? It looks like it should be in Athens, not Nashville!'

I told her about our Parthenon replica then and how it had been built for the Centennial celebrations. We could see that the park was full of people out for a stroll as always.

'The Parthenon seems a bit out of place here, I know, but the park is lovely. We spent hours there as kids.'

149

We rounded the corner and I showed her Vanderbilt University where my parents worked and Maggie, my sister, was a student.

My parents came out to meet us as we pulled up to the house.

'It's lovely to meet you, Rachel,' my mom said as soon as we got out of the car. My mom kissed Rachel on both cheeks after I introduced her, and my dad, ever the gentleman, took her hand and brought it to his lips.

'You're every bit as beautiful as Jackson said you were, Rachel.'

I rolled my eyes at him and Rachel blushed. We all laughed together, breaking the ice.

My mom took Rachel's arm and led her into the house, talking all the way. I shook Dad's hand, punching him playfully on the arm as well, after his showy display. Maggie joined us shortly afterwards, unable to contain her curiosity and we sat down to a simple pasta supper.

'So, Rachel,' my mom began, 'you're from Poole, Jackson tells me.'

'That's right, I've lived there all my life. I know you lived in Bournemouth when Jackson was young. Is that where you're from originally?'

'Yes, I was born and brought up there but I lived in a number of places around Dorset, including Poole for a short while, before Jackson was born. I haven't been back since I met Bob over here. I probably ought to do that sooner rather than later.'

'Rachel is an excellent guide to all the sights,' I mentioned, with a chuckle.

'I'd love to show you round sometime, Mrs Phillips,' said Rachel.

'Honey, you must call me Shelley, everyone does, except my students of course.' She laughed heartily.

'What do you lecture in, Shelley?' Rachel continued.

'French and European Studies. I took my first degree in the UK at Southampton and then completed my PhD here at Emory, over in Atlanta, after meeting Bob.'

The conversation continued without a pause, with Rachel filling them in with details about herself as we went along.

'What's Dorset like, Rachel? Is it near London?' asked Maggie, making everyone laugh.

'It's a good couple of hours away, Maggie, near the sea,' Rachel explained.

Maggie's face fell and I could see that she was mentally removing it from her list of places to visit even as we were speaking.

'It was lovely to meet you, Rachel,' said Maggie, as she kissed her goodbye. 'I sure hope we'll see you again soon.'

'Well, how about we get everyone together for a cookout this Sunday afternoon?' offered my dad.

'That sounds like a great idea, Dad,' I replied and it was agreed.

In the car on the way back home, Rachel snuggled up to me, and before too long, I sensed the change in her body and knew that she had fallen asleep. I couldn't bring myself to wake her when we arrived so I simply scooped her into my arms and carried her into the building. I was aware of every curve of her body as she wrapped herself around me, and when I laid her on the bed a few minutes later, I was consumed with desire for her once more. I lay awake for ages afterwards, listening to the sound of her breathing and waiting for the physical ache I had for her to subside.

Thanks to my noisy alarm, we both woke at seven the next day.

'Hey, sweetheart.' Rachel greeted me with a kiss on the back of my neck, pressing her body up against me and reminding me of the desire I'd felt last night.

I turned round to look at her, putting my hands lightly on

151

either side of her waist.

'Hey, beautiful,' I replied, savouring every detail of her face.

'I don't remember going to bed last night and I still have my clothes on. How did that happen?' She gazed at me, waiting for me to explain, which I did.

'You looked so lovely when I laid you on the bed, it was really hard to restrain myself.'

'And do you still have those feelings now?' she asked, giving me a very seductive smile.

I reached out to unbutton her blouse in answer to her question and she arched her neck towards me for a kiss.

We still made it to the office for nine o'clock after a leisurely walk in. Annie was already at her desk when we arrived and stood up to greet us. She smiled broadly at Rachel and I felt her relax with the warmth of Annie's welcome.

'Rachel, it's such a pleasure to meet you. I'm Annie, Jackson's assistant and dogsbody.' She grinned, making Rachel laugh by return.

'Well, I suppose someone had to have that job,' she replied good-humouredly.

'If there's anything you need, let me know,' Annie went on.

'Thank you, that's really kind.'

I showed Rachel into my office.

'Wow, Annie's a real catch, isn't she?' Rachel said as we went in.

'She sure is. I like to think of her as my office mom, always looking out for my best interests and a great friend to boot,' I said.

We sat down on the sofa and I quickly ran through the plan for the day.

'I've scheduled your live performance for ten o'clock which will give you a chance to meet the VPs and Alex. After that, around eleven, I've set up a meeting for you with Todd and Alex to discuss potential "Open Mic"/live performances in Nashville in the coming week, followed by lunch with Alex to discuss things so far. Then you and I can meet back at the office after you've had lunch to discuss progress.'

'That sounds good,' she said. 'Would I be able to go somewhere with a guitar or keyboard to have a quick run-through now?'

'Of course, sweetheart. Let's go to the studio and I'll show you where everything is. Jed, our engineer, may well be in by now to give you a hand settling in.'

We took the stairs to the lower floor and walked along to the studio. I saw Rachel glance at some of the staff as we walked along and some of them returned her look with a smile. As we walked along the downstairs corridor, she stopped in front of one of the framed posters on the wall. It was a colourful print of a guitar against the Nashville skyline.

'That's an amazing print. I love the guitar and I think I'd know those buildings anywhere now.'

I laughed and we continued on our way.

'Hey, Jed, are you in yet?' I called out when we went into the studio.

'Yup, I'm here,' his deep voice replied.

'Jed, I've brought Rachel down to get settled in before she sings for us later.'

'Hey, Rachel, nice to meet you,' he drawled, appearing from his office and putting his hand out. His massive hand dwarfed hers, I noticed, and she looked quite enchanted by his bear-like appearance.

I coughed lightly to get her attention and narrowed my eyes at her when she looked my way.

'I can trust you to look after Rachel, can't I?' I joked with Jed while staring fixedly at Rachel.

He laughed and she cleared her throat nervously in an effort to regain her focus.

'Of course, what can you mean?' Jed replied with a

twinkle in his eye.

Rachel seemed to recover some composure then. Jed definitely had a way with women but I didn't want him to work his magic on this particular woman.

'Okay then, well, I'll leave you to it. Jed, please make sure Rachel has everything she needs to perform. I'll be back at ten o'clock with the VPs and Alex, okay?'

'Yep, sure thing, Jackson, see you then.' He went off to look at his gear.

'Jed will sort you out. Don't hesitate to ask him for anything, all right sweetheart?'

'Okay.' She swallowed, looking nervous.

I gave her a hug and a light kiss before going back up to my office.

It wasn't long before I was winding my way back downstairs again to the studio, along with the VPs. Alex had already gone ahead to introduce herself and to check Rachel was ready.

We had some chairs set up around small tables in the studio area, making it like a café so it wasn't too daunting for performers and we all sat down in pairs around them. Rachel was sat on a high stool with her guitar in hand, tuning up as we arrived and she looked every inch the professional.

I remembered seeing her at that first gig and understanding that the music had the power to compose her in a way that nothing else could. Luckily, this was happening for her today too. She swept her hair over her shoulder, placed her pick in her mouth and focussed on tuning to her satisfaction.

She looked so stunning, I found it hard to concentrate on the job in hand but I willed myself to look away and take a deep breath. I noticed Alex giving me a look and I managed a tense smile in her direction.

'Hi, I'm Rachel Hardy, it's good to meet you all. Thank you for giving me the opportunity to sing for you today. As a warm-up, I'm going to start by singing one of my favourite songs, Lee Ann Womack's "I Hope You Dance".'

This song was also one of my favourites but we had no idea that we both liked it so much. I'd never heard Rachel sing it before and I realised I was holding my breath in anticipation of her performance. Well, I wasn't disappointed, she really knew how to do it justice. Damn, she was good.

I had a quick look round the others to see if I could gauge their mood. They were all smiling, if that was anything to go by. The applause was strong after her first cover and she looked buoyed up by that. Todd leaned towards me.

'She's even better live, Jackson.'

I blew out my breath then and tried to relax a little.

She moved on to sing some of her own songs, starting with 'My Turn', followed by 'Don't Let Me Go' and finishing with 'Too Late', which was the one I thought we could release straight away as a single.

At the end, we all stood to give rapturous applause because she'd been fantastic, there was no doubt about it and I could see that everyone was genuinely impressed, with a few people nodding in my direction. Rachel looked over at me then for confirmation and I winked at her to prove how well she'd done. She was beaming.

'You were right, Jackson. Rachel is an amazing singer,' Alex said to me when she joined me.

'I know and she wrote those songs herself. She is going to fit right in here in Nashville.' It was still true that for the Nashville music scene, it's all about the songs and the stories they tell, and Alex knew that as well as I did.

Everyone wanted to have a quick chat with Rachel before going so it took a while to get her on my own but when I did, I folded her into my arms and swept her off her feet. She giggled with delight mixed with a bit of relief, I think. When I put her down, we kissed and her excitement was infectious.

'That was the best feeling. I know I sang well and I really felt I did myself proud and when the applause came, it felt so good, you know?'

'I know, baby and you deserved every minute. Everyone was so impressed. It was great for them to be able to hear you sing live, rather than on a less than perfect recording.'

'Is there time for me to have a drink before my next meeting, do you think?'

I chuckled at her earnest face.

'You don't need to get permission, you're a free woman, honey!' I put on my best southern accent to tease her.

She flounced off up the stairs then, turning to give me a very sultry look over her shoulder and I chased her up the remaining stairs to the top. We were both a little breathless when we emerged into the main office and stopped suddenly, both doing our best to look calm. I glanced at her and she looked guiltily at me, pulling a face and making me laugh.

There was no doubt about it, Rachel Hardy was doing my damaged heart the power of good.

CHAPTER TWENTY

While Rachel was out at lunch with Alex, I walked down to Todd's office to ask how their meeting had gone. He invited me in and I took a seat across the desk from him so he could fill me in on all the details.

'Well, after Rachel's brilliant performance, it was easy to see where she would fit in for some live shows. We agreed to try for some "Open Mic" nights starting at The Bluebird Café next Monday, Douglas Corner on Tuesday and perhaps The Listening Room Café the following week. This would really get the community talking about her and promote some interest generally in the industry as well. We should get that demo CD recorded as soon as possible as well.'

'Yeah, that sounds good. This may well generate some interest among other record labels, which I think will be healthy too.'

'What do you mean, Jackson? Are you saying that you want other labels to be interested in Rachel, too? Doesn't that fly in the face of what we're trying to do?' Todd looked perplexed.

'Yes, I know it sounds crazy but I don't want Rachel to feel obliged to sign with my label out of loyalty to me. That's why I asked Alex to think about representing her. My theory is that if several labels are interested, she can then take a view about what's best for her, with Alex's help. That may well mean signing with us but it may not and I'm ready to accept that. Does that make sense?'

'Well, I understand where you're coming from, you don't want to railroad her, I get that. Have you told Rachel?' I nodded. 'And what did she have to say about your idea?' he asked.

'She didn't like it one bit,' I confessed. 'She said that she would be hurt if things were the other way round and I chose to go with someone else. I tried to explain my thinking to her, as I've done to you but she still wasn't convinced.'

Todd blew out a breath and continued to look confused.

'I do think that perhaps this is more about you seeking some kind of confirmation that she wants to be with you for the right reasons, rather than allowing her to make an independent choice of who she wants to sign with,' Todd told me gently.

'You mean that I'm afraid because of what happened with Stephanie?'

Todd nodded and shot me an embarrassed look.

'Okay, I hear you,' I said. 'I should be getting back now but I appreciate your honesty with me, Todd.'

I continued to ponder Todd's comments as I wandered back to my own office, worrying about whether I was doing the right thing with regard to Rachel's representation. In my heart, I wanted Rough Cut to sign her of course but I didn't want her to feel obliged to sign with us. I hoped that Alex would give her impartial advice so that she could make the best decision for herself.

As I neared the office, I saw Annie hovering by her desk looking concerned.

'Hey, Annie, what's up?' I asked, feeling worried myself by the unfamiliar look etched on her face.

She followed me into the office and closed the door.

'You received a phone call from Stephanie just now,' she said with a frown.

'What? What did she say?' I asked, feeling my heart pumping as I sat down heavily behind my desk.

'I think she thought I was lying when I said you weren't here so she was rude, of course.' She waved her hand as if dismissing Stephanie's rudeness. 'She asked again to speak to you several times before telling me to make sure to pass on the message that she'd called. She left her number.' She held out a note to me, which I stared at but didn't take.

'I don't ever want to talk to her again so I don't need that number, Annie.' I passed a hand over my face before banging my fist on the desk. 'Damn her. What the hell is she doing calling me again after all this time?'

'I'll get rid of this number then, shall I?' Annie asked me and I nodded. 'What do you want me to say if she calls again? I'm certain that she will.'

'If I am here the next time, you should put her through. But only so I can tell her that I don't ever want to speak to her again.'

I tried to put Stephanie's call out of my mind by working through lunch. Then, at two o'clock on the dot, Alex and Rachel appeared at the door of my office, looking ever so slightly conspiratorial and my mind switched immediately to them.

'Ladies, do come in and sit down,' I offered, in my best southern gentleman drawl. 'Did you have a good lunch?' I asked.

'Yes, it was lovely, thank you,' Rachel replied very politely.

'And did you make any decisions at all?' I went on, glancing from Rachel to Alex and then back again.

'Why, yes, Jackson, we did,' said Alex. 'I'm not sure whether you'll like our decision though.'

'Uh-oh,' I said out loud. 'Come on then, spill the beans. What did y'all conclude?'

'That Rachel should sign with Rough Cut and stop all this fannying around, if you'll pardon my expression.' She gave me a look that said she was prepared for a fight if that's what I wanted to happen.

I took a moment before replying and found them both staring at me intently when I looked up again.

'If we're being strictly truthful here, Rough Cut hasn't offered you a deal yet,' I said and I sat back in my chair in a victory stance.

'No, that's true,' Alex batted back, 'so we'll be on our way, shall we?' She motioned towards Rachel to stand up, which she did.

My jaw dropped at the way these two women were handling me. I threw my hands up in defeat and managed a smile.

'Okay, I know when I'm beat. I want Rachel to sign with us, you know I do. But are you sure that this is what you want to do?' I asked, looking directly at her this time.

She came towards me then but said to Alex, 'Would you mind giving us a minute please?'

As Alex left the room, Rachel came and took my hand, leading me over to the sofa. I waited for her to gather herself and explain her feelings to me.

'I need to sign with a label that will look out for my best interests. In the normal course of things, that would be really hard to find, wouldn't it?'

I nodded, swallowing nervously at the same time.

'But in this case,' she continued, 'I know that Rough Cut will look out for my best interests, above and beyond the normal call of duty because you own the company and not only that, but we're together so that's a double whammy. And there you have it. I don't want to sign with anyone else. I want you to look out for me and not just at work.' She raised her eyebrows a little and smiled which I found heart-warming.

'God, I love you so much, Rachel Hardy.' I leaned in for a kiss.

'I love you too, Jackson Phillips.'

I could feel her smile as she kissed me back to confirm it.

A short while later, Alex returned, and we quickly filled

her in on the point we'd reached in our discussions. She jumped up and down on the spot, clapping her hands with glee. Then she gave Rachel a hug and put her hand out to shake mine before laughing and pulling me in for a hug too.

'Way to go, Rachel,' she said. 'Now all we need is a contract to pore over, Jackson.'

'I know and I'll get straight on it as soon as I get some peace from all this harassment I've been experiencing this afternoon.' I grinned.

The afternoon whizzed by and soon six o'clock rolled round so I went in search of Rachel. I found her down in the studio practising some other songs I hadn't heard before. I was able to stand listening to her without her realising I was there. The song seemed to be called 'Driving Me Crazy' and had a really good up-tempo beat to it.

I coughed lightly as the song came to an end.

She swivelled in surprise to see who had been watching her. When she saw it was me, her face lit up. That special look she gave me would never grow old.

I crossed the floor towards her, and embraced her with a deep, passionate kiss that left us both breathless.

'Hey, baby, time to go home,' I whispered.

'That sounds like a great idea.'

The rest of the week passed quickly, with Rachel spending every spare moment rehearsing and recording tracks for her demo CD and me trying to finalise the details of her contract with us. It had been a busy but satisfying week and I had already suggested to her that we spend Saturday sightseeing like proper tourists in and around Nashville.

So we were up pretty early on Saturday morning to make the most of the day. I'd decided that our first stop should be The Country Music Hall of Fame and Museum, and because I knew Rachel would love it, I'd thought ahead and bought us Platinum Package tickets earlier in the week. This would allow us to take in the fantastic RCA Studio Tour as well which was worth the entrance fee alone.

We arrived at the museum a little after it opened at nine, planning to have a look around there first before our Studio Tour. We spent quite a while outside looking at the magnificent modern building, with all its musical references, most notably the windows designed to look like the keys of a piano. Rachel took a whole host of photos from different angles but, in the end, I managed to persuade her to go in so we could see some of the museum. She absolutely fell in love with the history and all the different collections, taking in every last item in the Taylor Swift 'Speak Now' exhibit on show at the time and marvelling at all the different artefacts.

We broke off to do the RCA Studio Tour then, taking the old-fashioned shuttle bus over there, with its life-size photo of Dolly Parton on the side of it. Watching Rachel's reaction to everything was such a pleasure because she wanted to drink it all in and remember it forever.

'I can't quite believe we're standing in the place where stars like Elvis and Dolly recorded some of their greatest hits,' she marvelled.

When she sat down at the piano and played a couple of chords from her own songs, I saw the look on her face as though she was being transported back in time to the days when some of those country music greats had sat there before her. She was a bit overwhelmed by it all then and had to pause to catch her breath.

When we got back to the main museum, we had lunch in the restaurant, taking advantage of their outdoor courtyard before heading back inside again for another hour to see some more exhibits before we left. Although we'd had a good look at each floor, as well as studying some of the hundreds of plaques for Hall of Fame inductees, I thought that we would need to go again soon for Rachel to see anything else she might have missed. We finally wandered back into the afternoon sunshine, tired out but happy.

'Are you up for a bit more sightseeing or was that enough for one day?' I asked her, smiling at the excitement on her face.

'Oh, Jackson, I enjoyed that such a lot, I really wasn't expecting it to be that wonderful. I'd love to walk for a while and have a look at anything else we see on the way if you're still okay?'

I put my arm round her shoulder and said, 'As long as I'm with you, watching your lovely face, I'll go anywhere you like, baby.'

We walked down towards the Cumberland river and caught the Music City Trolley Hop tour to save our feet for a while and to allow us to do more sightseeing more quickly. We took in the iconic red-brick Ryman Auditorium, known as 'the mother church of country music' from the days when it was a gospel tabernacle, Bicentennial Park, and the Centennial Park and the Parthenon again before finally jumping off at the Frist Center Art Museum. We went inside for a coffee and dessert then to talk over our day.

'I can't believe how much there is to see here.' Rachel was still full of wonder, as she stirred her sugar into her café latte.

'You're right and we only scratched the surface today. I had the feeling that you could have stayed at the Country Hall of Fame all day, so we'll have to go back there.'

'That's a definite date. Thank you for a lovely day today, you're a pretty good tour guide, you know.' She smiled and drank some coffee.

'Changing the subject slightly, what shall we do for dinner tonight?' I asked her.

'How about we stay in and cook something? We haven't used the kitchen together yet. I love to cook and your kitchen looks like it needs some TLC.'

'That's fine by me. We'll stop at a market on the way home and pick up whatever you need.'

We sat out on the terrace to eat the delicious meal that Rachel had cooked, with a little bit of help from me. I heard Rachel's intake of breath a couple of times, as though she wanted to say something to me but didn't quite know how to start. I glanced over at her to see her biting her lip.

'You sound like you've got something on your mind. What is it?' I reached out my hand to stroke her arm.

'It's just that…' She looked at me, changed position in her chair and began again. 'I feel a bit nervous about how quickly everything is happening between us. It all feels a bit too good to be true. Did you really mean it when you said you loved me?' She glanced anxiously in my direction and then away.

'I did mean it, Rachel, I wouldn't say something like that lightly.'

She nodded, looking back at me again, before covering my hand with hers. I had the feeling that I'd passed a test but I wasn't entirely sure which one.

CHAPTER TWENTY-ONE

I left Rachel to lie in the next day while I went for a run, leaving a note to tell her where I'd gone. I hadn't been all week but I had remembered one of my old routes through Centennial Park when we went past it again yesterday and so decided to take myself that way. I needed some time to think about the conversation we'd had the night before too. I knew she was a bit hesitant about moving too quickly in our relationship and I could only guess at the reasons for that because she hadn't volunteered that information as yet. I didn't want to put her under any more pressure by asking her about it but I did want her to understand that I cared and that she could trust me. What I wasn't sure of was how to do that well enough for her to believe me. By the time I came back an hour later, she was still in bed, obviously not yet caught up with her lack of sleep. I busied myself making us some breakfast and she wandered into the kitchen a few minutes later.

'Hey, sleepyhead, how are you today?' I kissed her gently on the nose.

'I feel awful for sleeping in so late.' She groaned, putting her arms around me.

The warmth of her body against mine made me want to groan too. Her body was so tempting, I had to stop myself from ravishing it at every opportunity.

'Don't feel guilty, you needed to catch up. I've been for a run and prepared us some breakfast so let's just enjoy it.' I moved carefully away from the temptation of her body and sat down at the table.

An hour later, Greg pulled up in front of my parents'

house. Rachel picked up the bouquet of flowers she had bought for my mom the previous day and we got out of the car. I took Rachel's hand and this time, we went straight into the garden, knowing that everyone would be gathered there for the cookout. As we walked through the wrought-iron gate, Mom glanced up and called out to us.

'Hey, it's lovely to see you both again so soon.' She reached out to Rachel first and took the flowers she offered before enveloping Rachel in a great big hug. 'Thank you for these pretty flowers. What a kind thought!'

'We wanted to thank you and Bob for putting in all this work for us today.'

'It's been our pleasure. Jackson, give your mother a kiss. You look more handsome every time I see you,' she gushed in the way that mothers do.

'Aw, Mom, don't embarrass me!' I blushed ever so slightly at her comment.

'Just speaking the truth, there's surely nothing wrong with that, is there, Rachel?'

'No, ma'am,' Rachel replied, putting on her best Tennessee accent.

We left Mom as she went to find a vase for the flowers and walked towards Bob, who was already cooking food on the brick-built BBQ. Maggie was sitting on one of the garden benches, chatting away to someone I didn't recognise.

'Hey, Dad, how's the BBQ going?'

'So far, so good, Jackson. Hello, Rachel, you look lovely. I won't kiss you right now 'cos I'm a little greasy. I'll catch up with y'all for a proper hug later.'

'Do you need a hand with anything, Dad?' I asked, knowing he was going to say no.

'No, no, I'm fine,' he confirmed and I laughed.

'Look, we'll go over and catch up with Maggie but promise me you'll holler if you want me to help, okay?'

'Sure thing, Jackson,' and he turned back to his grilled

meats like they were his babies.

I leaned towards Maggie to kiss her cheek and then I looked pointedly at her male companion. She laughed then at my big brother act.

'Rachel, Jackson, this is Ted, he's on my course at college.'

We both nodded at Ted and sat down on a nearby bench to enjoy the warmth of the sun. We chatted amiably for a while but when Ted went off to find the bathroom I jumped in quickly to quiz Maggie.

'Are you two dating?' I asked bluntly.

'We're just friends, Jackson. Relax, will you?' replied Maggie, rolling her eyes. Then turning to Rachel, she said, 'God, is he always this demanding? How do you put up with it?'

'I wouldn't call it demanding, maybe being a little over-protective, that's all.' Rachel smiled knowingly at me.

'I don't need you to protect me, Jackson, thank you.' Maggie stood up and flounced off.

I looked at Rachel and she raised her eyebrows at me.

'Am I over-protective?' I asked, a bit shame-faced.

'I guess you could say that but from my perspective, as your girlfriend, I like that. It's just that Maggie may not like it because she's your sister and so she has a different view, of course.'

'Just so we're clear though,' I replied, leaning in towards her, 'you are much more than my girlfriend.'

'How's that?' she asked, looking at me quizzically. 'I mean, we're not engaged or married, so the most you could describe me as is your partner. But I think that would imply that we were living together?'

She glanced at me from beneath her eyelashes.

'And that's what we're doing, isn't it? Living together?' I batted straight back at her.

'Yes, but I don't know if I like the sound of "partner". I'd rather be your girlfriend, if that's what's on offer.'

'I'm ready to offer you more whenever you're ready for more,' I whispered into her ear.

She turned towards me, placing one hand lightly on my chest.

'What kind of "more" do you mean?'

'I love you and you feel the same for me and I know I want us to be together all the time and, in my book, that means only one thing longer term.' I stuttered a little over my words, wanting to say everything I'd been thinking about earlier that day properly.

At that exact moment, Alex tapped me on the shoulder and said hello. I looked up, glad to see her but a bit frustrated at the interruption to my conversation with Rachel. I was only a bit surprised to see Todd hovering behind Alex but was momentarily rendered speechless. I'd kind of guessed that they might be dating from their reaction to each other around the office but it was still a bit of a shock. Rachel stepped in to cover my confusion.

'Alex, Todd, how lovely to see you both.' She stood up to kiss them.

They sat down and Todd put his arm around the back of the bench very casually. Rachel put her hand on my leg to calm me so I didn't put my foot in it with another of my sisters. I covered her hand with mine and gave it a little squeeze. She glanced at me and I could see what I thought was love shining in her eyes.

I desperately wanted to know how she felt, having bared my soul to her about where I wanted our relationship to go.

With Rachel's help, I relaxed a little and stopped being so overbearing. It turned out to be a really lovely evening, with great food and great company and pleasantly warm weather. I was really happy for Alex and Todd, they were a good couple and I told Alex that as soon as I could.

'Thanks for that, Jackson. I appreciate your support

because I know you and Todd are friends and I don't want to come between you. But it does feel good with him and I hope it's going to go somewhere.'

'Hey, kiddo, I'd be pleased as punch if you two stayed the course, you being two of my favourite people.'

We went in search of our other halves then and I found Rachel talking to my mom and dad, admiring some pretty yellow roses in the flower bed.

'So, Jackson, Rachel tells me she's going to try for The Bluebird tomorrow night. That is really exciting! Why don't Bob and I come along to the next one after that? I can't wait to hear her sing.'

'That would be great, Mom. Is that all right with you, sweetheart?' I had slipped my arm around Rachel's waist when I approached and I pulled her closer now.

'Of course,' she replied, 'that would be great.'

A short while later, we were getting into the car for Greg to take us home. We were both very quiet on the way back. I didn't quite know how to get us back to the mood of our earlier conversation, and from the tightness of her shoulders I could tell she felt the same.

All too soon, we were back at the condo and we still hadn't managed to revisit the conversation. I couldn't let us go to sleep on that though so I took a deep breath and turned to face her at the same time as she turned to me. I grinned stupidly and she laughed.

'I had a great time with you this weekend. In fact, I've been having nothing but great times since I first met you and I want that to continue.'

'I feel exactly the same. I definitely want our relationship to develop into something more but things are moving fast for me in so many ways at the moment. Can't we keep going as we are for a while longer, getting to know each other and enjoying each other's company before we commit to anything more?' She spoke gently but I was still surprised by that.

It sounded like she was afraid of commitment with me and I didn't know why. If anyone should be nervous of making another commitment, surely it should be me? What wasn't she telling me?

'Okay, sure,' I agreed and I turned away from her, desperate to hide my disappointment. I undressed quickly and climbed into bed.

'Goodnight then,' she said and I replied but I didn't turn round to face her. I heard her sigh before she rolled over and turned out her light.

That definitely wasn't the way I'd expected the day to end.

I was woken the next morning by the sound of Rachel cooking in the kitchen. I lay there listening for a moment. As I started to wake up, memories from our conversation the night before came flooding back and I couldn't stop the hurt I'd felt then from resurfacing. I closed my eyes for a moment and sighed. I didn't want to rush her into anything she wasn't ready for but I did want some sign of commitment from her. I sighed as I slipped out of bed and wandered into the kitchen.

'Hey,' she said softly, smiling when she saw I was up. 'How are you today?'

'How honest do you want me to be?' I replied before I could stop myself.

Her smile faded then and her face mirrored mine.

'Your face is telling quite a good story at the moment.' She pursed her lips and turned away.

'You hurt me last night,' I went on regardless, 'because you don't sound like you want to commit to our relationship as much as I do, which was unexpected.' I needed her to know what I was feeling, even if she didn't like it.

She suddenly threw down the tea towel she'd been holding and came round the breakfast bar to confront me.

'How can you say to me that you doubt my commitment to you when I have travelled thousands of miles to be with you and all but abandoned my old life to pursue my dream?' I could see her clenching her fists at her sides. 'I haven't told someone I loved them for a really long time and I don't think I've ever experienced what I'm feeling now for anyone else before. I do want to be with you and I'm really excited by the prospect of sharing these new experiences in my life with you. I don't think I could have conveyed that any more clearly than I have to you!'

'So why won't you commit to anything more right now?' I asked pointedly.

'I tried to explain last night and I realise that maybe I didn't do it very well.' She paused and swept her long, wavy hair over one shoulder and began to examine it. 'I'm frightened,' she whispered, refusing to look me in the eye. I took her hands in mine then and pulled her to me for a hug.

'What are you frightened of, baby?' I asked.

She pulled back a little to talk again.

'I'm frightened of pursuing my dream of being a singer and failing. I'm frightened of giving myself to you and leaving everything I know behind and it not working out between us. I still feel so out of my depth in your world and I don't even know the half of it after such a short time. It all feels so overwhelming.' She started to cry.

'Oh, please don't cry, sweetheart,' I told her gently.

I wiped her tears away with my thumb and then led her to the sofa so she was sitting next to me. 'I understand all your fears and how mind-blowing this must all feel for you. I'm sorry that I hadn't thought about that myself. But can I ask you why you think it won't work out between us? Have I given you any reason to think that?'

'No, of course not,' she sniffled. 'But my experience with men hasn't been good in the past and I don't know why you'd stick with me when you can have your pick of hundreds of women out there.'

'You're the only woman out there that I'm interested in. I

don't care about your background. You belong in this world as much as I do. Please don't put yourself down like that. I love you for who you are and I want to be with you. Can you tell me what happened in the past to make you doubt yourself like this?'

I offered her a tissue so she could wipe her eyes.

She took it gratefully and waited for a minute to compose herself before speaking.

'When I first went to college, I fell in love with someone on my course. His name was Nick. We did everything together.' She paused for a moment, looking like she was remembering that time in her life.

'After a year had passed, he asked me to marry him and I said yes without a moment's hesitation. We decided to wait until we'd both finished college but it felt good knowing that he was committed to me. I can't believe how easily I gave him my trust.'

A wave of bitterness crossed her face, something I'd never seen there before. I reached out to hold her hand.

'Then, gradually, I saw less and less of him as he gave me one excuse after another for not spending time with me. One day, he came round to see me and told me that when his finals were over, he wanted to go on a long holiday before settling down. I got all excited and asked him where we might go on our limited budget. But when I looked at him again, he said that he was going on his own, that we could pick up our plans when he got back but somehow I knew he was lying.'

I watched another tear roll down her face.

'I asked him what had changed his mind about being with me but he refused to own up. He went off to Europe shortly after that and I haven't seen him since. He contacted me a few times but then he stopped. I knew by then anyway but I was still so hurt, so let down and I felt stupid to have trusted all his empty promises about our future together.' She paused to let her words sink in.

'Is that how you feel about me too? That I'm making empty promises?'

'I honestly don't feel that about you but I'm scared of giving myself completely again in case everything comes crashing down around me another time. I don't think I could take it. After Nick left, I felt really vulnerable, especially when my dad died, followed so soon after by my mum and I made some mistakes with…well, with relationships that I'm not proud of and I don't ever want to do that again.'

'Listen, Rachel, I've been hurt too and let down to the point that I never thought I would trust anyone again and I've made some mistakes along the way so I understand how you feel. I also know that I've never felt the way I feel about you with anyone before. I want to do whatever it takes to show you that you can trust me and if that means going slowly, I can do that. I'd do anything for you.'

I leaned over and kissed her gently on the lips.

She put her arms around my neck and returned the kiss so tenderly that I knew we were okay but I also understood in that moment, that it was going to take some time for her to truly trust me.

CHAPTER TWENTY-TWO

Rachel went straight down to the studio when we got to the office the next day, to rehearse with Jed for the "Open Mic" at The Bluebird. Of course, there was no guarantee that she would be picked to play tonight given that it was such a small venue but we would give it our best shot because it was *the* place for all new singers to try for first. I kept myself busy in the office for most of the day, although I did go out to purchase a little surprise for Rachel in the morning while she was rehearsing.

At four o'clock, I went downstairs to collect her so that she could go home and get changed in enough time to get in the line ready to sign up at The Bluebird at half past five. She was packing away her guitar when I got there and she looked quite nervous when she saw me approaching.

'Are you okay, sweetheart?' I asked.

'I'm just hoping that I do get in tonight. It would be a dream come true for me to play at The Bluebird and I'll feel awful if I don't make it.'

I took her hand, gave it a quick squeeze and then led her back up the stairs and outside, where Greg was waiting in the car, patiently reading *The Tennessean*. We were back at the condo in no time and I sat out on the terrace while Rachel got ready.

When she reappeared, she looked fabulous, in skinny jeans and a simple blouse, and her hair still slightly damp from the shower.

I shook my head a little to make myself refocus.

'You look amazing.' I kissed her to show my appreciation.

'What shoes were you going to wear?' I asked her.

'Oh, I don't know, my old boots, I guess,' she said absently as she fiddled with her earrings.

'Hold on a second.' I went to my bedroom and returned with a box, which I presented to her with a flourish.

'What's this?' she asked surprised.

'Only one way to find out,' I replied, smiling in anticipation.

She pulled the lid off the box, her eyes widening as she saw what was inside. 'Oh my goodness, a real pair of cowboy boots and they're red! They're gorgeous, I love them, thank you.'

She gave me a thank you kiss, then bent to slip the boots on. Now she looked every inch a country star and I was already so proud of her.

'Ready to go, baby?'

We drew up at The Bluebird shortly afterwards and there were already lots of other people outside.

'It's not quite what I was expecting,' she confessed. 'It's quite unassuming for an iconic music venue, isn't it?'

'I know it looks a bit non-descript out here in this shopping mall but it'll be worth it when you get in, you'll see.'

Rachel joined the line with her guitar and waited for signing-up time. I hung around outside while Greg went in to check that Todd had managed to get us seats if Rachel was successful. He reappeared a few minutes later, confirming that Todd and Alex were sat at a table inside waiting for me.

Soon enough, sign-up time began and the line inched closer. There were lots of people in front of Rachel so it was going to be a nerve-wracking wait to see if she would be picked to perform tonight. The line was now much shorter and soon Rachel was signing up and the wait was over. Now we just had to hope that her name would be drawn.

We waited nervously as they started to pick out names and announce performers for tonight's session. Ten lucky people had already been selected and Rachel was starting to look disappointed. She looked over at me for support and I smiled encouragingly. Then, all of a sudden, it was her turn and we both whooped with joy. I ran over to give her a quick kiss and wish her luck and then she disappeared inside the building to get ready for her performance.

I dashed round to the front entrance, past the neon sign of the bluebird and inside to take my seat with the others before the start. I sat down on the familiar wooden chair, glancing at the fairy lights strung all around the room, lighting up the photos of famous country musicians on the walls. I blew out a breath I didn't even realise I'd been holding. Alex took my hand and gave it a squeeze and Todd clapped me on the back. I took a sip of my drink before sitting back and waiting for the show to start.

There was a good variety of talent on at The Bluebird that evening.

'I really liked that last artist, Todd. She had a nice mix of folk with a country twang, I thought.'

'Hmm.' He nodded but was deep in thought, no doubt weighing up where we would place someone like that in our list.

I always loved watching musicians playing 'in the round' with the audience so close to the music. People said that it was at The Bluebird that the tradition of having the stage in the middle of the audience had originated and it was special to Nashville.

When Rachel's turn came, I couldn't help but notice a slight change in the audience as she introduced herself. Her accent piqued their interest and she looked comfortable up on stage, even though the audience was so close, they were almost sharing the microphone with her.

She'd decided to start with 'Too Late' which was a good choice for this crowd. It wasn't long before they were singing and clapping along to the chorus and when she finished, there was great applause for her. Todd snapped a couple of quick photos of her as she stood smiling at the crowd.

'Man, she's great,' the guy next to me told me.

I gave him a big smile by return, pleased to hear such good feedback on Rachel's behalf.

I could see how pleased she was and she chatted a little about their reaction before introducing her second and final song of the evening. Performers were only allowed to play two songs on "Open Mic" night so I was curious about which song would be her next choice.

As she played the opening bars of 'My Turn' on her guitar, I knew that was the right choice and I smiled with pleasure at the crowd's response once again. She looked over at me then and I winked and nodded before she poured her heart and soul into the rest of the song, exposing her innermost feelings and showing the audience her true talent.

The applause at the end of her set lasted for several minutes and I knew that she had passed The Bluebird test. It took a while for her to leave the stage but eventually she had to and she disappeared into the darkness behind.

In the interval, she came round to find us and although I saw her come in, I didn't get to talk to her for some time because so many other people wanted to tell her how great her performance had been. She looked real happy with all the wonderful comments from the crowd and by the time she reached me, I only had time for a quick hug before we had to sit down for the second half again. Time flew though and we were soon discussing how well her set had gone with Todd and Alex.

'You were fantastic out there, Rachel. You looked like you were born to be singing on a stage,' Todd marvelled.

'The crowd loved you and it looked like you had lots of positive comments from people too on your way in,' said Alex.

'Yes, they were all lovely. I can hardly believe it and it felt absolutely brilliant to be up there, on that stage especially and for the crowd to like it so much. Wow!' Her eyes were shining with the thrill of it all.

'That was a wonderful début,' I told her, 'and I predict that there will be a lot of interest in you tomorrow. Shall we go and get something to eat now? I couldn't eat anything earlier, I was too wound up!' She nodded, still breathless with excitement.

We said goodbye to Alex and Todd and asked Greg to take us back into town. After saying goodbye to him, we stopped in at a little Italian restaurant on Church Street to share a quick pizza and to wind down after the gig.

'How are you feeling now about how it went tonight?' I asked as we tucked in to our pepperoni pizza.

'I'm still on such a high, I don't know if I'll ever come down! My adrenaline has been pumping since we first got there to sign me up but it was such a great evening, wasn't it?'

'It sure was and I hope that it boosted your confidence. You really are a great singer and songwriter and now you know that it's not just me and my employees who think so.'

'I have to be honest, I can hardly wait to do another show now,' she exclaimed.

After another fabulous "Open Mic" session at the Douglas Corner Café the following night during which Rachel performed two more songs to another packed audience that included my mom, dad and Maggie, I knew it was time for me to sort out her contract.

As she finished singing the second of her two songs, a slower more poignant one about her parents called 'Don't Let Me Go', you could have heard a pin drop among the audience. When I turned to look at my family to see their reactions, their eyes were full of tears from the touching song but also from their pleasure at Rachel's obvious talent.

'Hey, son,' my dad said when he'd gathered himself together. 'She's damn good. I think she's going to go far.'

'Rachel, you made us all want to dance with the first song

and cry with the second! You were wonderful, sweetheart.' My mom embraced her and kissed her on the cheek.

Before dropping us home, Alex made it perfectly clear what her expectations were as Rachel's manager.

'I'll come into the office tomorrow morning,' she said once we'd set off, 'because I want to find out why you still haven't had your contract yet.' Alex raised her eyebrows at me and I gave her a knowing smile by return.

I shut the door behind us as we went into my office the next morning.

'Come and sit with me on the couch, there's something I want to show you,' I told Rachel.

I handed her a large envelope.

'Go on, open it,' I said when she hesitated.

She opened it and read the title out loud, 'Contract between The Rough Cut Record Company and Miss Rachel Hardy.' I heard her sharp intake of breath.

'This is what you and Annie have been up to while I've been rehearsing, huh? This is amazing. And it's...it's massive,' she stuttered, leafing through all the pages.

'A lot of it's standard legal stuff but you'll need to look over it with Alex. You may even want a lawyer to look at it for you too.'

'Why, are you trying to take advantage of me?' Her eyes twinkled at me.

'I like the sound of that.' I grinned back at her. 'But I haven't tried to do that in this contract, no.' I put my arm around her and drew her to me for an embrace.

'Thank you, I couldn't have done any of this without you,' she whispered softly, her warm, hazelnut eyes glowing with excitement.

I bent my head down so my lips could meet hers, but when she pressed her body against mine, the kiss became deeper and when we finally broke apart after several minutes, I was breathless and she was too. We held on to each other to steady ourselves and I heard her laugh softly.

Shortly afterwards, there was a knock on the door and Alex and Todd appeared from behind it. They both smiled broadly when they saw us together.

'Hi, you two, you look good today.' Alex looked from Rachel to me and back again, as if trying to figure out what our secret was.

'Thanks, yep, we're both good today,' Rachel said, smiling and taking my hand. She waved the contract at Alex.

'Ah, I see you've given Rachel the contract at last. Have you had a chance to look through it real carefully yet, Rachel?' she asked.

'No, I think I'm going to give it to you to do that for me instead because it really looks quite boring,' she whispered the last part.

'Hush your mouth!' I cried in mock shock. 'That is a seriously important document for you to look over, boring or not, so make sure you do, please.'

'Okay, bossy,' she said, grinning at me and rolling her eyes, before going off to lunch with Alex.

I was finishing off some paperwork when my laptop pinged to tell me I'd received an email. I glanced over at it, switching to see who the message was from and my heart almost stopped at the sight of Stephanie's name at the top of the list. The title of the message was a simple 'Hello!'

'As you won't answer my calls, I'm sending you an email instead. I only want to say hello, Jackson and to see how things are with you now that some time has passed. I regret what happened between us so much and would love to meet you in person to say how sorry I am. I'm travelling on business with my daddy at the moment but could be back in Nashville real soon, if you'd say the word. So, how about it? Let's get together, even if it's only for old times' sake.

Love Stephanie x'

180

I could hear her spoilt little rich girl voice as I read every word and I knew without any doubt in my mind that she had some ulterior motive for getting in touch with me that had nothing to do with her apologising for what happened between us. I realised that Annie must have been blocking her calls to me, which I couldn't blame her for, and in all honesty I didn't want to speak to her or see her. On impulse, I deleted the message and made a mental note to talk to Annie about the calls later when she returned from lunch.

After lunch with Alex, Rachel asked if she could talk to me about the contract some more.

'Do you have some questions?' I asked her.

'I'm concerned that you've been too generous, from what Alex has told me.' She frowned at me. 'A royalty rate for a new artist is normally around 10%, as you know, and yet you've offered me 17% and on top of that, you're giving me an advance of $150,000 against sales from my first album, which is also way above average.' Her hands went to her hips and my eyes followed. 'Alex also tells me that the manager's cut you're offering her is below the usual but she did say this was normal because she hadn't discovered me. So my question is: are you sure you aren't being blinded by your feelings for me?' she asked shrewdly.

'Hey, you sound like an old pro already!'

She slapped my arm gently.

'I don't want you to give me preferential treatment, that's all and I don't want you to lose money on me either.'

'There's no need for you to worry,' I reassured her. 'I have every confidence that I will get back a great return on you. You're very talented and I have high expectations. As you said, Alex knows that's a good rate for an unknown and she knows that I discovered you so that's the deal.'

'No, she wasn't complaining, she was very fair and honest in her appraisal of the contract. She's going to show it to her usual lawyer, in case you are trying to take advantage of me.'

She batted her long eyelashes at me then and I swear I could have made mad, passionate love to her right there and then in my office and she looked like she might be up for that too. Instead, I took a calming breath and put my hand on her arm to still her.

'I have twelve months from now to make my first album, is that right?' she asked me, turning serious again.

'Yes, that's fairly standard and then you're expected to be gigging and promoting yourself while making that album.'

'Well, I think I already have enough songs for an album so spending the next year drawing attention to those songs sounds good to me.'

'Shall we go out to celebrate tonight? It's not every day you get a recording contract, is it?' I asked her, sitting down on the edge of the desk and pulling her towards me.

'That sounds like a great idea. Where did you have in mind?' She fell into me, wrapping her arms around me for another breathtaking kiss so I had no chance of answering that question for quite some time.

After work the next day, Rachel and I took a cab to the movie theatre over near the university for six o'clock to meet up with Alex and Todd. They'd already bought tickets for the movie for all four of us so we went straight on in. We were going to see a love story set in Italy, a film I'd never heard of but I didn't really care, as long as I was sitting next to Rachel, feeling the warmth of her hand in mine.

Halfway through the film, she pulled her hand away and when I looked over at her, I could see she was crying. She wiped away her tears, before offering me a wobbly smile. I took her hand in mine and she held on to it for the rest of the film.

I held her tightly to me as we left the theatre, with her emotions decidedly the worse for wear.

'Did you enjoy the film?' I asked.

'I loved it, it was really sad but so romantic at the end.'

I had to smile at the way that she loved the romance, even though it made her cry.

We settled on a cosy Italian restaurant for dinner, agreeing that it was the right choice after seeing an Italian film and it was only a short walk away. Inside, the restaurant was packed with local families and so we knew the food must be good. After we'd been eating for a little while, Todd brought up the subject of one of our other artists who was based in New York.

'Jay has been pressing me to ask if you could pop up there for a couple of days to sort things out face to face,' he told me.

I sighed as all eyes turned to me.

'I guess a couple of days away wouldn't be too bad. How would you feel about me being away, Rachel?'

Her face fell at once but then she tried to hide her emotions so as not to upset me, I guessed, but I already had my answer.

'Sweetheart, I know the timing could be better. But listen, I wouldn't need to go till Tuesday and I'd be back by Thursday so I'd only be gone for a short while.' I took her hand to soften the blow.

'I understand you have to go, I'll miss you, that's all, especially as I don't know many people.'

She looked forlorn and Alex and Todd looked uncomfortable. I wished Todd hadn't brought it up now.

'Why don't you go together?' Alex suggested. 'Rachel can always pick up on any press interviews when she gets back.'

'Of course, how stupid of me,' I said. 'Would you like to come with me, Rachel?'

'To New York? I'd love to,' she said and smiled.

'That's settled then.'

CHAPTER TWENTY-THREE

We pulled up outside my apartment building in Lower Manhattan about twenty minutes after leaving the airport. Rachel got out and stood on the sidewalk while I paid the cab driver. I grabbed our bags from the trunk and took her hand. She stared up at the building.

'This is…awesome! There's no other word for it.'

'C'mon, let's get you inside. I think you might be even more amazed.'

As we walked into the apartment, Rachel let out a gasp of surprise. The main reason I'd bought it was for its great view of the Hudson river, and Rachel's reaction was exactly the one I'd had the first time I walked in. We dropped our bags and walked out on to the terrace to take in the fabulous view in all its wonder. The view of Jersey City across the water and the late summer sun reflecting off the buildings there never failed to draw me in. It was still quite warm in New York but a lot less humid than at home. I put my arm around Rachel's shoulder and pulled her close to me.

'I can't tell you how much it means to me that I can share these things I love with you and that you feel the same as I do. For me, that's all I need to know that we're meant to be together.'

Her body relaxed into mine and I sighed, feeling happier than I had for a long time. We stood together for a few more moments and then, reluctantly, I pulled away.

'Sweetheart, I have to get to this meeting, I'm sorry. I thought we could perhaps share a cab to the nearest stop for the Hop On Hop Off tour so that I know you're safely there and then I'll go on to my meeting from there. Is that all right with you?'

'Absolutely. I need five minutes to get ready, okay?'

We went back down to the street and hailed a cab ten minutes later. I dropped Rachel off at her stop and then carried on to my meeting. For me, the afternoon passed very slowly because all I wanted to do was to get back to her but I tried very hard to focus on the business I'd come for. It seemed to me that it had all been exaggerated out of proportion, but sometimes my presence lent some sway and it didn't take long to sort matters out.

I chatted afterwards with Jay, our rep in New York.

'I think that went well, Jay, don't you? They seemed happier at the end anyway.'

'Yes, I agree. It's like you always say, sometimes they just want to meet the boss and hear him say the words. I did want to talk to you about something else though.'

'Okay, shoot.'

'Well, I hope that I haven't acted out of turn here but I agreed on your behalf for you to attend a charity dinner tomorrow night in aid of Phoenix House. The thing is, I only asked for one ticket because I thought you'd be coming on your own but I'm sure we can get you another ticket for you to take er...I'm sorry I don't know her name.'

'Her name's Rachel.' I sighed. This was definitely a dinner I would want to attend under normal circumstances. I just had to hope that Rachel would understand. 'It's fine, Jay. Please could you look into getting me another ticket and in the meantime, I'll discuss it with her.'

I said goodbye to him and sent a text to Rachel to find out how she was getting on. She replied straight away.

'Ready to come home whenever you'll be there. I'll get a cab. Can you text me the address?'

I texted back the address and set off for 'home', loving the way that Rachel made any place we were together our 'home'.

Later that evening, we were enjoying a meal in the heart of Chinatown, trying out soup dumplings for the first time.

'I'm sure this is dribbling down my face,' Rachel complained and I looked up from my own struggle to dab her chin with my napkin, smiling at her discomfort.

We shared our news from the day, while tucking into some pan fried noodles and finally I got round to telling Rachel about the charity dinner the following evening. She looked disappointed but understanding all at once.

'I'm sorry, I know there's a million other things you would've loved to do. But listen, we can come back whenever you like, I promise and, next time, I'll make sure I don't have any business or any engagements to carry out.'

'Don't worry, I know this is only a flying visit but I'll hold you to that promise.' Then she gasped. 'I don't have anything suitable to wear to a charity dinner and I don't want to spend tomorrow shopping for clothes.' She frowned then with concern.

'I'm sure we can contact a personal shopper at one of the big stores and get them to send some things over for you to try on for tomorrow evening. They'll know the right sort of thing.'

'How about you?' she asked. 'What will you wear?'

'I'll wear a tux. I have several here to choose from.' She was staring at me, with her eyes narrowed. 'What, Rachel?' I laughed.

'Well, I can't wait for tomorrow night now. I'm just imagining how gorgeous you'll look in a tux.'

Our knees brushed under the table and all of a sudden, desire overcame me and I couldn't wait to get back home again. I glanced up at Rachel to see her standing up, getting ready to leave. We caught a cab back to the apartment and it was all we could do to keep our hands to ourselves during the short journey back. No sooner had we closed the door, than we abandoned ourselves to our feelings, hardly able to keep our clothes on for a minute longer. We stumbled through to my bedroom, where our lips met with renewed passion, our bodies entwined and our love for each other revealed itself without any inhibitions.

As we lay in each other's arms afterwards, I knew that I didn't want to be without her in my life. I hoped she knew how much I cared for her now and that this was only the beginning of a long future together too.

'Rachel?'

'Mmm?' I brushed my fingers through her hair, watching as her eyelids drooped.

'I love you, you know.'

'I love you too.' I could hear her smile in the darkness and I held her closer to me then as we both fell asleep.

I sent a quick text to Alex early the next morning, asking her who she would recommend for personal shopping in New York. I rang Neiman Marcus a little bit later on her advice and Rachel spoke to a personal shopper there for about five minutes, explaining her requirements. The shopper agreed to send over half a dozen outfits, with shoes, by five o'clock.

Having sorted all that out, we set off for a full day of sightseeing. I planned to make sure that we did as much as we could in the day that we had available, starting with the Empire State Building. Although we had to wait in line for about half an hour, it was worth it when we reached the observatory on the 86th floor. The views of New York were fabulous whichever direction you looked in.

'This is my favourite view,' I told Rachel. 'There's Fifth Avenue leading past the Flatiron Building all the way down to the 9/11 Memorial and the sea beyond.'

Rachel took what seemed like hundreds of photos from all different angles. I explained to her that the building was open till the early hours of the morning and we made a plan to come back at night-time next time.

Next, Rachel wanted to go and see the Statue of Liberty so

we took the ferry from Battery Park to Liberty Island. We spent a good couple of hours exploring the statue and the museum but decided to pass on the trip to Ellis Island this time. We picked up a couple of chicken wraps to go from the café and ate them while waiting for the ferry back to Manhattan.

On our return, we decided to go and visit the 9/11 Memorial to pay our respects. Although once again we had to wait a while in the line, we were not prepared for how moving an experience it would be. The pools and the waterfalls created such a calm atmosphere but reading the names of all the people who had died upset both of us, even more than we'd imagined it would. We went for a coffee afterwards at a nearby café to catch our breath.

'It's been a great day, with some highs and lows, I guess. Is there anything else you'd like to see before we head back to get ready for tonight?' I asked her.

'Do you know, I'd really like to see Central Park, even if only for a little while so I can say I've been there?' She smiled her special smile at me that usually made me do anything she asked. We took another cab after we'd finished our drinks and set off north again towards the park. We'd been really lucky with the September weather and the park looked wonderful as we strolled through the small part of it we could do that day. The leaves on the trees were already starting to change colour, signalling the start of fall and it was heavenly to see folks enjoying the park as much as we were.

'So, what do you think of New York?' I asked as we walked hand in hand.

'I love it, of course and I can't wait to come back again.' She sighed with contentment.

'I'm glad we managed to spend this time together. I've really enjoyed today especially.' I lifted her hand to mine and kissed it and she leaned into me for a hug.

Our final cab of the day dropped us home just before five

o'clock. I'd received a text from Jay, confirming that he'd secured an extra ticket for Rachel for the evening. She'd wandered into the bedroom with the outfits sent over by Neiman Marcus when we'd arrived and I heard her cooing over them as she took each one out of the wrapper. After a while, I noticed that she'd gone quiet and I called out to her.

'Hey, Rachel, are you still all right in there?'

'Yes, I think I am.'

I stood up and walked towards the bedroom.

'What do you mean, you think you are?' I asked curiously.

'No, don't come in!' She shut the door against me. 'I don't mean to be rude but I only want you to see me when I'm all ready, sweetheart.'

I stopped in my tracks and went back to the lounge, leaving her to it. Shortly afterwards, I heard her go in the shower and I made my way to the other bathroom to start getting myself ready. I didn't take quite so long so I was back in the lounge at half past six and sat down to read some newspapers on my laptop while I waited. About fifteen minutes later, I heard the door from the bedroom open and I looked up in anticipation. When Rachel did finally appear in front of me, nothing could have prepared me for the heavenly vision that I saw. The dress she'd chosen was stunning: a one-shoulder gown, with a striped lace bodice and a bow on the left shoulder. The skirt was black and satiny looking and flared at the knee, with a mini train at the back. She looked completely transformed and I was speechless as I took in all the different elements. She'd piled her hair up and there were little tendrils framing her face. She lifted up her dress then to show me the black strappy sandals she was wearing which finished off her outfit perfectly. I walked towards her and took her hands in mine, leaning into kiss her softly on the cheek.

'You look absolutely fabulous. You're the most wonderful vision I've ever seen,' I said breathlessly.

She looked so happy, she was fit to burst. I pulled myself

together and cleared my throat.

'I have something else for you, too.'

She looked at me quizzically then as I went off to get my gift from the bedroom. I returned with a Tiffany bag and I heard her sharp intake of breath.

'You didn't need to get me anything else. This is a Carolina Herrera dress and I'm wearing Manolo Blahniks on my feet. Never in my life did I dream that I would be spoilt like this. To give me anything else would be too much, Jackson.'

'But Rachel,' I protested, 'it gives me such pleasure to spoil you and you deserve that more than anyone I know. Here.' I passed her the bag, hoping that she would like my purchase.

When she opened the gift box, her face lit up and she looked at me in surprise before looking back at the eighteen carat white gold heart-shaped pendant filled with round diamonds I'd bought for her to wear.

'This is far too generous of you but thank you, I love it. Would you put it on for me please?'

I went towards her and took the necklace in my hand, undid the clasp and refastened it around her neck. I kissed her neck before turning her round to face me.

'Shall we go, sweetheart?'

She took my hand, her face shining with happiness for the evening ahead.

CHAPTER TWENTY-FOUR

The cab pulled up outside the Plaza Hotel a few minutes after seven. I went round to Rachel's door to help her out of the car and we climbed the stairs to the entrance gracefully together and then turned back to smile for the photographers. We both paused before going in, taking a deep breath at the same time and smiling at each other as a confidence boost. Once inside, a waiter offered us cocktails. I opted for the non-alcoholic one of course and Rachel decided on a champagne cocktail.

'Dutch courage,' she said, raising her glass towards me.

'Don't be worried, you look amazing and I'm here to look after you.' I grinned at her, taking her hand in mine.

We wandered around the anteroom, greeting a few people I knew and relaxing gradually into the setting. Soon, we were being called in for dinner and I took Rachel's hand again, looping it through my arm to walk her in.

As I glanced down at her, something caught my eye in the background. I looked over to see a couple arguing heatedly under their breath. I was about to look away again, not wanting to stare, when my insides went cold with dread. It surely couldn't be her but the longer I watched, the more I knew for certain that I was looking at Stephanie, my cheating ex-fiancée. Her long, blonde hair was straighter and shorter than I remembered. She also looked like she might have lost some weight, making her already slender frame seem gaunt. Her usually flawless style seemed askew as she argued with her companion.

Rachel had already turned when she heard my sudden intake of breath. She glanced behind her to see what had upset me. She turned back to me, with a slight frown on her face and gently urged me onwards because people were waiting behind us to go in.

'Who was that woman? You look like you've seen a ghost,' she muttered under her breath as we walked in. I didn't answer immediately because I was still in shock. She continued to frown at me in concern.

'It was her, Stephanie. It's the first time I've seen her since we split up.'

'Oh, God, no!' She only loosened her grip on my arm as we arrived at our table.

I sat down heavily and tried to recover myself. I hadn't thought for one minute that I would see her here. Still, I knew she had family here so it might make sense that she'd gone to New York or perhaps this was where her business trip with her father had taken her. I just wasn't ready to talk to her. In this setting, I was afraid that I might over-react and embarrass myself or worse still, embarrass Rachel.

'Look at me, sweetheart, please.' I turned towards her and shook my head a little to clear it of my thoughts and help me focus on the present. 'Would you rather leave now? I don't mind,' she offered.

'No, no, I'll be all right, really, it's thrown me a little, is all.' I tried to smile but it may have come out as a grimace. 'There is no way we're leaving anyway, not because of her.' I couldn't tell Rachel that Stephanie had been trying to contact me. I hoped that she wouldn't see me among all the other people there.

Our starters arrived shortly afterwards and we used them to keep me focussed on the here and now. One or two of the other guests tried to engage me in conversation but I found it difficult to concentrate for longer than a few minutes. After the main meal, there was a speech from the charity organisers, which, thankfully, was quite short. Then Rachel excused herself to go to the bathroom and anxiety threatened to overwhelm me all over again, as I glanced nervously around me all the while for signs of Stephanie approaching. As soon as we had eaten dessert, I took a final glance around the room.

'I think it's best that we get out of here now. C'mon, sweetheart. We've both had enough for one night.'

I stood up, taking Rachel's hand.

We made our way as calmly as possible towards the exit. Just when we thought we were home and dry, we saw Stephanie emerging from the stairwell and looking straight at us. I turned and squared up to her then. I wasn't going to stand for any of her nonsense.

She sidled up to us, her face and hair looking a mess, as though she'd been crying and, quite clearly, she'd drunk too much as well. I couldn't believe that they hadn't asked her to leave.

'Jackson,' she whined. 'It's really good to see you.' Her whole demeanour oozed danger, and fear started to spread through my body. My hands were clammy so I let go of Rachel's.

'I'd have to disagree with that statement, Stephanie. Nothing about this feels good to me.' I spoke quietly, trying to keep calm.

'Jackson, don't be mean, I've had such a bad evening and I know you could make it all better. And it's such good luck that I've seen you when you haven't been returning my calls or emails.' She fluttered her eyelashes at me in the most unattractive way and I suddenly thought I might be sick.

I took a step back from her, pulling Rachel with me. When I risked a quick look at Rachel, I saw that she had gone very pale and she was staring at Stephanie with dismay. I could only assume that was a reaction to the news about her trying to contact me. My heart sank.

'Stephanie, let me make this very clear,' I went on, trying to put an end to this meeting. 'Everything there once was between us is now well and truly over. I've moved on from the mess you made of my life and I don't ever want to spend time with you again. do you hear me?' I waited, hoping that I'd said enough to make her go away. I wasn't sure how much longer I could keep this strong-guy pretence up.

'Okay, Mr High and Mighty,' she sneered at us. 'I've moved on from *the mess you made of my life* too.' She mimicked my words in a squeaky high-pitched voice and I felt nothing but hatred for her in that moment. 'I can have a real man any time I want. I don't have to go scraping the barrel like you obviously have with your new plaything. Anyway, she's welcome to you, you're not worth it. It won't be long till she finds out how weak and pathetic you really are.' She'd switched back to her alter ego in a second and the look she gave Rachel was poisonous.

I gripped Rachel's hand once again.

'Stay away from me and my family, Stephanie.' I glared at her for a moment and then I turned abruptly, taking Rachel with me, and left the hotel.

We stood outside for a minute, allowing me to catch my breath. Then we hailed a cab and set off home. Neither of us spoke on the way back, we were both too shell-shocked to say anything after Stephanie's verbal attack. By the time we arrived back at the apartment, my shock had turned to anger and I knew that I would not be a good person to be around right now.

I turned to Rachel and said, 'Honey, you go on up. I need to be on my own to let off some steam for a while, I'll be back soon.'

'I really don't think it's a good idea for you to be on your own right now. Whatever you're feeling, come in and talk to me about it. We can handle it together,' she protested.

I wavered for only a second.

'No, this is something I need to do on my own.'

I gave her the keys, trying to give her hand a squeeze for reassurance as well but she snatched it away and climbed out of the cab without saying another word. I watched her go in, knowing that this was probably not the best decision. I didn't want her to see how angry I was or how vulnerable I felt after seeing Stephanie again. She had a way of taunting me that I couldn't seem to handle, making me frustrated at my weakness before her and yet furious all at the same time.

Of course, then I had to decide where to go to vent my frustration. The cab dropped me off a few minutes later at a bar nearby. I went on in, sat down and waited for the bartender to come over. When he asked for my order, I paused. I wrestled with my demons and wanted desperately to resist them but all I could think about was drowning my sorrows in alcohol. I looked up and asked for a beer. Then I sat there looking at the bottle for what seemed like the longest time, trying to persuade myself of the right thing to do. Eventually, I gave in and took a sip. The next thing I knew, I had downed several bottles, as well as working my way through half a bottle of bourbon.

My cell vibrated with a text at that point. It was from Rachel and she was furious.

'Jackson, where the hell are you? I am worried sick. Please let me know you're okay. Better still come back home.'

By this time, it was two in the morning and something in her message appealed to my inner common sense and I staggered up from the bar, unused to the effect of the alcohol after so long without it, and made my way outside to find a cab.

When I let myself into the apartment a short while later, I found Rachel in her pyjamas, sitting on the couch waiting for me. She jumped up, looking like she would run to me but when she saw the state of me, she stopped short.

'You've been drinking,' she stated as a matter of fact.

'Yes, ma'am, I have.' I grinned a little sheepishly, with the idiot humour of the drunk.

'Sit down there and don't move,' she ordered. She came back with some water and some headache tablets and made me take them and then drink all the water. She helped me to get into bed and the minute my head hit the pillow I fell straight into a deep sleep.

I woke in the middle of the night certain that I needed to be sick. Luckily, I made it to the bathroom in time. After emptying my insides, I felt better. I washed my face, rinsed out my mouth and returned to the bedroom, going via the kitchen to get some more water. There was no sign of Rachel in the bed and it didn't look like there had been all night.

I went to check the other room then and was saddened to find her asleep in there. I turned as quietly as I could to head back to my bedroom. Once I was back in bed, the enormity of my actions weighed down on me and it wasn't long before despair at my stupidity set in. Rachel probably wouldn't forgive me for breaking her trust like this. I tossed and turned for the rest of the night, finally getting up at eight o'clock when I heard her stirring.

I went out to the lounge to find her already dressed and finishing off her last bit of packing.

'Hey, Rachel,' I ventured, desperate to explain myself.

She turned to look at me and I could see that she'd been crying at some point. I went towards her automatically but she backed a step away and I stopped, chilled by her reaction.

'I figured that we need to be at the airport by nine o'clock for a midday flight so you'll need to get a move on to get yourself ready,' she said, focussing on practicalities.

'Please, I'm sorry,' I whispered.

'So am I. More than you can know.' With that, she turned away from me and went back to the other room.

The rest of the day was unbearable, with us hardly exchanging a dozen words. I wanted to put things right but she wouldn't talk to me. I hoped that she might have thawed by the time we got back to Nashville but as soon as we walked into the condo, she went and retrieved her other larger suitcase and started filling it with all her things. I couldn't take the tension between us any longer.

'What are you doing?' I demanded.

'I'm moving out of here to a hotel. I can't be with you right now.'

'Why do you want to do that? That's only going to make it harder for us to talk and sort this mess out. Please don't go,' I begged her. I waited a moment for her reply, as she considered how best to tell me what she wanted to say.

'I'm going because I need some time to process the change that came over you last night,' she said quietly, breaking my heart with every word. 'You told me that I could trust you and that you'd always talk to me, be honest with me. But at the first sign of real trouble, you turned to alcohol instead of me. My dad used to drink whenever things got tough, rather than talking things over with someone who loved him. That's what hurt me the most, that you wouldn't talk to me. I need to decide how I feel about that before anything else. You also need time to think about the "mess" you've created.' She grabbed both her cases and walked towards the door.

'Where are you going to stay?' I asked.

'I've booked a room at The Hermitage for now. I'll call you tomorrow.'

'What about the gig tonight?'

'I've cancelled it. I can't really face that now.'

And then she was gone.

I fell on to the couch and put my head in my hands, wishing I could take back the last twenty-four hours.

I didn't know what to do with myself once she'd gone. I kept going over and over it all in my head but coming up with no solutions. I had let her down and she had every right to be mad at me. Not only that but now she had cancelled her gig as well which meant that everyone would be wondering what had happened and I would have to be the one to tell them. Sure enough, my phone started going crazy with texts and calls shortly after that but I left them all while I went to have a shower and to try and get my head together. This time though, nothing seemed to help.

I finally decided to look at my cell around four o'clock and was staggered to see texts and calls from Alex, Todd, my parents, Annie and even Maggie. I decided to call Alex first because she would want to know about the show.

'Alex, hi, it's me.'

'Okay, this had better be good. What the hell happened between you two that caused Rachel to cancel the gig?'

'We bumped into Stephanie in New York and I went on a minor bender, coming home drunk in the early hours of the morning. Is that bad enough for you?'

'Oh my God, Jackson. Seeing Stephanie must have been bad. What was she like?'

'I'm sorry to say it but she was a complete bitch. It really threw me and I was really angry. But now Rachel has left and I can't believe what an idiot I've been.'

'She's left? What do you mean?' she gasped.

'Not left, left but moved out of the condo to The Hermitage while she thinks things through. She said she'd call me tomorrow.'

'Okay, well, you just have to hope that tomorrow you can put things right. Look, your behaviour was wrong of course but you're only human and it was completely understandable in the circumstances. Rachel loves you, she'll come round.'

'I don't know, Alex. She was more upset by the fact that I didn't want to talk to her. Instead, I went and got drunk on my own and I think she feels let down because of that more than anything else.'

'Well, let's hope she feels better about it all tomorrow. Call me and let me know, okay? You're not going to drink any more are you?'

'No, I think I've done enough damage.'

We said our goodbyes and then I rang my mom and had the same conversation with her.

'Mom, I'm just so ashamed of my weakness. I'm better than that, I know I am.'

'Yes, you are but we can all be weak and at least you can see that you've made a mistake here. Maybe tomorrow, you and Rachel can talk this all through. She needs some time, honey.'

I couldn't face anyone else but I did want to text Rachel before going to bed for an early night.

'I'm sorry for being such a fool. I know I've hurt you and I never meant to do that. I hope you'll believe me and that we'll be able to talk more tomorrow. I love you x'

I turned off my cell and climbed into bed, hoping that sleep would help me escape my self-inflicted misery.

CHAPTER TWENTY-FIVE

Dorset
Rachel

I was exhausted by the time I arrived in London and filled with sadness after leaving Nashville so abruptly.

The taxi had just pulled up outside the hotel in Nashville when my phone had buzzed as it received a text. I'd expected it to be from Jackson, pleading with me to come back so I'd taken a deep breath before looking at it. I was completely unprepared for the name I'd seen on the screen. It was from Jenna and as I read it I knew I would have to go straight home to Dorset.

'Rachel, I'm sorry to be the one to tell you but Sam's in hospital. He's critical. Please can you come home?'

'I'm sorry,' I'd said to the taxi driver, 'but there's been a change of plan. Please could you take me to the airport?'

'Sure thing, ma'am.' He'd pulled off once again into the traffic.

During the journey, I'd gone over again and again how everything had seemed so perfect between me and Jackson, and now it all seemed lost. I completely understood his anger and his vulnerability around alcohol but I didn't understand him abandoning me like that. Hell, I'd been as shocked as he was by the way that Stephanie had behaved but he hadn't spared a thought for me.

Now here I was, back in London and freezing because I'd left in such a hurry and hadn't given any thought to what the weather would be like back in the UK. The flimsy cardigan I was wearing was no protection against the light drizzle that was falling as I arrived but I had no choice but to keep going until I got to the hospital. I still hadn't managed to charge my phone and I was starting to worry now because I knew that Jackson and Jenna would be trying to get hold of me and I couldn't let them know I was okay.

My final taxi ride of the day dropped me outside the hospital just after half past six. I gave them Sam's name at the reception desk and then followed their directions to intensive care. I found Jenna in the family waiting room, pacing the room nervously and looking exhausted.

'Rachel, thank goodness you're here safely,' Jenna cried when she saw me. 'I've been trying to get hold of you and was worried sick when I couldn't.'

'My phone battery died,' I said as I threw my arms around her for a big hug.

We held on to each other like that for a long time, giving each other strength. Eventually, we pulled apart and I sat down so she could fill me in on what had been happening.

'Mum and Dad are both in with Sam at the moment. He's still being sedated for the time being to give his body a chance to recover from the shock of the fall at the building site and for them to assess how bad the damage is. We know that he's broken a few bones so he's going to be in here for a while.'

'How did it happen though, Jenna and what was he doing on a building site? That's not his usual kind of job, that's what I don't understand.'

'His carpentry jobs had slowed and someone offered him a few weeks work, just general labouring, and I think he felt he had to take it. He's been quite low since you left and he wanted something to take his mind off things.'

My face fell as I listened. I knew she wasn't blaming me for him taking the job but I still felt guilty.

'Anyway, he was working on the roof,' she continued, 'and as he was walking along the scaffolding, he tripped and fell down to the next level, about six feet below. He landed face down, breaking his left leg and probably quite a few ribs. They've been able to set his leg without surgery and that's good at least. His face is quite torn up too but what they're most worried about are his lungs.' Tears were in her eyes as she finished and she wrapped her arms around herself, no doubt trying to push away her worries.

'I'm sorry this has happened, Jenna. How are your mum and dad holding up?'

'They're okay. It's just that we've been trying to make sure that there's always someone here and it's hard going, what with me working and Matt having to worry about his family as well.'

'Whose turn is it to stay now?' I asked.

'I'd just swapped shifts with them when you arrived. I'd best say goodbye to Mum and Dad before going home,' she said. 'You could come home with me and get changed and perhaps catch up on some sleep and then we could come back and relieve them later,' she suggested.

'That sounds like a good plan to me,' I said.

She disappeared out of the room, leaving me alone to collect my thoughts.

When Jenna returned, she asked if I'd like to see Sam before we left.

'I would like to but I didn't know if I would be allowed, not being direct family.'

'You're family to us and that's all that matters. Why don't you go in for a minute?'

She showed me to Sam's room and I went in, exchanging hugs and kisses with his mum and dad, Sarah and Dave, as we swapped over.

I sat down on the chair at the side of Sam's bed, taking hold of his hand very gently. He looked very pale compared to his normal tanned skin and he had bandages and tubes everywhere. I talked to him for a few minutes, telling him my news, until the constant bleep of the machines in the room became too much for me.

'I love you, Sam. Please get well.' I stood up then and kissed his damaged face. I left a minute later, afraid to say any more in case I broke down in tears.

'We'll see you again later,' Sam's mum, Sarah, told me and I kissed her goodbye before setting off home with Jenna.

It felt odd to be going back to my old cottage after a few weeks away and even though it was still full of my things, it felt like it belonged to Jenna now. I unpacked my stuff in the spare room, making my priority to plug in my phone to charge while Jenna made us both a cup of tea. As soon as it had been plugged in for a while, I was able to send a quick text off to Jackson.

'Hi, Jackson, my phone battery died. I know you must have been trying to get hold of me. I've had to come back to Dorset. Sam's in hospital, in critical condition. I'll call you later.'

Jenna was waiting for me in the living room when I returned.

'How has it all gone over in Nashville? I kept meaning to ring you but it's been so busy lately,' she said.

I told her the whole story then of my short time in Nashville, from my musical success and signing to the label to the developing but complicated relationship between Jackson and me. I finished by telling her what had happened in New York and how I'd moved out.

'I love him, Jenna, but it has been quite overwhelming all this change, you know, and now I feel let down that at the first sign of trouble, he shut me out.' I shrugged with the disappointment of it all.

'What are you going to do now? Is it over in your mind?'

'No, no but I can't see how to move forward with him at this point.'

We continued talking over a quick supper, planning to go back to the hospital shortly afterwards. I was so tired that

Jenna told me to get off to bed for a nap. I woke up with a start just before midnight. The house was eerily silent. When I went downstairs, I found a note from Jenna, telling me she'd gone back to the hospital and would see me in the morning. I was alone and I knew I'd been putting off calling Jackson so I had no other option but to get on with it now.

'God, I've been really worried about you, especially when the hotel told me you hadn't even checked in!' I heard him release a sigh of relief and I felt bad for not contacting him sooner.

'I'm sorry, but I had no way to charge my phone until I got back to the cottage after visiting Sam in hospital. I really didn't mean to worry you.'

He was silent for a moment at the other end of the line and I didn't know what to make of that.

'And how is Sam? Is he still critical?'

'Yes, he's sedated and they're waiting for him to wake up on his own so they can see the full extent of his accident and decide how to treat it.'

There was another pause. We both had such a lot to say but neither of us knew where to start.

'Rachel, I...I'm so sorry about the other night. I was stupid and I know I've hurt you and let you down. Please can you forgive me?'

'I know you're sorry but you're right, I do feel let down at the moment. I can't talk with you about it over the phone and I can't answer your question right now. I need some time to think things through before we talk about it.'

'Will you come back though or can I come over? I can't bear not being able to see you or talk to you. I want to make this right.'

'Can you give me a couple of days and then I'll know more about what's happening here and where that leaves me?'

'You don't want to speak to me for a couple of days?'

He sounded broken and I immediately felt guilty.

'It's not that I don't want to talk to you. It's just that I have to think about Sam now.'

'So Sam's well-being is more important than our future together? Is that what you're saying?' He sounded angry now.

'I don't have time for this. I'll call as soon as I can. Take care of yourself, bye.' I managed to stop myself slamming the phone down on him but only just.

After speaking to Jackson, I'd fallen asleep again for a couple of hours and when I woke on Saturday morning, it was with a heavy heart. I was worried about Sam of course, but I felt awful about the way I'd treated Jackson too. The timing of all this was terrible and even though there was nothing I could do about it, I still felt bad.

Jenna was in the kitchen making breakfast when I went downstairs.

'Hey, Jenna, I'm sorry about last night. I really wanted to come back with you but I was more tired than I realised.'

'Don't worry about it,' she replied. 'I only relieved my mum and dad for a couple of hours so they could go home for a shower and a change of clothes. They were back in no time and insisted on me coming home again. I want to get back as soon as I can this morning though.'

So we set off for the hospital straight after breakfast, wanting to find out the latest about Sam and also to give Sarah and Dave a break. They were both wearing big smiles when we arrived which cheered us up immediately.

'What's happened, Mum?' asked Jenna.

'Your brother's woken up, love.'

We could see the relief in her eyes and we all relaxed with that great news.

'Oh, that's wonderful.' Tears sprang to my eyes as I reached out to give her a hug.

'The doctors said that they'd come round again this afternoon to give a full diagnosis so that gives Dad and I a chance to catch up on some sleep and we'll see you both back here later. Is that okay, girls?'

'Of course it is, Mum. Is Sam awake now? Can we go in?' asked Jenna.

Her mum nodded and smiled, looking exhausted but clearly more reassured about Sam's condition. We said goodbye to them both and Jenna went in to see her brother.

I took a seat in the waiting room and no sooner had I sat down than my thoughts turned to Jackson once again. On my own, the doubts crept in. Wasn't I doing exactly the same as him by running away instead of staying to talk? I couldn't believe what a mess we'd made of things in so little time. I knew I'd had a good reason for leaving Nashville, but in my heart I knew it had also been a convenient way of leaving everything behind, rather than dealing with what had happened.

I managed to pop in briefly as well to talk to Sam later that morning after Jenna had been in. He seemed in good spirits but obviously very tired and shaken by his ordeal. We all waited anxiously together in the afternoon for the doctors' verdict.

'It's good news, everyone,' Sarah reported. 'Sam's fall wasn't too severe, thank goodness. He only has the broken bones we knew about and his lungs are okay. He should be able to come home in a few days but he won't be mobile for quite a few weeks.' She smiled and her face lit up with a whole host of emotions, revealing how she'd felt over these past few days. 'He wants us all to come in and see him. The doctors said it would be all right.'

'Hey, Sam, how are you?' asked Jenna, approaching the bed first as we all went in.

'Well, I've been better,' he replied with a roll of his eyes. 'But it's the shock of it all that's hit me the most.' He glanced around the room at everyone, sharing a rueful smile. His eyes came back to me, as if noticing I was there for the first time.

'Hey, Rachel, it's good to see you.' He reached his hand

out to me.

I went forward at once to take it.

'Listen, why don't we wait outside for a minute to give you and Rachel a chance to catch up?' said Sarah, nodding at the other members of the family.

Sam watched them as they left the room, before turning back to look at me. His handsome face crinkled into a smile.

'If I'd only known that this was all I had to do to get you to stay...' Sam laughed and then grimaced from the pain.

'That serves you right,' I replied, sitting down carefully on the bed. 'How are you feeling, seriously?'

'I'm okay, I'm trying to deal with it all bit by bit and not get too carried away with what ifs. Do you know what I mean? When I first had the accident, it was so overwhelming and when they were bringing me to the hospital in the ambulance, I couldn't stop myself from thinking the worst but now that a couple of days have passed while I've been sedated, I'm feeling calmer, especially now it's only about broken bones which will heal in time.' He paused before going on. 'I've missed you, you know.' His clear, blue eyes looked so sad that for a moment, I didn't know what to say.

'I've missed you all too,' I said, including the whole family rather than just Sam, although I knew that wasn't what he wanted to hear.

'And how are things with you? How did it all go over there?' he asked.

I looked up at him then, trying to gauge whether he really wanted to know and he smiled as if to reassure me.

'It's been great in Nashville, the music's going really well and I just agreed to sign to Jackson's label but I haven't signed the contract yet.'

'Wow, that's amazing news, Rachel. Well done!'

I'd expected things to be a bit awkward between us, given the feelings he'd previously expressed for me, but there was no resentment there, only happiness for me.

'And how's Jackson?' he went on.

'Umm, not great actually. We had a row the other day and I moved out of his place. I was on my way to a hotel when I got Jenna's text about you.' I looked up at him, not sure what emotion I would see on his face but, once again, he surprised me with a look of sympathy.

'Oh, Rachel, I'm sorry.'

I couldn't tell how he felt about Jackson but his feelings for me were clearly just as strong.

'Anyway, you don't want to know about all that.' I coughed nervously to try and change the subject.

'Will you be staying here then?' he asked me, taking my hand in his.

'I don't know what I'm going to do, Sam, to be honest.'

I leaned towards him and rested my forehead on his and he put his arm gently around my shoulders.

We sat like that for a moment before I pulled back and stood up.

'I'll be back to see you tomorrow,' I said as I turned for the door, giving him a last smile and seeing his face light up in return.

CHAPTER TWENTY-SIX

I decided to call Jackson when we returned to the cottage, knowing that I needed to put his mind at rest on a number of fronts.

'Hi, Jackson. How are you?'

'I'm okay, you?' It was lovely to hear his voice but I felt nervous about how the conversation was going to go because of what I wanted to say to him.

'I'm missing you, to be honest but I'm also glad to have had some time to think.'

'How's Sam doing?' His tone was firm and unemotional, which I supposed I deserved after the way I'd spoken to him earlier.

'He's awake and off the critical list now. He should be home soon but he'll be in recovery for a while.'

'Are you going to come back to Nashville then, now that Sam's on the mend?'

'Not for the time being, no. I need some more time here.'

'I see. Well, actually, no, I don't see. I made a mistake and we need to talk about it, face to face, not keep running away from it.' I was surprised by his irritation.

'I think I know that better than anyone but now that I'm here, it's helping me to put things in perspective which I was finding difficult when I was with you, not just about our relationship but about my future. I need to decide what I really want.'

He blew out a long breath. 'This is all news to me and not what I was expecting you to say.'

'I know and I'm sorry but...if you truly love me, then you

need to leave me alone, please.'

'I do love you but you're making me nervous about what's going to happen next for us.'

'I'm sorry but I need to think about you, about my career, about Sam...' I sighed as my sentence trailed off.

'Hang on, what does Sam have to do with anything? He wasn't in the picture before.' He sounded really spooked.

'Look, you knew that Sam had feelings for me before, and since coming home I've realised how much I missed him so I need some time to think about all that.'

'About whether to choose him or me you mean?'

'No, look...I don't know...Can we not do this over the phone, please? I'll call again soon.'

After that, we brought the conversation to an end pretty quickly. I knew I had to be honest if there was to be any future for us but I couldn't blame him for not liking what I'd said and I regretted even having mentioned Sam.

I went downstairs to find Jenna and discuss what we were doing for dinner to try and take my mind off things.

'I'm starving, I don't know about you,' I declared on walking into the kitchen, where I found her rooting through the cupboards.

'Yes, me too. I was looking to see what we had to eat and, sadly, the answer is not a lot. Shall we get a takeaway or go out?'

'I'd be happy with a takeaway if you would, how about a pizza?'

'Great. I think I've even got a bottle of red somewhere, and by the look on your face, you need a glass of wine. I'll go and look for it and you order the pizza, okay?'

Our pepperoni pizza arrived by bike just as Jenna was pouring me a second glass of red. We divided it up and sat down to eat. I was surprised by my sudden appetite.

'Will you be going back to Nashville soon, now that Sam's getting better?' Jenna asked, catching me off guard.

I paused dramatically, as I was about to take a bite of pizza, aware of her waiting expectantly for my answer.

'I haven't really decided yet. I do need to clear the air with Jackson after what happened and I have a contract to sign too.' I'd only told her that we'd had an argument, not the full extent of it and I knew she was leaving it up to me to tell her when I was ready.

'Your music must have gone down really well over there. I'm so pleased for you,' she said.

'Yeah, although I've only actually played a couple of "Open Mic" nights so far but they did go really well and I can't wait to play some more.'

'And what's Nashville like?' she asked.

'I love it, you know, even more than I'd hoped I would. I love the feel of the place, the food, the people, the music everywhere. Jackson's family have welcomed me so warmly too and that's been a relief because I was quite nervous about meeting them all. The people at the record label have been really positive as well and I felt that I fit right in there. Now, I'm one step away from signing a recording contract. It all seems quite incredible still.'

'Do you think I might be able to come and visit you while you're there if you do go back?' she asked hesitantly.

'That would be wonderful, Jenna. Would you be all right to take the time off though?'

'Yes, a few days would probably be okay, as long as I plan it with Mary.'

We both went quiet for a bit as we finished our pizza and I pondered what I would do next. She topped up our wine glasses and turned to face me.

'Is everything really all right between you and Jackson? You haven't said what you argued about and I don't mean to pry but if you want to talk about it with me, you can.'

'Well, no, not really.' I sighed and then told her the whole sorry story. 'Now that I'm here, I really miss him but I've also realised how much I miss home and all of you. And then there's Sam.' She raised her eyebrows. 'Before I left, he told me he loved me and begged me to stay but I knew I needed to go, Jenna. I needed to know if I could make it over there and I knew that Sam wasn't interested in that, despite what he might feel for me. Then yesterday, I could see that he still felt the same for me and he said that he'd really missed me. So now I'm really confused.'

'Do you have feelings for Sam?' she asked.

'I thought I only cared for him like a brother but when he kissed me, I did feel something.'

'He kissed you!'

'That wasn't all we did either.' I flushed under her surprised look. 'But that was ages ago, Jenna, a drunken one-night stand. For my part, I worried then that if we'd continued with a relationship, we would have lost our friendship and I didn't want to take that risk. After you told me that he had feelings for me, he eventually told me that he would have liked it to go further. That's when he kissed me before I left for Nashville.' I took a gulp of wine.

'God, I had no idea. It sounds to me like you have a huge dilemma on your hands and I can't advise you what you should do for the best but you will need to be careful, otherwise someone is going to get hurt.'

I started the next day feeling confused after my conversation with Jackson the day before. Now that Sam was out of danger, I did feel ready to think about going back to Nashville. Being in Dorset again and so far away from Jackson had made me realise how much I missed him so maybe it was the kick I needed to stop me dithering. I loved him and he loved me. The question I had to deal with was whether I loved him as he was or if his faults were too much for me to get past.

There was also the question of me and Sam to deal with so, later that morning, I gathered up my keys and set off for the hospital. The bus dropped me outside about half an hour later and a noisy grumble in my stomach reminded me that I hadn't eaten anything yet. Still, food would have to wait for now. I made it up to Sam's floor quite quickly, checked in with the nurse at the desk and went along to his room. I peeked in first through the window and seeing that he was on his own, I knocked gently before going on in.

'Hey, Rachel. I'm glad to see you, I'm so bored.' He groaned.

'Well, you sound much more like your normal self so you must be feeling better.'

'Yeah, I am but I want to go home, not be stuck in here. Come and talk to me please!' I smiled and walked around the bed, taking a seat in the chair alongside.

'I need to talk to you about us, Sam,' I said, putting my bag on the floor and looking him clearly in the eye.

'I didn't think there was an "us" or am I wrong?'

He said it kindly but I knew I must sound confused.

'When Jenna let me know you were in hospital, I was out of my mind with worry and then, after I spoke to you yesterday and you said you'd missed me, I realised that I'd really missed you too and it got me wondering about my real feelings for you. And now I don't know what to think or what to do about anything.' I felt the tears prickle at the back of my eyes and struggled to keep them at bay.

He reached out across the bed to take my hand and I let him. Before I knew it, I was crying and he'd stretched his arms out towards me. I moved to sit next to him on the bed and he put his arms around me as best he could.

'Do you want to talk about what happened between you and Jackson?'

'Sam, I'd love to talk to you about it but it wouldn't be fair on you to do that,' I managed to stutter out between sobs. 'Nor would it be fair on Jackson to tell you what we argued about, would it?'

213

I buried my head in his chest, unable to say any more. After a few minutes, we drew apart and he gave me a scratchy hospital tissue to dry my eyes. When I looked at him, his eyes were sad but also full of an unmistakable love for me, which made me feel even more wretched. I sank back on to the chair beside the bed, trying to put some distance between us.

'I don't want to put you on the spot. I care for you and I want you to be happy. Just tell me that Jackson's not hurting you or anything terrible like that.'

'God, no, it's nothing like that. He does love me, Sam, and I...I think I love him. We just have an obstacle to get over and I have to give us the chance to try and do that. I don't know if we can but we owe it to ourselves to try.' I smiled tearfully.

'Does that mean you're going straight back to Nashville? Because I don't think you should.'

'Why not? I need to talk to Jackson and sort things out with him. I have the contract to sign as well.' I sniffed as I thought about everything.

'Look, I can take care of you, perhaps better than Jackson can. I've known you a lot longer and I think I know what you need. I wouldn't ever hurt you either. I love you and I want to be with you. I know that means giving up on the Nashville dream maybe, but it doesn't have to mean giving up on your career dream altogether. We could still make it happen for you here.'

'Are you saying that you'd support me in that dream now?'

He nodded, a determined look in his eyes. 'I understood after you went how much it means to you and if I want to be with you, I know that you'll need me to back you all the way. I know you have a lot to think about but I want you to know that you can trust me to take care of you. You do know you can call me at any time, don't you?'

Although I nodded, I was frightened by this new information and the impact it had on my situation.

I stood up and leaned over the bed once more to kiss him

goodbye before walking to the door.

'Jackson! What on earth are you doing here? How did you...? I only just...' I shook my head a little, trying to clear my confusion at seeing Jackson in front of me. It didn't make any sense.

'What the hell is he doing here?' I heard Sam complain behind me.

I glanced over at him, pleading at him with my eyes not to make a scene. He threw his hands up in despair and I let the door close behind me, as I went out to talk to Jackson.

'Can I talk to you, Rachel, please?'

I was still unable to comprehend how he'd got here so quickly when I'd only been speaking to him yesterday evening and he'd been in Nashville then. Obviously, he must have thought it was important to see me face to face and my heart skipped a beat at the thought that I meant so much to him that he'd come all this way. I led Jackson to the waiting room, which I was thankful to see was empty, and sat down opposite him, waiting to hear his explanation.

'You must have left pretty soon after we spoke to get here so quickly,' I said.

'Yes, I suppose I didn't waste any time,' he agreed. 'I could hardly believe what you were saying to me about Sam and I knew I didn't want to be apart from you a moment longer.' He looked down at his hands to compose himself before continuing. 'Rachel, I love you such a lot and I don't want to lose you but I know I've been stupid about how I dealt with seeing Stephanie again and I can only hope that you'll forgive me that in time.'

He swallowed before continuing. 'The most important thing for me at the moment is not seeing you throw your talent away because of a moment of madness on my part. I want you to follow your dream and make a go of your music career regardless of what happens between you and me. So I'm here to ask you to come back with me to Nashville to sign the contract and to do what you were meant to do with your life, to sing. I promise that I'll leave you alone, even though it will be the hardest thing I'll ever have to do, but if that's the deal, then I'll take it.'

I stood up and went over to the window to look at the street below, struggling to take in everything Jackson was saying to me. If he meant what he said, his love for me was even greater than I'd realised. What he wanted more than anything was for me to be happy, even at the expense of his own happiness. As I turned back round to look at him, the tears were threatening to spill over.

'I can't believe you would do that for me when it would hurt you so much.'

'I'd do anything for you, I mean it and I'm only too happy to put you first.'

He stood up, his broad frame expanding to fill the space, and he took a step towards me. He looked so pained, it was all I could do not to throw myself into his arms. Instead, I reached out my hand and he took it, raising it to his lips. I had to wipe away my tears then, so reluctantly I let go of his hand.

It was time for me to make a decision now. I was still reeling from Sam's sudden change of heart about supporting my dream of pursuing a music career but in my heart, I didn't really believe he meant what he'd said, not when he'd been so against me pursuing my dream of going to Nashville before.

Now I had all the facts and I knew I was ready.

'Okay.' I cleared my throat before going on. 'I will come back with you but I do have some conditions.' The smile on his face fell a little in anticipation of what I was about to say. 'Firstly, we must keep it strictly business and secondly, I want to stay in a hotel when we get back. Is that acceptable to you?'

He didn't reply straight away as he considered what I'd said. Then a look of such regret and sadness washed across his face that I was left feeling terrible.

'I wish you didn't feel that way but I guess I understand why you do. So you really are going to come back with me?' he asked, looking uncertain.

I nodded. 'I have to go and tell Sam what I've decided and then we can go.'

CHAPTER TWENTY-SEVEN

Rachel

It had been an emotional morning, having to leave Jenna, and as the taxi weaved its way through the morning traffic towards the airport, I remembered our tearful goodbye.

'I really hope you can come and stay with me over there. Let me know how things progress, won't you?' I'd said to her, giving her a big hug.

'I will and I hope things go all right with you and Jackson. Take care.'

I'd still been raw from saying goodbye to Sam the day before and now I felt wrung out. I knew of course that Sam would be upset that I wasn't taking him up on his offer but going back to Nashville with Jackson instead, and as I'd walked back into his room I knew that there would probably be no going back from this point. I couldn't see him forgiving me now. He looked up as I came into the room but there was no smile for me this time which meant he'd already worked out that I was leaving.

'I wanted to see you again before I left, to try and explain my decision.' I stood before him, wringing my hands.

'You don't owe me an explanation.' His voice was clipped and I could see the tension on his face as he wrestled with his emotions. 'But now you're here, I would like to know if you're sure you've made up your mind about going back with Jackson?'

'I think I have, yes. We've agreed to keep things strictly business for now so I'm going back to sign my contract and to get on with my music career.'

'But are you still together, the two of you?' he asked.

'I...I don't really know how to answer that and it's probably best that I don't.' I saw irritation pass across his handsome features.

'What I said to you meant nothing then? You know when I told you I loved you and I want to look after you, none of that made any difference?'

'Sam, please don't do this. Of course it means something to me but I want to try and make a go of my music career in Nashville and maybe I have to accept that I can't do that and have a relationship as well.' He let his head fall back against the pillows.

'I don't get why you have to go to Nashville when I can help you make a success of your music career right here.'

'It's what I want, Sam, and for the first time in my life, I'm going to put myself first and go after it. I'll be in touch with you again soon. Take care of yourself and concentrate on getting better.' I leaned forward to give him a kiss on the cheek but he didn't respond and his body remained stiff.

The rest of the journey back to Nashville was fairly quiet, with Jackson and I finding little to say to each other after all that had happened. Despite all my efforts to try and forget about my complicated love life for a while, it was the only thing on my mind. I fretted constantly about whether I'd made the right decisions about my future. I wanted to pursue my musical career as much as ever but it would be a hollow success if I had no-one to share it with.

Jackson

I was desperate to ask Rachel how her goodbye with Sam had gone at the hospital yesterday but knew that she probably wouldn't have told me anyway so I left well alone. I couldn't stop thinking about what might have happened between them. If I were Sam, I know I'd have been begging her to stay but thank goodness she had already decided to come back with me, even if it wasn't going to be on the same terms. I just had to hope that she would come round again in time.

While Rachel was saying her goodbyes to Jenna, I had been in touch with Annie to make arrangements for Rachel to stay at The Hermitage and even though I knew it would annoy her, I'd asked Annie to book her into a suite. She hated me paying for things as it was, so when I went the extra mile and indulged her even more, she only seemed to be more cross with me. I saw it as spoiling her whereas she seemed to think I was being over-indulgent and that somehow she didn't deserve these little luxuries that I could easily afford. Annie had texted me to confirm that she had booked the suite and to tell me that The Hermitage wanted to check whether I had any special requests for the suite to make Rachel's stay there more comfortable. I gave Annie the go-ahead to contact them and go with what she thought would be best.

Greg picked us up from the airport but even his jolly manner couldn't cheer us up.

'Is it straight back to the condo, sir?' he asked as we settled into the back seat of the car, this time at opposite ends of the seat.

'No, Greg, sorry. Could you go via The Hermitage please?' I looked at him in the rear-view mirror, catching the almost imperceptible raise of his eyebrows.

We drew up outside the luxury hotel not long afterwards. Its many windows bathed the car with light as I jumped out to help Rachel with her bags.

'Thanks,' she said as I passed her the last of her two bags. 'We do still have a lot to talk about so I'd prefer to stay here until we've done that, okay?' She was at her most assertive right now, putting me on the back foot, which wasn't a place I liked being in.

'Will you come into the office tomorrow?'

'I don't know yet. I need to get myself sorted first.' My heart sank. This was going to be a lot harder than I'd thought.

She turned to go inside then and I watched as the doorman greeted her and called a bellboy to take her bags.

Rachel

By the time I went into the hotel I was dead on my feet so when the receptionist told me that I was staying in one of their executive suites, I didn't have the strength to argue. I sighed, knowing that Jackson had organised this further extravagance but I couldn't be cross with him when it was really just what I needed.

I thanked the receptionist and turned to follow the bellboy up to my suite. My eyes were immediately drawn to the bedroom, where I could see a four-poster bed adorned with masses of fluffy pillows and a very inviting looking duvet. Once the bellboy had gone, it was all I could do to change into my pyjamas before falling into the welcoming arms of the bed and letting sleep claim me.

I was disorientated at first when I woke in the morning, forgetting for a moment that I'd checked into the hotel. Then it all came back to me and all of a sudden, loneliness enveloped me once again. Here I was in a foreign country, with no real friends to speak of and the man I loved had already abandoned me at the first sign of difficulty. What's more, I had left behind a perfectly good man who had never hurt me. Was I mad? I dragged myself up out of bed and had a shower to try and wake up. I switched my phone on, even though it was early, and was surprised to see a message from Alex.

'Hey, Rachel, Jackson told me you were back. So sorry to hear about what happened with Stephanie. If you need to talk, I'm here for you. Take care and stay in touch.'

Her kind words touched me so I replied straight away and asked her to join me for breakfast at the hotel if she was free. I was about to go downstairs to the dining room when my phone pinged with another text, this time from Jackson checking how I was today. Well, he'd have to wait till after breakfast. Alex joined me a few minutes later, giving me a quick hug and a kiss before sitting down opposite me.

'How are you, Rachel? You look wrung out,' she said gently.

'I am wrung out after leaving home again and the long journey here and now it's dawned on me that Jackson and I finally have to sort out all this mess. I do feel better now that there's been some space between us and I've had some time to think. I was surprised when he followed me home to the UK and impressed by his offer to put his feelings for me to one side.'

'Jackson definitely missed you but he knows you needed time to sort out your feelings as well. I was surprised that he could be so impulsive and jump on a plane just like that. I think it shows how much he cares for you, if you don't mind me saying. Anyway, I'm sorry about your friend, Sam. How is he now?'

'He's definitely on the mend, thanks for asking.'

'I think when Jackson couldn't get hold of you at first, he thought that you'd decided to go back home because of what happened that night, you know.'

'Well, he would only have had himself to blame,' I argued heatedly. 'At the first sign of trouble, he decided to go out and get drunk rather than talking to me and sorting things out and I'm finding it really hard to forgive him for that. He doesn't seem to understand that I was hurt by Stephanie as well. She was absolutely vile to me and she ruined what was meant to be a lovely evening.'

'Tell me something. Do you still love Jackson?' she asked plainly.

'I love him more than anything but this is a big hurdle to overcome.' I'd blurted all that out without even thinking and I'd only said what I knew to be true in my heart.

'If you love him and I know he loves you just as much, then you will overcome it,' she said gently. 'C'mon, let's eat now to take our minds off all this and then I want to schedule in another gig as soon as possible.'

I'd sent Rachel a text as soon as I got up the next day, hoping to speak to her before I came into work but she hadn't replied. I knew she would get in touch when she was ready but I wished she understood how it was killing me trying to be patient.

I'd hardly arrived at the office when Annie called me to say that Rachel was on the line for me.

'Hi, how are you today? Did you sleep well?'

'I'm fine, thanks and yes, I did sleep pretty well. Thank you for booking the executive suite for me, I really needed that, even though I know it's terribly expensive.' There was a slight pause and then she went on, 'Would you like to have dinner tonight at my hotel, say about seven o'clock? It would give us time to talk.'

'I would love that. Where shall I meet you?' I replied.

'I'll be in the foyer. Umm, I won't be coming into the office today, if that's okay so I hope you have a good day and I'll see you later.'

I was pleased to hear from her and to know that she still wanted to talk to me. I hoped that she wasn't going to tell me it was all over. I tried to be optimistic instead and went home promptly at the end of the day to get ready for dinner.

I walked from my loft to the hotel, figuring it would help me clear my head, as well as calm my nerves. On entering the hotel, I saw Rachel at once and watched her for a minute before she noticed me. She was captivating and my arms ached to hold her again. She stood up, smiled tentatively and walked towards me.

'Hey, how are you?' I asked nervously.

'I'm good, thanks, how about you?'

She seemed to see right inside me so there was no point in pretending I was fine.

'I'm nervous, to tell the truth,' I said honestly. Then she took my hand and said,

'C'mon, let's go and eat.'

I started to feel better from the minute she took my hand in hers.

CHAPTER TWENTY-EIGHT

<u>Rachel</u>

When Alex had asked me at breakfast if I still loved Jackson, my heart seemed to know the answer before my head did. It was only when I'd seen him at the hospital once again that I'd realised how much I'd missed him since leaving Nashville. Although I cared for Sam, he didn't have the power to make my heart beat faster like Jackson did.

On top of that, Jackson wanted what was best for me and now, all I wanted was to sort this out between us as soon as possible so that we could move on. I'd told him we would keep things strictly business when I returned, but I couldn't keep it up. He looked so nervous when I saw him in the lobby that I took his hand, which seemed to immediately relax him.

We sat down on opposite sides of the table in the candle-lit restaurant and looked at the menus for a few minutes. When we'd placed our orders and got some drinks, I looked over at Jackson to see him staring at me expectantly.

'Why are you nervous about meeting me?' I asked gently.

'Because I don't know if you're going to tell me that it's all over between us and that you can't forgive my stupidity.'

'I don't want things to be over between us but we do need to talk about what happened and, more importantly, how you chose to handle it, I think.'

'I know what upset you most was that I chose not to talk to you, not so much that I went out and got drunk.'

'Yes, although I'd rather you didn't go out and get blind drunk every time you see Stephanie. But you didn't even stop to think that I might have been upset too, that I might have needed to talk it all over with you. We could have talked to each other and shared our feelings but instead, at the first sign of trouble, you ran away from me.'

'Haven't you done that to some extent as well?' Jackson asked hesitantly.

'Yes, you're right. I ran away too, although I did have to go and see Sam, but once he was out of danger, I knew I'd been running from dealing with our troubles.'

Our food arrived then, causing a break in our conversation. As soon as we were on our own again, Jackson asked:

'So why did you come back?'

'I was so surprised when you came after me but more than that, I was touched when you said you were prepared to put my happiness before yours. That was really selfless of you and it made me see how much you care for me. It also helped me to focus my own feelings. In the end, I guess it was your love for me that persuaded me to come back and that's why I texted you today about meeting tonight. There's no point in dragging this out any longer. We need to deal with it and move on, otherwise we'll both just carry on being miserable.'

'I'm sorry for not staying with you and talking about how I was feeling. I didn't want you to see how angry I was. I felt ashamed of myself for that and then for getting drunk and letting you down.'

'But I love you, with all your flaws included and I was angry with Stephanie too. I completely understand that.' I took his hands in mine. 'I need you to promise me that we'll always deal with things together and not shut each other out, otherwise I can't do this any more. If you want me to commit myself to you, you have to be totally honest with me. If you want to be angry, tell me. If you're tempted to drink, tell me. I want to help you when you're feeling vulnerable but I can't deal with you shutting me out.' I was almost in tears by the time I'd finished.

'I love you, I really do and I promise I won't shut you out

again from how I'm feeling.'

I breathed a sigh of relief and smiled at him.

'We also need to talk about Stephanie and what you'll do if she tries to contact you or you see her again,' I said.

'Do you really think she'd try and see me again after what I said to her?' he asked me.

'She seemed like a really mean-spirited woman to me and she was obviously jealous of us being together. I wouldn't put it past her to try and wheedle her way into your affections again.'

'I'm clearly being naïve here because I can't believe she'd be so stupid as to try anything else. But I'll go with you on it because it's better for us to be prepared for her turning up again, especially now she knows I've moved on with you. What can we do though?' He looked really concerned about this possibility.

'Well, we can't stop her turning up but we do need to manage how you react to that. I thought you handled yourself well in front of her, it was just afterwards that was difficult so that's where we'll work together if there's a next time, all right?'

'Okay.' He paused. 'Will you be staying here now or will you be coming back with me?'

'I don't know. It's been quite nice having my own suite to do what I like in.' I grinned wickedly at him. 'I can invite whoever I like up to my space.' Under the table, I slid my bare foot up his leg to show him what I meant. I saw his eyes darken with hunger for me after all the time apart.

I signed the bill after that and we hurried upstairs to my suite.

Once the door was closed, Jackson took me in his arms and gave me a long, slow kiss, leaving me breathless and filled with longing when he pulled away. He reached out towards me, starting to undress me slowly, tantalisingly slowly, and I had to stop myself from helping him. Then he was stroking my skin and his touch was at once soft and passionate. I began to remove his clothes as we kissed again and soon we were lying together, our bodies entangled and growing hotter by the minute. Making love with Jackson brought me back to life and I knew I didn't ever want us to be apart again.

Jackson

When I woke the next morning, Rachel was still fast asleep so I was able to watch her. I knew how lucky I was that she'd been prepared to forgive me so quickly after what had happened and I'd already promised myself that I would never do something as stupid again. I wanted to spend the rest of my life with this woman and I didn't want anything or anyone to get in the way of that plan. She stirred so I turned on my side to face her.

'Hey, beautiful,' I said as she opened her eyes.

She smiled at my words.

'Hey, it's great to wake up with you in my bed for a change.' She chuckled at the idea.

I gave her a hug and a kiss on the cheek before slapping her behind playfully and jumping out of bed to get in the shower.

'Hey, that hurt,' she cried as I disappeared into the en suite bathroom.

Twenty minutes later, I reappeared to see her eating room service breakfast. She beckoned me to join her, as she swallowed a mouthful of croissant.

'Mmm, I'm starving, I can't think why.' I grinned, picking up a croissant and putting it on my plate. 'Would you mind if I went into the office today? There's some things I need to finish up,' I asked.

'Not at all. I have some things I need to do as well. I can come and meet you at the office after that, if you like,' she said mysteriously.

'Now you have my interest piqued. Are you going to tell

me what you're up to?'

'No, sir, I am not,' she replied, teasing me before she sloped off to the shower.

By the time she'd finished, I was ready to get off to work.

'Well, I guess I'll be off and I'll see you later, sweetheart, unless you're going to tell me what you're doing?' I tried again to get her to reveal what she was planning.

'Good try, but no, that's a fail.' She kissed me lightly on the lips, guided me towards the door and with a final wave at me, she closed the door behind me.

I made my way towards the elevator with a very satisfied smile on my face.

Rachel

I leaned against the door for a moment after Jackson had gone, savouring the time we'd spent together since making up last night. Then I went to pack. By the time I'd finished, it was ten o'clock so I went down to the reception to check out and caught a cab back to the apartment. It was strange being there without Jackson because it wasn't my home, I suppose. That made me wonder what it would be like to choose a home together. I stood for a moment then, daydreaming about a longer-term future for us.

It was late morning by the time I finally arrived at the office. Annie greeted me with a great big smile, as usual.

'Rachel, I'm glad to see you,' she said kindly.

I guess she knew what had happened and was happy that we'd managed to sort it out.

'It's good to see you too, Annie, thank you. Is Jackson in his office?'

'He is, yes, he's doing some paperwork, go on in.'

I knocked lightly and opened the door. Jackson's face lit up at once with obvious relief.

'Did you think I wouldn't come?' I guessed.

'I was worried, yes but I'm really glad you're here now.

Alex popped in just now looking for you. She wants to talk to you about the contract, I think.'

'I'll go and find her. She'll probably be with Todd, won't she?'

I wandered down the corridor to Todd's office and knocked tentatively.

'Come in,' he called.

When Alex saw me, she smiled and gave me a hug. Todd looked really pleased to see me as well.

'How are things with you two now, if that's not a rude question?'

'Things are good again now we've talked. I've moved all my stuff back to the apartment but he doesn't know yet so keep it quiet, won't you?'

'Of course we will and, Rachel, thanks for not giving up on Jackson. He loves you and I think you've been incredibly good for him, you know. He needs you in his life to take him forward into the future and away from that scheming cheat of a woman!'

'What could she be scheming to do next do you think?'

'Well, I don't know what exactly but I don't think we've seen the last of her, especially now she knows that you and Jackson are together.'

'Anyway, Jackson said you wanted to talk to me about the contract.'

'Yes, have you signed it yet?'

'No, I still haven't signed it yet but I can do it now.'

'No, no, my lawyer friend has some minor concerns so we'll need to hold on for a few more days but we should be able to get it signed soon.'

Jackson

As the end of the day drew near, I started to wonder whether Rachel might decide to come home with me. I hadn't asked because I didn't want to keep on about it. I packed up my things and we went out together to the street and started walking in the direction of the apartment. When we got there, I turned to look at her.

'Would you like to come in for a while?' I asked.

'I think I'd better,' she replied.

I was about to ask another question when she put her finger sensuously to my lips, took my hand and led me inside the building. As I unlocked the door, my eyes fell on her two suitcases and I whirled round and took her in my arms.

'How did they get here?' I asked breathlessly.

'That's what I did this morning before coming into the office. I wanted to surprise you this afternoon.'

'Oh, sweetheart, I'm so glad you've come back. It was horrible here without you.' I kissed her with so much force then, we lost our balance and tumbled on to the couch. One thing led to another and soon we were basking in the aftermath of our lovemaking, back in my bed once again.

'Jackson, this morning, I found myself thinking about what it would be like to choose a home together.'

I stilled next to her at this new revelation.

'And what did you conclude?' I teased her because I thought I already knew what she was going to say.

'I concluded that it would be rather nice to choose a new home together and that I could see a future for us where we would do just that.'

I pulled her into my arms then and hugged her tight.

'Rachel Hardy, I love you!' I almost yelled at her.

'Hey, I'm not deaf you know.' She was laughing and everything seemed good again in the world.

Later on, I decided to bring up the subject of my birthday.

'Hey, it's my birthday next weekend and I'd like to take you to my beach house near Charleston for the weekend. Would that be okay?'

'Of course it would, that sounds lovely and if that's what you want to do for your birthday, then that's what we'll do.

What about your family, do you usually see them?'

'Yes, I do and I thought we could maybe see them on the Friday evening and then fly down to Charleston early on Saturday, maybe coming back on Monday morning?'

'It will be wonderful to be near the sea again, even if it's a different sea!'

CHAPTER TWENTY-NINE

<u>Rachel</u>

Later that evening, I made a point of calling Jenna to bring her up to speed on what had been happening to me since my return.

'Hi, Jenna, how are you?'

'I'm fine, Rachel. How are things with you? Did you manage to sort everything out with Jackson?'

'Yes, we talked things over and I've moved back into his condo now. I didn't want to keep dragging things out and making our lives miserable. So we've moved on now and I think I should be signing my new contract next week.'

'That's brilliant news. Have you decided about the longer term yet, like with your job, I mean?'

'No, but I can't imagine going back to that now, to be honest. My life is starting to be more here. Next weekend, we're going to Jackson's beach house in Charleston to celebrate his birthday. Can you believe it? I keep having to pinch myself to prove it's real!'

'I'm so happy for you but I do miss you. You're so far away.' She sounded really glum.

'Hey, I miss you too, Jenna. There have been so many moments when I wished you were here to keep me company. But we talked about you coming to visit didn't we? Any news on that front?'

'You know I'd love to but I am worried about leaving Mary on her own at the shop, even though I know she could manage it. The business is going really well at the moment. I'm not sure I could drop everything and go.'

We paused for a moment while we both absorbed this fact.

'We were only talking about a few days though. Surely Mary could manage that, with some help from your mum, say?'

'Yeah, maybe. Sam's out of hospital now too so that's made life a bit easier for everyone.' I could almost hear her mind working.

'I'm glad to hear that about Sam. Well, how about you give it some thought and we'll speak again within the next couple of days to see what you've decided?'

'I will. I could really do with a break. Although it's been lovely living in my own place, it is quite lonely at times. I don't suppose Jackson has a friend you could recommend?' She laughed and I knew that it would do her a power of good to escape.

We hung up a short while later and I couldn't help but feel excited about the prospect of my best friend coming to visit.

Jackson

Rachel had been booked for a short slot on a radio show mid-morning on Saturday. It wasn't far to Music Row, where the radio station was located but it made sense to go by cab so that she arrived looking as good as she had when we'd left. She'd taken even longer getting ready but it was worth it when she came out.

'You look gorgeous. You do know it's a radio interview, right?' I winked at her and she patted my arm, knowing I was trying to help her relax.

Alex met us at the station to add to Rachel's moral support and about half past ten, they took her off to prep her for the sorts of questions the presenter would be likely to ask and then suddenly, she was in the studio getting ready to go on air.

'We're joined today by Rachel Hardy, a talented new singer/songwriter all the way from the UK. Welcome, Rachel.' The presenter's accent was even more of a drawl than mine, which I hoped she wouldn't find too off-putting.

'Thank you, it's a pleasure to be here,' she replied.

I could tell from her body language that she was trying to relax but at the same time, she didn't want to be caught off guard by an awkward question.

'Tell me, how did you make it here, all the way from a little seaside town in Dorset? It's a place I suspect that not many of our listeners will have heard of before.'

'I was really lucky in that Jackson Phillips was over in the UK for his cousin's wedding and he heard me singing at a gig, encouraged me to enter the "Open Mic" competition and I went on to the national final. Then he offered to help me cut a demo CD and the next thing I knew, I was out here, singing at The Bluebird Café!' She laughed and the presenter joined in with her.

'And Rachel, is it true that you and Mr Phillips are romantically involved as well? That had to help, didn't it?' His gaze never left her as he waited to hear what she would say in reply.

I sucked in my breath, wondering how Rachel would deal with it. She couldn't even look to me for support.

'I'm here in Nashville because of my songwriting and singing talents mainly. Mr Phillips has certainly been very generous and supportive but he wouldn't have done any of that for me, if I hadn't had the talent to start with. Maybe you should come along to my next gig and find out for yourself.' She laughed and he joined in again with her but he knew she had won that round.

The interview went on for another few minutes and then he shook her hand and it was all over. She rushed back to us and we both smiled at her. I swept her up into my arms.

'You were so cool, sweetheart, you handled him brilliantly. Well done.'

We decided to have a lazy day on Sunday, enjoying spending

time together. I went out to get a newspaper and some croissants first thing but that was it. It was as we were leafing through the sections of the paper that I came across a photo and article that made my blood run cold.

'Listen to this, Rachel:

Nashville socialite, Stephanie Shaw, has returned home, like the prodigal daughter. She was last seen here when her engagement to respected independent record label owner, Jackson Phillips, came to an abrupt end after she was caught cheating on him. Snapped here at a charity ball last night, she looked like she was back for good.

I looked up at her and found her staring back at me carefully.

'Alex told me she was a schemer and that she expected we would see her again before too long, after seeing her in New York. Now we have to be ready for her when we do see her.'

'Yep, I feel so annoyed, I guess. I don't want her here but I have no control over her, do I?' I fell silent but it had unnerved me and I didn't relish the prospect of seeing her again one little bit.

Rachel

Alex was already at the office on Monday by the time we arrived and she whisked me off to a meeting room as soon as she saw me, bringing coffee with her that she had picked up on the way.

'Let's get straight down to it, shall we?' she said all business-like, the minute we sat down. 'Don't look so worried, Rachel, it's all good.'

I breathed a sigh of relief because I'd been concerned about how we would deal with any big problems.

'So, largely speaking,' she continued, 'he had no major concerns. There are a couple of minor points which I'd like to go over with you and then, if you're happy, we can go ahead and sign!'

It took only half an hour to discuss the finer details and we were done.

'I can't believe I'm on the brink of doing this, Alex. It's all nerve-wracking for me, to be honest,' I confessed.

'Well, you obviously have the talent, there's no doubt about that but it does also commit you to Jackson for the next year. Is that what's worrying you?' Her voice had become very quiet and I tried to frame my words carefully.

'I love Jackson very much and I know I want to be with him. It's just that for me, this is a complete change of life, moving country, leaving my close friends and my old life behind and trying my hand at something I'd only ever imagined myself doing in my wildest dreams. And on top of that, it's about starting a new life with someone I hardly know really and putting my trust in him completely. I'm not saying I don't want to do all of that but I'd be lying if I said I wasn't frightened by the prospect of all that change at once.'

'Have you told Jackson all this?' she asked me gently.

'I've tried to tell him but he thinks I'm afraid of commitment and when I try to explain, it all comes out wrong. I asked him to give us time to enjoy our relationship for a while before we take things to the next level but I think he saw that as a kind of rejection when we talked about it once before.' I sighed deeply.

'Well, look, there's no rush to sign this if you want to take some time to think about things,' she reassured me.

I took the contract from her again and signed it with a flourish before putting it back in the envelope. In my heart, I knew that was what I wanted to do.

'You know you've been a good friend to me, Alex, thank you.' I smiled at her and she returned it. 'I can't ask you not to talk to Jackson about what we've discussed. That wouldn't be fair as you're his sister. But will you be careful about what you say to him? I don't want to hurt his feelings.'

'Rachel, I won't break your confidence. I know he's my

brother but you're my friend as well, which puts me in an impossible situation. But I care about you too.'

She stood up then and gave me a hug, before adding, 'You'll get there, you know. You and Jackson are good together and I think you'll work it out between you. If you want my advice, try saying to him exactly what you said to me and I think he'll understand.'

'Okay, I'll give it a go this weekend, maybe. Talking of which, I still need to talk to you about his birthday present and now I have the means to pay for it as well!'

Jackson

Rachel gave me back the signed contract as soon as she came out of her meeting with Alex.

'Rachel, this is fantastic! You won't regret this, I promise. We'll tell everyone at the weekend and celebrate your new contract then as well.' I pulled her to me and kissed her, knowing what a big step this was for her. As I stared into her eyes, I didn't feel any concern from her. 'Are you okay?' I asked.

She nodded and kissed me again.

The rest of the week passed quickly, and soon it was Friday afternoon and Rachel and I were getting ready to leave for my birthday weekend. I knew that she had been plotting something with the rest of the family but I was trying not to be apprehensive about it.

We got home to the condo at half past four and packed our bags for a weekend at the beach. Rachel was being very coy about her packing and I suspected she was hiding things she had bought for me in her bag. I was like a little kid all of a sudden about the prospect of sharing my birthday with this wonderful woman who had just stepped into my life out of the blue. I was certain that she would love the beach house in Charleston and, what's more, I had a little surprise of my own for her.

Greg picked us up at five and we set off to my parents' house, except that a few minutes later, I noticed we weren't going in the right direction.

'Er, Greg, where are you going? This isn't the way to my parents' house.'

'Hey, relax, everything is in hand,' Rachel said. 'Try to go with the flow, sweetheart.'

She laid her hand on my thigh in an effort to still me but her touch only served to ignite me further. I took some deep breaths and reassured myself that she wouldn't let them arrange anything I wouldn't like. Shortly afterwards, we turned up at the airport and I started to get nervous all over again. Greg bid us farewell and we were suddenly standing in the departures terminal, ready to go somewhere unknown.

'Honey, I can't stand it any more! Please tell me where we're going,' I begged.

'Okay,' she said, smiling. She took my face gently in her hands. 'I thought it might be nice for everyone to come to your house in Charleston and for us to celebrate together there tonight. I hope that was a good idea? I did check it with your mum first and she said she thought it would be all right. She's been there all day getting things ready with your dad.' She paused, biting her lip nervously, waiting for my approval.

I breathed out in relief.

'That is a brilliant idea, I couldn't have come up with something better myself. Thank you.' I kissed her gratefully for thinking so carefully about what to do.

'Everyone's coming in tonight but going home after breakfast tomorrow, leaving us on our own after that, like we planned.'

'Oh, sweetheart, this is going to be the best birthday ever. I can't wait to show you the beach house. When's our flight?'

'Well, that's the other piece of news. We arranged for a private jet to ferry everyone back and forth so we can go when everyone's here,' she smiled hesitantly.

'Wow, you sure know how to surprise a man!' I pulled her in for another kiss.

When we boarded the plane, I was even more surprised to see Alex, Todd, Shelby and her husband Josh already on board, together with Maggie and her friend, Ted. I smiled broadly at them all. It was six o'clock by the time we set off and after a very smooth flight, we were touching down in Charleston at half past seven. The weather was more balmy than Nashville when we stepped off the plane and the gentle breeze was very welcoming. I looked over at Rachel and took her hand as we walked across the tarmac and through the airport to find our waiting car. The journey from the airport to the house was short but exciting, as we crossed the two rivers and islands separating us from our destination. As we crossed over the last bridge on to Sullivan's Island and could finally see the sea, I sensed everyone's mood lift, especially Rachel's.

CHAPTER THIRTY

<u>Rachel</u>

Jackson's house was in an area of Charleston called Sullivan's Island. As the people carrier drew up outside, it was starting to get dark and the fairy lights scattered all around the outside of the pale blue coloured house made it even more enchanting. I drew in a sharp breath of delight and excitement, glancing over at Jackson as I did. He squeezed my hand, pleased at my reaction to his incredible beachfront home. It was a truly magnificent house, with steps leading to a first-floor verandah and a second floor with another verandah above that. We wandered across the lawn, past a number of palm trees and up the steps to the entrance. Inside, the house was even lovelier, with warm antique pine flooring and mahogany doors, giving the place a really cosy feel. I fell in love with it at once. I whirled around and found Jackson waiting right behind me.

'I love this house, it's absolutely beautiful and you've furnished it so well. I really do love it.' I was excited but I couldn't help myself.

'I'm glad you like it and it feels good bringing you here at last. Now, come and see the rest.' He put his arm around my shoulder and hugged me as we went towards the kitchen to find everyone.

Soon we were all hugging and kissing our hellos and marvelling at the wonderful job Jackson's parents had made of the food. The granite counters were heaving with the wonderful buffet spread of all kinds of salads and cooked meats and fish. We all helped ourselves to a plateful of food and then went upstairs to sit on the enormous verandah or

241

porch, as I was learning everyone else called it. There were numerous rocking chairs and wicker chairs to choose from and, together with the twinkling fairy lights and the ocean view, it was a simply magical atmosphere. Bob came round offering everyone a cup of fruit punch that he'd made earlier, and soon we were all relaxing and enjoying each other's company.

We'd hardly sat down before another car pulled up on the driveway. Out tumbled two boisterous young men, calling out as they glanced up and saw us all.

'Rachel, meet my younger brothers, Jamie and Ben,' Jackson informed me.

These were the last two members of Jackson's family I had to meet. They came bounding up the stairs and were with us in a matter of minutes, staring at me with interest. Jackson performed the introductions but I was suddenly shy, like I was meeting everyone for the first time again.

'Rachel, we've heard such a lot about you and it's an absolute pleasure to meet you at long last,' charmed Jamie.

I said hello and smiled at their boundless energy. They both embraced Jackson in a man-hug before sitting down and tucking into their food.

Jackson

It had been a lovely evening with my family and I'd really enjoyed the surprise trip by private jet and the get-together here in Charleston. It felt good to have introduced everyone to Rachel now as well and I was so pleased that she seemed to really love the house. I was looking forward to showing her round, once everyone had gone home. I was hoping that all my surprises were done now but after dinner, everyone started talking about birthday presents. Even though I'd told them all not to bother, they had anyway and that did make me feel good, if undeserving.

'You guys, I did tell you not to get me anything, you

know!' I complained half-heartedly.

'Where's the fun in that, Jackson?' Ben called out, grinning. 'Here, open this one first, it's from me and Jamie.'

He handed me a large gift, which was all soft and squishy. I opened it slowly just to wind them up. When I could see what it was, I let out a low whistle.

'Oh, now that really is a perfect gift. I'm going to try it on now.' I stood up to try on the soft, black suede bomber jacket they'd bought for me and it fitted perfectly.

I glanced over at Rachel for her seal of approval and she gave me a big thumbs up. I think I saw another look in her eyes too and I returned her gaze, finally giving her a cheeky wink.

'Thank you, you guys, I really appreciate this.'

Next up was a gift from my mom and dad, a handsome leather satchel, very understated, in my style and something I would use a lot for work. Then Shelby and Josh gave me a platinum line Mont Blanc fountain pen, engraved with my initials.

Finally, Maggie, Alex and Rachel gave me a joint present from all of them. I had no ideas about this one. When I opened the box, I laughed. It was a brand new iPad, nestling inside a soft, black leather case.

'Wow, ladies, you do know how to spoil a man. I might need some help to get it set up.'

'No problem, that's where younger sisters come into their own,' laughed Maggie.

I stood up to go round to them all and thank them for their presents, finishing with a special kiss for Rachel.

'Put her down, Jackson, for goodness' sake,' teased my brother, Jamie.

Just when I thought all the excitement was over, my mom and dad went inside for something else and reappeared holding an impressive-looking birthday cake, covered in what looked like hundreds of candles but was in fact only thirty. They all sang me Happy Birthday while my dad videoed my embarrassment and they insisted on me blowing out the candles while making a wish.

'Okay, I'll indulge you but only to make you all stop harassing me!' I groaned.

I glanced over at Rachel as I made my wish and was rewarded with a little smile, tugging at the corners of her luscious lips. Then she mouthed 'I love you' at me and I think I actually blushed.

Rachel

After all the excitement of the presents and the cake, we sat and chatted while watching the magnificent sunset over the marina together. It had been a truly perfect evening. I suddenly realised that we hadn't told everyone about me signing with Jackson's label so I leaned over to whisper in his ear. He jumped up then to make the announcement.

'Hey, y'all, I completely forgot to tell you that we have other exciting news as well. This is business news really, I suppose, but it's just that we signed a new artist this week and I'm really looking forward to working with her.'

He smiled knowingly around the people there and when they realised he was talking about me, everyone leapt up and came either to me or to Jackson to give their congratulations. By the time that was over, we were all exhausted and ready for our beds.

Fortunately, there were four bedrooms, which sorted out Jackson's parents, Shelby and Josh, Alex and Maggie, and finally, Jackson and I. Todd and the other guys shacked up in sleeping bags in the main living room. They didn't seem to be overly worried about sleeping on the floor. I guess they were just used to it.

After saying goodnight to everyone, Jackson led me to the master bedroom. It was another amazing room, with windows on three sides and painted in a delicate shade of mint green. I could hardly wait to see the sun come up in this room. The wrought-iron bed was very romantic, and when I sat down on it I almost melted into the duvet floating on top of it. Jackson joined me and we lay back on the bed facing each other.

'How have you enjoyed your birthday so far?' I asked him.

'It's been the best birthday ever, I'd say. And when you say "so far" that seems to suggest there's more to come.' He looked at me hungrily and I laughed at his obvious need for me.

'Well, yes, I hear you loud and clear on that front but I do have another gift for you that I wanted to give you on our own.'

Jackson sat up then and turned to pull me up into his arms.

'You're the best birthday present I could have. You didn't need to get me anything else, baby.'

'I think you'll really like this one though,' I whispered, looking deep into his eyes.

He swallowed and I could see I had his interest aroused, among other things. I stood up and went to my bag to retrieve my final gift. I returned with a distinctive Tiffany gift bag. His eyes went wide when he saw it.

'It's my turn to give you something special now,' I told him and passed him the bag.

He looked inside at the small box lying there. He took it out and opened it very slowly to reveal a sterling silver knot ring. His eyes met mine and he looked unsure for a moment.

'This is to tell you that I really do love you and that I want to be with you. Just because I asked you to take things slowly doesn't mean that I'm any less committed to you. This ring is to say that I'm yours for the long term.'

'I...I don't know what to say,' he stuttered. 'Except that this means so much to me and if it's possible for me to love you even more than I already do, then I do. Which finger shall I put it on?' he asked hesitantly.

I took it from him and slipped it on to the fourth finger of his right hand. He swept me into his arms then and we made love as though we were doing so for the first time, discovering each other all over again.

'You make me so happy,' I whispered just before we fell asleep.

'Ditto.' I heard his soft reply in the darkness.

Jackson

In the morning, I left Rachel sleeping and crept off quietly downstairs to the kitchen. It was a tradition in our family for the guys to get up early the next day and cook breakfast for all the ladies. As I walked in, I could see my dad lightly whisking eggs that he'd turn into delicious scrambled eggs with salmon and chives later on. After greeting him, I set about preparing a pancake batter. Josh joined us shortly afterwards, having been reminded the night before by my dad and he started cutting up some fruit. Soon, Todd, Ted, Jamie and Ben were also with us, woken no doubt by all the wonderful cooking smells.

'Can one of you boys take care of the bacon for me please?' asked my dad. 'And someone else needs to prepare the salmon too.'

He gave the orders out and everyone jumped to attention. We finished by putting on some fresh coffee and filling jugs with juice. Just when we thought we'd have to go and call the girls, by some miracle, otherwise known as my mom, they appeared. Rachel came directly over to me, surreptitiously checking that I was wearing my ring before giving me a sweet good morning kiss.

'Hey there, baby, I hope you're hungry!'

'I am, actually. This is really lovely of you to do this for us.'

We gathered around the large kitchen table to tuck in to our sumptuous breakfast.

'What time will y'all be having to leave to catch your flight back?' I asked.

246

'Can't wait to get rid of us, hey?' teased Maggie. I poked my tongue out at her.

'I'd like to know what our plans are going to be for the day, that's all. I've had a wonderful time getting together with all of you, which I hope you know. We really should make the effort to do this more often.'

'I couldn't agree more, Jackson, honey,' my mom concurred. 'Anyways, to answer your question, the jet will be available to take us back from noon so really, we need to get there around then or shortly after, I think.'

'Okay, that sounds good. We have some more time together this morning then.'

While everyone was clearing up after breakfast, my dad drew me to one side.

'Son, I hate to bring this up while we're all having such a lovely time but did you see that Stephanie's back in town?'

'I did see it in the paper, Dad, yeah.' I didn't really want to think about this now but I knew my dad was just looking out for me.

'And how do you feel about it?'

'To be honest, I'm worried that she's up to something but I'm powerless to do anything to stop her scheming.' I blew out a long breath. I saw Rachel glance over at me and a look of concern passed across her beautiful face.

'Does Rachel know about her being back?' my dad asked, looking in her direction.

'Yes, I told her straight away.'

'Good. Well, I guess all you can do is hope she leaves you alone now.' He didn't look convinced and I didn't feel it either.

I wandered back to Rachel and the rest of the family, eager to put Stephanie as far from my mind as possible.

'Is that a new ring you're wearing, Jackson?' Alex shrewdly pointed out for everyone's benefit. She smiled knowingly and I realised she'd probably helped Rachel decide on what to buy me.

'I think you know the answer to that one,' I replied. 'Rachel gave it to me last night.'

All the women came over to look at the ring and oohed and aahed about it being stunning. I smiled at Rachel through it all, remembering the words she'd said when she gave it to me. I felt on top of the world, knowing that she felt that way about me and I was more hopeful now that she would like my gift as much as I'd liked hers.

CHAPTER THIRTY-ONE

Rachel

As we waved goodbye to the family, Jackson grabbed my hand and pulled me to him.

'It's time for the tour of the house!'

I laughed and followed him happily as he led me round the first floor, taking in the library (a library in your own home, how cool!), the great room as Jackson called it, furnished with lots of soft leather sofas to cuddle up on and a fireplace for those cold winter nights, and there was also a dining room and an office. We went on upstairs to check out the other bedrooms and the numerous bathrooms (how many did one man need?) and we ended up on the second floor porch looking at the fabulous view of the ocean.

Jackson put his arm round my shoulder and hugged me to him. 'What do you think of the house, then?' he asked.

'I love it. You've made it into a wonderful home and it's great to be here. I'd love to go and get some photos on the beach. Could we go and do that now?'

'Of course we can. Let's grab our things and head out. We can stop somewhere for a seafood lunch as well, if you'd like to.'

'Mmm, you're making me hungry, already.'

We wandered barefoot along the beach for the next hour and I took hundreds of photos of the sea, the marina and the view back towards town. When I thought he wasn't looking, I snapped a few of Jackson as well. He looked so happy and carefree and I managed to take some wonderful photos of him as a result. We had lunch at a lovely restaurant, sitting on their patio looking out to the sea. It was idyllic. After lunch, we walked lazily home again along the beach, watching the families with small children playing together in the sand. I sighed.

'Hey, that was a big sigh. What's up?' Jackson asked, stopping me so he could look at my face.

'I was just thinking that that could be us one day in the not-too-distant future.' I paused to consider what he thought about that.

'With kids, you mean?' he asked.

'Yep, I'd love to have a family one day.' I waited to hear what he would say about the subject, aware that I was holding my breath.

Then he reached out and pulled me to him.

'I can't imagine anything more wonderful than making babies together with you.' He smiled at me and I was glad that we were on the same page about that.

'Do you know something else I've always wanted?' I said, changing the subject ever so slightly. He looked at me intently once more, keen to hear this new revelation. 'I've always wanted a dog!' I burst out laughing at the surprise on his face.

'Well, that definitely wasn't what I thought you were going to say!'

'It's seeing all these people on the beach, walking their dogs. It's made me remember how much I love watching people do that. They always seem so happy together and I could never have a dog as a child because we were all out all day. I'd love to be able to do that in the near future. Do you like dogs?'

'Yes, but it would have to be a proper dog, not a yappy sort of dog that you can carry in a handbag, if you know what I mean.'

'So you wouldn't want to carry a dog in a handbag, huh?' I grinned at him. 'What's the matter, don't you like handbags?' I ran away from him and he chased after me along the beach.

The wind blew through my hair as I ran but I'd forgotten that Jackson was a practised runner and he caught up with me in no time, grabbing me around the waist and swinging me round to face him.

'You can't get away from me that easily, you know,' he said almost breathlessly. He kissed me deeply, so that I almost swooned right there but luckily we were just about home.

We ran the rest of the way and, once indoors, it was only a matter of time before we were in bed again, having strewn our clothes all over the house in our desperation to show each other how we felt.

Jackson

I was nervous about when to show Rachel my surprise because I didn't have any idea what her reaction would be and I didn't want anything to spoil this wonderful weekend we were having. Lying in my arms now, snoozing after our lovemaking, she was the closest to an angel I'd ever seen and I loved her so much. She stirred then and turned to look at me, smiling lazily at our decadence.

'Hey, gorgeous,' she said.

'Back at you, sweetheart.' I kissed her gently on the lips.

'Are you all right? You looked deep in thought about something when I opened my eyes.'

'I'm fine but I was deep in thought about something, you're right.' I closed my eyes briefly, steeling myself for this. 'I bought something for you too and I want to give it to you now but I don't know how you'll feel about it.'

She sat up then and the sheet dropped to her waist. God, she was beautiful. When I raised my eyes to her face again, she was smirking at me as she pulled the sheet back up again.

'Well, you'll have to concentrate on the matter in hand first before you can do anything.'

She was trying to put me at ease so I stood up and went to get yet another gift bag from my drawer. When I returned with it, her eyes were wide with surprise.

'You're not supposed to be buying presents for me, it's your birthday!' she scolded.

'Open it, please.'

She took the Tiffany bag from me, muttering about how we ought to get shares in the company, and looked inside excitedly. Then she gasped and looked up at me.

'That looks like a ring box,' she said.

I bit my lip nervously and said nothing while she took it out and slowly opened it. Then she sat back and laughed joyously.

'It's almost identical to the one I chose for you.'

I nodded. It was a sterling silver triple band ring, meant to show that our love was going to last forever.

'I wanted to tell you how precious you are to me and that I'm in this relationship for the long term too. Last night, you almost stole the words I've been rehearsing this past week right out of my mouth. We could have practised together if we'd known,' I chuckled. 'Do you like it though and is it okay for me to give you a ring like this?' I worried, still nervous because I hadn't let her say anything yet.

She moved towards me and came to sit in my lap, bringing the box with her.

'I love this ring because I know exactly the reason you bought it for me and it is more than all right for you to give it to me. In fact, it's fantastic! Will you put it on for me?'

I slipped the ring on to the fourth finger of her right hand so that we were matching and then I kissed her. We made slow, deep love after that, bringing the day to a beautiful close.

Rachel

Sunday passed too quickly and before we knew it, it was Monday and time to go back to reality. We were planning to be back at the airport for midday as the others had been on Saturday so we only had a few short hours left before we would have to be on our way. We sat down to breakfast on the porch for one last time and I couldn't help feeling glum about the prospect of going. Jackson picked up on my mood at once.

'You okay? You seem kind of down.'

'Yeah, I don't want this lovely weekend to end that's all. It's been good to spend all this time together with nothing else getting in the way.'

'I know, I've really enjoyed it too but we can come back whenever we like, it's not far and maybe we should make more of an effort to do that regularly, you know.'

He smiled at me and I loved him so much for understanding me.

We were back in Nashville by mid-afternoon and Jackson went off to do some work in his office while I unpacked. I decided that I needed to speak to Jenna again to see if she was going to come and visit as I'd suggested. I had such a lot to tell her.

'Hey, Jenna, it's me. I'm sorry it's late but I wanted to hear your voice.'

'It's never too late for you to call me, don't be silly. How did this weekend go? What was the house like?'

I told her everything about the weekend, finishing with the part where Jackson gave me an almost identical ring to the one I'd given him.

'Wow! It sounds to me like you two are engaged in all but name and fingers!'

'I guess you could say that, yes. Do you think we're both afraid of commitment?'

'Not at all, I think you're both totally committed to each other but you're scared to say it in the traditional way as if there's no way back from that in your minds. Does that make sense?'

'Yes, I think you've gone straight to the point. I do want to be engaged but I don't want to get hurt again, you know, and I'm sure that Jackson feels the same.'

'Well, sooner or later, you're going to have to decide whether you're both prepared to take that risk because it is a risk to love someone but it's not without rewards.'

'Oh, Jenna, tell me that you're coming to visit soon! I need you here to help me with all this.'

'I can come, yes, but only for a week, I think. I can't leave Mary in charge of everything for longer than that and Mum's tied up with other stuff obviously right now. I was thinking about coming over next weekend, what do you say?'

I squealed in delight, unable to contain my excitement. I promised to call her the next day to talk further about the details and rang off, going in search of Jackson to tell him the good news.

Jackson

As soon as I heard Rachel saying goodbye, I quickly returned to my desk, hoping she wouldn't guess that I'd accidentally overheard her conversation. I'd come looking for her, missing her after only a short time apart, and had almost walked in just as she was telling Jenna about our exchange of rings this past weekend. I knew I shouldn't have listened in but I couldn't help myself. It was definitely how I felt too but I needed to work out when would be the best time to admit this to Rachel and to persuade her that we should go ahead and take this risk on each other. It was crazy the way we felt this but couldn't say it to one another.

'I just came off the phone with Jenna and she's thinking about coming here to stay for a week this coming weekend!'

She looked so excited, it was catching.

'Oh baby, that's great news. We need to get thinking about arrangements for her, if you think she'll be okay with us helping her out.'

'Do you mean paying for her ticket and other stuff?'

'Yep, that's what I was thinking but I don't want to overstep the mark. You know her better than I do, of course.'

'I do but you're right that she would find it difficult to pay for her ticket. And where's she going to stay? Would you be happy with her staying here or would you prefer her to stay in a hotel? Come to think of it, she might prefer to stay in a hotel!' She ran her hands through her hair in concern.

'Hey, sweetheart, don't sweat it. Just ask her if she would mind us paying for her ticket and whether she'd prefer to stay with us or in a hotel. We could pay for the hotel of course.'

She looked at me for a long moment then and finally smiled.

'What is it, baby? What are you thinking about?' I asked, intrigued by her look.

'I just noticed how you're talking about *us* paying for her ticket and *us* paying for her hotel, like we're a proper couple, sharing everything, including our money, like you're saying what's yours is mine. And that feels kind of nice, like we really do belong together already.'

'Well, I think we do and what's mine *is* yours, forever.' I paused for a moment, then I continued. 'I have a confession to make. I came looking for you just now and accidentally overheard some of your conversation with Jenna.' I tried to look suitably guilty.

'You did?' Her beautiful hazel eyes went wide with surprise. 'And what did you hear?' she whispered.

'I heard you telling her about our exchange of rings.' I heard her sudden intake of breath and I instinctively closed the gap between us. 'And my next confession is that I had a different plan originally for what I was going to do and say when I gave you that ring.'

'You did?' she said again.

I went down on one knee then and took her hands in mine. 'What was it you were going to say?' she said so softly, I could barely hear her.

'Rachel, will you marry me?' I replied.

Her left hand flew to her mouth and her eyes filled with

tears about to fall.

'That's what you were going to say?' she managed to choke out. 'Why didn't you say it then?'

'I didn't think you were ready and I didn't want to rush you. But after hearing your conversation with Jenna, I think I was wrong and that maybe we both just need to have faith in each other. So, will you marry me?' I looked up at her tenderly, waiting for her to reply.

She lowered her left hand by way of an answer and removed her ring from her right hand and gave it to me. I took a moment to catch on to what she wanted me to do, then I slipped the ring on to her wedding finger and I kissed her hand.

She pulled me up then and we kissed deeply.

'I haven't heard your proper answer yet, you know.' I smiled down at her.

'Nothing would make me happier than to be married to you for the rest of my life.'

She confirmed what I'd been waiting to hear and, with a whoop, I swept her into my arms and whirled her round the room.

'Thank you for making me so happy,' I cried.

When we came to a stop, she took my right hand in hers and removed my ring, slipping it on to my wedding finger.

'Now we're promised to each other forever.'

CHAPTER THIRTY-TWO

<u>Rachel</u>

I could not believe all that had happened between us over the last few days and now we were engaged! To be married! We had overcome quite a few hurdles to get this far and this seemed to be the next step for us.

'I think this calls for a celebration! Let's go out to eat tonight, what do you think?' I asked.

'I think that's a great idea. How would you feel about asking the family along too?'

'That would be lovely. I'll call Alex.' Jackson said he would call his mum, which would include Maggie as well.

We went into separate rooms to make our calls and when we returned about ten minutes later, Jackson had managed to get his mum to call Shelby as well.

'Did you tell them what the occasion was?' I asked.

'No, I managed to get away without revealing that. How about you?'

'No, I kept it close to my chest,' I confirmed.

'Well, that sounds like a nice place to be,' Jackson quipped flirtatiously.

'Mmm, so that's the kind of mood you're in, is it?' I queried, tilting my head to one side, quizzically.

'You know me, I can always be in that mood but I'm trying really hard to focus here, honest.' He held up both hands in surrender.

I kissed both his palms in response before bringing us back to the conversation.

'What about Jamie and Ben? Could we get them to come?

Is it too far for them to come back?'

'I've already dealt with that one, baby.'

'You have?' I asked, not understanding how he could have dealt with it already.

'They hadn't left my folks' house yet, so no problem.'

I took a step towards Jackson, wanting to feel his arms around me once again. 'So we're all sorted for another family celebration,' I whispered against Jackson's chest.

'Yep, all sorted and if you keep whispering against my chest like that, I don't think I'll be able to control myself any longer.'

'How do you mean?' I continued, whispering against his muscular chest as I'd been doing before.

He suddenly swept me up into his arms and carried me through to the bedroom.

Jackson

A few hours later, we were walking into The Hermitage hotel, towards the Capitol Grille restaurant, where the whole family had gathered. We kissed and hugged and deflected their questions as smoothly as we could, making our way to our table quickly. Once we were sat down, I was able to take charge.

'Thank you all for coming at such short notice. I know that we've only just said goodbye and now Rachel and I are asking you to get together again.' I paused to smile at Rachel.

Then we both held up our left hands for them to study. It took only a moment for Jamie to realise.

'Wait a minute! You both have rings and they're on your left hands now, are you two engaged?'

We both grinned and nodded. Suddenly, there were whoops of joy all round, followed by backslapping and lots of hugs and kisses. Eventually, we all sat down again and I coughed politely to get everyone's attention so that I could speak.

'I asked Rachel to marry me earlier today and she said yes. We know that this is all we want for our future and we want to share our good news and fortune with all those we love.'

I glanced contentedly round the table at my family and friends and then back again at Rachel, as we all tucked into our meals. Rachel was glowing with happiness and had never looked lovelier to me.

'Have you set a date for the wedding then, Jackson?' asked Alex who was sat on my left.

'No, no, we haven't got that far yet. But I guess that will be next on the agenda,' I replied, looking over at Rachel for confirmation. She nodded looking a little bit worried.

'Hey, what is it, baby?' I asked her.

'Well, we'll have to think about the logistics of including everyone here and everyone in Dorset in our celebrations. I've only just thought about that and it's not going to be easy, is it?' Her brow creased a little.

'What about having two weddings then, one here and one there?' suggested Alex. 'Mom and Dad could come to both,' she continued.

'What do you think about that idea, Rachel? It sounds like it could work to me.' I looked at her again to try and gauge her thinking.

'Yes, I think that could work. We'll have to give it some more thought.'

'Don't worry about it now, let's enjoy tonight.' I smiled at her.

We finished our meals, chatting all the while and we were just pondering whether to have dessert when a dramatic hush fell over the table. I turned to see what had brought this on and looked straight up into Stephanie's eyes.

'Well, what do we have here? A Phillips family celebration with a few hangers-on, I see.' Her sarcastic voice cut through the air as she leered at everyone. She looked drunk again.

I tried to stand up to confront her but I simply didn't have the strength.

I was surprised to see Rachel already on her feet.

Rachel

'You're right, Stephanie, this is a Phillips family celebration but you seem to be the only hanger-on in sight.'

She leered at me, swaying dangerously close.

I took a small step back before continuing. 'Jackson and I are celebrating our engagement tonight. I've chosen to be part of this wonderful, loving family and they've welcomed me with no hesitation.' I looked round briefly at them all, noting how surprised they looked by this turn of events. 'That could have been you, Stephanie, but you rejected their love.' She rolled her eyes at that. 'That was your mistake, which you seem to recognise now but it's too late for you to come back. You need to move on, like Jackson has, and find your future because it isn't here. Your future is somewhere else.'

I hadn't broken eye contact with Stephanie as I came to the end of my speech so I hadn't noticed that Jackson had stood up next to me while I was speaking and that his mum had joined me on the other side.

Stephanie swallowed hard, looking like she was about to launch a counter-attack but after glancing over at Jackson's mum and then at Jackson himself, she seemed to think better of it.

'Well, you folks go ahead and enjoy the rest of your evening,' she muttered, her words slurring and, turning on her heel, she started to walk away, wobbling ever so slightly as she did. As she reached the door, she looked back one last time before saying, 'Oh and don't worry, Jackson, your secrets are safe with me.'

Then she slipped through the door and disappeared. I saw Jackson wipe his hands on his jeans, and I noticed everyone exchange a look of concern.

I fell back into my seat at the table, feeling exhausted with the effort of standing up to Stephanie like that. I never would have thought I had it in me to do that and in front of so many people but it had been my gut reaction. I didn't want this cloud hanging over us any more and it was time someone told her straight. I didn't want to crush her but I did want to make the message loud and clear and it seemed that I'd succeeded.

Jackson's mum knelt down next to me.

'Rachel, I'm really proud of you for doing that and I'm so happy that you're joining our family. I couldn't have wished for a better daughter-in-law.' She squeezed my hand and kissed me on the cheek. Jackson helped her back up and sat back down next to me. He leaned forward and kissed me gently on the lips, holding my face in his hands. He gave me a reassuring smile.

'I love you, Rachel. I can't wait to make you my wife.'

I didn't smile back at him though. I was wondering about Stephanie's last comment. Did Jackson have secrets he was keeping? And if he did, why? I had no choice but to push my concerns away for the time being.

The rest of the meal went smoothly with desserts and coffees following along. I gave some more thought to Alex's suggestion of two weddings and the more I thought about it, the more I liked it. It would be lovely to get married in Nashville so everyone here could attend but it would be complicated to get everyone over from Dorset as well, and anyway, I wanted to get married at St James' so I would feel like my parents were there too and, more to the point, Jenna would kill me if she couldn't do the flowers! I would have plenty to talk to Jenna about then when she came to visit next weekend. I was looking forward to seeing her and I gave a little smile in anticipation.

'Penny for them?' Jackson was looking at me intently with his deep, brown eyes. I wanted so badly to ask him what Stephanie had meant but I was frightened.

Taking a deep breath, I talked about our wedding plans

instead.

'Oh, I was mulling over the idea of two weddings and asking Jenna to do my flowers. You know, most men find the idea of one wedding hard enough to deal with and here you are possibly agreeing to two!'

'I would do anything for you, you know that. And if that means two weddings, who am I to argue?' I kissed him gratefully then.

'Thank you.'

'What for?'

'Just for being so wonderful mainly but for understanding that I need to include everyone back home as well.'

'Well, of course you do but I think this could work really well. And if Mom and Dad are at both weddings, that will join the circle once again from Nashville back to Dorset. I think it will be quite fitting. Why don't we mention it to Mom now?'

So we turned to Jackson's mum, Shelley, and put the idea to her. To say she was delighted was an understatement. She threw her arms around us both with obvious pleasure.

Soon the evening was over and Jackson and I were wandering slowly back to the condo.

'Are you going to tell me what she meant?' I asked after a few minutes calming myself. I stopped and turned.

'In all honesty, I have no idea what she meant. I promise you that I'm not keeping any secrets from you.'

'Why do you think she said that then?'

'I don't know but it's got me worried about what she might be scheming to do next.'

I took his hand to show that I had accepted his answer. But I knew instinctively that he was right about Stephanie. The doubt which had sowed its seed at the back of my mind when she'd said those words, began to grow.

Jackson

I was still reeling from seeing Stephanie again at the restaurant when Rachel asked me about her parting shot. I wasn't keeping any secrets from Rachel but I could see the suspicion in her eyes, which was exactly what Stephanie had planned. Damn that woman! Would I never be free of her?

I felt powerless and I hated being in that position. Stephanie was up to something but I had no idea what. This was the last thing we needed now when we'd only really just got back together. Not only that but I wanted the focus to be on our future, not on my past.

We were into the office bright and early the next day because Rachel wanted to get down to work on her new EP which was what her demo CD had turned into and, by extension, her album. We were also planning a special gig for her at the end of the week, as well as some more press interviews so we were going to be kept real busy.

Annie was sorting out Jenna's travel arrangements so that she could be with us by the weekend. I knew that Rachel wanted to tell Jenna all about our plans for the two weddings and we'd both agreed that we would press ahead with them as soon as possible, hopefully before Christmas.

Meanwhile, I started to contact some real estate agents so that Rachel and I could start looking for a house together to kick off our married life. I'd just finished making a batch of phone calls when I heard Rachel's cell phone ping with a text. Realising she'd left it on my desk while she was in the studio, I pulled it towards me to see who the message was from. It said it was from Jenna and I decided to take it downstairs to she could read it straight away.

Rachel read the text out to me as she read it herself:

'Hey, Rachel, any news on flights? Everything is in place at this end so I can come as soon as you're ready for me!'

She clapped her hands together in excitement and then ran towards the stairs. 'I'm going to ask Annie to arrange a flight for Jenna tomorrow if possible!'

Rachel

Annie managed to book Jenna a flight for the following day, arriving late at night like I had. I sent her a text to confirm the details and to ask where she'd like to stay.

'Thanks for arranging ticket. Can't wait to see you! Happy to stay at condo if that's not awkward but a hotel's fine too :) See you at the airport tomorrow!!! Xxx'

I couldn't wait to tell Jenna that Jackson had asked me to marry him and that we were planning two weddings as well. I wanted her to do the flowers for both if possible so we'd have plenty to talk about in terms of practical arrangements.

We set off for the airport the following night about ten, driven by Greg as usual.

'Have you had any ideas about what you'd like to do with Jenna while she's here?'

'I thought we could do some sightseeing, I want her to come to my gig on Friday, of course, and she'll be able to meet some of your family then too, as well as maybe seeing them at the weekend. What do you think?'

'That sounds good to me. Why don't you do some sightseeing tomorrow and then come into the office for some rehearsal time on Friday. I'll be able to keep Jenna company if you need me to. Then perhaps we could do something all together on Saturday and see the family again on Sunday.'

'Yes, that all sounds good. I can't wait to tell her our news as well and to make some plans with her for the weddings.'

Jackson took my hand, raised it to his lips and kissed it.

In no time at all, we were at the airport and standing by the arrivals gate, looking for Jenna.

'Should we go and check the arrivals board?' I asked Jackson anxiously, after we'd been waiting for about half an hour with no sign of her.

'Yeah, maybe we should, sweetheart.'

He took my hand and we wandered over to the nearest board, only to find that her flight had been delayed.

I felt my shoulders sag in disappointment.

'Hey, it's only another half hour delay, why don't we go and grab a coffee while we wait?'

He was trying to keep my spirits up but I wanted her to be there and to know she was safe.

We sat down at the nearest café, waiting for our coffees to cool.

'Shall we go and check the board again?' I asked for about the tenth time, standing up and smoothing down my skirt. Luckily, it said Jenna's flight had now landed so we made our way back to the arrivals gate and a few minutes later, there she was, pulling her suitcase along behind her while busily scanning all the people looking for us.

'Jenna, over here,' I called and waved and her face lit up. I ran towards her and gave her a great big hug. Jackson leaned over and kissed her on the cheek in welcome and we set off to look for Greg and make our way home.

CHAPTER THIRTY-THREE

Jackson

I could hardly get a word in edgewise as we travelled home, for all the talking the girls were doing on the way. Rachel explained that we'd be delighted for Jenna to stay with us and that we were heading back to the condo now. Then they were chatting about news from Dorset and about all their plans for the coming week and before we knew it, we were being dropped off by Greg and heading inside. I said goodnight to Jenna and left Rachel to get her settled in. They must have chatted for a long time because I had no memory of Rachel joining me in bed when I woke up the next morning. She stirred a little when I got up to get ready for work but she didn't wake up. When I went through to the lounge, Jenna was already awake.

'Morning, Jenna, did the jet-lag get you up this early?'

'Yes, it did, unfortunately.' She pulled a face for a moment but was instantly smiling again.

'I'm heading off to work but you girls should take it easy for today and get reacquainted.'

'That will be lovely, as long as Rachel doesn't lie in too long!' She laughed then and I was struck by her easy-going nature.

'Have you two known each other a long time?' I asked, realising I didn't really know much about how they'd met.

'Since we were at high school.' She nodded. 'We've been through a lot together. I'm glad that she's met you, Jackson, it's wonderful to see her so happy.'

'Rachel has made me happy too. In fact, I don't think I've

felt happier than this, ever.'

Rachel appeared then, looking absolutely gorgeous. She came straight over and kissed me good morning, as if to confirm the point I was just making.

'Are you two talking about me? My ears are burning.' She grinned at both of us.

'Yes,' admitted Jenna, 'but in a good way. I'm glad to see the pair of you so happy. I would love to have some of what you two have between you so, any tips, please send them my way!'

'We have some news for you, actually.' Rachel held up her left hand for Jenna to see and I did the same.

We were both smiling like lovesick teenagers by this point.

'Oh my goodness,' Jenna squealed as the penny dropped. 'You're engaged?' She jumped up and ran over to hug each of us in turn.

'When did this happen and why haven't you told me?'

'Just after I spoke to you about it but I wanted to tell you face to face and see this reaction!'

'Sorry to interrupt you, ladies but I'd best be going. Have a nice day catching up and I'll call you later, Rachel, okay?' I kissed her, feeling her body respond to mine then, reluctantly, I pulled away to leave.

Rachel

By the time we'd had breakfast, I'd filled Jenna in on all, well not quite all, but most of the details of our weekend in Charleston. I told her about the engagement celebration we'd had with Jackson's family as well.

'Then, you'll never guess who decided to show up to try and spoil things?'

'No, she didn't? Stephanie, I presume.'

'Yep, and what's more, I stood up to her and even though I was shaking on the inside, I felt strong on the outside, strong enough to tell her to get lost, anyway! By the time I'd finished,

I had Jackson on one side of me and his mum on the other, like bodyguards ready to protect me. I really do hope that's the last we'll see of her but I have a feeling it won't be. Her last words to Jackson were that his secrets were safe with her.' I pulled a face as I remembered it.

'And what did she mean by that? Did you ask Jackson?'

'I did and he said he had no secrets from me and had no idea what she was talking about.'

'Well, it sounds like you left her in no doubt about the fact that she didn't belong there. As you say, hopefully that's the end of it but if it isn't, you'll be ready for her.' After a slight pause, she continued, 'How are you going to organise the wedding? We'll all want to come too, you know, and that could start to get expensive.'

'We've decided to have two weddings! One here and one at home, in Dorset.' I paused then, realising that I was referring to Dorset as home again. I mean, it was my home for nearly thirty years but things had moved on and I was going to have to think differently from now on. I bit my lip and tears sprang to my eyes. I tried to swipe them away but Jenna noticed at once.

'Hey, what brought that on? What's the matter?'

'Oh, I don't know, I'm being silly, I guess. It's just that Dorset is still the place I think of as home but it's not going to be my home any more, is it? Every time I think about it, I get upset because I want my home to be where Jackson is but I also have my memories from the past twenty-odd years of my life in the UK. It's going to be hard to move on from that and start afresh over here, without you and your family and everything I've ever known around me.'

'It's natural that you'd feel scared as well as excited by that prospect but you will be able to come back to Dorset and see us, won't you? You'd better, anyway.' She laughed and I smiled, feeling reassured.

'How's Sam doing?' I asked her, desperate to know but

hardly daring to ask.

She blew out a breath before replying. 'Physically, he's well on the mend but...' She paused, looking hesitant.

'What?' I whispered, guessing what she was going to say.

'Well, he's hurting in his heart. I had a long chat with him about his feelings for you. Don't worry, nothing you wouldn't want me to know. Look, he asked me to give you this letter actually.' She dug in her bag for a moment and pulled out a slightly crumpled envelope with my name on it. She looked so torn between her love for her brother and her friendship with me that I didn't know what to say.

I took the letter from her, trying not to cry. 'I didn't mean to hurt him, you know,' I managed to say after a minute.

'I know. He needs some time to get over it but he will in the end.'

'C'mon, let's get dressed,' I said, trying to lift the atmosphere. 'Why don't we go out for a nice lunch and maybe, if you're not too tired, we could do a little mild sightseeing after that. What do you think?'

She nodded and we went off to our separate rooms to get ready.

I closed the door of the bedroom behind me and sank on to the bed. I stared at the letter for a long minute, not sure if I was brave enough to open it but knowing that I had to read what Sam wanted to say.

Dear Rachel,

I'm sorry if this seems a bit strange but I didn't want to say all this in a text or email and I haven't got the courage to call you yet. I heard from Jenna that you and Jackson are back together and from what she said, I think it sounds like you've committed to each other for the long term. I have to be honest and tell you that I'd been finding it hard to accept that you don't love me the way I love you but when I heard this news, it was the push I needed to move on. I want you to know that I wish you every happiness in your life but a part of my heart will always belong to you. I hope you know that I'll always be here for you, as a friend, if nothing else. Take care and good luck with everything.

Love Sam x

I looked up as I finished reading, hardly able to see for the tears streaming down my face. Sam was such a good man and a great friend to me too and I felt such sadness that we wouldn't ever be together in the way that he wanted. I knew I'd made the right decision for me but it still hurt to know I'd caused him such pain. I reached for a tissue to wipe my eyes and then folded the letter up very carefully and put it in my bag, resolving to call him at the first opportunity.

Jackson

I'd set to work as soon as I arrived at the office and had managed to get quite a lot done. Just before lunch, there was a knock on the door.

'Come in,' I called out and I stood up to greet whoever was there. 'Hey, Will, what's up?'

Will, my VP for Marketing, looked uncomfortable with whatever he was about to say.

'I think you'd better sit down, you're not going to like the news I have to tell you.'

'What's this all about?' I frowned at him but sat down as he'd asked.

Will went on, 'I just heard that *Gossip* magazine, which is published online, is going to be running an interview with Stephanie in next week's issue and in it, she says some pretty scathing things about you and Rachel.'

'What the hell?' I stood up again, immediately angry and turned to look out the window to hide my frustration. 'Do you know what she says about us?' I said quietly a couple of minutes later.

'Yes. Do you want me to read it to you?' He waited for my nod before continuing. 'There are two main things she says.

270

Firstly, she says that the real reason you dumped her is not because she cheated on you but because she wanted a family and you told her you didn't want to have children. She goes on to say that she needed a real man, blah, blah, blah. Obviously, she's trying to win back some sympathy for the way that she behaved by making up another lie. Secondly, she says that Rachel's nothing but a gold-digger and that she's wormed her way into your affections to get at your money and that you've been fool enough to fall for it.'

He fell silent and waited for my reaction.

I let out the most almighty roar of anger at this new betrayal by the woman I'd come to hate.

Annie appeared at my door at once. I signalled that I was okay and she disappeared again but she didn't look like she believed it.

'Is there anything we can do to stop them publishing this, Will? I don't give a damn what she says about me but I do care about Rachel and I don't want them saying this sort of stuff.'

'We should check with our lawyers about libel but if it isn't, I don't think there's anything we can do. You'll have to keep your head up and try and rise above what she's said about you. It might be an idea to issue an official statement about your engagement to Rachel, or perhaps to organise an interview for you both in one of the more respected newspapers or magazines to set the record straight. What do you think?'

'I need to speak to Rachel and then I'll come back to you. Thanks for letting me know. It can't have been easy for you, telling me all that.' I smiled tightly.

'I'm sorry I had to be the bearer of that news,' Will said, looking miserable. 'Let me know what you want me to do and I'll get on to it at once.'

I sat down heavily at my desk and put my head in my hands. Would we never be rid of this woman? I heard the door open and looked up to see Annie there, looking really

271

concerned.

'What on earth has happened?' she asked.

I gave her the main points and she sank down into the chair opposite me then, unable to believe how spiteful Stephanie was being.

'What are you going to do?' she asked.

'I'm going to have to tell Rachel, of course, which I'm not looking forward to one bit. Will has come up with quite a good idea that Rachel and I should give an interview to set the record straight in one of the better magazines. I'm going to head off home now.'

'I'm sorry, Jackson. I think that's a good idea on Will's part but see what Rachel thinks first, as you said.'

'You do think I should tell her then?' I asked.

'Oh definitely. She needs to know before it's published for everyone to see.'

After Annie left, I thought about how I would break this news to Rachel, especially as I was so damn mad about it all. I needed a run to get my head straight really. An idea formed in my mind about how I might tackle things. I picked up the phone to Annie and asked to be put through to Will again.

'Hey, Will, I was wondering whether you're busy tonight?'

'No, I haven't got anything special on. Why?'

'I'll tell you on our way out. I'll be with you any minute, I just have to send Rachel a text.'

Something came up again with Stephanie. Will's coming home with me to sort out how to deal with it. I need to go for a run first so he'll fill you in then. I thought we could all go out for dinner later maybe x'

Rachel

After listening to Will's account of what had happened and his suggestion of how we should deal with it, I was stunned into silence. I could not believe the animosity that this woman had towards me but worse than that was what she was saying about her relationship with Jackson. She clearly had a different view about Jackson's feelings with regard to starting a family.

I felt like I was being kept out of the loop and as my mind whirred I began to feel very angry with Jackson. I had trusted him with my heart and, once more, it seemed like he had kept things from me. I stood up and walked over to the window, clenching and unclenching my fists as I paced up and down the length of the glass, impatient for him to come back from his run and explain himself. I knew that I couldn't talk to him with Jenna and Will there though.

'Will, Jenna, I need some time alone with Jackson, I think. Would you mind going on to the restaurant without us?' I felt guilty about sending Jenna away with Will when I'd only just introduced them but I knew he'd look after her.

'If you're sure,' Jenna replied and then turned to check that Will was okay with the idea.

He nodded and she went to get her coat.

'Try and keep calm, Rachel, and let Jackson explain first,' she said when she came back, taking my hands in hers.

I nodded but I couldn't speak. It was taking everything I had to keep myself together for speaking to Jackson.

When he returned, I was torn between relief at seeing him back safe and looking much calmer, and anger at this new turn of events, which was making me doubt him once again. I kept my arms tightly folded and waited for him to come into the lounge.

'Hey, baby. Where's Will and Jenna?' he asked, looking around as he towelled himself dry after his run.

'I sent them on to the restaurant so that we could talk,' I said quietly.

'Okay, that was probably a good plan. What did you think of Will's idea then about us doing an interview with another magazine to try and set the record straight?'

'It would be difficult for me to set the record straight seeing as I don't actually know what the record is, do I?'

'What do you mean?' His handsome face was etched with worry now as he started to understand that I was angry.

'Why did Stephanie say that she didn't cheat on you when that's what you've told me all along? Is it true that you told her you didn't want children? Again, that's not what you've been telling me.'

He swallowed but didn't speak for a moment.

I didn't know if he was preparing another lie or if he was about to tell me the truth at last.

'I did tell her I didn't want children, yes,' he whispered finally.

My mouth dropped open.

'What? You said she cheated on you and that was why you dumped her.'

'She did cheat on me, she's lying when she says she didn't and in the aftermath, we both said some terrible things to each other, including me telling her that I didn't want to have children but I meant with her, not with someone else. I do want to have children with you. I wasn't lying about that.' When I didn't reply, he carried on. 'Haven't you ever done or said something in the heat of the moment which you regretted later, Rachel?'

And all of a sudden, I remembered that I'd done just that. With Sam and I'd never told Jackson about it. It was all before I met him of course, which was how I'd rationalised not telling him whenever I wondered whether I should. I tried hard not to let it show in my face but I couldn't quite manage it.

'What is it?' he asked me.

'Jackson, I…I haven't been totally honest with you either.' I watched as his face fell, and worried whether to go ahead but it was too late to back out now.

'What haven't you been honest about?' He'd gone pale as he waited for me to answer.

I could feel myself shaking but I tried to pull myself together to tell him.

'Before I met you, I had a one-night stand with Sam but I regretted it instantly because I knew I didn't want that kind of relationship with him.'

'And why didn't you tell me this before, when I asked you if you'd ever dated each other?'

'I hardly knew you then but I should have told you when we came back to Nashville together. We both promised to be completely honest with each other then but neither of us have been. For my part, there never seemed to be a good time to tell you when it wouldn't hurt you and perhaps ruin everything we had together.' I fiddled with my engagement ring, unable to look him in the eye.

'And that's how I felt about Stephanie. My relationship with her was over long before we met, as I told you, and I haven't lied about what happened. It's just that now she's trying to stir up trouble and we can't let her do that, not if we want our relationship to survive.'

'Even if we can get past the things we've kept from each other, if the press go ahead and publish that interview with her, my career will be in pieces before it even gets started, along with your reputation.'

He stood up then and came towards me, arms outstretched and I instinctively walked towards them.

'I wish you'd told me about you and Sam but I knew the minute we came back to Nashville that you'd forgiven me and that we were going to be together so I'm happy to leave the past where it belongs. How about you?'

'I can forgive you too but what are we going to do about Stephanie?'

His big arms enveloped me and we hugged silently for a few minutes, both of us glad that everything was now out in the open.

'At first, I thought Will's suggestion sounded like a good plan but when I was out running, I wasn't so sure. I don't feel it's going to be that easy to make her go away, you know.

What about you, how do you feel about it?'

'Well, she's going to say some pretty unpleasant things about us but if we rise to her bait, trying to defend ourselves, we may only make things worse. I hate attention from the press at the best of times.'

'I know, and if we don't say anything, it sounds like she's telling the truth and what's more, we'd be letting her get away with it.' He paused for a moment, groaning at the seemingly hopeless situation we now found ourselves in. 'Look, let's go and catch up with Will and Jenna and see what they think.'

CHAPTER THIRTY-FOUR

Jackson

We arrived at the restaurant a few minutes later and found the two of them sitting at a quiet table in a corner, nursing some drinks and deep in conversation. I took a moment to absorb the scene and smiled a brief smile before joining Rachel at the table. Once we'd said our hellos and then placed our order for food and more drinks, I spoke up.

'First of all, I'd like to apologise to you, Jenna for having this horrible mess take over your stay with us and I'd like to welcome you to Nashville properly with a toast.'

We all clinked glasses.

'Thanks, Jackson but please don't worry about it on my account. I'm your friend and it pains me as much as it does the both of you. What I want to know is what are we going to do about it?' She gave us all a look that showed she meant business and we all laughed, glad of the icebreaker.

'Jackson and I were just saying that we're worried that we might be playing into her hands if we rise to the bait but if we don't say anything, then she'll think she can do and say what she likes.' Rachel looked really miserable about the dilemma we were in through no fault of our own. I took her hand.

'You've got an important gig tomorrow night, Rachel, haven't you?' Will asked her.

'Yes, why?' she replied.

'Well, I was wondering if you could use that as a platform to present your side of the story without going to the extra trouble of an interview which might look like you were trying too hard.'

'That sounds like quite a good idea, Will, thank you. What do you think, Jackson?'

'Yeah, that might work. We couldn't tackle everything but we could deal with some of the things she's going to raise. I guess we'd have to leave people to make up their own minds after that. Okay, how about we leave it there for tonight and try and enjoy the rest of our evening?'

The next day flew by in a whirl of rehearsals and preparations for Rachel's show that evening so there was no time to worry about Stephanie. This was to be a charity dinner and show performed by Rachel and had been set up by my parents on behalf of the university. It was by invitation only and we were expecting about two hundred people to attend. I knew that Rachel was nervous but I also had every confidence in her. After spending the morning rehearsing, she appeared in my office just before lunch.

'Hey, sweetheart, how's it going? You look exhausted.' I went over to her and drew her into my arms, losing myself in her hazel eyes.

'It's gone well, I think but I'm dead on my feet, to be honest. Where's Jenna, is she okay?' She pulled back slightly, looking guilty at the thought of having left her friend on her own all morning.

'She's more than okay. She spent some time with me but when Will came and asked her if she'd like to go on a tour of the office, she jumped at the chance.' I gave a little smile and Rachel raised her eyebrows slightly.

'Do you think...? Do they...?'

'Yes I do and yes they do!'

We both laughed.

'Well, I'm pleased about that. Is Will coming tonight?'

'He is and so is almost everyone else from the office. It's going to be a great night. I heard that there's a great new singer performing as well.'

'I'm very nervous. It will be such an important audience,

although I know I've performed in front of larger ones before but I know and care about a lot of these people and I'm scared of mucking it all up.'

I tipped her chin up so that she could see my face.

'You are not going to *muck* up, you will be fantastic as always. I believe in you and so does everyone else at the label. Our family and friends will be there and we'll all be rooting for you so try not to worry. Is there anything else you need me to help you with before tonight?'

'No, I think I'm all right. I'd like to get some lunch and then probably get off home mid-afternoon to get ready, if that's okay?'

'Let's go and find Jenna then and see if we can tempt her away from Will.'

We wandered down the corridor towards Will's office but when we got there, it was empty.

'Perhaps they're still doing the tour?' Rachel commented. We turned around to see if we could see them across the open-plan office and saw Annie speeding across from my office.

'Jackson, there you are, I've been looking for you to give you this message. Will and Jenna have gone for lunch at the deli and said for you two to join them if you wish when you're ready.'

'Thanks, Annie. What would you like to do, Rachel? Shall we join them or leave them to it and lunch on our own?' I touched her gently in the small of her back and was rewarded with an unexpectedly sultry look in return.

'If you touch me there, I will not be responsible for my actions,' she whispered seductively in my ear. My eyes lit up at her flirting but I had to drop my hand, given our current location.

'I guess I'll have to take a rain check on that wonderful offer.' I smiled and touched her cheek.

'In answer to your question then, how about we go somewhere and eat on our own, and leave Will and Jenna to get better acquainted?'

'That sounds like a great idea.'

Rachel

By five o'clock, we were on our way to the country club where the dinner was being held. It was over near the university and quite close to Jackson's parents' house so Greg was taking us there. Will had offered to pick Jenna up and take her there so Jackson and I were alone in the back of the car.

'Are you going to introduce me tonight then?'

'I want to introduce you anyway, sweetheart, but I don't know how much to say about the other stuff. People might think it odd before there's even been any sign of an article, do you know what I mean?'

I nodded and sighed.

'Maybe it's best to try not to get drawn in to all this bitching with Stephanie because we could end up getting more hurt by her. Perhaps if we try to ignore it and rise above it by proving that we're not like her, she'll get bored and move on.'

Jackson nodded but neither of us seemed any more convinced.

There were lots of people milling around when we arrived but I was able to find Jed quite quickly and carry out my soundcheck without any hitches. Jackson was listening and gave me the thumbs up. We'd chosen the six songs on my setlist together and I was confident that we'd made a good choice. Our next stop was to find Bob and Shelley to say hello before people started arriving in earnest. They were out in the foyer, greeting guests as they arrived for drinks. Dinner was at seven so it was a good time to mingle and meet new people.

'Rachel, you look lovely, dear and I love those cowboy boots. Have you done your soundcheck? Was everything okay?'

'Thank you. Yes, I have and it was fine. Thank you again for doing this for me, Shelley, it's a great opportunity.'

'Sweetheart, you have nothing to thank me for. You earned it. Just try and enjoy yourself, you look nervous.'

She gave me a hug and then Jackson took me round to introduce me to some of the music industry people who were attending. We bumped into Will and Jenna on the verandah and I took a moment to check how things were going, pulling her off to one side, leaving Will to talk to Jackson for a minute.

'How are you two getting along?'

'We're having a lovely time, Rachel. I can't believe how much I like him even though we've only just met. He's such a wonderful person.' Her eyes glowed with the enjoyment of a new romance and I was happy for her.

'How about you? Are you feeling nervous about tonight?'

'A bit, yes. It's just that it's a really important crowd this evening and I could do without this whole thing with Stephanie hanging over us.' I swallowed but tried to smile.

'Is everything okay between you and Jackson after all that came out yesterday?' I nodded in reply and she took my hands in hers and gave them a little squeeze to try and reassure me and then we went back to join the guys.

It was soon time for dinner but I hardly ate a thing. Bob gave a short speech, telling everyone about the charity he and Shelley were involved with and thanking them for their generous donations to their cause. Before he went to sit back down, he introduced Jackson who went on to the stage where my small band of session musicians were settling into place. He looked calm and gorgeous, all at the same time and I took a deep breath as he started to speak.

'I'd like to take a few minutes of your time to introduce Rachel Hardy who will be singing for you tonight. I first met Rachel in the UK, only a couple of months ago and I was so impressed by her singing and songwriting talents that I persuaded her to come out here to Nashville to pursue her dream. She performed in a couple of "Open Mic" nights when she first arrived and these were all a great success. Shortly afterwards, I signed her to my record label and she's already started work on her first album.' He paused and smiled as the audience gave a round of applause.

'Rachel and I have come to know each other real well over these past couple of months and it wasn't long before we both realised that we were meant to be together, which is why I recently asked her to be my wife. Luckily for me, she said yes! Ladies and gentlemen, please give a warm welcome to Rachel Hardy.'

I stood up amidst the rapturous applause and made my way to the stage, holding my head up high.

Jackson

Rachel looked absolutely beautiful as she stood up to make her way to the stage. As I'd thought, the minute she was there and the intro to her first song was playing, she became calm and focussed solely on the music. She was singing only her own songs tonight at my suggestion because she'd made it now and needed to show the audience what a good songwriter she was. She sang her first three songs, 'My Turn', 'Don't Let Me Go' and 'Too Late', stopping only to tell the audience the names of the songs and to introduce the band members. Then there was a short interval. She was congratulated by lots of people on her way back to our table and she was smiling confidently by the time she returned.

I took her into my arms for a hug and whispered into her ear, 'Baby, you were sensational. Well done!' I kissed her gently and felt her body lean into mine with relief at her success.

We only had time for a quick drink before the second half.

She kicked off with 'Driving Me Crazy' which really got the audience going and then she paused to say a few words.

'I'd like to thank you all for the great welcome you've given me tonight, you've been a fabulous audience. I'd also like to thank Bob and Shelley for this opportunity to perform in front of you, I really appreciate it. Most of all, I'd like to thank Jackson for turning my life upside down and for showing me that dreams can come true.' And she blew me a kiss from the stage.

I hardly heard the applause because I was so taken aback by the declaration of love she'd just made in front of all these people. Someone slapped me on the back, bringing me back to reality and I gave a little smile to Rachel as she began her next song on the guitar. It was one I remembered hearing her sing in her little cottage all that time ago, 'Without You'.

'Before we met, I felt so alone,
I didn't even realise just how much,
I yearned for someone who would love me,
And fulfil me with their every touch.

Now we're together and so much has changed,
I was one and have become two,
I can't begin to imagine, I wouldn't even dare,
To consider living without you, without you.'

It was another wonderful song and Rachel gave it everything so the audience was hanging on every word and every note. I was so proud of her talent and I knew this audience was on her side and would spread the word about her to all their friends and family.

She had come to her final song now and I could feel an anticipation in the audience as they waited to hear what it would be. She coughed gently to get everyone's attention.

'This is my last song of the evening and it's called "Empty Promises". Thank you.' She glanced quickly over at me and then went to sit down at the piano.

I remembered when we'd talked about empty promises and I hadn't heard this one before. I felt a tiny flutter in the pit of my stomach.

'I want you to love me like there's no tomorrow,
Just in case you're a dream and gone when I awake,
Can I trust you or are you just making empty promises?
Are you here to stay or am I making another mistake?

Tell me that you love me again, it won't ever get old,
Make sure that you mean it, please don't let me down,
My fragile heart is easily broken and I
Don't want to be your clown.'

She had a way with words that went straight to my heart and all I wanted to do was show her how much I loved her and wanted to be with her forever. At the end of the song, I jumped to my feet along with the rest of the audience to give her a standing ovation. We were stood there for several minutes and then someone called for an encore. Rachel responded at once, turning to the band to confirm what she would sing. I knew she would have prepared for this, just in case.

'Well, this has been an amazing evening, here in Nashville, with y'all!' Everyone laughed with her, as she tried out the accent. 'Here's a Dolly Parton classic which seems a good one to finish on.' She went straight into 'Here You Come Again' to lots of whooping and some hat throwing and everyone was singing along and, in that moment, I knew that Rachel Hardy had well and truly made it.

Rachel

We didn't talk much in the car on the way home. I didn't think there were any words for the excitement I felt after the show or for all the emotions I was feeling. I held Jackson's hand tightly to show him I needed some time and I think he sensed that. When I'd come down from the stage, he'd been right there to take me in his arms and kiss me so intensely that I knew he'd

284

understood what I'd been trying to tell him in my newest song and that he just wanted to reassure me.

Once we were inside the condo, we kissed again, more passionately this time and we kept on kissing all the way to the bedroom, closing the door behind us to save Jenna from any embarrassment later, and we made love like never before. As we lay there afterwards, gradually recovering from the strength of our desire for one another, I managed to put how I was feeling into words.

'I love you. We feel so right together and I want us to be together forever, as soon as possible. Can we set dates for our two weddings?'

'Sure we can, baby.' Jackson propped himself up on one arm to look me in the eyes. 'I hope you know that I feel the same and that I'll never make you an empty promise for as long as I live. I want to be with you because you make me whole and I've never felt as good as I have since I met you. I love you and I always will.'

'I was wondering about setting a date for the weekend of Thanksgiving or do you think that's too soon?' I bit my lip as I pondered this thought, seemingly rendering Jackson completely weak out of need for me once again. So it was some time later when he was able to answer my question.

'Thanksgiving is a wonderful idea. That would be a fantastic family celebration for that weekend. I'd like to keep it to close family and friends if you're okay with that and we could maybe hold the wedding at my parents' house because there's plenty of room. What do you think?'

'Oh, yes, that would be lovely and everyone would feel at ease but I don't want your mum getting stressed by any of the arrangements. It would have to be on the condition that she let us organise people to do everything. Do you agree?'

'I do, honey. I have another idea too which I'd like to run past you.' I looked at him eagerly, loving the direction this conversation was taking.

'Well, you know how we said that we'd have a second wedding in Dorset? How about if we do that as the start of our honeymoon and then spend the rest of it visiting Europe? I've never been and there are so many wonderful places I'd love to go with you to create shared memories for the future.'

I kissed him then to show him what a great idea that was before we fell asleep in each other's arms.

CHAPTER THIRTY-FIVE

Jackson

The next morning, everything went mad. Will called me at seven on my cell to warn me about what had happened.

'I'm sorry to call you so early, Jackson, but I thought you'd want to know that Stephanie's article has been published in *Gossip* magazine but it's even worse than we'd expected and there are comments about it all over the internet. Speculation is rife about the things she said about you, which includes an accusation that you made her have an abortion when she fell pregnant but it's Rachel that people are really going for. They really seem to believe that she's after you for your money. I'm sorry. Do you want me to come over so we can work out a plan of action?'

I was speechless for a moment, in the wake of these new revelations. I climbed out of bed and walked into the living room as I gave him my reply.

'That would be great, Will, if you don't mind. I'll see you later.'

I ran my hands through my hair, unsure once again of what to do. I'd been staring out the window for some time, watching the city wake up and trying to come up with a plan, when I felt Rachel next to me as she put her arm round my waist.

'Penny for them, sweetheart?' she whispered by way of greeting.

I looked down at her trusting face and wondered how on earth I was going to break it to her. I couldn't hide from her how I was feeling, she could see it written all over my face.

'What is it? What's wrong?'

When I told her, she sagged against me and I put my arms around her to hold her steady. I felt her breathing quicken and I stepped back so I could look at her face. Tears were streaming down it and it broke my heart to see her so upset. I gently wiped them away with my thumb and tried to pull her close to me again but this time, she resisted. I heard her sniff as she tried to pull herself together and I knew how hard she would be finding this. I needed to be strong for both of us now.

'Listen, Will's coming over to help us work out what to do. I need to have a shower and get dressed. Why don't you have some breakfast with Jenna and see what you both think?' She didn't say anything so I led her to the lounge where we found Jenna already preparing something to eat. I quickly told her what had happened, gave one final glance in Rachel's direction and went off for a shower.

By the time I returned, I was still no clearer about the best course of action to follow but I was glad to see Rachel looking calmer. Will arrived a few minutes later, telling us that there were already some paparazzi stationed outside the building. It was then that I noticed the pair of suitcases by the door. I swung round to Rachel and found her staring right back at me.

'Rachel, what...?' I began but she cut me off.

'I can't take this, Jackson, I don't know what's real any more.'

My face fell at the thought of Rachel leaving me again, I didn't want her to go but I didn't know how to persuade her to stay either.

'Is that what you really want to do, Rachel? Where will you go and what about the weddings?' I asked.

'I want to be away from all these lies and accusations. As for the weddings, well...'

She brushed past me, stopping only to pick up her suitcase before disappearing through the door. I watched in shock as Jenna approached Will, kissed him goodbye and then followed after Rachel, suitcase in hand.

Rachel

As we descended in the lift and made our way to the taxi waiting for us at the back entrance, I became more and more overwhelmed by this new turn of events. I climbed into the cab and sat back in the seat, feeling as if my breath had been knocked out of me. This whole situation was so unfair and I felt like such a victim, which wasn't like me at all.

I knew that I was running away again but I needed the time and the space to think about everything. I desperately wanted to give Jackson the chance to explain but I didn't know if I could trust what he said any more. I'd been such a fool for believing that he'd told me all the secrets Stephanie was keeping and I'd gone and declared my love for him in front of all those people last night as well. That would teach me to let my guard down.

'Where to, Rachel?' I was suddenly aware of Jenna's hand on my arm but I had no idea how long we'd been sitting there. 'Do you want to go to the airport?' she continued.

I glanced in the mirror to see the cab driver looking more than a bit impatient.

'No, I don't know. Could you take us to The Hermitage hotel please?'

The cab took off but I wasn't any more sure whether this was the right thing to do or not. My mind was in such a mess. Jenna and I were both very subdued on the journey. We both received texts on the way but while Jenna busied herself sending a reply to Will's, I didn't even read mine.

'Please don't tell Will where we've gone for the moment, Jenna,' I pleaded with her when I realised that she might want to let him know that we hadn't left the country.

'That's not fair. I know you're cross with Jackson but you can't take it out on me and Will as well. Besides, you ought to speak to Jackson, you know.'

'Why should I? He's only going to lie to me again and I

don't want to hear any more of that.'

'How do you know he's lying? Surely he deserves more credit than Stephanie does. He loves you, I'm sure of that and I don't think he would hurt you by lying to you about something as major as that. Trust works both ways you know.'

I stared at her for a moment, hurt that she would say that to me and I thought about saying so but then, I just gave up. I had no more energy left to fight with anyone. We said no more on the journey but I did think a lot about what she'd said.

The cab dropped us off in front of the hotel and a bellboy appeared from nowhere to take our luggage inside. I'd booked us into a suite with separate rooms so that we could both have a bit of space. No sooner had I sat down in my room than she was back knocking on the door.

'Come in,' I called.

'I'm going to meet up with Will for the day. I hope you don't mind too much but I'll be going home soon and I don't want to miss out on any time I could spend with him. I thought that you could probably do with some time on your own anyway. I've asked him not to tell Jackson where you are but I can't force that point really.'

All I could do was nod weakly and she turned and closed the door behind her.

Once she'd gone, I took out my phone and saw that there were at least a dozen messages from Jackson but then nothing during the past half hour. It seemed like he'd given up too. I scrolled through the messages until I reached the last one.

'You told me once that we should always deal with things together and not shut each other out so why won't you do that now?'

I couldn't believe his nerve so I bashed out a reply, letting my guard down once again.

'I also seem to remember telling you to be completely honest with me so why weren't you?'

His reply came back immediately.

'I am not lying to you about this and it hurts me to think that you could believe I would lie to you about something like that.'

Tears filled my eyes as I realised that I should have talked to him before leaving and not run away again. I should have given him the chance to explain and now it was probably too late. I didn't bother to reply and neither did he. I lay down on the bed and cried myself to sleep.

Jackson

Once they'd left, I sank on to the nearest sofa and put my head in my hands, trying to figure out why Rachel had reacted like that. I knew that she'd been shocked by the new revelations in the interview but surely she wouldn't believe that I had forced Stephanie to have an abortion, surely she knew that I wasn't capable of such a thing? Stephanie had never been pregnant with my child and even though it would have been the last thing I would have wanted, which was what I told her, I would never have tried to make her have an abortion if she had been pregnant. She'd tried to make me believe that she was pregnant by me of course after she'd cheated on me but it had been long since we'd had sex that it was a laughable claim and she knew it. I'd seriously underestimated her desire for revenge because now she was using that same ridiculous claim against me, and Rachel had left me again because of it.

I took my cell out of my pocket and sent off a barrage of texts to Rachel but heard nothing back. I slumped back against the chair, defeated. It was only then that I realised that Will was still with me.

'Man, I'm sorry, you don't have to stay and see me like this,' I told him, standing up and trying to pull myself together.

'I know I don't, Jackson, but I don't want to leave you in this state either. If it helps, I've had a reply from Jenna telling me that they've gone to a hotel, not back to England.'

'Oh, that is a relief. Where are they staying?'

'She hasn't told me for the moment. I think she's finding it hard to be caught in the middle between the two of you.'

'Okay, well, thanks for telling me, I know it's awkward. You can get back to your weekend, honestly, I'll be fine.'

'Are you sure you don't want me to call anyone to come and be with you?'

'Yes, I'm sure. I can do that when I'm ready. I'll need to give some thought to what to do next so can I contact you about that later maybe?'

'Yes, of course. Ring me any time.'

Shortly after he'd gone, I received a reply from Rachel at last but it wasn't what I wanted to hear and I switched my cell off then, not wanting to discuss it any further.

I threw on my running gear and left the building by the back entrance to try and run off my latest nightmare, or at least to come up with a way of making it go away. As I pounded the streets, everything became a bit clearer. I would have to issue a statement of some kind to put straight the most toxic comments Stephanie had made but not before I contacted my legal department to get them to force the magazine to remove the article and publish a public apology to myself and Rachel. Having made a plan in my mind, I picked up my pace to get back to the condo and get to work on sorting out this mess once and for all.

Rachel

When I woke up, I was disorientated at first, unable to remember where I was. Night had fallen and the soft bedspread underneath seemed unusually luxurious. I lay there for a moment, trying to gather my thoughts and slowly, it all came back to me. The misery of my situation threatened to stifle me and I sat up quickly, gulping for air. I ran my fingers through my hair, trying to tidy the curls a little but knowing it was a pointless task. I switched on the little bedside light and was surprised to see that it was only half past seven. My stomach rumbled then as if to confirm the time and I went out to the main living room area to look for Jenna.

The living room was empty and uninviting, causing another wobble in my emotions as I was reminded of how alone I was and felt too. I found my bag and took out my mobile. There was no message from Jackson, which made my heart sink but there was one from Alex not very long ago.

'Hi, Rachel, can you give me a call when you get this? Feeling v. worried about you x'

The message brought tears to my eyes at once and made me glad that Alex was on my side. I knew that Jenna was a bit annoyed with me but I could have done with her support earlier and instead I'd been left feeling abandoned by her. I found Alex in my phone book and pressed her number.

'Alex, hi, it's Rachel,' I began.

'Oh, thank goodness. I've been really worried. Where are you?'

'I'm in Nashville, staying at a hotel. I'm sorry but I can't tell you where because I know you'll want to tell Jackson.'

'Well, at least you're still here. Have you spoken to Jackson since you left?'

'No. We texted but after that, there didn't seem to be much else left to say.'

'Ah, so Jackson hasn't told you what he's been doing then?' I could hear a smile in her voice but didn't know what to make of that.

'What do you mean? What has he been doing?' I knew I was falling into her trap but I couldn't help myself.

'First of all, go and take a look at the company website. Jackson's issued a statement there and when you've read that, click on the link at the bottom of the page. Then call me back, okay?'

I hung up and then went on to the internet on my phone. I hated doing it because it was so small but I found the site and on the front page, there was a short message from Jackson, next to a gorgeous picture of him, which made my heart ache with longing.

A Message from Jackson Phillips, CEO, The Rough Cut Record Company

As some of you may know, an interview with my former fiancée, Stephanie Shaw, was published today in an online magazine. This interview contained some serious allegations against myself and Rachel Hardy, a singer/songwriter from the UK, recently signed by our label. I could not let these allegations pass me by without setting the record straight and, given their libellous nature, I have also asked my legal team to contact the magazine in question. They have now agreed to remove the article and they have also published an apology, together with a modified version of this press release.

However, out of concern for Rachel's blossoming career and my good reputation in this city, I want to make a few points clear for those people who wish to know the facts. I was engaged to Miss Shaw but following her infidelity, I broke off our engagement last year. Miss Shaw was never carrying my child but if she had been, I would never have tried to force her to have an abortion. One day, I do hope to start a family with the right woman.

When Rachel came second in the UK final of the "Open Mic" competition, I was sure that she could make it big in Nashville and following very successful performances at a few "Open Mic" nights here, we signed her to my label. Rachel performed last night at a charity dinner over in Bellevue to a crowd of over 200 people and she is now about to start work on a new EP, as well as her first album. She has a contract with our company which was professionally negotiated on her behalf by her manager and makes her financially independent. She has no need of my wealth or anyone else's, for that matter, and she would never lower herself to marry for money. Rachel is a talented artist and the success she has had so far is all of her own making.

I trust that this clarifies the situation and thank you for your time.

I swiped my hand across my face to clear it of tears before clicking on the link to the magazine's website. Jackson was as good as his word: there was now no evidence of the article, just a grovelling apology from the magazine, promising to check their facts more carefully in the future. I owed Jackson an enormous apology too of course but I had no idea whether he would accept it after all that had happened between us. I sent a text to Alex, rather than calling, because I had somewhere more important to be. I stopped in front of the mirror in the hallway to check my appearance before leaving, regretting that decision immediately. I smoothed my hair down as carefully as I could before slipping on my shoes and stepping out into the corridor to walk to the lift.

Jackson

The tension of the day was beginning to slip away from me now that I had put everything right. In the end, it had all been very easy because once the lawyers were involved and started talking libel and damages, the magazine backed down straight away. Will had helped me draft the press release and Jenna helped out once she returned from the hotel Rachel was staying in. I didn't embarrass her by asking where Rachel was and she didn't betray her friend either. Once they'd gone back to the office, I waited for the website to be updated and then double-checked the magazine's site as well. Then I called Alex to tell her what had happened.

'Jackson, I knew that scheming woman was up to

something else but I am really proud of you for handling it all so calmly.'

'Yeah, I'm pretty proud of myself too. Now all I need is for Rachel to see what I've done and forgive me. Can you help out with letting her know about it, please?'

'Of course and I know she'll forgive you.'

'Thanks, Alex, for everything. I owe you.'

I settled down to wait for some message from Rachel that she'd seen the statements I'd put in place, keeping my cell close to hand but there was nothing. About eight, I started thinking about going out for something to eat, as it looked like I was going to be on my own after all. My mind was whirring with what might have happened when Alex called Rachel but maybe she'd gone out and Alex hadn't been able to reach her. I had to keep clinging on to the hope that everything would be sorted out between us because I had nothing else without Rachel in my life. I made my way down to the street, lost in thought about everything that had happened that day.

'Jackson!' I heard my name being called and it sounded a bit like Rachel but she sounded far away and I couldn't see her. 'Jackson!' I heard her call again and looked all around me trying to find her, frowning at the struggle I was having. Then a cab pulled up right in front of me and suddenly, there she was, leaning out of the window, looking straight at me. I opened the door to help her out and she took my hand gratefully. The cab drove away and we were left on the sidewalk staring at each other, neither one of us brave enough to speak first.

'I'm sorry I couldn't see you,' I ventured and she laughed, a sound that filled my heart with joy.

'I was calling from the window of the cab so I suppose my voice kept being carried away by the wind. It was funny watching you looking for me.' Her face lit up with a dazzling smile. We both paused again.

'I saw the statement on the website and I came to say I'm

so sorry for not trusting you and for running away again earlier. I know I hurt you but please can you forgive me?' She was breathless by the time she'd finished her speech and I knew she was nervous and must have repeated it over and over to herself on the way. I brushed one of her long curls out of her face and leaned down to kiss her gently on the lips.

'Nothing would give me greater pleasure, Rachel Hardy.'

CHAPTER THIRTY-SIX

Rachel

Once Jackson and I had got back together, things settled down again pretty quickly. I made things up with Jenna and enjoyed the remaining time with her before she left to go back to Dorset. She and Will grew even closer and she was heartbroken when she had to go.

'It won't be long till you're flying back again for the wedding, Jenna. The time will pass so quickly, you'll hardly notice.' I tried hard to reassure her but her long face and tear-stained cheeks showed how sad she was and I felt sorry for them both.

I managed to summon up the courage to give Sam a call too, having let enough time go by after reading his letter.

'Sam, hi, how are you?' I screwed up my face in anticipation of him refusing to talk to me.

'Rachel, it's lovely to hear your voice. I'm fine. How are you?'

'I'm good now, after a couple of hard weeks here.' I paused and blew out a long breath. 'Thanks for your letter, it made me cry but I accept what you said. You were right about me and Jackson, we're getting married.' I heard his sharp intake of breath at the other end of the phone. 'Sam?'

'I'm still here, it was just a surprise to hear you say that, that's all. I did kind of expect it though, if I'm honest.'

'The thing is, we're going to have two weddings, one here and one in Dorset and I wanted to ask if you would come. I'll understand if you say no but...'

'I'll be there, Rachel, don't worry.'

In the month before the wedding, I made my mind up that I was going to focus on my debut album as much as possible so I hid myself away in the studio, rehearsing and trying to lay down tracks. One particular day, I was finding it hard to concentrate and I was glad to see Jackson appear mid-morning to talk to me.

'Hey sweetheart, what's up?' I asked. He looked unusually serious.

'I just watched a news update on the TV in my office which Will told me I ought to watch.' I frowned a little at this because Jackson hardly ever watched TV.

'What was it about?' I had a worrying feeling in the pit of my stomach.

'It was a report about Stephanie. She's been arrested for driving while drunk.'

My hands flew to my face. 'Oh my goodness, was anyone hurt?'

'No, no-one else was hurt but the photos of her injuries looked horrendous. Apparently, she had over twice the legal limit of alcohol in her blood so it's a miracle that she survived.'

'Where is she now?' I asked.

'She's at the hospital under the careful eye of the police. They're waiting for her dad to arrive from Texas.' He winced as he said it.

'Her dad's not going to be best pleased, I guess.'

'Hell no! He'll hate all the bad publicity.'

'I hate to admit it but I actually feel a bit sorry for her. Does that make me mad?'

'Not at all, it's what makes you special.'

He pulled me towards him for a lingering kiss then and I let myself sink into the warmth of his arms.

'How's everything going for you today?' he asked after a few moments.

'Not well at all. I can't seem to concentrate today.' I pulled a face to show him my frustration.

'Do you want something to take your mind off things for a while?' He raised his eyebrows and I grinned back at him.

'What did you have in mind, Mr Phillips?' I asked, walking my fingers up his chest, until he caught my hand and kissed it.

'Come and have lunch with me and you'll find out!' he replied with a smile.

We emerged on to the street outside the office a few minutes later where Greg was waiting in the car.

'You know, I've been thinking that I should probably sell my New York apartment now,' Jackson said once we were settled in the car. 'I don't really need it any more and if I am going up there again, it will definitely be with you and there's no shortage of luxury hotels for us to stay in. What do you think?'

'I think that's a really good decision but it's up to you, it's your apartment, not mine.'

'Well, that's something else we need to talk about, worldly goods and all that. I take the view that what's mine is yours, you know that.'

'I know, it's hard for me to get used to, that's all.' I paused for a moment, trying to work out where he was taking me. 'Where are we going then? This looks like the road to your parents' house.'

'You're right, it is but we're not going there.' He smiled cryptically at me, looking like he could hardly contain his secret any longer.

Just then, Greg made a left turn and we started down a long driveway.

When the car drew up outside an impressive colonial mansion, I had to sit for a moment to catch my breath. I looked at Jackson in disbelief. The house was so stunning that I could hardly believe my eyes. It was a colonial brick building with bottle-green shutters and two magnificent pillars on either side of the entrance, rising from the ground right up to the roof. On each side of the house were two smaller wings, adding to the overall grandeur of the building. I loved it on sight and couldn't wait to see the inside.

A woman came to meet us from the car, shaking my hand and then Jackson's in greeting. She introduced herself as the realtor in charge of selling the property before taking us on a tour of the house and grounds. We didn't say much because there was such a lot to take in. I was delighted with everything I saw and I could see that Jackson was too.

'The house is laid out perfectly and there's plenty of room for a family,' she declared, smiling at me.

By this time, we were outside the back of the property. The grounds were as wonderful, with two acres all in all, including a very enticing pool area and tennis courts as well. When the tour was finished, Jackson told the estate agent how impressed he was with the property.

'How about you ma'am?' she asked me.

'I absolutely love it!'

Jackson

It felt funny to be back in the condo again after living in the new house for a while. The worst thing was how cramped it felt after all the space in our new five-bedroomed mansion. Still, it had only been for last night because Rachel wanted to stick with tradition and not let me see her before the wedding. I could have stayed at my parents' house but I preferred to be on my own to collect my thoughts before today, the most important day of my life.

I was glad that we'd held our 'hen' and 'stag' nights last week, a good time before the wedding so that we could recover in plenty of time. I hadn't drunk anything of course but the guys had kept me up pretty late, visiting honky-tonk bars and the like and I'd been shattered the next day.

Now, I felt refreshed after a good night's sleep, although

I'd woken up early, unable to contain my excitement any longer. I'd already checked that I had everything ready at least ten times, most importantly the rings to give to my best man, Todd. I'd also checked our plane tickets for the honeymoon and my luggage, since we would be departing straight after the reception. What Rachel didn't know was that I'd booked for us to stay overnight in New York at the Ritz-Carlton. We would be staying in a suite overlooking Central Park and flying out the following afternoon to London which would break our trip up a little.

By nine, I was all ready to go and waiting for Greg to arrive to take me over to my parents' house. The wedding was to be at eleven so I knew I was in plenty of time and I didn't want to be hanging around when I got there. I was thoughtful in the car on the way over, thinking about how far Rachel and I had come in such a short space of time and how much I'd changed under her influence. She'd sent me a text earlier that confirmed for me that she was the one and that she felt as strongly for me as I did for her.

'Good morning, my almost husband! Hope you're okay today and looking forward to getting married as much as I am. I love you, I can hardly wait to see you later. Lots of love till then x'

I walked into my parents' house and was relieved that things were calm, in fact it was an oasis of peace and quiet which was exactly what I needed. I found my mom and dad in the kitchen, along with various other family members and I was glad to see Todd there. I walked over and shook my dad's hand and then kissed my mom. After that, all the women wanted to kiss me and coo over my appearance until I couldn't stand it any more and, gesturing to Todd, we escaped out to the garden. It was a cool but sunny day which I was glad about for Rachel's sake. The marquee was set up in the garden and Jenna had done a fantastic job with the flowers. Since her return, she had worked with the caterers over the last couple of days to decorate the marquee and the tables with glorious purple, orange and yellow flowers in arrangements of all different sizes. The seating area in front of the marquee where the actual ceremony would take place, was also lavishly decorated with a red carpet scattered with rose petals and a single pink rose attached with a ribbon to the back of each chair. I knew that Rachel would be delighted with it all. My mom and dad had really done us proud by overseeing everything and taking the strain off us.

'Todd, I need to give you the rings so you can put them somewhere safe for later on,' I said when I'd stopped marvelling at the setting for a moment.

'Sure thing, Jackson. How are you feeling? You look very smart by the way.' He smiled and winked at me.

'Don't you start fawning over me as well. I feel great, Todd, but I can't wait to get started, you know.'

'I know, man, but try and keep calm, it's not long to go now. Let's go and sort out your buttonhole and check that everything else is in place, shall we?'

An hour later, the seats were almost full and I stood nervously waiting for Rachel to arrive. The opening strains of Etta James' 'At Last' suddenly began and I turned to gaze at Rachel as she slowly started to make her way down the aisle towards me. She looked utterly breathtaking in an ivory silk dress and matching bolero jacket. Her hair was piled in soft curls, with just a few tendrils hanging at the sides and she was wearing a simple tiara in it with a short veil hanging down behind her. I noticed that she was wearing the Tiffany pendant I had given her in New York all that time ago too. Will was beaming at her side, looking very proud in that role and I felt so lucky as I watched the pair of them walking towards me, Rachel's eyes not once leaving mine. Alex and Jenna followed right behind Rachel, both of them taking to the role of bridesmaid with ease. As Rachel and Will came alongside me, Will shook my hand and went to sit down with Jenna, and

Alex took her place next to Todd. I leaned in to kiss Rachel's cheek.

'You are so beautiful and I'm very lucky.'

'Me too,' she replied.

In no time at all, Todd was stepping forward with the rings and we were exchanging our vows. We'd chosen the rings together from our favourite shop, Tiffany's, choosing one that would fit with Rachel's ring I had given her previously while I chose a simple wedding band and moved my knot ring to my right hand. When we kissed to seal our vows, I knew that this was a life-changing moment for us both.

The rest of the day flew by in a blur of greetings, celebratory drinks, speeches and food. I was glad when it was time for us to start the dancing because it seemed like the first time I'd really had Rachel to myself all day.

I took her hand in mine and held her close to me, wrapping my other arm around her waist.

'How are you feeling now, Mrs Phillips?' I asked with a grin.

'I feel wonderful and so glad that everything has gone according to plan.'

'I still can't get over how fabulous you look,' I said, gazing into her eyes.

She kissed me tenderly and laid her head on my shoulder and we stayed like that for the remainder of the dance.

It was the best day of our lives but by the end, I could hardly remember a thing. All too soon, it was time for us to go. We went to our room to get changed and it was all I could do as I helped Rachel out of her dress not to take her in my arms and make sweet love to her there and then but we had guests waiting to see us off and a plane to catch. We changed into more comfortable outfits and went back outside to find our families.

We kissed my mom and dad goodbye and there were some tears on all sides but we'd be seeing them again very soon for wedding number two. Rachel tossed her bouquet of roses and then turned to see Alex catch it. Both their faces lit up in surprise and Todd actually blushed! It had been a wonderful day and I still had another surprise for Rachel.

Rachel

As we drove off towards the airport, I was wondering when I would stop smiling. It had been such an amazing day, one that I would remember for the rest of my life and it wasn't over yet.

'So, Jackson, are you happy?'

'Yes, Mrs Phillips, I truly am a very happy man. Hasn't it been a fantastic day?'

'It has been a perfect day, yes, in every way, thank you.' I brought his hand up to kiss it and I leaned into him.

'You made it perfect for me and I have another gift for you now, Rachel.'

I sat up in surprise.

'There can't be anything else left to give me, surely.' I smiled at him, wondering what it was going to be this time.

'You know we're on our way to the airport, right?'

'Ye-es,' I stuttered, wondering where this conversation was going.

'Well, we're not going to the UK till tomorrow. We're staying somewhere else tonight.'

'Are we? What have you got up your sleeve?' I narrowed my eyes at him but he laughed his usual sexy laugh and kept me waiting. 'C'mon, the suspense is killing me.'

'I've booked us a suite at the Ritz in New York for tonight overlooking Central Park.'

I let out a little squeal before leaning in to kiss him with all my heart.

A few hours later, we were pulling up outside the Ritz and being whisked up to our suite in a private lift. It was late by this time and we were both exhausted but once we were in bed, luxuriating in the feel of the crisp, cotton sheets, it wasn't long before our love for each other took over and we made love to seal our union once again.

'I love you, Jackson,' I whispered sleepily.

'Back at you, Mrs Phillips.'

When I woke the next day to my first full day as a married woman, I felt confused at first, having arrived so late and not had time to check out the suite. I got up promptly and, having visited the marble bathroom, I then wandered into the separate living room, where to my delight I discovered the magnificent view of Central Park below. I was even able to see it closer up with the use of a tabletop telescope so thoughtfully provided for that purpose. I was amazed at the size and the utter luxury of the suite. Even Jackson's old apartment in New York hadn't been as magnificent as this. I didn't dare think how much this had cost but I had to get used to the fact that I now had plenty of money and didn't need to worry about it. Still, that was going to take some time. Jackson joined me shortly afterwards, laughing at all my oohing and aahing but the panoramic view of the park took his breath away too.

'What time's our flight today? Will we have any time to go to the park?' I sounded like a little kid but I really wanted to go and explore even if only for a short while.

'We'll have time, baby, I made sure to book an evening flight so we're going to have a leisurely breakfast and go out some time after that, okay?'

A sumptuous breakfast was delivered minutes later so we were crossing West 59th Street into the park by eleven. We spent a lazy few hours exploring, taking in as much as we could of the south end of the park before working our way towards the John Lennon 'Strawberry Fields' memorial. After a few moments of reflection there, we went out of the park to pick up a couple of hot dogs when we got hungry so that I could say I'd had that experience. By about three, we were starting to feel the cold and so we stopped in at a café for hot chocolate and a slice of cake.

'We really do need to come back here again soon,' I sighed. 'There's so much for us to see and do still.'

'I promise we'll be back again soon, honey. For now, I want us to concentrate on starting our new life together, just you and me.'

'Yes, you're right, it's time for us to move on from our past lives and to forge a new one together. I can't wait!'

Jackson

We arrived to a cold, rainy day in the UK and I felt our spirits sink a little as we drove from the airport south to the coast. Rachel's cottage seemed cold and forlorn when we got there, especially as there was no-one to welcome us but she switched on the heating, as well as an electric fire in the lounge and it felt cosier in no time. We snuggled up together on the sofa and the next thing we knew, we'd both fallen asleep and the sound of a key in the front door woke us up.

'Oh, look at you two, you're like an old married couple,' joked Jenna as she poked her head round the door.

Will followed her in, holding her hand and laughing at the joke.

'Hey, you guys. How are you? Sorry, we're just both so tired.' Rachel groaned, rubbing her eyes gently to help herself wake up.

'We're fine and ready for another wedding whenever you are!' Jenna sounded very bubbly, which was a bit grating when we'd only just woken up.

'What time is it anyway?' I asked.

'It's eight o'clock now. Shall we get a takeaway in rather than cooking?' she suggested.

While we ate, Jenna and Will entertained us with tales from the wedding reception party after we'd left. We didn't stay up too long, knowing that we had to get up for church the next day to hear the final reading of our wedding banns.

After a good night's sleep, we both felt better and even the weather had improved so that we could walk to the church. It was freezing inside the church though and I worried that Rachel would be cold on the next wedding day but she didn't have any concerns about it. Maybe she was just used to the colder weather. The banns were read for one last time without incident and we had a quick chat with the rector afterwards about final arrangements.

Rachel and I stopped in for some lunch in town on the way back home.

'Is there anything else we need to do before next Saturday, do you think?' I asked her as we started eating.

'I don't think so, really, it should just be a case of checking that everything's organised. Did you contact Tom and Meg?'

'Yep and that's fine, they'll both be there. I can ring the restaurant this afternoon to check that's all set up or we could pop in if you like, before we go back to the cottage?'

'I love that you're so organised.' She nodded and sighed contentedly. 'Is there anything else you'd like to do before the wedding?'

'We could explore the coast together perhaps, if we hired a car. I know the weather's not so good but the coastline will be spectacular whatever the weather, won't it?'

'That sounds wonderful. It's been a long time since I did that.'

Over the next few days, Rachel took me to lots of interesting places along the coast, starting with the iconic Corfe Castle.

'I used to love visiting this castle as a child and roaming among the ruins,' she told me as she drove, a wistful look on her face.

From her description, I thought I knew what to expect when I got there but nothing could have prepared me for the spectacular setting of the medieval castle and the breathtaking views across Purbeck from the keep. It was my first visit to a British castle and the memory would stay with me for a long time.

We continued as far as Lyme Regis, stopping off at various tourist must-sees along the way. We managed a short walk along the Heritage Coast, giving me an idea of why the coastline is so special, before we had to set off back to Poole.

'It's been good to have this time together here. I hope we can make time to do it again soon,' I said as we pulled up outside the cottage.

'I hope so too but it won't be easy to get back here that often, will it?' Rachel replied.

'I think we ought to buy a new house here as well,' I said quietly. I was sure that this was something she'd been worrying about and I wanted to set her mind at rest.

She stared at me. 'Do you mean that?'

'Of course. I know you'll want to come back regularly and see Jenna and her family.'

She threw her arms around me for a hug then and I was glad that I'd cleared that one up for the future.

Rachel

The day of our Dorset wedding dawned bright and clear. Jackson and Will had taken themselves off to a nearby hotel so that we would only meet at the wedding and as this was also where Jackson's mum and dad would be staying, it made sense. Jenna helped me to get ready once again and this time she would be the only bridesmaid. Jenna's dad had hired a vintage Rolls-Royce to take us all to the church and we arrived just after eleven o'clock. Jenna handed me the lovely bouquet she had created especially for me, this time a mixture of roses, peonies and gerberas in various shades of pink, before making sure my dress was straight at the back.

Sam appeared, fresh from his role as usher to escort his mum inside and gave me a quick good luck kiss before setting off just ahead of us towards the church. I noticed that he was still limping slightly as he went.

On the way, I stopped briefly at my mum and dad's graves and laid a single ivory rose there for each of them, saying a silent prayer to ask them to be watching this important moment in my life.

This time, we'd gone for traditional processional music to accompany my walk down the aisle of St James' and so it was that I walked in to the Trumpet Voluntary. Jackson looked every bit as gorgeous as he had done just over a week earlier and I thanked my lucky stars for having found such a good man and one that I now knew I could trust completely.

I could not help but beam as I walked down the aisle, I was so happy, and Jackson looked like he felt the same. It was such a good feeling knowing that we'd already done this once and the second time was an absolute bonus, especially with Jenna's dad, Dave, giving me away. We said our vows and exchanged the rings again and although it was a small wedding group, it felt every bit as poignant as it had done the first time.

As we turned to walk back down the aisle, The Band Perry song 'All Your Life' played and I smiled at Jackson and we both let out a soft 'whoop' together.

We went on to the restaurant after chatting to people outside the church for a while during the official photos. It was a wonderfully intimate meal with just Jenna's family and Will, Jackson's parents, Tom, Meg and Jackson and myself around the table. We didn't go for formal speeches this time but Jackson did stand to give a short speech when we were finishing our desserts. He thanked both sets of parents and he thanked Tom for being his best man and acting as usher, along with Sam. He then turned to Jenna.

'I'd like to finish by thanking Jenna for being such a great friend to Rachel through all these preparations for both weddings, as well as overseeing flower arrangements on two continents. I have a feeling that Jenna's business is about to take off and she might need someone to hold her hand through all that. So, just to let you know, Jenna, I've asked Will to set up a UK office for our record label in London and I wondered if you might be able to find him somewhere to stay?'

Jenna's hands had flown up to her cheeks and her mouth had fallen open in shock. She looked at Will for confirmation to find him smiling and nodding all at once. He pulled her into his arms, seemed to ask her something at which she nodded and then they kissed to a thumping round of applause from everyone else around the table. It couldn't have been a nicer ending to our day. We danced late into the night until we were so exhausted we could no longer stand up. There were two people I had to speak to though before calling it a night. First, I went in search of Jenna.

'Jenna, I just want to thank you for everything. I don't know what I would have done without you.'

'Don't be silly, it was my pleasure for my best friend.'

'And what about that with Will, huh? Are you pleased?'

'Are you kidding? I'm over the moon. Didn't you know about it then?'

'Not at all, Jackson kept that secret very close to his chest but I'm so happy for you. I expect to have lots of updates. Will you ask him to move into the cottage?'

'If that's okay?'

'Of course it is, don't you be silly, now.' We both laughed. 'Anyway,' I continued, 'I think the cottage is more yours than mine now so take care good care of it, won't you?' Her eyes filled with tears as we hugged and said goodnight. I was glad I'd been able to do that for her.

Next, I went in search of Sam, while Jackson went to see Tom and Meg off.

'Hey, Sam, I just came to say goodnight and to thank you for today. I really appreciated you coming.'

'I wouldn't have missed it for the world. I hope you'll both be happy, you deserve to be.' We hugged and said goodbye for perhaps the last time in a while.

Finally, Jackson and I went upstairs with his parents, and

after thanking them too, made our way to our suite and collapsed into bed after another long, full day.

As I drifted off to sleep, I thought how far we'd come in a few short months and I fell asleep dreaming of Paris and of the new adventure we would start together the next day.

Acknowledgements

It has been a long journey to publication for my debut novel and I couldn't have reached this point without the help of lots of other generous people along the way.

I'd like to thank Cat, Tanya, Julia, Mandie, Hannah and my mum, for beta reading for me right back in the very early days of the story and for having faith in my idea. I'd also like to thank Kate for beta reading the almost final version for me, along with Cat who liked it so much, she read it again! I'm so grateful to you all for your time and your support.

As many of you will know, I successfully joined the Romantic Novelists' Association's New Writers' Scheme in January 2014 and I've been lucky enough to have so much help and support from many RNA writers during the past year as a result. I'd like to thank my RNA reader for her positive report especially and I'd also like to thank Ros and Heidi-Jo for befriending me right from the start. Thank you to all the RNA members I've met and come to know over the past year for your generosity of spirit. It really is a great organisation.

Thank you also to everyone who has followed me on Twitter, on my Facebook page or on my blog and taken the time to interact with me. It has been such a pleasure to meet so many new people as a result of social media.